Come away, O human child!

To the waters and the wild

With a fairy, hand in hand

For the world's more full of weeping

That you can understand.

The Stolen Child
William Butler Yeats

To Ed &
Linda,
In memory of
all our times
Together
Love
Kathleen

D1417511

ISBN: 978-0-692-17580-4 (Paperback)

Any references to historical events, real people, or real places are used fictitiously. Names, characters, and places are products of the author's imagination.

Printed by Sheridan, United States of America.

First printing edition 2018.

Whales Tale Press
P.O. Box 144
Lake Villa, IL 60046

Cover illustration by Anne FitzGerald, Studio/Gallery in Mungret College, Limerick, Ireland
Cover design: Meghan FitzGerald Wiegold
Book design: Pam McGinty

For these dear people who made my life so rich

My Irish Angel, Phil Moran, 1934 – 2018

My *Anam Cara*, Marguerite Phelps, 1926 – 2014

My dangerous pal, Mary Curtin, 1942 – 2017

My best priest buddy, Tom White, 1933 – 2014

My beloved son, Garrett FitzGerald, 1975 – 2015

With the deepest gratitude to all those who made *Martin* possible

My sister Molly who never let Martin disappear and held high the lantern so I would never lose sight of where we were going.

To Dr. Dolores Christie, Vicki Eiden, Patty Burt, Dr. Monica Oblinger, Noel Rose, Mary Beth Rakoczy, Rosemary Ellis, Mary Agnes Dalton – for their sharp eyes to see where I was going, their warm hearts when I grew cold and their strong arms when I grew faint.

To my family - my dear husband Tom, my daughter Meghan and Brad Wiegold and their children: Phalen, Cia'n and Annie and Garrett's daughter, Bridget FitzGerald; the Whalens – Ellen, Tommy, Molly; Tim Armstrong; the FitzGeralds – Anne, Gerard and Pauline.

The Moran family – Declan, Breda, Mary, Kerry, Kieran and Tommy, all the children of Angel Phil.

To John Hooper who shared with me what a Roman education was all about and to Pat Harrington who has always kept the juices flowing.

To Pam McGinty who so wisely drew the blue-prints, so cleverly built the book and finished it with great aplomb!

To Benedictine Father Kevin Murphy who first escorted me through the Abbey at Benet Lake, Wisconsin, and enabled me to dream of a holy place where priestly amends could begin.

To Anne FitzGerald, who so artistically captured what young Fr. Martin Sweeney was all about.

A Note to My Readers

I am now an old Irish priest, up here in the green hills and blue lakes of Wisconsin, much like the land at home.

You may be an Active Catholic, a Passive Catholic or no Catholic at all. Whatever you are is just fine with me.

I want to tell you right off the bat that I have never, in my long life on this earth, ever raised a fist in anger nor lowered a hand in lust to a child of God, regardless of his or her age.

So rest easy and come along with me and I'll tell you about my very long life as a priest in these troubled times.

Signed:

Martin Sweeney

TABLE OF CONTENTS

Part Four: The Least of My Children

Part Five: The Welcome Home

Epilogue:

Martin Sweeney Family Tree

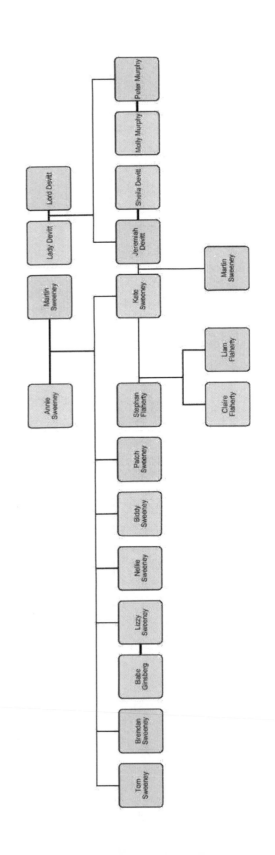

PART ONE

Chapters 1 – 10

Oh, Danny boy, the pipes are calling
From glen to glen and down the mountainside.
The summer's gone and all the roses falling,
'Tis you, 'tis you, must go and I must bide.

CHAPTER 1
Long Ago in County Clare

It was in the year of our Lord 1936. General Francisco Franco marched through Spanish Morocco and sailed into Spain, initiating the Spanish Civil War. Hitler invaded the Rhineland. In January King George V of England had died and oil was discovered beneath the burning sands of Saudi Arabia.

An Irish Catholic playwright, Eugene O'Neill, won the Nobel Prize for literature, as his powerful works reflected an "original concept of tragedy". Another Irish Catholic, John Kennedy, enrolled in his freshman year at Harvard. His young, brilliant life was to end in tragic death, casting the entire world to its knees.

As the black waves crested and tumbled onto the shore, my family slept soundly in a small thatched cottage high in the hills of Clare on the west coast of Ireland. Dreams tumbled in their heads as they drew closer to each other for warmth and protection. The turf fire glowed silently in the hearth.

A wounded cormorant tucked herself into a crack in the black cliffs and gray speckled seals rolled in the waves and dove beneath the sea. Black clouds blocked the light of the moon as a German U-Boat prowled the waters beyond Mutton Island. 1936 - two years before I was born.

Martin and Annie were my grandparents and they slept in the small room beyond the hearth. Before she climbed into bed beside Grandpa, Grannie banked the sods of turf together in the hearth, for a fire once lit was never to go out. And it was the mother's task, for she was the heart of the family as the hearth was the heart of the home.

Martin Sweeney and Annie Delaney had met 25 years before at the fair in Ennis. Pale and wispy Annie was selling honey and large blue duck eggs. Martin with the black and wild beard was looking for a sturdy dairy cow, but he found a wife instead. Poor Grannie must have been so innocent in those old days, but where else could her life have led her, but right into Grandpa's arms?

Before I go on, I need to tell you that I was named after my grandfather, Martin Sweeney. I've always been proud of my name, but I'm still sad that I never laid my eyes on him. I always wondered if he would have liked me. Through my whole life, if I get a whiff of a pipe, I know that my grandfather is near.

Martin Sweeney and Annie Delaney were married by our priest, Uncle Paul, in 1915, the year before we declared our Independence from England. Quilty is near the sea in West Clare and up the road from Ennis. It was there they settled into a small, neglected farm with their backs to the sea.

They had seven live children: Tom, Lizzie, Nellie, Brendan, Biddy, my mother Kate, and young Packy. There were many more that never saw the light of day. Each time that Grannie brought forth an unfinished or dead baby, Grandpa would place it on soft cotton, then wrap it in heavy brown burlap and slowly carry it down to the sea.

With his long, black beard flying into his face and his marble-blue eyes filling with tears, Grandpa would lift the baby above the water and walk in up to his waist. He then placed his small, fragile bundle on the open sea, careful to lower it between the waves so it be carried out into the arms of the Blessed Mother. He prayed, "May the Blessed Mother receive into her loving arms this young one and forgive me my sins."

Then the lifeless baby slipped farther and farther away from her father's arms. The stars fell into the sea and the moon grew pale. On the flat rocks beneath the cliffs, the gray speckled seals with their long, black eyelashes watched mournfully, their ghostly wails filling the dark night air.

Holding his head in his empty hands, Grandpa would scream and scream and scream into the black and godless heavens, like the red-shawled women on the islands, keening and howling in the face of death. Then he would look out to sea and the baby would be gone.

Uncle Tom saw his father wrap a dead baby in burlap and carry it down to the sea and walk in up to his waist to be with her as long as he could. He listened as his father screamed over the waves and the gray seals barked along with him, rending the heavens with their grief.

3

Tom Sweeney watched the little bundle bob upon the waves until he could see it no longer and he prayed for his uncle Liam and his aunts Jane and Rosie and for all his brothers and sisters who had been set upon the waters. He vowed that he would never go through what his father was going through and he would never put a woman through what his mother was going through. There'd be no children for Tom Sweeney in this lifetime.

My Mammie, who was Kate to all the rest of them, told me how she and Nellie would sneak out the door and hide in the bushes and then follow him down to the sea by the light of the moon. They'd stick a cloth in their mouths to keep from screaming and they'd lie quietly next to his over-turned *currach* to watch their little brothers and sisters be placed on top of the waves.

Mammie and Nellie would then cry their hearts out and try to understand why some of them were alive and why some of them died before they even got started. I think this is where it all started – Mammie trying to figure out the right from wrong and never really being satisfied with any choice that she made, big or small. I think I caught some of that from her, the back and the forth, the forth and the back. It nearly drives me mad.

Every time Mammie told me this story, I'd cry and hide my face in her lap. I couldn't understand why they couldn't be buried in the graveyard with all the other dead people.

Every time I'd ask her, she'd tell me over and over again that since they hadn't been baptized before they died, they weren't really Catholic, so they couldn't be buried with the other Catholics. I'd tell her I thought that was so cruel, because it was not their fault that they died, but she'd tell me to hush up and not say anything bad against the Catholic Church.

******

Grandpa had a younger brother, Liam, who drowned. They had met a black-toothed woman on the way to their boat and she stopped them dead in their tracks along the crooked path down to the sea. She had smiled and nodded to them as she made her way up from the water.

The Irish believe that a black-toothed woman means nothing but trouble, "Sure she's a killer one," said our old neighbor Patchy Quinn. So they got into their boat, rowed out to the fishing fields and within an hour, poor young Liam met his fate as the black-toothed woman's presence had fore-shadowed.

And for all the years and nights to come, as the people of Quilty were sound asleep under their warm quilts, Grandpa Sweeney, thrashing against his wife, was back on the sea in his dreams, shouting at his brother Liam to grab his hand, grab his oars, reach out 'for Chrissake'.

Liam was after bobbing up and down. Then Liam would smile one last time, wave and let the sea have its way with him. Grandpa would crash to the floor as he'd reach from the *curragh* for his young brother's hand. Grannie could only bless him with holy water, *"Bail o' Dhia ort,"* and struggle to pull him back into bed.

When Tom would hear his father shouting, struggling and crashing to the floor, he would jump down from their loft and run to help his mother lift Grandpa back to bed, for his father was growing heavier with the years.

Tom knew that Liam would never be free as long as his father's guilt kept him bound to the Earth. Tom said that Grandpa wore his guilt like a red flag wrapped around his neck for all the world to see. Sure, if he at least felt guilt, then his sin of not saving his young brother was lessened.

When he was younger, each time his mother lost a baby, Tom would ask her where the baby went, and she would tell him that the angels had come to carry him home to God. He would listen for the angels coming but heard only the wild Connemara ponies snorting to the pounding sea.

Uncle Tom knew that his mother, our Grannie, was lying to him, but only to be kind. And Grannie knew that her son knew she was lying. She feared that one day he'd make a liar out of her, but she needed to protect him from the losses that marked her every breath. She could handle it – they were her children and she had enough love in her heart for all of them, living or dead.

5

All the Sweeney children were forbidden to go near the water. It was traditional for the Irish not to be taught to swim. Death was easier if you found yourself far out in the sea and did not struggle to swim for land. You could just close your eyes and surrender to the rolling waves.

Grandpa had a twin sister, Rosie, who was on *The Titanic*. She and seven others from the village were going to go on to Chicago to marry and raise their families. The entire village had been beside themselves with grief, as eight families were losing their young to America.

As shouts of, "Not even God can sink this ship!" rang through the village, mothers and fathers blessed themselves at the blasphemy rising from the lips of their own children. The Irish traveled in steerage and when the ship's officers realized there were not enough life-boats, they locked the Irish down below to save space for the wealthy.

They never heard a word about Rosie, so they presumed she had drowned with the rest. Whenever anyone would mention the *Titanic*, a silence dropped like lead upon us. We were never allowed to even mention the name of that ship, and as books and movies came out, they were forbidden to us.

Grandpa hated the sea, as it had taken his brother Liam, his sister Rosie, and all his stillborn children. Yet if he were far from it, he grew restless and irritable, as if the blood in his veins thickened, darkened, grew sluggish. If he could then only breathe in the salty air, his blood would roar to life and he'd be the Lion of Clare, stalking the wild cliffs, sniffing the wind for his enemies.

So this was the beginning of me so very long ago. No one knew that I was just a little ball of life, growing day by day inside of my dear mother's womb. When they found out, sure the cups got thrown, the voices got loud, and the fists got raised, but the blessings of God Almighty filled every cell of my body, as I was selected to be born in the most wonderful home on God's green earth. I often wonder if I ever really left there, as I was forever drawn to our little old cabin, so full of life, at the very edge of the sea.

CHAPTER 2
Blood is Thicker than Water

Tom Sweeney knew his place as the eldest son, the eldest child. Concern and care were sculpted across his handsome face which made him look so much older than he really was. His features were perfect, so perfect that his mother would tease him, "Now, Tommy, even the ewes and the cows fancy you! You'll be swattin' the girls off like flies on a hot summer day!" Uncle Tommy never got married and I don't think he even had a lady-friend. He'd have made a good priest. Better than myself anyhow.

I never in my life ever saw a man so at peace. Uncle Tom loved the little white cabin with the thick, thatched roof where the blue-birds would nest above him and sing their hearts out. Grannie would tell him to get them with the broom handle, but he could never do it. "Mammie, please leave the little birds alone – you wouldn't like some giant poking at you like that."

The blue-green hills and black valleys, the misty rains and salty prayers, the mournful lowing of the cattle at dusk and the golden blessings through the wind and the snorting of the tired horses and the pure and simple grace of every single day, of every minute in West Clare. He would never leave, for here his heart was completely at peace.

****

Uncle Brendan was quiet. Some thought him stupid. He had bright red hair, almost the color of ripe strawberries and his eye-lashes were a pale yellow, like tender, little threads of wheat growing out of his eyelids. He thought this make him look foolish. He loved to argue, but no one understood that he was not looking for a fight, but he just liked the battle of minds. Grannie always said, "You watch that one, he'll be makin' his mark in the world, sure 'e will, God bless 'im."

Brendan loved the little school in Dunsallagh and the day he was able to read was the happiest day of his life. He was never without a book stuck in his belt and when he was lost to them, Tom would find him under a tree or by the strand, looking out to sea with an old book in his hand. He never paid much mind to me, so I kept my distance from him.

There was something pure about Brendan, as if he breathed a different air. He lived in his head, as his own thoughts were sweeter that any that we could offer to him. We'd find him on the endless strand at Spanish Point, the spot where the Spanish Armada, 130 ships sent by Philip II of Spain to invade England, was destroyed.

They say the blood of those Spanish sailors created the "Black Irish." Some of us Sweeney's have that black Spanish blood roaring through our veins and the rest have the red blood of the Vikings who conquered us so long ago.

****

At 20, Aunt Lizzie was the oldest of the four girls. She hadn't a "pick" of flesh on her and was as hard as the sheets of limestone in the Burren. She walked with great fury, heels first, and thought ill of everyone, including herself. When she was barely ten, she chopped away at her thin, straw hair which sharpened her already pointy features. Old Mrs. Hickey would ask Lizzie to take the horse out for a little run, as she'd be getting too restless in her old barn. Lizzie was more restless than the horse and her only release was tearing up and down the strand on Maeve, the charcoal mare with the blazing red eyes and long white tail.

Everyone stayed away from Lizzie, fearing her tongue or a swift kick in the behind. I was always afraid of Lizzie and she would stick her tongue out at me when no one was looking. I'd notice when Grannie walked behind her, she'd look at Lizzie's head to see if she had sprouted horns over-night and she'd have to be taken to the priest.

While everyone stayed far from the Fairy Fort on the back side of the road, Lizzie would march right up to the raised mound of dirt and jump on top of it, unafraid that the fairies would be angry and carry her off to their underworld. But if you looked closely at Lizzie, wouldn't she be carrying a snatch of the white hawthorn for protection? The old fairies did love their hawthorn and wouldn't hurt Lizzie a bit, as she was probably one of their own.

8

Grannie always said that Lizzie was "a heart scald" and she caused a lot of trouble in the family. But Auntie Lizzie changed so much when she got to America and it helped me understand why she had been so crazy and angry with all of us. I really grew to love her and I know she loved me. Lizzie was the original Shape-Shifter!

******

Nellie was 18 and as quiet as the blue-bells that grew on the low side of our crooked, little cabin. Not a day went by that Grandpa didn't say to Grannie, "Now that one's afraid of her own shadow." Brendan tried to understand how anyone could be afraid of their own shadow, but soon gave up and went back to his books.

While Lizzie was a "big, strap" of a thing, Nellie was tiny and dark and looked to Lizzie for her orders and protection. When she was a baby, she would curl herself into a soft, little ball, a kitten asleep in the sun. Grandpa would sit on the hob by the fire, smoking his pipe, saying to whomever would listen, "Now that wan' never spoke a word to me in her whole life, and I'm her only father, be God!"

Nellie was the smallest of all the Sweeney sisters and the easiest for Lizzie to shove around. She would kiss Biddy and Baby Patch when no one was looking and give her mother a little hug before she went out to gather the warm eggs every morning. She'd wink at me and tickle me under my arm when we were alone. Nellie would hear them call her "the little nun" behind her back - I thought then that must have hurt her feelings, but I know now that she was proud of it.

Nellie was Lizzie's shadow. Days would go by and no one would hear a sound out of Nellie. She would look to Lizzie for permission to speak and if Lizzie withheld, Nellie was silent. Aunt Nellie had wavy nut-brown hair with streaks of red that shone when the morning sun struck it just right.

And interestingly, when they got to America, Lizzie changed into a completely different person and Nellie became more of her true self. I often have wondered what America has done to me. Have I been a Shape-Shifter like Lizzie, or have I just come into clearer focus like Nellie?

9

And the one I loved the very most was Aunt Biddy, oh, dear Biddy, with a profile like the lady of the cameo. People would wait for her at the market on Saturday and smile at her passing. Then they'd look at me with envy that I got to be so close to beautiful, beautiful Biddy.

She would lift her eyes, the blue of the finest porcelain in all of China and nod her elegant head with the fullness of shiny black curls like a nymph rising out of the sea, and move like a black swan gliding over a silver lake. Sometimes Grannie would put her rough hands over my eyes when she'd find me staring at Biddy.

Biddy was the best looking of all her sisters and she was healthy and strong. The great tragedy of Auntie Biddy was that her mind was little more than that of a child, but her smile would put a smile on the very Face of God. I'd hear Grannie say she and Grandpa would have Biddy for the rest of their lives. God was good, and they'd be well able for it.

Biddy had come out feet first with the cord wrapped around her neck. Grandpa Martin had grabbed her, tore the cord apart with his own hands and fell on his knees with the baby in his arms, begging that God spare her, spare her, don't let her die as he couldn't part with another baby and have to release her back out to the cruel sea.

Biddy turned her new little face to her father and cried and kicked and thrashed her little pink hands. If Grandpa had lost his brother Liam, he had saved his daughter Biddy and she would remain his favorite until the day he died.

As poor Biddy was so simple-minded, little was expected of her. We could always find her rocking the baby. They called him Packy, short for Patrick. When the fire got low, she'd reach down with her left hand and throw in a few sods of turf from the peat bog.

Delighting at the hiss and bubbles the damp peat would make, she'd begin to sing, "Ah, da durty black bog, da durty black bog, da durty black bog, da durty..."

"Biddy! Biddy! Stop it! You'll have me out of me mind with dat 'durty black bog' song! Please, dear Biddy...no more of it, Love, no more," cried her mother, grabbing at her old curly gray hairs and bending over the little white sink to hide from the litany of the dirty black bog

Biddy held Packy closer and whispered in his little pink ear, "Ah, Packy little pet, da dirty black bog, da durty black bog goin' to come and get ye and ole Biddy herself will come and save ye from the durty black bog."

Grannie would rub lemon balm on Biddy's temples and prepare a nice bowl of rosemary tea with honey for her to sup. Anything at all to get her brain working. When Grannie heard Lizzie or Brendan say that Biddy was "gormless", she would swat them with her tea towel.

All the same, they kept their eyes on Biddy lest she wander off and one of the Tinkers would grab her or she'd fall off the cliffs and they'd never know what happened, just like Grandpa's Aunt Jane so long ago. When Grandpa had the drink taken, he'd call Biddy "Crazy Jane." That would hurt her so and Grandpa would hate himself, fearing that he had set a *pishogue* on Biddy, cursing her as it had his Crazy Aunt Jane.

Dear Crazy Jane was blown off the cliffs and sailed out to sea and the sharks had a feast on her fat bones. A fisherman reported seeing a big, black balloon lifting over the cliffs and being blown out to sea. Like a moth to the flame, Jane had to be with the wind and the waves and the sharp, black boulders. She slipped out in the dark of night and got her wish.

****

My dear mother Kate was the youngest of the girls. It was her job to make everyone happy and when Kate threw back her head of ginger-red curls and closed her baby-blue eyes, they all laughed along with her, for she knew that life was to be enjoyed and that all of God's marvelous creation was only to be celebrated!

With the hearing of so many stories and watching them bump up against each other over the years, I've come to understand how they coped with the small house and small lives they were dealt. The old folks would say, "After the gathering, comes the scattering", and scatter they did.

They all had to find their own safe place to hide and to scrape out a tiny private spot to call their own. Grandpa hid in his grief, Grannie in her work, Tom in the land, Brendan in his books, Lizzie in her rage, Nellie in Lizzie, Biddy in her fireside chants, and Packy in Biddy's bosom. Kate was left with nowhere to hide until she met my father, Jeremiah Murphy, who later became Cardinal Jeremiah Devitt.

Grannie would look out the small kitchen window and forget her troubles as she saw my mother skipping through the potato drills or trying to get up on Sally, the old brown cow. "Full of the joys of life, that one is, just full of the joys of life is our own dear Kate."

Now I know all of this to be true. Mammie, Grannie and all the aunts and uncles have told me these stories over and over again and I do know that I walked those green hills of Clare even before I had the legs to walk on, before I was born back in 1938.

I was in that cottage and watched my mother from the time she was small. They say that all our cells remember what our ancestors have lived through and I've grown to believe it. I know I took it all in and I still wear all my people as close to me as the old white hairs that blanket my chest. Besides, when I'm deep in the hard earth, a part of me will forever haunt that little green and misty space across the sea. The place of my people.

CHAPTER 3
The Holy Ground

Lord and Lady Devitt came down the dark green Connemara marble steps to greet the carriage. As the Devitts were Catholics, they could not be in line to inherit British titles. Their titles were literally purchased before the Famine of 1849 when Lord Philip Devitt's grandfather bought Graymour Manor; like the parlors and pillars, the titles came with the estate

The stately black carriage drew up to Graymour Manor. The coachman reined back the elegant white horses as they snorted and reared back. The grounds-keeper Peter Murphy ran out to steady them so Bishop Ronan Devitt could descend his episcopal carriage with dignity. Both Lord and Lady Devitt began to kneel at the foot of the carriage to kiss his ruby red ring.

"Good God! Mary, would you ever get on your feet? Philip, please! Off your knees! Off your knees! Have I just come home to be treated like a king? I'm hot and dry and me tongue is parched for a Guinness, Mary! And would you not have something here for Fr. Davis, my assistant? He's anxious to get out on the course before the sun goes down, God help him."

The ornate hand-carved golden oak doors were slowly opened by Molly Murphy, Peter's wife, who served as the Devitt's housekeeper. The Bishop stepped aside so his sister-in-law could go through before him. He looked up the mahogany staircase with the graceful green oriental runner, swept her up in his arms and twirled around the elegant foyer.

"Ronan, dear Ronan! Put me down right now! Act your age, Ronan! Philip, tell him to leave me down!"

The Bishop lowered Mary onto the thick, round dusty pink Persian rug and kissed the top of her small head with her thick hair pulled into a tight black bun. She held him tightly and gasped, "It's been so long, Ronan, so long. Never leave us again! We've missed you so much! Don't ever go again, Ronan!"

Young Mary O'Connor had met tall, handsome Ronan Devitt at the 1904 Dublin Horse Show. Like the turf stacked at night

13

so the flame would be alive in the morning, Mary's heart had burned with love for Ronan Devitt for over 40 years.

He had been home on his summer holiday from his studies in Rome to be a priest; Mary O'Connor simply knew she could stop him from returning to the priesthood. Nothing ever got in the way of what Mary wanted. Defeat and rejection were as foreign to her as the dirty little urchins, begging for 'tuppence' along the musty canals in Dublin.

Ronan knew better - he would be going back in September, for his vocation to the priesthood was as strong as an oak tree. No woman would ever stand between him and the church. The church meant power and privilege and renown, far greater than being a land-owner in poor County Clare.

Philip Devitt remembered the dread that played out across Mary O'Connor's black eyes when Ronan introduced Mary to him. Mary knew instantly that she was being "handed off', regardless of what their overt intentions were. She knew exactly what was happening and the deepest part of her froze like black ice for the rest of her life. The Dublin urchins had it better.

The Devitt brothers looked so much alike, yet Philip's features were softer and kinder, making him look slightly effeminate, like a faded version of his younger brother Ronan. In voice, gait, and manner, they were so similar, yet to the hungry eyes of Mary, they were as different as night is to day. Philip was a eunuch of sorts, while Ronan, the celibate, was charged with a sexual energy that could pierce a boulder.

Mary O'Connor was haunted by the words of Shakespeare's Romeo and Juliet that the nuns in the Loretto convent in Dublin had made her memorize:

All the entire world will be in love with night
And pay no worship to the garish sun.

Philip was the garish sun and Ronan was the black night that Mary desired to the point of madness. Philip was used to being a step behind the dark one, so when Mary was handed over to him, he knew what his role was – again to pick up the pieces that Ronan left in his wake.

14

Ronan was ordained a priest in Rome in 1916 and was made a bishop in the spring of 1919, immediately after the war. Philip and Mary were married by Ronan in the ProCathedral in Dublin that autumn. They stayed at the Shelbourne Hotel on St. Stephen's Green for their honeymoon, being content for long walks together through Dublin.

The older Devitt's youngest son, Aiden, was killed in Flanders in 1918, the same year that both the first Lady and Lord Devitt died of the Black Flu. The brothers Philip and Ronan were all that were left of the family. Hopes were on Philip and Mary to continue the Devitt line.

The First World War ended on September 29, 1919. Ireland had sat out the war as a neutral nation. They wanted their independence from England as much the lowland countries of Europe did not want to be controlled by Germany. The Irish Proclamation of 1916 stated, "Ireland …summons her children to her flag and strikes for her freedom." The Irish were getting restless to be done with England.

Soon English ships sailed into Dublin, Queenstown and Limerick full of the cruelest of British soldiers, known to the Irish as the "Black and Tans, or just "Tans" because of their uniforms. These English soldiers had nothing to do back in England and liked to wage war and throw their weight around. Forty-nine thousand Irishmen were killed fighting for England, but that was of little consequence.

Mary O'Connor was frightened as these "big galoots" who were all over Dublin, like a plague of locusts landing on her soft, white neck. Wanting Mary to feel safe, Philip assured her that the Black and Tans would be gone by the first of the year. Ronan lifted his eyebrow to Philip and Philip shook his head at Ronan. Mary was his to protect now. The hand-off was complete and now Ronan had to attend to his church and not to sweet, delicate Mary.

Philip came into the room with a plum sherry for Mary and two tumblers of Guinness for themselves. Ronan threw his back with one thirsty gulp and raised his glass to Philip. As Philip left the room to refill his brother's glass, Ronan turned toward Mary and asked how long it had been since they'd all been home together in

15

Graymour.

"Don't you know, Ronan? It was for Lord Devitt's funeral and then Aiden dying a few weeks later and you had to come back from Dublin again. They'd just made you an Archbishop and you thought you'd get a rest after all the goings-on in Rome and the Troubles around here with all the other big houses burned to the ground."

"I remember it all, very well, Mary."

"Then why did you ask, Ronan? Are you after tormenting me again? Are ye?"

As Philip brought in another tray of Guinness and as Mary sipped her sherry, the French doors flew open and four-year-old Jeremiah Murphy tore into the room with chicken feathers stuck in his curly black hair, his hand in the shape of a gun. He whooped and hollered like an Indian and his mother Molly darted in the room, curtsying to the Bishop and attempting to kneel and kiss his ring, chasing Jeremiah and shaking him by the ear. She grabbed her chest as the pains were on her again and shooed Jeremiah out of the room with her good foot.

"Ah, Molly, would you ever leave the young one with us? I'm never with a child, only the priests and the old folks who want something out of me. I just want to get to know your one here."

"Oh, of course, Your Excellency, whatever you wish!"

"Molly, would you ever call me 'Ronan'? You've always known me as Ronan, so please leave off the 'Excellency' business.

"Well, now, welcome home, Ronan, Ce'ad mi'le fa'ilte romha! Oh, you are so very welcome to be home and if there is anything you want...Jeremiah, you behave yourself for the Bishop now!"

Bishop Devitt reached his arms out for the young boy and Jeremiah jumped up into his lap. He stuck the Bishop's gold cross in his mouth and ran his fingers down the purple piping on his cassock. "Whoa, young fella', you're not a priest yet! Will we have another in the family?"

Mary uncrossed her legs and nodded to her brother-in-law with a knowing smile. Ronan smiled back and kissed little Jeremiah on the neck. As Mary opened her small pearl snuff box and placed a pinch of snuff in her nose, Philip looked out the window at old Peter Murphy carrying young Fr. Davis's clubs for him.

******

As Jeremiah Murphy aged, he grew to hate his parents. They were too old, too poor, too stupid for his tastes. Peter and Molly took care of the Big House up the hill and they were only servants and they shamed him. Peter had a gift with horses and Molly could put a shine on the silver that would blind a beggar, but that didn't make them part of the nobility.

By the time he was eleven, Jeremiah was mortified that he even *knew* Peter and Molly, much less be their only child. Not a day went by that Molly did not tell Jeremiah that he was "putting on airs" and he would shout back at her, "better than that stink from you, you old boggy hag."

When his father would attempt to swat him, Jeremiah would run around the big table until Peter grabbed his chest and plunked himself into his old chair by the fire, trying to grab fresh air for his wet lungs. "I hope ye die now, Old Man! The world'd be better off without ye, ya old Bollix!"

As the pains grabbed Peter's heart, Molly would reach for the hawthorn tea that she kept for him beside the open hearth and offer it to him in a tin ladle. It was thought that Christ's crown of thorns was made from the hawthorn tree and the ancient Irish revered it as a ward against evil.

As he struggled to swallow the tea, Molly's trembling hands spilled some on his shirt. Eleven-year-old Jeremiah snickered and kicked the old dog asleep by the fire. As he moved into his teen years, Jeremiah Murphy had the looks of a young Tyrone Power, with the heavy, sultry eyes and cleft chin that made women light-headed and men jealous. He carried himself like a king and spent hours correcting his West Clare accent.

There was something powerful about Jeremiah, that even as a young child, he was noticed in a crowd. He was aware of his own presence and authority and relished the powerful impact he had on people. Jeremiah was a magnet, snatching up the scattered filings of innocent minds and hearts, to control and absorb them as he pleased.

17

Bishop Ronan Devitt saw in young Jeremiah a mirror of himself as a child and knew that with Jeremiah's intelligence and personality and with Ronan's strong arm to guide him, Jeremiah would go far in the church. But the *Murphy* name would do him little good – he had to be a *Devitt* if he were to go places.

******

When Mary Sullivan, the young mid-wife, delivered Jeremiah that dreadful winter night of 1916, she thought she heard the Banshees howl so long and so loud that the stars tumbled from their place in the heavens and the moon hid her face in the sea.

The baby was bright and pink and loud and turned his head about to see where he was. Jeremiah was the most beautiful, intelligent baby that Mary Sullivan had ever held, yet there was something strange about him, like he wasn't a real baby – more like the son of a wild boar or a gray, whiskery seal.

Slowly she handed him over to Molly, wondering if she had made a mistake and that the child was in fact a changeling who belonged in another dimension. The mid-wife forced a smile, so as not to alarm his mother, but Molly Murphy had already read the doom on the mid-wife's face.

Peter came into the room, kissed his wife, and leaned over Mary's shoulder to see his new-born son. The baby looked up at his father and peed right in his eye. While Molly and Mary laughed, Peter turned his face and headed out the door.

With a pinch of bitter tobacco in his left cheek, he spit on the roots of the sacred oak trees as he made his way to the holy well, hidden deep within the side of the hill.

Carved into the entrance to the well was a small figure of a smiling woman, her legs splayed apart, ready either to give birth or to receive a male. This was an occulted remnant of the ancient Celts, the *Sheela na Gig*, the Goddess of Fertility, New Life, the earth's fullness. The *Sheela* is the Female Creator which is neglected at great peril. Peter Murphy smiled at the *Sheela*, as the old unconscious Druid within him recognized her power.

18

He knelt before the tumbling waters of the well and prayed, "Dear Mother of God, spare us from the wrath of this one now, for I can see it in him already. Give us the strength to rear him rightly, Sweet Mother of Jesus, whose only Son caused ye no trouble, only joy. But sure, He caused you pain, Dear Mary. That one caused ye plenty of pain, He did."

Peter blessed himself with the cold mountain water, raised himself from his aching knees, yanked his old tweedy black cap over his soft pink ears and made his way back to his own place by the quiet fire. *"Go sa'bha'la Dia sinn,* yeah, God help us, God help us all!"

Peter and Molly did rear him rightly. As a young child, Jeremiah was beloved of his mother who held and rocked and sang the old lullabies to him, who cared for his bumps and bruises and hurt feelings, who delighted herself with his hearty appetite for the warm bread and butter, for the sweet puddings and bits of peppermint, for the tender leg of the young chicken prepared especially for him with fresh butter and sea salt. Her old face was covered in his wet kisses and she never wiped one away.

Peter Murphy was delighted with himself for having sired such a strong, handsome youth in his advanced years. When Jeremiah could barely walk, Peter lifted him up on the Devitt's prize horses and he sat like a king. Later, Peter would give young Jeremiah a "leg up" and watch as he guided the gentle gray filly up and down the long drive. Peter would tell Jeremiah that his time was up, but Jeremiah always pleaded for just one more round that Peter was helpless to refuse.

Jeremiah would then fall into his father's waiting arms and hold him tightly around his strong, red neck. "I love ya, Da, more than anything in the whole, wide world! I just love ya to pieces, Da! You're the best Da forever!"

Jeremiah was a beautiful, loving, tender child, generous with his love for both of his dear, old parents. They never dreamed they would be so blessed in their old age, like Elizabeth and Zachery, the old parents of John the Baptist. All of them were probably in their late 30's or very early 40's, old when folks didn't usually make it all the way to 50 years of age.

19

As Jeremiah Murphy moved out of his sweet boyhood, he radically changed into an arrogant, ambitious, hateful young man. He held his own, dear parents in contempt, a factor that may have contributed to their untimely deaths. He became Jeremiah Murphy **Devitt**, a name he hungered for from the first day that he began to understand the power of a name.

Jeremiah Murphy **Devitt** was my father, a fact that was hidden from me for the first 25 years of my life.

CHAPTER 4
Courting in the Kitchen

Kate joggled in the two- wheeled trap beside her brother Tom on the way up the stony mountain to Graymour Manor with their fat duck eggs. Old Peter Murphy waved to Tom from the stables as he was grooming the last of the horses. Molly Murphy met them up the back and invited them in for a spot of tea, as the Devitts were away up to Dublin for the horse show.

As Tom tied the trap, Molly Murphy linked her arm in Kate's and shooed the chickens out of their way. Standing in the corner was their son, Jeremiah, back home from the seminary up in Maynooth for his holiday. Kate saw the tall, beautiful young man in his red riding clothes and caught her breath. As she placed the wicker basket of eggs in the porcelain sink, brown and white duck feathers flew out of the basket.

Kate lowered her eyes and hoped he couldn't see her heart racing. She bent over to collect the feathers and could see only his shiny black riding boots keeping time with the beats of her heart. And he knew it.

"Kate, now, have ye ever met our son, Jeremiah? Jeremiah here is studying to be a priest."

"My name is Jeremiah, Kate," he carefully articulated so she wouldn't miss the echoes of his Maynooth schooling. "I'm most pleased to meet you."

He extended his hand. Kate lowered her eyes and curtsied. Molly grabbed her arm and raised her up. "Ah, we'll have none of that in here, Kate! He's just full of himself and expects everyone to fall on their face before him. God help us all!"

Jeremiah tossed his fine China teacup into the sink on top of the eggs. Broken eggs and shards of the China ran down the sides of the wicker basket. Molly held her face in her hands. Jeremiah stamped down the outside back stairs to see if his father, Peter Murphy, had the horse ready for him. Kate's heart pounded like the waves of the sea.

21

Coming up the stairs, Tom Sweeney bumped into Jeremiah.

"Tom," Jeremiah said.

"Jeremiah," Tom replied, as he extended his hand.

"Tom, now, have you seen that old fool, himself? He's late in getting the horse ready for me."

With his hand on the railing, Tom planted his feet and didn't look up.

"Now would you move yourself, Tom Sweeney, as I'm already behind schedule. You're just as thick in the head as all the rest of them from 'up da cuntry' Get out of me way, Sweeney!" He aimed his riding crop at Tom's head.

Tom grabbed the crop and Jeremiah flew down the steps and into the muck of geese and goats. Gray and brown lumps of animal waste streamed down his contorted face and onto his crisp, white riding shirt. Tom Sweeney slapped his knee and let out a roar of laughter that woke the old greyhound sleeping under the stairs.

Molly and Kate opened the kitchen door as Jeremiah lifted his big, beautiful self out of the muck. He hurled down his stick, kicked the old dog and, reinforcing his upper-class accent, shouted, "Ah, Sweeney, I'll return this favor if it's the last thing I do!! You won't be wanting for anything from me!" And under his breath, he cursed, "D'anam don diabhal! The devil take you!!" Tom dusted himself off and motioned for his sister to hurry along. "I'm sorry, Mrs. Murphy, I mean ye' no harm."

"Ah, don't ye worry a bit of it, Tom. Jeremiah here is only getting what he's long deserved. His is a black heart pumping in that mean, wily chest of his. Now go on with the two of ye and the blessing of God be with you on your wild path down this old mountain. And my love to all the Sweeneys, especially your poor mother, dear Annie herself."

Kate and Tom waved to Peter Murphy in the stables and Peter tipped his old cap with a wave himself. A soft rain began to fall. Never in all the 15 years that Tom had known Jeremiah Murphy had the meeting been sweeter.

Jeremiah knew that he was more Devitt than Murphy and his place was to belong to the small group of Catholic aristocrats. The

Devitts did not belong to the socially elite enclave of the many Anglo-Irish aristocrats, Protestant nobility who owned the big houses and the land and charged exorbitant rents to the poor Catholic farmers. It was this latter group who were robbed and pillaged during the Irish fight for independence.

Jeremiah was most pleased with himself that he had been born in such proximity to the Devitts – near to their power and wealth, not into poverty and shame, huddling in a poor, stinking cottage by the sea. He was wanting in nothing – not in looks, brains, style.

Everyone knew that he was going far in whatever he did, but the Roman Catholic Church had claimed him long before he was even born. He knew that the Devitts would make their claim on him, as the son they had never had in the flesh, but their rightful heir and mirror of their commitment to the church, of their worldly power amidst the Protestant gentry. And he set his sights high within that power structure, as anything less would have been wrong for him.

Lady Mary Devitt had fastened her eyes on young Jeremiah from the first instant she saw him. Denied her own her own flesh and blood, Jeremiah Murphy, the child of her spirit, would climb that golden ladder to the stars faster and more gracefully than did Bishop Ronan Devitt, the old devil himself.

A storm rolled in over the cliffs and rattled the old trap as it made its way down the narrow, muddy mountain. Tom pulled up his collar and Kate wrapped the old gray shawl tightly around her thin shoulders. Contented, Tom breathed deeply that many an old score had been settled with Jeremiah. Kate's heart continued to hammer in her chest. Neither knew that many more scores to be settled lay in wait for the both of them.

****

The whinchat whistled through trees on the old mountain road. Kate pushed the black-faced sheep out of her way and ran behind the pile of stones from the old chapel. Jeremiah Murphy was waiting, his white shirt blowing on the rusty iron hook. He was kicking off his riding boots as Kate flew into his arms. He tore at her bodice until her breast was in his face like a sweet, plump melon.

23

Kate was a young woman starving and wanted nothing more than to devour him, or to leap inside of him and become him and he would become her, and they would be one, not just two hungry kids on a mountainside. Kate was driven mad with desire for Jeremiah. As she marched up and down the hillside, in and out of the cottage, she felt herself floating like a wounded cormorant, battered until she would find shelter in his arms.

Jeremiah Murphy had first appeared at the Sweeney's as he walked his horse back from the sea. He stood by the old stone wall and watched Kate pulling potatoes from the black soil, her face streaked with dirt and sweat. She looked up and he waved to her. She waved back and brushed her hair back from her face. He tied up the horse and jumped the wall.

Kate blushed a deep crimson. Jeremiah walked to the potato drills and smiled down at Kate on her knees. He offered her his hand and she took it. She came up to his shoulders. "I hear tell that there's a holy well to St. Bridget near here, Kate. Would you ever lead me to it?"

Kate nodded and away they went, across the fields, over the stone walls, down the steep side of the glen and following the creek to the falling waters of the holy well at the back of the dark cave hidden in the side of the rocky mountain. The high black cliffs were on the other side, facing the sea.

Kneeling on the damp, uneven flagstone before the well, they blessed themselves and prayed with only the sound of the splashing waters to cut the stony silence of the cave. Kate cupped her hands and covered her face with the cold, brown water. Her red hair clung to her forehead. She began to wipe her mud-streaked face on the sleeve of her frock, but Jeremiah held her face and began to dry it with his soft handkerchief, like he would dry the dirty face of a little girl.

They stepped into the light, filtered through the thick, leafy trees. Jeremiah lifted Kate's face and kissed her ever so gently on her full, red lips. She had never been kissed before and felt her knees slide out from under her. She crumpled into a ball at his feet.

When she came to, he was sitting quietly next to her. His hand was on her soft hair. She didn't know what had happened to her. She looked around and when she looked into his eyes, it all came back. "I'm sorry," she whispered. "I never done that with anyone."

"Sure, Kate, it won't be the last time, either. It's only the beginning of what's between us. I knew it the minute you came into the kitchen with the bluey duck eggs. Sure, there's a wild, stormy pull between us, isn't there?"

Kate nodded and covered her face with her hands. Jeremiah took her hands away, leaned over and kissed her on top of her head. "I'd better get you home before that brother of yours has my scalp. But we'll meet again, now won't we?"

"Indeed, we will. When you have the time, I'll be here waiting for you, Jeremiah. I've got nowhere else to go, sure, I haven't. I'll be here waiting. Just waiting." They walked together, hand in hand, up the sides of the glen and over the stone walls. Shaking, Kate made her way alone back through damp fields. Jeremiah Murphy was flying away like a hungry raven, smiling that he had caught his willing prey.

Kate's mind and body belonged to him and him alone. When she was at home, she was beyond them all. Her mother would shout, "Kate, you're away with the fairies!" and Kate would whisper, "Sorry, Mammie, so sorry."

And just as wildly, Kate hated him for making her so desperate. She pictured herself with her father's long blue steel blade that he used for slaughtering the pigs, whipping it around Jeremiah and tossing his limbs into the sea or back to the pigs for a treat.

Jeremiah treated her sweet brother Tom like cow dung. He thought the church was lucky to get him. The Devitts ate out of his hands. Bishop Ronan Devitt treated him like his very own son, so improper for a man of God. Jeremiah Murphy thought only lofty thoughts of himself and plotted to have Devitt as his surname

The arrogance Kate hated about him drove her to a state of madness, of passion and desire that would have scared the salt out of the sea. She had become a wild woman with feelings she did not know even existed, wild feelings that flamed with abandon within herself.

As the wind tore in over the cliffs from the sea, Jeremiah covered her with his naked body and kissed her roughly. He entered into her waiting self and roared in his climax, matching the crest of the waves crashing on the rocks below. When he finished his pleasure, he rolled over onto the wild grass and fell into a deep sleep.

Shivering, Kate lay still, staring up at the weak, formless clouds rolling in from the sea. Her legs felt sticky, like she had sat in a bowl of honey-cream. She was at a loss for what to do – Jeremiah was sound asleep, his stallion was pawing the ground, she was half-naked in a lonely Irish field of clover and burrs, a desperate thirst came on her for a cup of her mother's strong tea. Was this what it was all about?

Suddenly Jeremiah jumped up, pulled on his shirt and boots and flung one of his monogrammed handkerchiefs at her. It was always, "Thanks Kate...I hear someone comin' down the old path. Tom Sweeney will kill me. Thanks again, Love" and away he flew on the back of the snorting stallion, his welcoming prey left to mop up.

Kate would often lie on the cold stones of the old chapel, her face and breasts scratched from his heavy beard, the sheep bleating with the gathering storm. She had him and he had her and yet she felt as empty as an old milk pail.

When she would ask him if a priest in the making should be with a woman that way, Jeremiah would rumple her hair and tell her that she wasn't a woman yet, still a girl and he loved her like a girl, the most "darlin' girl from Clare".

And Kate would persist, asking him how it was not sinful that they were doing this and he'd say he wasn't a priest yet. One time he told her that his spiritual advisor said he would make a much better priest if he had a woman all to himself.

The last time they were together, Jeremiah told Kate that he needed her more than he needed God Himself. She caught her breath and slapped him in the face, "Ye blasphemer! Ye dirty sinner, ye!"

He pinned her arms down, held her tightly between his legs and spit in her face. "It's back to the pigs with you, fat Kate, back to the pigs! You Sweeneys are dumber than pig shite! I've always known!"

Jeremiah lunged from the top of the stone wall onto the back of the stallion, kicked him in the ribs and galloped up the laneway to the gray stone mansion waiting for him on the mountain top. He hadn't the time to waste on her.

The tiny, tiny cells of my body began to cluster within the soft, pink womb of my dear mother and it was there I would live for the next nine months until I was strong enough to breathe alone and drink her warm, rich milk. Jeremiah had no idea what he had done.

CHAPTER 5
Down Where the Bees are Humming

Grannie was at the table, mixing the flour and eggs for her brown bread. She chased Rosie, the *Rhode Island Red* hen, off the top of the table. Squawking at Grannie, she flew into the air, red feathers flying. Grannie caught one and stuck it into her white hair. Rosie pouted under a chair. Grannie smiled – this was her kitchen.

Grannie often thought of how blessed they were now with the potatoes and parsnips and hens and pigs and the head of cattle and the few black-faced sheep to call their own. She had a heart that over-flowed with gratitude, for she knew how fragile their existence was.

She'd heard tell of the Potato Famine, just 80 years before, with folks dying by the side of the road, green juice streaming down their chins from eating weeds and grass. Coffin ships taking half the country to America and dumping them, dead or alive, on foreign shores.

To this day, I can't sit myself down before a lusty, fat spud, drenched in melting butter and sprinkled with sea salt, and not call to mind the Famine and those poor, dear souls, starving to death for the want of a potato, their only nourishment. While the ships, groaning with the weight Irish beef and eggs and wheat, sailed for England, leaving the Irish people watching in horror.

Before Grannie laid the dough in the heavy iron pot and swung it on the crane over the turf fire, she made the sign of the cross on top of the bread with her little knife. "*Dia linn*, God bless us, *Dia linn*."

One day, Lizzie was in a wicked humor, as usual. Her sharp features could slice you in half with a glance. Weeding out the cabbage and carrots, she'd swat the chickens and kick the goats and shout terrible curses to the wind.

"Shite and damn it to hell. Those bloody fuckers, all of them! I'll kill them, I will. Crikey to hell, Crikey to hell. They can all go to hell!"

28

"Lizzie, mind your tongue! There's a babe here sleeping and poor old Biddy will hear ye!"

"And that stupid damn fool can kiss me arse, she can!"

Grannie looked out to the chickens, scratching in the dirt. Speaking to only herself, she said, "Ah, that one will have it coming to her someday, she will. The way she hurts them poor animals will all come back at her. She's done it since she was a babe, gnawing at that poor old dog's ear and him taking it from her. Sure, but all the same, isn't Lizzie's a good, strong worker, God help us all!"

Every time Lizzie came into the house, she would go to her mother's medicine box and gulp some of the teas that Annie had brewed, taking lavender for her migraines, primrose and chamomile for her nerves, valerian tea to sleep. She always had a sprig of parsley between her teeth to keep her breath fresh and some hyssop in her hair for good luck.

"Easy, now go easy, Love, with all them flowers and such. It's all them teas what's making you so nervous," Grannie would warn her daughter. Lizzie couldn't be bothered with her mother's goings on. She would stick her tongue out at her mother when she wasn't looking.

Papa and Tom and Brendan would be in for their noon-day meal before long. Grannie shouted to Kate to get the cabbage and bacon in the pot. She went around back and shouted for Kate again. Her ginger-red head appeared over the hedge on the girl's side of the land they used when Nature called them.

Kate waved to her mother and bent over the cold spring, washed her face and hands and rinsed out her mouth. She had been vomiting every morning for weeks and fresh mint leaves were the only thing to settle her stomach. She ran into the house, frantically sucking on a little piece of mint.

"I'll have it done in no time, Mammie. I'm sorry, Mammie," she said as she kissed the baby and Biddy on top of their heads.

"Are ye sick, lame or lazy, or what the divil ails ye, Kate?"

"Ah, Mammie, it's just my time of the month, you know."

"But you never threw up like that."

29

"The milk tasted a bit off last night, don't you know?"

"None the else of us got sick."

"I'll be right as rain in just a few minutes, Mammie."

"God help us, I hope so! God help us all!"

Grannie stared at her daughter as she washed the green onions and cabbage and tucked the small side of fatty rashers into the heavy, black pot. Kate avoided her mother's sea-green eyes, not wanting to welcome the trouble that was just around the corner.

Biddy nodded her head and smiled up into the rafters as the old gray dove cooed down on the family. Biddy thought the bird was Crazy Jane come back to keep an eye on them, perched up there where she could see all the comings and goings of her little family.

Grannie placed her hand over her heart and wished above all else that Kate be as happy in her whole life as she was that morning. Then she placed her thin hands on her own taut belly, praying that she would be able to deliver her own new baby whole.

The tea had been steeping long enough. Grannie poured the first little bit out the half-door as an offering to the gracious God who had blessed them so. Then she sat down with Biddy at the fire to enjoy a nice hot cup.

They could smell the new cabbage and green onions starting to boil. As the tide came in, Grannie fell fast asleep in her old rocking chair, the hot tea spilling into her lap, her head bouncing on her plump, full breasts.

I often saw her standing up straight as a board, her tummy against the hard, old sink, sound asleep in herself. She'd jump awake when she'd hear herself snoring. Biddy would laugh so loud the rafters would shake and Grannie would tell her to mind herself.

So this was the beginning of me so very long ago. No one knew that I was just a little ball of life, growing day by day inside of my dear mother's womb. Sure the cups got thrown, the voices got loud and the fists got raised, but the blessings of God Almighty filled every cell of my body, as I was called to life in the most wonderful home on God's holy green earth.

I often wonder if I ever really left there, as I was forever drawn back to our little old cabin at the very edge of the sea. So full of

30

life in every room, yet death was always stalking us – sometimes like a flash of lightening and at other times like a slow roll of the drums. It wasn't for us to say.

CHAPTER 6
The House of the Rising Sun

It was Kate's 16th birthday. She sat on the curve of the old stone wall that separated the Sweeney's few acres from the Conley's. It was a dry day with a gentle breeze coming in from the sea. With her bare feet tracing the clefts in the rocks, she played with her willowy hair and dreamed of love in a faraway land.

The quick and heavy crunch on the gravel alerted Kate. A black stallion cleared the mountain turn, sweat glistening on his haunches like white rain. Jeremiah Murphy was riding low on his neck, leaves and flowers clinging to his wet shirt and black hair.

"Greetings, Lassie!! I've come to kill your brother, that Tom Sweeney, the daft man of the little world!"

Kate leaped down from the wall, tearing her black frock as she jumped from the pile of rocks onto the soft grasses. She bolted through the narrow gap into the Conley's green oats, shouting her brother's name as she ran.

Her foot caught in a rabbit hole hidden in the oats and her ankle snapped. She could do nothing but hold her ankle and stare back at the mother rabbit, scared and twitching her long brown ears.

Jeremiah opened a spot in the stones for his stallion and walked him slowly to where Kate lay. She hid her face in her hands. He stooped down and placed his hand on her ankle, smiling as they both knew that she had caused this misfortune all on her own. She had no one to blame but her stubborn self.

Kate hauled off and slugged him on the cheek and back-handed dirt into his eyes. "You dirty bastard, go on out of here! I'll kill you myself, I will!"

Jeremiah scooped her up and lifted her up on the stallion. He mounted behind her and tore through the tall grasses and off up the mountain. Kate screamed with the fright. No one heard her.

"Now, Kate, Dr. O'Boyle is up at Graymour right now, looking after Lady Devitt herself. He'll have time for you and I'll take you right back to your gentleman of a brother." Kate was in shock from the pain and drifted off.

Jeremiah pulled the stallion up to the front of the mansion, kicked open the oaken doors and carried Kate into the sitting room where Lord and Lady Devitt were having sherry with the doctor. Black mud from the mountain and horse-hairs covered the pink Persian rugs. Jeremiah placed Kate on the red velvet sofa.

Dr. O'Boyle raced over to Kate, spilling his golden sherry on the rugs. Her ankle was wrenched from its bearings and hung limp in his hand. Kate hid her face in her black apron, streaking dirt and tears into her hair and onto the red sofa.

With all the commotion, Molly came running into the sitting room, wiping the wet mud with a fresh tea-cloth and telling Jeremiah to get out and leave Dr. O'Boyle to his business, that he had no right to be with Kate.

Molly Murphy was the only one who was permitted to use her sharp tongue to speak to her son, Jeremiah. The Devitts never ceased to be shocked that their prince would elicit such rough language from his very own mother.

"And you with your fancy airs and Glenstall Abbey monks and girls and handsome looks. You've no right to take advantage of Lord and Lady Devitt. They have their own concerns and don't need to be bothered with the likes of you. And Dr. O'Boyle, please forgive his rudeness. Ah, he'll never learn!"

"Get yourself into the kitchen where you belong, Molly." Jeremiah shoved his mother, their house-keeper, out of the room and smiled at Lady Mary Devitt. She smiled back and patted Lord Philip Devitt on the knee with her thin hands, as delicate as a robin's breath. Philip placed his soft, white hand on top of hers and bit his thin bottom lip.

Dr. O'Boyle leaned over Kate and spoke privately, "Tis a nasty break you've got here, Kate Sweeney. The best I can do is to tape it tight and give you some tablets for your pain. It will bother you for a while, now, but you're young and will heal over." And even more softly, "Now, Love, be sure that Martin Sweeney gets the old bone-setter down from Killaloe."

Dr. O'Boyle tugged at his left ear and made the sign of the cross on her ankle. He knew well that Jeremiah was up to no good and Kate Sweeney would walk with a limp for the rest of her life. He put his left hand across her stomach, closed his eyes and hoped he was wrong about another diagnosis he was making to himself.

****

Annie and her daughter were at the kitchen sink. It was not large enough for both with their long black frocks and sleeves rolled up to their elbows. "Make yourself small, now Kate. You're taking up too much space around here, Love. You're eating' too much for your tiny size."

Kate ran up the back where the grass was soft and green and climbed up into the young pear tree. She hid her face in her long black skirt to stifle her tears. She thought of how she could kill herself. Maybe the cliffs...or the dirty black bog.

"Come down, Love, come down now. Nothing is so bad with you. Ah, sure aren't you loved and cared for by all of us, sweet Kate. Do come down now, Love. We can let those worries all go out with the tide, now Pet."

Kate slid down the smooth tree and fell into the arms of her mother. Annie felt Kate's large breasts against her own and held her even tighter. She lowered her hand and placed it on Kate's belly and made a small sign of the cross.

They both sat under the pear tree without saying a word. Biddy came to the door with the baby Packy and joined them on the ground. "Ah, Biddy, that young one will sleep his life away in your arms, so he will." Biddy smiled with her mother's approval and looked over at Kate. She was sad because her little sister was crying. Lizzie was in the front snarling as she and Nellie swept the pebbles on the path. The men were up the back.

"Who is it, Pet? Who done this to you?"

"I don't know."

"Don't lie to your mother, Mary Catherine. Sure it wasn't the Holy Ghost!"

"I can't tell ye, Mammie!"

"Then who are you going to tell, this one here?" pointing to Biddy. Biddy smiled back.

"Tell her to stop it, Mammie! I can't stand her smiling up at

34

the sky all day long!"

"Sure and wouldn't you be in a better place if you'd been smiling' at the sky instead of at some bollix with nothing else on his mind?"

"Mammie, please don't, please don't!"

Annie placed Kate's head in her lap and Biddy placed young Packy's head in her lap. Annie closed her eyes and prayed...the pear tree smells like something out of China or Japan and me here with another baby on the way and Kate herself only a babe. Dear Lord, guide me with her father, because if it was one of them damn Tinkers, Martin Sweeney will kill him.

She heard Tom and Martin washing up the tools from cutting the bog. Brendan had begun to stack the dry sods beside the house. Martin poked his head around the side of the shed and blessed himself. He looked at his wife and she shook her head, placing her hand on Kate's belly. There was no sound. Even the animals were still.

"WHO IS IT! WHAT'S THE FUCKER'S NAME? GIVE ME HIS NAME AND I'LL KILL THAT BLOODY FUCKER TONIGHT!"

"Martin, in the name of God, would you mind yourself, please Martin."

"I'LL KILL THE BLOODY FUCKER!!"

With Nellie close behind her, Lizzie carefully placed a basket of soiled handkerchiefs in Kate's lap. Each held a monogram with fine silk thread: J.M.

Tom Sweeney picked up one of them, studied the monogram and slammed his fist into the sweet pear tree. Biddy frowned, and the baby cried. Brendan squeezed a sod of turf until it crumbled in his hand and the brown bog water ran down his arms. I kicked a few kicks in a soft spot next to my mother's heart.

CHAPTER 7
The Gray Mountains of Dark Donegal

Martin wired for our uncle, his brother Paul Sweeney, to come home to Quilty, for the family was in need. Paul Sweeney was a Jesuit priest who had been banished to a small parish up in Donegal. His superior hoped the clean, mountain air would sort him out and help him get a handle on his drinking. Paul had been on a path of scholarship in Rome when his life derailed with alcohol.

Paul was tall for the Sweeneys. His red hair and snowy red beard made him resemble an ancient Druid, chanting beneath a great oak tree, more than a Jesuit priest trying to get sober. His long fingers were those of a musician, although he couldn't play a note. They said that his smile could charm the skin off a seal and that his temper could chase the wild *Pookas* into the sea.

Martin and Tom took the pony and trap down to Ennis to pick up Paul. As they made their way from Quilty to Kilkee and on to Ennis, they stopped for the noon *Angelus* three times, as the times in each village were set by a different reading of the sun. They were afraid that if they didn't hurry, they'd be caught again at 6:00 and must pray again and again.

This was the first time Martin had turned to his younger brother for anything. While the telegram had been brief, Paul knew that there was trouble afoot and he was glad to get down to Clare and be with his family. Martin and Tom filled him about Kate's condition on the road back to Quilty.

As they came up to the house, they saw a strange horse tied to the old apple tree. They went in the house and saw Fr. Hayes from their local parish ranting at Kate and Annie, Biddy humming about the dirty black bog and Rosie hopping on the table, feathers flying. Lizzie and Nellie were outside, their ears to the window.

Martin, Paul and Tom Sweeney towered over Fr. Hayes. Fr. Paul Sweeney blessed himself and said, "God save all here!" and the family responded, "God save you kindly."

Paul introduced himself to the parish priest and inquired as to his concern at the family home. Fr. Hayes shouted that Kate was nothing more than a common slut, she was going to be "read" from the altar on Sunday and the following week she'd be sent off to the nuns at the Magdalene laundry in Limerick for the rest of her life and the life of that dirty bastard inside of her.

Martin lunged for Fr. Hayes. Paul stepped between them and asked the parish priest if he wouldn't care to step out to the garden. The family watched through the half-door as Paul smiled down at Fr. Hayes and Fr. Hayes clenched his teeth as his face fell and his bald pate reddened.

"Now, Father Hayes, I'm sure there has been a grave error somewhere in your information. There will be no more of your *pagan* reading from the pulpit, there will be no sending of my niece off to the nuns and sure the child's father died when that old bullocks ran him off the cliff last month, don't you remember?"

Fr. Hayes said nothing and moved not an inch. He then nodded, "We'll see, indeed, we'll see."

"Ah, Fr. Hayes, there is nothing to see, don't you see? Don't you see at all? It would be a shame if all that Devitt money dried up and your fancy trips to Rome to see himself there waiting to be a priest, then a bishop and probably a cardinal. Maybe even the first Irish pope, Jeremiah Murphy Devitt, himself!"

"And if it were to become news for all your parish, it would soon fly into the very ears of Bishop Barry in Ennis, as Michael Barry and I are friends from long ago. Ah, sure, Fr. Hayes, it'd be a bloody shame for all of you, now wouldn't it? Then there is the matter of the altar boys and your fondness for your boney fingers down the front of their trousers!"

All eyes were on Fr. Hayes, waiting for a response. What more was there to say? Revenge filled his lungs as the old priest stormed off, slapping his old brown mare on the flanks and never looking back.

Annie had the tea made, the bread cut and fresh golden butter in the blue-flowered bowl. The cream was from the goats who ate the ivy down by the stone walls. Never was a spot of tea so lovely and never a victory so sweet.

Paul reached over for his niece, "Ah, Kate, whenever a child comes into the world, Christ Himself appears again and the whole messy lot of us is made whole. Martin, you yourself know it better than me, an old celibate up the mountains."

Paul pulled out his rosary and the entire family knelt before the hearth. Afterwards the younger ones went off to leave them alone by the fire. Only beautiful Biddy was there, smiling into the glowing turf. Paul began to tell them about his first night, years ago, up in Donegal.

****

There was a frantic knock on his door and a young boy was shouting at him to hurry, his mother was screaming, and his father was out fishing for the mackerel and the doctor was cold drunk on the surgery floor. Paul followed the boy down the dark and twisted lanes to a small cabin tottering at the edge of the sea.

The mother lay on the floor by the fire, water gushing out from between her legs, her hands grabbing her face in pain and thrashing her hips on the floor. Her heavy sighs and sharp screams frightened both Paul and the boy. He sent the boy for some clean, dry cloths and prayed to know what to do.

A little head was making its appearance between its mother's legs. The mother shouted, "Pull him out, not too hard! Let me push! Pull him out in the name of Jesus! Just pull him out!" Paul steadied the little head and gently tugged as the baby's one shoulder, then the other slipped out and quickly the little blue body was in the priest's two hands.

"Graham, Graham! Quick, get the knife for him, get the knife!" Paul did as the mother directed - cutting and tying the thick, blue cord and gently guiding out the placenta. He tossed it in the dog's dish.

"Christ, Almighty, get the baby to cry! Slap him on his arse! Suck the stuff out of his nose! Dear Mother of God, I'll lose this one, too! Get him to cry, would yous to hell!!" The mother screamed and screamed.

"Slap him on the arse, you old fool, ye!"

Paul did as he was told, working quickly to save the baby.

38

He covered the baby's face with his mouth and blew the gift of life into the little creature. She began to cry. Graham hid his face behind the thin stack of turf.

"Give him to me, would you? Give me the little man!"

"I think he's not a boy...not at all. Here's your little girl, Mammie!"

The mother held her only daughter to her lips, her cheeks, her breasts. She put her finger into the little rose-bud of a mouth and urged her to take her nipple.

"Ah, now, are you the new doctor? Where is Dr. Nolan? I told Graham to run, get Dr. Nolan."

"Would you not know that I'm the new priest, Fr. Sweeney? I just arrived here today. I thought you sent for me."

"Oh, Holy Jesus, Mary and Joseph!! Ah, Father, sure I'm ashamed of myself, shouting at ye and making ye look at me parts."

The mother buried her head in the back of the old dog lying next to her before the fire. "Ah, I'm ashamed, making a bloody show of myself right in front of a holy priest, Jesus forgive me, ah, forgive me Father..." She began to cry and then quickly wiped her eyes.

"Now, Father, what's the name of your own earthy mother? What's her name?"

"Molly, Molly Sweeney"

"Would ye be so kind to baptize our own little Molly right now, Father? It's a good, old name for our strong little girl! Molly it is to be! Oh, the sweet Mother of God sent our own little Molly to us."

Graham brought a little cup of water to Paul. He baptized the baby and kissed her on her little bald head. He blessed the mother and young Graham. The boy opened the door and took the priest by the hand and walked him down the dark path to see that he found his way home.

CHAPTER 8
The Old Maid in the Garret

Kate sighed and moaned as she lifted herself off the coarse, burlap-covered straw and went outside for the third time that evening. "My bladder's shrunk up on me, it has," she'd nudge Nellie or Biddy, but never Lizzie who always placed herself over by the wall so she had only one other sleeping body to contend with.

Kate would limp out to the girls' side of the hedge and frequently wet herself in the dark of night. When she'd roll back to bed, Lizzie never failed to proclaim how "disgoosting" she was, fat as a cow, smelling like a pig, dumb as a mule. Kate tried to ignore her and softly cried into Biddy or Nellie's back. Biddy would pat her little sister and Nellie would rub her back so Kate went back to sleep.

It was the middle of October with the rays of the sun faltering and the winds from the sea cutting into stone, tree and flesh. Kate was cold most of the time, but a flash of heat, like a bolt of lightning, would come upon her in the worst of times.

In the kitchen, she asked her mother what she could do to make the baby come faster, as she couldn't stand it one more day. When Annie told her that God has His time with every hair that falls from her head, Lizzie shouted over the half-door, "Just jump off the damn table, would you? Jump off the damn table!"

Annie bolted toward her with the wet tea cloth, shouting "I'll swat that sassy one across her mug and give her what's coming!"

Lizzie, jumping high over the drills of potatoes like a young colt, was far gone as she headed out to Nellie who was weeding the cabbage. Nellie was tearing off the weathered leaves of the fat, green cabbages and wiping her eyes with the back of her hands. Her little nut-brown head wasn't as large as a head of cabbage.

"Ah, now, where's our little garden snail?" Lizzie taunted Nellie, kicking her on the side and sending her rolling, face-first, into the black, loamy soil.

"Ah, Lizzie, why are you giving out to our poor Kate all the time?"

"Sure, don't you know I'm only giving the fat cow an idea to get her out of her misery? And I'm after praying that that little bastard will be born dead, like Biddy should have died, she's so stupid, rocking herself to death by that damn fire."

Nellie pulled herself up on her elbow and threw a fat cabbage at Lizzie. She caught it and with great force, hurled it back at Nellie's face. Nellie dropped into the cabbages, face-first. Lizzie knelt at Nellie's head, slapping her face and shaking her shoulders. Nellie didn't stir.

Lizzie flew over to the stream and back to the cabbages to throw cold water on Nellie's face. She began to stir, but her big, brown eyes remained glazed over. Through the hedges came their big brother Brendan with a look of surprise on his face. He saw Nellie lying unconscious and Lizzie beside her. He asked what the matter was.

"Nothing at all, nothing at all! Ye mind your own business, you Brendan, you! Just go piss on yourself, you damn thing, and just leave poor old Nellie alone, for the heats gotten on her again! Go piss on yourself and leave us alone, you hear?"

Brendan ran for his father. Martin and his son Tom made for the cabbage patch to see Nellie not moving, still as a dead lamb. Martin looked at Lizzie, his eyes glaring at her stony face. "You'll get what's coming to youse, you' will, just youse wait and see!"

Martin picked up his middle daughter and carried her over to the cold stream. He held her head as young Brendan cupped his hands and poured the cold water over Nellie's face in the sign of the cross. As they began the *Hail Mary*, Tom chased Lizzie into Conley's fields and tackled her amidst the sharp cornstalks.

"I've never seen such a look of evil as you're wearing today, Lizzie. Your heart is black as pitch, you're the very worse of us, the very worse, God help you and God help us all!"

Lizzie followed the shafts of wheat as they meandered to the edge of the sea. She looked out over the water. Dark storms were gathering in the west, the sun was blinding in the east.

Sometimes Nellie made Lizzie's skin crawl - always hanging around her, taking her orders, keeping her secrets. When Nellie saw

41

Lizzie hugging and kissing Mary Conley behind the barn, Mary pushed away from Lizzie and whispered, "Fences have ears."

Nellie tore off home, tripping over a rusty milk can in the field and slashing her arm. That should have taught her not to spy on her older sister. When Nellie saw Lizzie crying on the hillside with a young lamb who had lost her mother, she ran away so as not to let Lizzie know she had seen her tears. When Lizzie would slip out at night to meet Mary Conley in the shady glen beside the cliffs, Nellie would lie awake, still as a stone, waiting for her return.

Nellie kept Lizzie's secrets. Her own life was plain and simple, next to her sister's deep secret, mysterious life. Nothing was ever said by either of them. Nellie knew to keep her mouth shut. Maybe Lizzie's knocking Nellie's eye out with the green cabbage was her punishment for seeing too much.

The smile on her face began to fade as tears rose in her cold, steely blue eyes. Lizzie scorned Nellie's simplicity, yet she loved her younger sister and would have killed anyone who ever tried to hurt her. "God help me, *Go sábhála Dia sinn*, God help me," she prayed. "Don't let Nellie die, I'll kill myself if she does."

****

Nellie always knew she was different from the others - it was almost as if she were of a different family altogether. Brendan with his books, Lizzie with Mary Conley, Kate with her baby, Biddy by the fire. Nellie wasn't a nothing, although they all thought her empty-headed and vacant, but Nellie was not lacking in intelligence.

Nellie didn't mind what they thought of her. She was just quiet and dreamy and always "away with the fairies," as her mother so kindly named her vacancy. Nellie knew that she bothered her father, but she just could never think of anything to say to him. If the truth be told, he frightened her with his loud voice and heavy footsteps and thick, hairy arms.

Nellie loved them all so dearly, but she just didn't want to be troubled with all their worldly ways. She loved her prayers and her dreams of the world beyond this world. That other world was more real to her than that world of Sweeneys and cows and sheep and babies and dishes and noises from every quarter.

The Sweeney sisters received their early education at the hands of the Dominican nuns at the small country school near Doonbeg. Sr. Mary Grace, a tall, willowy nun in her long, white habit and black veil, also knew that Nellie Sweeney was different from the other girls. She was a child of the Spirit and when Nellie was gazing out the window, Sr. Mary Grace knew that she was seeing angels and the holy saints that once walked the green, green hills of Clare.

When Sr. Mary Grace spoke of holiness and of the great spiritual ways of the Celtic people, Nellie's heart raced in her thin chest, so much so that she felt the angels placing their soft wings around her to keep her heart from flying out the window. Nellie wanted nothing more than to be a holy martyr for the Good Lord whom she loved more than anyone.

In the small classroom, young Nellie Sweeney did her work, but without a sound, as if she were listening to something that no one else heard, seeing things that no one else saw. Sr. Mary Grace never raised her voice to Nellie because she understood her and did not want her to be any different than she was. Nellie was perfect just the way she was.

Sr. Mary Grace was so unlike her own mother, Annie, who was troubled by her quiet daughter's mysterious ways. After their tea, Nellie would dust the table and throw the crumbs to the chicks. Then she would steal back into the kitchen and wash the table over, fixing her eyes level with the top of the table as she may have missed a few crumbs.

When the Sweeneys knelt each evening for the family Rosary, Nellie would bless herself twice and kneel like a board was strapped to her back and hold her eyes closed like she was asleep. She ate only half of her small portion and never once caused her mother any trouble.

Sr. Mary Grace shared with the small class that the ancient Irish monks taught that there were three martyrdoms, three paths to union with God: white, red and green. While others in the class snickered, Nellie's face flushed with desire.

The *ba'n martra*, the White Martyrdom, was the self-sacrifice where all earthly pleasures and comforts were relinquished for the love of God. The most drastic renunciation was that of their very homeland, thus becoming missionaries to carry the word of God to faraway lands. St. Brendan was a white martyr, for he sailed to America long before Christopher Columbus, bringing the Word of God to the pagan Indians in America.

Red Martyrdom was the spilling of blood for the Kingdom of God. This was rare in the Christianizing of Ireland. However, many Irish monks and nuns died in Africa and India, and other foreign lands spreading the Word of God to the heathens. Nellie prayed for the courage to die if that was what God would choose for her.

Green Martyrdom described the harsh life of penance and fasting and hard work that the early Celtic monks endured on the harsh and rocky islands off the coast of Ireland. Nellie grew feverish with desire to suffer, physically and mentally, in union with the strong spirit of St. Bridget who was made a bishop of the church in those former times.

When Nellie tried to explain this to her mother, Annie whispered in her ear, "Sure, Love, now don't we all here in our poor country have not a pick to eat and us here working our fingers to the bone from sun up to sun down and sure, aren't we just the same as them Greenie Martyrs, as you say?"

Tears filled her little eyes as it hurt her that her own mother didn't understand her desire for a life of prayer and penance and Irish martyrdom. Nellie sometimes wished that Sr. Mary Grace was her real mother and then she would fall to her knees and ask God's forgiveness for such a terrible sin against her own flesh and blood.

Nellie Sweeney's soul was a receptacle for the life she was given. While she appeared passive to the more ambitious Sweeneys, she was spiritually alert, sensitive to the still, quiet voice within that spoke constantly to her. The breath of the Spirit of God was infusing her life with a joy that defied description.

While Nellie shared their flesh and blood, her soul was older than the caves up the road in Ballyvaughan, carved out of the limestone of the Aillwee Mountains. While others saw only emptiness, the walls of the caves told a story millions of years old, stories of floods and heat, of sand, silt and salt, of the earth formed by the force of nature. Still Nellie Sweeney was a hidden force of nature, formed by the many incarnations she had experienced over ages. Nellie Sweeney was a very old soul.

CHAPTER 9
When I was a Boy with Never a Crack in My Heart

Annie heard her youngest daughter whimpering through the thin wall. Her husband Martin had been dead some three months now and would miss the coming of his first grandchild. She knew Kate's time was drawing near and that I would come by the end of the week.

She had been giving her cups of comfrey tea and Tom had again brought the old bone-setter from Killaloo to fix Kate's ankle. It was swollen and throbbing with the extra weight from carrying me. My birth was going to be hard on my mother, but thank God she wasn't thrown in with the old laundry nuns in Limerick. The whimpering grew louder and soon she was crying.

Grannie sent Tom out on the old horse to fetch the midwife from over the hills. Grannie made Kate some strong comfrey tea and sent the others out of their room below the hearth. Kate was screaming with every minute.

Annie breathed softly in her ear, "Now, Love, the baby is on the way. It'll only take a few more minutes, breathe for me now, Love, just breathe, Pet... now just let me see between your legs...Jesus! She's coming now! Just breathe, Love, breathe, breathe..."

Tom and the midwife were nowhere to be seen. Brendan hid under his covers and Lizzie went out for a stroll, a smirk on her face and a bright red shawl across her sharp shoulders. Nellie put the kettle on to boil and Biddy sat at the end of their bed with fresh rags on the ready and began to rub her sister's legs.

Annie knelt between Kate's legs and caught me as I flew out of my mother like a silver salmon swimming upstream. Annie lost her balance, but Biddy caught me before I hit the floor.

She held me tight as Grannie cut my cord with her favorite little white paring knife. There was a slippery covering over my face, almost like a veil that hid me from the world.

"Oh, Sweet Mother of God, he's got the caul, the caul, the sacred caul!" shouted my grandmother, lifting the small membrane from off my face. She kissed it and handed it to Nellie for safe-keeping. Nellie kissed it and placed it on her blind eye.

46

"And I'm not finished with ye, Love," Annie whispered to Kate. "Now just open your legs again and we need to get the rest of it out of you." Annie held her one hand firmly on Kate's belly and with the other, pulled ever so gently on the placenta. It came out with a rush of blood.

Nellie soaked up the warm blood with the cloths and set them outside the back door to frighten the Fairies away. They needed none of them to come stealing into the house and swapping new little me for one of them. With all their troubles, a changeling would be the last thorn in the Sweeney's crown.

Biddy placed me on Kate's chest and my mother kissed me and held me and told me she would never let me go. Tears streamed down her cheeks. Kate smiled at her mother and Biddy and Nellie. I was sound asleep on her soft white breast.

Rushing through the half-door, the midwife took out her worn leather prayer-book and began praying. Into the house burst Tom and Brendan. They joined the crowd at the back of the cabin. Mary asked the Sweeneys if I had a name. They all looked at each other and then at Kate, "Martin, sure my young one is Martin Sweeney, just like his granddaddy, my own daddy, not yet cold in the ground, just like him is our new Martin."

Kate breathed her warm breath into my ears and rested her cheeks on my little bald head. She closed her eyes and silently made a vow in her heart of hearts: "I will never, ever tell him who his father is. My Martin will be a Sweeney through and through. I vow to keep this secret until the day I die and wild horses will never be able to pry it from my lips. So help me God!!

Annie reached for me, little Martin Sweeney, her first grandchild. Kate closed her eyes and fell asleep with a beautiful smile on her face. She knew that she would keep her secret vow and this would protect me all the days of my life. Little did she know she was making a deal with the devil.

CHAPTER 10
The Barren Barony

From the 14th Century, the Devitts could be traced back to the Barony of Raphoe, Co. Donegal. The family crest sported the mighty Irish elk with the 12-foot span of antlers and whose mullet denotes a Divine quality bestowed from above. The Devitt motto, *AR NDUTHCHAS,* in Irish, means "Our Heritage."

Their innate sense of entitlement was as natural to them as the mighty antlers that sprung from the crown of the majestic Irish elk. While the Devitts remained fiercely Catholic, they entertained no moral conflict in buying from the wealthy Protestants the noble titles that were attached to Graymour Manor.

Philip and Mary tried for many years to have children to inherit the wealth and noble name. Philip's family had all girls, many of whom had either died young or immigrated to Australia or America. They married or became nuns, ceding their Devitt name to following generations.

Mary's families, the O'Connors, had great wealth, but were poor in progeny. As Mary's health grew weaker with the years, Dr. O'Boyle advised them to stop trying, regardless of their money. The good priests could always use the money to help the poor. Mary and Philip nobly accepted their fate and fastened their hungry eyes on young Jeremiah Murphy.

With her black hair turning white, Lady Mary Devitt asked her house-keeper and lady's maid, Molly Murphy, to brush it for her every evening after tea. Molly would loosen Mary's tightly wrapped bun and holding the gracious pearl handle, gently pull the camel's hair bristles through Mary's thinning hair.

Lady Devitt would nod as Molly's steady stroke lowered her into an easy sleep. Molly would motion to Lord Devitt and he would tenderly lift her and carry her like a small child back into her bedroom.

Smoking his pipe, Peter waited on the back steps, swinging his paraffin lantern to drive away the Banshees. Peter's feet hurt and the soft pain in his chest was becoming sharper. It was a two mile

48

walk home and they both found it more difficult with the passing years and all the aches and pains of attending to the daily wants of the Devitts.

Lord Devitt came out from the back of the manor and offered Peter some fresh tobacco for his pipe. It was a clear night with the blue turf smoke from the small cottages in the valley curling up the mountainside. Both men stood silently, nodding to the moon as they filled their pipes.

"Peter, ah, Peter now, Mary was askin' if I'd talk to ye about something the two of us had been discussin.'

Peter knew something bad was about to happen with Lord Devitt putting on his old country accent as if they were really brothers under the skin and Peter hadn't been shining his boots and mucking out his stables for these many years.

"Oh, yes, m'Lord, of course."

"We are proud of young Jeremiah, Peter, proud of him as if he were our very own."

Jeremiah had been away at the Gregorian Papal Institute in Rome after studying for two years with the Jesuits at Mungret College in County Limerick and then out to Maynooth, the National Irish Catholic Seminary. This was an honor given to few. It was the Devitts that saw that no stone was left unturned for young and handsome Jeremiah Murphy.

Before ordination, Jeremiah had to be immersed in philosophy, moral theology, spirituality, sacramental theology, ecclesiology, church history with an emphasis on the Church Councils, patronymics and the rubrics of the church. He became fluent in Latin and Greek and spoke Italian with a Roman accent.

Jeremiah had begun to call Archbishop Ronan Devitt, "Uncle Ronan". The Archbishop had supervised not only his education, but his full development as a man of the church. On his many trips to Rome, Archbishop Devitt whetted Jeremiah's appetite with the subtleties of church politics, canonical structures and personalities, the future of the church, all plied with good food and fine wine.

49

Jeremiah knew that Archbishop Ronan Devitt was grooming him to be not only a priest, but a bishop and most probably a Cardinal, a Prince of the Church. If he stuck close to his mentor, the top of the ecclesiastical ladder was not a reach beyond his grasp.

Peter nodded, realizing that the two of them had never discussed the money it took to educate and support Jeremiah in his elegant style. *The old bugger just wants his money back, with interest. I'll damn well just let him ask, I will.*

Then a wave of remorse swept over Peter, angry with himself that he had never been man enough to sit down with Lord Devitt and work out the terms of the loan for the fortune it had cost to support and educate Jeremiah.

"Ah, Peter, I hate to bring this up to you like this, but her Ladyship and the Archbishop and myself have been discussing this for quite a while. I'm sure you understand, 'as a nod is as good as a wink to a blind horse'."

Saying nothing in response, Peter scratched the old greyhound that slept beneath the back porch and continued to puff on his clay pipe. A shooting star caught his eye.

"Well, what I'm getting at is that we have never had a child of our own and I know well that you and Molly have only the one son, but Mary and I want to adopt Jeremiah. Certainly he'll keep the Murphy name with the addition of Devitt at the end. We want to continue to provide for him in the way we have, Peter, and certainly with additional funds for you and Molly as the years are fast coming on you."

Peter cleared the rumblings in his throat, looked his Lordship straight in the eye and said, "Philip, you shame me."

Peter Murphy opened the back door, called for his wife to come and gently took her hand. Ever so slowly, with their old knees aching, they walked home together with their heads held high in the light of the pale white moon and never returned.

PART TWO

Chapters 11 – 19

O beautiful for gracious skies
For amber waves of grain
For purple mountains majesty
Above the fruited plain!
America! America!!
God shed His grace on thee!

CHAPTER 11
The Sea of Sorrow, The Trail of Tears

1948. I was 10 years old and on my way to a new life in America. There was nothing wrong with my old life in Ireland. I really loved it and, even though I didn't have a real father, I had Uncle Tom and he treated me like a son. I was afraid of what I'd be getting into in America.

World War II had been over for three years and the Cold War had begun in earnest. Israel had declared itself an independent state and the *Diaspora* of Jewish people were called home. Mahatma Ghandi, the spiritual and political leader of India, was murdered for his policy of non-violence.

The Marshall Plan brought billions of dollars to Europe to assist in war recovery. The World Health Organization was begun by the United Nations. The Cleveland Indians won the World Series, defeating the Boston Braves.

Eamon deValera, the New York born *Taoiseach*, lost his 16 year leadership in Ireland. The Hells Angels, the motorcycle gang, was formed in California. Harry S. Truman defeated Thomas E. Dewey for the presidency. Dewey was described as "the little man on top of the wedding cake".

My mother wrapped her scratchy, old gray shawl tightly around the both of us as we stood on the deck of *The Maryland* that crawled into New York Harbor. I could hardly breathe. Tears rolled down Mammie's pale white cheeks as she squeezed my hand and breathed into my ear. I grabbed the railing even tighter, as she was swaying like she did at home whenever she got faint.

As I put my head on her boney chest, I could hear the rattle in her lungs. I heard that all my life, almost like that distant rumbling that echoed over the cliffs before the storm hit. I thought that she would have left that at home and not brought it with her to America. I heard them call it *consumption*.

Then I saw what I had been waiting for but it was crawling with green stuff, like the slippery lichen that covered our stone walls at home. "But look, Mammie, "I asked her, "I thought the Statue of Liberty would be white like they are in church!"

"Ah, sure, now Son, doesn't that tell you that us Irish are her favorites? We'll make a whole new life for ourselves, isn't that right?" Mammie coughed and looking down at the churning black waters, told me again of how we had just crossed that vast *Sea of Sorrow* and followed the *Trail of Tears* as millions of Irish had done before us and millions will do after we are long gone.

I wished she would stop all that blather about the tears and the dead, but I couldn't say anything to her. She had to talk about that old stuff. Maybe she was terrified of forgetting her other life, her other people and if she shared it with me again, then there'd be the two of us to remember against the dark forgetting.

"Sure, the Irish are great shape-shifters, are we not, Martin? We must survive wherever fate drives us and sometimes we become strangers to ourselves. What shape will we take now, Martin? What will we look like when we start to be Americans?"

During every minute of our journey, all Mammie could talk about was what had brought us to this place in our lives, the twists and turns that had brought her to make this hard decision to leave Ireland.

Grandpa, her father, Martin O'Connor, had been coughing up blood for weeks before they found him in the small green field with Sally, his favorite brown cow, keeping vigil over his still body. Sally nudged him with her nose, moaned and breathed warm air over him as she would a still-born calf.

Tom said that when he found his father, Martin had his face turned toward America and his arse toward the Devitts. He was 48 years old. I wasn't even born yet, but they called me after him, "Martin Sweeney".

Mammie told me that she prayed daily that I would never be plagued with the ugly guilt that choked Grandpa to death for letting his brother Liam drown and for letting his dear sister Rosie sail on the *Titanic*.

Grannie, her mother, Annie O'Connor, died from pneumonia when she, too, was only 48. I was seven years old, but I

55

remember her well. Mammie would make Grannie mustard plasters to lie on her chest by mixing the mustard powder with water and honey and spreading the paste on a soft cloth.

Grannie would fall asleep with the cool pack on her chest. It would grow hot from the warmth of her body and she would wake screaming with the heat. When she died, her chest was burned purple and her lungs were filled with fluid that rattled like a child's toy.

Mammie talked about us being shape-shifters, but I never really knew what shape I was in to begin with, so how could I change from being nothing into being something? I'd ask her again and again about my father. Who was he? Where was he? First she said he had been a hero in the war with the Black and Tans, but at other times he had died at sea when his boat was lost in the fog.

When I asked her what my father's name was and where he was from and weren't there any relatives, she would cough and wave her hand before her eyes, like she were swatting a fly or dispelling images of him. I put my left hand over my jaw so she wouldn't see my old tooth, the Delaney *fiacail*, throbbing in my mouth as I took in her stories, God love her, her simple lies.

Mammie lied to me over and over again. She said his name was Frank, then Peter, then Martin. He was from Sligo, then Cavan. His family had all immigrated to Australia and left him behind. His family had caught the Black Flu or the Blue Flu.

"What? What? Why are you asking me again, Martin? Aint I enough for you, Martin? I brung ye all the way over here and you're still after me about your father. I told you all I know, now let the poor man rest in peace!"

With every inch of sea we crossed, I moved farther and farther away from ever finding my father. And to my tender, young soul, I was the one turning my back on my father, leaving him back there in Ireland, abandoning him as he had abandoned me. Within me, thin layers of guilt began to gather like silt, just as they had in the soul of my old grandpa, the first Martin Sweeney.

The vagueness about my own father left me vague about myself. As the English poet wrote, "I wandered lonely as a cloud". My mother, for all her good intentions, had wrapped my father's life in anger, mystery and lies. To be a good son, I funneled all that into myself and stayed vague, cloudy. I could even make my eyes glaze over when it would suit me.

I knew that he was bad – Tom and Brendan and Lizzie all referred to him as "that dirty son of a bitch up the road". Whenever I brought him up, everyone grew silent and looked to Kate for an answer. My mother had made her vow of silence the day I was born and wild horses would never pull it from her.

Sometimes I'd pretend my father was a great soldier, a great hurley player, a hero for all times. I'd walk down the boreens, those little twisty pathways, with a stick in my right hand, cap on straight and firm, my head held high and my left hand out to wave to the crowds - like deValera or Michael Collins.

And I'd catch the eye of a mucky lamb or an old cow and nod to them – I was the great hero, acknowledging my grateful people. But if an old farmer caught me, I'd duck behind a tree or roll on my back in the oats, anything not to be seen. "Makin' a show of himself," they'd say and, of course, I wouldn't want that.

If my father had been so horrible that they could not even speak his name in my presence, then I would be good, even exceptional. I would be a priest and be able to deflect from the Sweeneys all the bad things about my father, whoever he was. My father was a source of shame; I would be a source of honor. Half of my blood was his, my ever-present stranger.

I knew that I would be a priest the day of my First Holy Communion. I was only seven. As was the tradition, I visited all the relatives and neighbors in the small village, collecting a sweet or few pence as they were able. Then there was the lovely dinner back at home, with ham and eggs, spuds, carrots, turnips and a great current cake. Again, I was the center of attention and the day of my First Holy Communion was no different.

After I had changed out of my good clothes, I slipped out of the house to visit the well of St. Bridget in the shady glen near the cliffs. I needed to be alone and quiet. Carved into the entrance to the well was a small figure of a smiling woman, her legs splayed apart, ready either to give birth or to receive a male. This was an occult remnant of the ancient Celts, the *Sheela na Gig* the Goddess of Fertility, New Life, the earth's fullness. The *Sheela* is the Female Creator which is neglected at great peril.

As I stood at the entrance to the cave, *Sheela na Gig* was the same figure that had watched Jeremiah Murphy Devitt kiss Kate Sweeney, although I didn't know it then. I walked into the dark cave and knelt by the deep, splashing water. I stuck my fingers into the holy water to bless myself and lost my balance, nearly tipping straight into the cold, black water.

Shaken, I righted myself and looked square in the eyes of a statue of the Blessed Mother poised above the small ledge of the waterfalls. She stared at me. I stared back. My heart raced. My eyes filled with tears. My ears itched.

In that instant, I knew that I would be a priest. I knew beyond a shadow of doubt that my young hands would someday change bread and wine into the Body and Blood of Jesus, I would baptize babies and lay the dead to rest in the graveyard. I would be a good and holy priest, just like Jesus Christ Himself.

Then everyone would know that my father must not have been such a bad person if he could have produced a priest! Then I would really be a person of worth if my father had been such a wonderful man. Then I could be proud of myself, at ease, not worried. I'd be certain and speak with authority and stop being so vague and get my head out of the clouds.

****

In 1945 Lizzie, Nellie and Brendan had already come to America to join Grannie's sisters, the Delaney girls, who were set to welcome us to Chicago. There was no work, no money and no future in Ireland. Its greatest export was people - missionaries to Africa and India, and nurses, housekeepers, laborers to Australia, South Africa, America, Canada and England.

The *American Wake* was held in the mountains and valleys, in the towns and villages across the country. The night before a young son or daughter was to leave for America, family, friends, and neighbors from near and far would gather for a night of drinking, dancing, songs and great food.

As dawn broke, the new emigrants would gather their things and a horse and trap would carry them to the train for Cobh in County Cork where ships sailed for America. It was formerly called Queenstown until Ireland was free of English rule and English names.

Overlooking the quay towered St. Colman's Cathedral, an imposing neo-Gothic church facing the harbor. It was a proud, ominous building of blue Dalkey granite with Mallow limestone, gray flying buttresses, gargoyles, spirelets and pinnacles, roofed with blue Belgium slate.

Young Irish men and women leaned against the rails of ships sailing west and strained to see the very last patch of their home. As the green hills of Cork faded from view, the forbidding cathedral of St. Colman pierced the low-hanging clouds. Their very last picture of Ireland was St. Colman's Cathedral, never letting them forget that they were on their way to a pagan land and must never, ever abandon their faith, their one, holy, Roman Catholic faith.

Most of these young Irishmen and women would never return home, so they would indeed become "dead" to everyone. They had no choice but to go, leaving in their wake mothers and fathers, brothers and sisters who would grieve for these lost children for the rest of their lives.

Guilt at abandoning those who remained at home mixed with excitement to start a new life across the seas and to be joined again with those who had already left. Most left part of their souls back in the little cabins clutching the hillsides or resting in the rich valleys of their home. Without their souls, many dove into deep depressions or took to the drink.

They soon found that the streets of America were not "paved in gold," but they had an obligation to work – as housekeepers, gardeners, laborers - anything to provide for themselves and to send the bulk of their earnings back home. And if they were fortunate enough to return, to retrieve their lost souls, they had become outsiders, frequently called the "Yanks" by those who stayed at home.

We jumped at the three blasts from the ships' horns. Kate blessed herself, her mind in a whirl remembering those left at home in

Quilty – Tom, Biddy by the fire and young Packy. Papa and Grannie growing cold in the Quilty graveyard with no one to tend their graves.

My mother blessed herself again. I watched as the gulls swooped into the black waters of the Hudson River and the horns blasted again. I squeezed my grandfather's black rosary in my left pocket and in my right pocket, I clutched the round white stone that Packy gave me that dark and rainy morning we left poor, sweet Quilty behind and sailed for America.

CHAPTER 12
New York, New York

The sun had been up for nearly an hour as the *Maryland* was towed into New York harbor. Skyscrapers shot into the sky like giant stone fingers. I held my ears at the ships blasting, bells clanging, men shouting and women screaming. My mother covered my hands with her own and pulled me closer.

I looked over the railing. Six men with very dark skin were securing ropes around the big posts sunk into the river bottom. I squeezed her hand and pointed to them – I had never seen black skin.

"Hush, now Martin, hush now."

"Why do them have black skin?"

"Hold your whist, Martin, or they'll come after us!"

The gang plank was lowered and after the 1st and 2nd class passengers descended, we walked down the shaky path to our future. I squeezed Packy's stone and when my foot touched America, a wave of betrayal swept over me. Packy had to stay in Ireland and I had to come to America.

The sounds, sights and smells of Dock 54 bombarded us. I buried my face in my mother's tired shawl and planted my feet on the pavement.

"Mammie, let's go home! Let's go home!"

"Hush, Pet – we'll be fine, with the help of God, we'll be right as rain, now Love."

As they were no longer using Ellis Island, Mammie had to show again our diphtheria shot certificates, our passports, name of the person collecting us who agreed to provide for our home and board. The different accents, complexions, expressions and nearness of so many crushing bodies overwhelmed my poor mother.

As we left the staging area, Mammie closed her eyes and bit her teeth, not wanting me to see her fear. Lizzie had written that she would meet us when we got off the boat. She was nowhere to be seen. What the bloody hell! Where had she gone?

"Now, Martin, hold Mammie's hand, Love – don't let yourself go….Ah, stop pulling on the old shawl! Jest grab me hand! Grab me hand, Pet."

As soon as we went through the immigration gate, someone grabbed Mammie's arm. She did not recognize the tall, fashionable woman at her side who called her "Kate". The hair gave her away: what was once an angry, self-administered chop was now a chic, angled bob.

"Lizzie! Lizzie! Oh, for Crikey sake!"

They embraced and held each other and cried. Lizzie put her hand on my shoulder and pulled me toward her. I did not recognize her and pulled away as fast as I could.

"Now, Kate, Pet, would you ever introduce your son to his aunt?"

I frowned as I tried to replace my mean and miserable Aunt Lizzie with this smiling, warm woman.

"Auntie Lizzie? Auntie Lizzie?"

"The very one, Love, I'm Lizzie Sweeney, your old Irish auntie!"

A big, fat woman with short, curly black hair, a tiny, hooked nose and a strange, large mannish face stood next to us. She smelled pleasantly of face powder, but there was not a touch of make-up on her face. There was a lot of turquoise and silver jewelry hanging from her. She smiled at the three of us, back together after so long apart and so far away. She nudged Lizzie.

"Oh, Kate! Here's Babe, my friend." Babe and Lizzie were obviously "thick as thieves," good friends, but a different sort of friendship. I couldn't figure them out. Maybe this was how it was in America.

"Pleased to meet you, Babe", my mother offered her hand as graciously as she could. Babe took her hand and held it firmly. The angry Lizzie of home had vanished. Mammie had to admit that her sister seemed happier and nothing like she used to be.

"Martin, shake hands with Babe."

She bent over slightly, looking me straight in the eye. I offered my pale, thin hand to her. She took it gently, "Welcome to America, Martin. I've heard so much about you."

I buried my face in my mother's scratchy shawl while I continued to shake her hand. Her deep voice scared me, though she addressed me like a real person, not a child. When I took my hand back, I opened it and found a small Tootsie Roll from Babe.

"Liz, let's grab a taxi and go to Times Square and then to Schrafts for lunch – Wadda' ya' say? We're catching the 8:35 train tonight and we'll be in Chicago by noon tomorrow!"

Babe reached for Lizzie's hand, but she pulled away and put her arm around my thin shoulders, her other arm around Mammie's waist. Babe stood apart from us and said nothing.

I squeezed my eyes closed at the flashing lights, blaring sounds and people, people, people. I needed to get away to that silent place where me and Packy would be lying on the high cliffs of Clare, with only the crashing of the sea, the sweep of the gulls' wings and the shivering wails and squeals of the gray seals as they tumbled in the sea.

I still could hardly recognize Lizzie. She used to be so skinny and mean, but now she was rounder and kind. Her prickly hair was soft and longer, but she didn't seem to be Irish anymore. And she made Mammie nervous...I could tell because she'd talk faster and point her fingers into the air. I wondered if she were thinking what new shape was waiting for us. Would she turn out to be like her sister? Then who would I be? Shape-Shifting scared the life out of me.

A yellow taxi screeched to the curb and we jumped in. I was in the back seat of the taxi between Mammie and Lizzie. Babe was in the front with the driver. I couldn't understand either of them as they both talked too loud and too fast. Lizzie's finger rested on Babe's tailored shoulder.

Babe shrugged her off and reached down for something in her floppy black bag. She twisted around to the back of the cab and in a blink of an eye, a small black gun was pointed at Lizzie. She screamed as Babe shouted, "Bang! Bang!" and squirted water in

Lizzie's face. I started to shake and was shrieking hysterically within seconds.

The driver swerved with the commotion, nearly missing a delivery truck. "Cut it out, Lady!! You wanna' get us all kilt? Put the goddamn think away!" Sufficiently chastised, Babe stuffed her squirt gun back into her bag. She felt me kicking the back of her seat and pounding my fists on my knees. What had she let lose?

As the driver turned on 5th Avenue, Babe shouted to the driver to stop at St. Patrick's. We all got out of the taxi and stood open-mouthed in front of the colossal yellow marble cathedral. The spires shot up beyond the clouds and the massive front doors swung before us like castle gates.

People were dashing in and out, blessing themselves on the run. Babe held the door open and the three of us entered the church that would have shamed even God Himself. The Holy Water fonts were bigger than birdbaths and the magnificent stained-glass windows were a look into the very courts of Heaven.

Masses were being said at the various side-altars and women in black babushkas were kneeling before the Stations of the Cross. Wood and marble statues towered over the altars like a tribe of mammoth warriors. Dirty, poor raggie men who smelled of whiskey were sleeping in the back pews.

I could only think of our tiny church in Quilty, Our Lady Star of the Sea. In 1907 the men from Quilty had risked their own lives saving the sailors clinging to the bow of their doomed French ship, *The Leon XIII,* which floundered and was swept upon the Quilty reefs during a tumultuous October storm. The small, simple chapel with the faint, flickering altar candle was more filled with the very presence of God than this shameless castle that reeked of pride and wealth and power. So this was America!

Babe sat on the hard benches in the back with the poor men who were sleeping and mumbling and shouting to monsters in their dreams. Indeed, being inside the church itself was humbling, almost terrifying. It gave Babe the same sense of awe and smallness she experienced as a little girl at Temple Sholom on Lake Shore Drive in Chicago with her family. Really, it didn't look all that different,

64

except for the huge crucifix with the brass body of Jesus nailed to the wood.

Babe's heart was racing. She had never seen this part of Liz - the big Sweeney part, the big Catholic part. What had she been missing? She had always had Liz all to herself, except for Nellie and Brendan, who were off on their own.

****

Babe thought of when they had first met...Liz was on her hands and knees under the massive mahogany dining-room table at their home. Judge Nathanson, Babe's father, had hired Liz on a recommendation from Judge Harry Hogan who had hired Mayme Delaney, Liz's aunt.

The Nathansons needed the extra household help this time of the year. It was Spring, time for Spring-cleaning before Passover or *Pesach*. Every remnant of every crumb of *hamotz* or leavened bread would be hunted down, cleaned away until the last dustpan was empty.

At that very second, Lizzie and Babe's eyes locked and their hearts were ready to explode. Babe was immediately embarrassed that this beautiful, wild woman was on her knees at their house.

"Who hired you?"

"Judge Nathanson, Ma'am."

"Well, I'm going to let you go!"

Lizzie got off her knees and inquired as to what she had done wrong.

"Nothing, nothing at all – I just don't want you cleaning up after us."

Lizzie looked Babe in the eye, threw her damp rag down on the mahogany table, ripped off her starched white apron and cap, hurled them on the floor and stormed out the front door, not the back door reserved for the servants' use.

Babe ran after her, shouting, "Wait! Please wait, just a minute!"

Lizzie did not look back, but shouted, "You can just go to hell. Fuckin' go to hell, so!"

65

After pleadings from Babe, Judge Nathanson called Lizzie. She came to his office and he apologized for his daughter's actions. Babe was waiting in a back room. She came into her father's chambers and expressed her regrets.

The Judge reached into his vest pocket and pulled out a $5.00 bill and "ordered" the two young women to go out for lunch at Stouffers and "do try the apricot chiffon pie, a bite from heaven."

He winked at Babe...though the Nathanson's didn't follow Kosher dietary laws, they did observe the Passover restrictions of no leaven breads or baked goods during the time of Remembrance of bondage and repression under the pharaohs of Egypt. Their Passover was to begin in two days, the house had been cleaned and there was nothing to do but follow the judge's orders.

Babe savored the memory of the apricot chiffon pie with Lizzie over the next week of Passover potato breads and matzo sandwiches. But sweeter was the memory of their conversation, their sharp minds comparing the histories of their tribes: The Jews had the Pharaohs and the Irish had Oliver Cromwell; the Jews had Holocaust and the Irish had the Famine.

Their different, but shared religious and political histories put both Lizzie and Babe outside the main-stream. But they both sensed there was something deeper, more personal, much more personal that thrust them farther out of the conventional, acceptable flow of normal life. And as they were both bloody-minded, they took a perverse delight in being distinctive, but distained by most.

When they came back to the Nathansons home, Babe's father understood. Babe had few acquaintances, much less friends. The Friday night dinners his wife had engineered in hopes of landing Babe a nice Jewish husband were all for naught. "From your mouth to God's ears," she'd say fervently.

"Ah well," thought the Judge, "I think this is a match...a *mazel* for my Babe, always calling her own shots, finding a *shiksa* right under our own nose. Now she'll be happy, a happy, happy *mensch* of a daughter, my Babe."

Babe graduated from Northwestern Law School and had just passed the Bar. She was going into practice with her brother and uncles at Nathanson, Hogan and Miller, a Loop firm that specialized in Personal Injury and Criminal Law. Babe loved the fact that she was now able to right wrongs and to bring justice to injustice.

She had always been the one who could hold her own in a debate, a game of chess or kick-the-can with her brothers and their buddies. She could be as aggressive as she wanted and would never hold herself back to please anyone. No one in the family had tried to discourage her from going to law school and she always knew that a place in the family practice would be waiting for her.

Lizzie and Babe had been together for nearly three years. Lizzie worked part-time at the Nathanson law firm while she was studying at Mundelein. The Judge, who was on the board of the small, progressive Catholic women's college, had made a call to Sr. Thomas Gerard, President of Mundelein, and Lizzie was admitted there immediately.

Now Babe watched the Sweeneys genuflecting, kneeling, blessing themselves and lighting candles. What was that all about? She had never gone to church with Lizzie as prayer and religion were a private matter.

It was a very different religion from that which Babe had known, but there were strong similarities - men in charge, the strange, archaic languages, and guilt that hung over every thought, word and deed. She shivered at the realization of the claim that religion held over all their lives.

****

As my mother and Lizzie walked slowly and stopped before a statue or Station of the Cross, I slid into a pew and knelt before the Blessed Mother. I hid my face in my hands and prayed to be good my whole life so I could be a priest. I peeked at the massive marble altar through my fingers and dreamed of the day I would say Mass and forgive sins and baptize babies.

Looking up, I suddenly realized my mother was nowhere to be seen. I frantically searched the massive cathedral as hot tears flooded my eyes and my heart thumped wildly in my chest. A strong hand pulled at me. I looked up into Babe's strange face and threw my

67

arms around her, just like the frightened French sailors in the storm greeting the Quilty fishermen who saved their lives in foreign waters.

CHAPTER 13
In the Bruised-Colored Dusk of the New World

The engine of the *20th Century Limited* groaned as it pulled out of Grand Central Station and sped westward to Chicago, with stops in Buffalo and Cleveland. Steam from the engine curled around the steel wheels like fog arising out of the moors. In her lower bunk Mammie lay still as a corpse.

Above her, I cried myself to sleep, knowing that with every turn of the wheel I was moving farther from Packy and my old life in Ireland. I was afraid that I would change like Lizzie with her new friend and her new words and her American accent. When I'd come back to Quilty, they'd call me the "Yank."

Kate was raw on the inside and raw on the outside. Doubts haunted her: What if we had stayed at home with Tom and Packy and Biddy? Am I fair to Martin? Will he get over this idea of being a priest? Am I far enough away from his father? Will Jeremiah find us? Who will tend the graves of Ma and Pa? Who is this Babe? What came over our Lizzie?

Kate fell into a deep, deep sleep with images of the Statue of Liberty chasing her into Lahinch and Liscanor and herself trying to hide behind the hay ricks and inside the holy wells. She swam like a dolphin across the Atlantic Ocean and just as she was about to run up the Empire State Building, the Statue of Liberty tackled her and squeezed her so she could hardly breathe.

I woke up to hear Mammie gasping for air and shouting below me. I jumped out of my bunk and got in beside her. She was having a hard time breathing, so I wrapped my thin arms around her. I didn't want her to die. I was now almost the same size as my mother.

She whispered to me in Irish, "*Cad ata' ag cur ort?*" – "What's the matter with you?"

"Mammie, you were the one who was shouting in your dreams. It must have been a nightmare. I heard you shouting away! Mammie, I want to go home! I hate America! It's not right for us here!"

"Hush, Pet, hush now, it will be good and we'll be happy again, Love, right here in America." She then told me about her dream, her first dream in America. We started to laugh, at her swimming like a dolphin and she never really put her foot in water her whole life. All the drowning and ship-wrecks and storms had all of us frightened to death of the sea. Plus Rosie on the *Titanic*.

"I know, Love, now go back to sleep. Go back to sleep, Martin, little Pet. I'll never let a single soul harm you here in America. Besides, I can swim like a dolphin and you'll be as safe as the periwinkles on the strand at home."

"Sure, don't they eat the little periwinkles with a pin?"

"Ah, now, Martin, ye know what I mean. Don't be startin' a fight at this hour of night."

I fell into a dead sleep and Mammie climbed over me and up to the top bunk. She lay still as her old life began to fade into the distance and her new life was becoming real for her in Chicago. She closed her eyes and prayed:

"I am lying down tonight with Mary mild and with her Son,
I will not lie down with evil nor shall evil lie down with me,
But I will lie down with God and God will lie down with me."

****

"Arriving in Chicago in one-half hour, arriving in Chicago in one-half hour, at 11:45 exactly," announced the porters as they made their way through the rocking trains.

I was so frightened by these dark men with their crispy, black uniforms and shiny black shoes. Again, like a little lost goat, I hid behind my mother. She yanked me out in front of her and told me to behave myself. Did I want to hurt their feelings? Oh, how I wished that I had a father to teach me to act and not be the coward that I am.

The train slowed, came to a stop, lurched forward and stopped again. Babe and Lizzie from the next compartment joined us as we gathered our bags and readied ourselves to step into Chicago at LaSalle Street Station.

A tall, young man in a Navy blue suit with thick auburn hair shouted, "Kate! Kate! Sure, Martin, over here!" When Mammie saw

70

her older brother, she ran limping and threw herself into Brendan's arms. He kissed her and hugged her and grabbed for me.

"*Ci' he' sin?*"

"I'm Martin! Did you forget me, Brendan?"

"How could I ever forget you, Martin? Come here and give me a strong Irish hand-shake! Did you go and leave Packy behind?"

Mammie kicked him in the shin and shook her head and pursed her lips. Getting the message, Brendan tousled my wild hair and pulled me closer, "Sure, don't we know that ol' Packy will be over here with us before we know it, right, Kate?"

I nodded shyly and grabbed Packy's white stone in my pocket, but knew it was untrue. People always lied to me to make me feel better, but it only made me feel worse, knowing the truth and smiling at their lies.

Brendan towered over Mammie now, but three years ago when he left Ireland with Lizzie and Nellie, he had been only a few inches over her. He was at DePaul University and had a job through Babe's brother at the Nathanson law firm. Brendan would be on his way to Law School in the coming year.

Brendan directed us to the big, black car, on quiet loan from Lou Nathanson. Babe recognized it but said nothing. Mammie asked him if he wanted to know anything about Tom and Biddy and Packy. He put his index finger in the air for her to wait while he crammed our bags into the back of the car.

We heard Brendan cough and blow his nose. He packed his tears down as deep as they would go. Down as deep as that 'deep heart core" where an Irishman's grief and tears turn to stone. It was there he could feel nothing and he could stay safe forever. My mother had vowed that this would never happen to me. She let me feel shame or pride or grief so I would never be a stone. But still she lied to me about my missing father.

Brendan got into the car, humming:

"Oh, the summertime is coming and
the trees are sweetly blooming
And the wild mountain thyme grows
around the blooming heather

71

Will ye go, Lassie, go? Will ye..."

"Stop it, Brendan! Stop it right now!" cried Lizzie from the back seat. She swatted him on the back on the head and told him to behave himself. Babe did not know what it was all about, but she could only imagine.

The Sweeneys were a foreign tribe, so different from the Nathansons. And yet, Babe had to laugh to herself, as her father had often said that the Irish were one of the lost tribes of Israel.

I squeezed my eyes closed so I wouldn't see the lake from the back window of the car. My tweed coat was scratching my neck and I was boiling with the heat. Babe kept talking about Lake Michigan and Lizzie told about how lovely it was in the summer with picnics and games and strolls in the park. Everything was going around in a circle, spinning and spinning and I couldn't make it stop. I was getting sick.

Brendan looked in the rear-view mirror, jammed on the brakes and pulled over to the side of the road. Mammie opened the door and shoved me out onto the pathway. I vomited pink and orange on the car door, on the street, on my mother's skirt, on myself.

A pale young mother wheeled her baby-buggy around me and walked faster. Three teen-agers laughed and imitated my vomiting. An old whiskery man uttered, "disgusting, disgusting," as he hobbled passed me.

I wiped my mouth with my sleeve and jumped back into the car. I hid my face in Mammie's soiled skirt. "Nice job, Lad, nice job!" shouted Brendan into the back seat. "Are you just marking your territory, like the dogs and the cats?"

"Mind yourself, Brendan! Enough, enough, enough! Can't ye see that he's had enough for the day!" And Mammie slapped him with the back of her hand on his red neck.

Duly chastised, Brendan drove north on Lake Shore Drive and after a few turns, pulled in front of a tall, red-brick building on a straight, leafy street. On the steps going up to the first floor stood four stout women, all with gray hair rolled up in buns and flowered aprons on their flowered house dresses. They wore fleshy lisle stockings and their shoes were thick black brogues, the kind that nuns wore.

Babe grew silent as she observed these strange rites of passage – from the old land to the new. Brendan opened the trunk of the car and I buried myself in the backseat. Lizzie took Mammie to meet the aunts, Grannnie's sisters whom Mammie had never seen. Brendan rapped on the window, asking me to help him carry in the bags.

Lizzie introduced Kate to the Delaney sisters - Josie, Mayme, Norah and Kitty. The four Delaney sisters bore a striking, almost frightening resemblance to their youngest sister Annie, my grandmother, Mammie's mother. They were a human prism, all reflecting pieces of Grannie. My mother burst into tears and clung to as many of her aunts as she could hold, scooping her own long-gone ghost of a mother up in her arms.

Sober, the Delaneys were not in the habit of displaying emotion. Emotions embarrassed them, as the hot, old injustices bubbled right below the surface and they might scald them. They all nodded and patted her head and her shoulders. None of them cried and none of them knew why she was crying. They were empty inside, soulless, as the small cabin in ClareCastle held all their precious soul parts they had left behind so many years ago.

"Sure, come on in, Child, Josie's after making ye some sweet currant cake and we'll have a nice cup of tea," declared Mayme as she led the way to the living room, darkened by the closed drapery and heavy oak furniture, through the ornate dining room and into the bright lace-curtained kitchen. She took the yellow broom and knocked three times on the ceiling. Three knocks returned.

"Nellie'll be down in a minute. She's getting the rooms ready for ye now. She'll be down faster than three shakes of a dead lamb's tail," Mayme laughed.

Out in the front hallway, Brendan was speaking softly to me. Brendan handed me a coin. I followed him into the dark and stuffy room. The sour vomit on my tight, green tweed jacket was making me sick again.

73

As the currant cake and tea were laid out on the oval dining-room table, the four Delaneys, Kate, Brendan, and myself sat down. There was an empty place setting. Lizzie went out the front to get Babe. She had disappeared. Lizzie returned as her own sister Nellie poked her little brown head into the kitchen.

Lizzie stirred her tea with her finger, as she looked over the furry African violets on the windowsill and looked out the window down the street for Babe. This was unlike Babe to disappear. Had they made her feel unwelcome?

"Oh, dear Jesus' sakes alive, Nellie!" shouted Kate and flew from her place to hug her sister. Nellie had grown even thinner and when Kate kissed her on the cheek, there was no padding, just a sunken hollowness that stretched from her cheek bone to her jaw. White Martyrdom, the nun had called it.

"*Bail o' Dhia ort,*" whispered Nellie, "God bless you over and over, Love. Yes, God is good to bring us all together. Now, where is the Lad? Where is my Martin? Sure, now isn't he after having a terrible journey?"

They looked around for me. I had fallen asleep at the table. Brendan lifted me up and carried me upstairs to the apartment on the second floor. Brendan lowered me onto the bed and began to remove my shoes.

I half-opened my eyes and asked my uncle, "Are ye me father?"

Brendan slowly shook his head, saying "God bless you, Martin, have yourself a nice sleep, a sweet sleep, Martin."

He blessed me with Holy Water in the small bottle on the dresser as I closed my eyes again. Brendan thought of Jeremiah Murphy again and wondered if he would ever know that he had a son in America. He kissed me on the forehead and prayed that Jeremiah Murphy remain a stranger to us all. He had caused enough trouble in the past and even now, Jeremiah Murphy was tormenting me with his absence.

When I awoke, I sat up, wondering where I was. I found the black squirt gun and four Tootsie Rolls on the dresser next to the Holy Water. I couldn't remember that lady's name. Was it Baby? How could a grown woman have that name? Well, she was nice. I didn't think Americans were like her. O.K., "Baby" it is.

CHAPTER 14
On Raglan Road of an Autumn Day

Babe turned into the short alley-way off Sheridan Road, parked and turned off the ignition. She and Lizzie had not spoken a word since leaving the Delaneys. Lizzie's family kept expanding and with each expansion, Babe saw another side of Lizzie that she had not expected. With all her attempts to become Americanized, Lizzie remained Irish to the core.

Babe was confused. She thought she knew Lizzie well, as they had been together for nearly three years. Between them there was a delicate balance, like the little bubble in the middle of the carpenter's plane that warned when the power between them was out of whack.

They climbed the back stairs to their spacious third floor apartment. As they neared their back landing, Babe lost her balance and fell against the banister. "Damn Klutz...damnit to hell," she chided herself. Lizzie opened the door for Babe and went straight for the stove and put the kettle on. Babe opened the refrigerator and pulled out the cheese-cake. She plopped it on the table.

"Ah, sure now, Babe, is she comin'?" Lizzie knew that every time that Babe began her period, she went right for Eli's Cheesecake.

"I got on the *schmatto* this morning after we got off the train."

"It'll be over before ya' know it, Love. Thank God it doesn't last that long."

"I just need a slice of cheesecake. Cut me one there with some tea, Lizzie. I'm getting cramps. Oh, God, how I hate this thing!"

"Go sit out there on the porch, Babe. I'll bring it out to you as soon as the kettle boils. Just put your feet up now and you'll be better in no time."

Their screened-in porch ran the width of the building. The white wicker furniture, bleached yellow bamboo rug, dark red-tiled floor and whitish stucco walls, the green potted ferns and bamboo ceiling fan made a South Seas refuge from the noise of the city.

As it jutted out toward the lake farther than the apartment buildings on either side of them, their porch became a ship, quiet, idyllic, their escape from the world of noise and strange, contemptible looks of scorn, tossed so easily into their faces. Two women together, as Babe and Lizzie were, drew judgment, as if their very existence was a sin.

Babe would look out on the lake and Lizzie would bring her old Irish pipe, stuffed with sweet tobacco and Babe would light up her Cuban cigars that she had pilfered from her brother Ira's desk.

Babe sighed, "I'm *k'velling* here on my front porch with my Lizzie and a good Cuban cigar, oh, to me a real *michia!*" And the two of them sat together, just *k'velling* until the chill came in off the lake and it was time for the Nightly News on Channel 5.

As she sat looking out over the choppy water and the little sailboats negotiating the winds and waves, Babe closed her eyes, and, despite her cramps, she smiled at how her life was, the good *mazel* that had come to her since she and Lizzie were together. All those 'push-pull' struggles were finally over, and they were learning to trust each other.

Babe had always thought herself the more powerful one, the one with the money, law degree, family connections, the real American, although a Jew. Could a Jew be a *real* American? Lizzie could never be a *real* American, as she was an immigrant with an accent and different ways of doing things. And she was Catholic.

The balance of power…Babe had always loved that concept. When power was not balanced between countries, there was war. When power was not balanced in personal relationships, there was war. Then divorce.

Within a short time of their meeting, Babe had asked Lizzie to come and live with her. It was Babe's apartment, Babe's home, Babe's money, Babe's city, Babe's family. Lizzie had nothing, just herself, her history, her old Delaney aunts, her brother Brendan and her sister Nellie.

Lizzie had just started as a freshman at Mundelein College, adjacent to Loyola University, embarrassed that she was so much older than the other girls. The boys at Loyola called the girls the "Mundle Bundles."

As she was cutting the soft, creamy strawberry cheesecake, Lizzie remembered the first time she had seen Babe so vulnerable and so wounded. Babe had lost her first case – it was an ugly divorce and the judge had awarded the children to their abusive father.

Babe kicked open the back door, threw her briefcase on the kitchen table and began to berate herself for losing. *"Nebbish, Nebbish, that's all I am, a real *Schmuck,* a real nothing. I couldn't protect those kids from that bastard."* She ran into the bathroom, slammed the door and sobbed.

Lizzie pulled Babe out of the bathroom and led her to their citron green velvet couch. Lizzie held her and rocked her and when she tried to get up, Lizzie held her tighter and hummed softly as Babe cried and cried and finally cried herself out. Babe came up for air and blew her nose. Lizzie released her and moved to the side.

Babe was embarrassed at her display of emotion. "I don't know what came over me, Lizzie. I've never cried like that before. Never. I've always had to be so tough, just like the boys. My father taught me to be tough or the world would have killed me for being who I am."

Lizzie held her hand softly, "Sure, you were like the mother sheep at her first lambing and her bleating and crying with the pain and not knowing what had happened to her. And I'd sneak up the mountain and hold her and help her throw off her little lamb, and sure, wouldn't she lick off the stuff around the little one and then give him her milk.

"Sure, you had just lost your first little lambs, with the Judge sending the kids to their father and all that. But my Babe is not a *Nebblie* or *Schmuckie* or whatever you go callin' yourself. Sure, don't them mother sheep lose their young ones but they have to go on. Sometimes they be born dead and sometimes they go wandering off the mountain and the mother is forlorn and ends up wailin' for her babies. It's just a natural thing, Babe. Sure, you're no different from her."

They sat quietly under the gold and silver framed pictures of the Nathansons on the mantle. Their darker, heavy Eastern European faces looked so different from the fair and fine Irish faces of Lizzie's family. They looked serious and proud and defensive, "Don't mess with us" was written all over them, their faces and necks and shoulders tight and firm. Lizzie was frightened every time she looked at them. And she was learning that they were her new family now.

****

Babe was the youngest of the three Nathanson children. The two boys, Louis and Ira, were born three years apart. Three years after Ira, Barbara joined the family. Judge Ira Nathanson and his wife, Maxine, were socially prominent in Jewish political and social circles. They lived in a tall, gray-stone mansion in a section north of the city called Rogers Park.

Judge Nathanson called his only daughter "Babe" after Babe Ruth. He had taken her to Wrigley Field for the third game of the Yankees – Cubs World Series on her 12th birthday, October 1, 1932.

They watch as the Babe, with a count of 2-2, stepped out of the batter's box, paused, gestured toward center field, stepped back in the batter's box and then hit the ball out of the park onto Graceland Avenue. Babe Nathanson, who had always liked to call her own shots, was never again referred to as "Barbara", but simply as "Babe".

Her mother, Maxine Kronheim Nathanson, was named after her uncle and was just as tough. Max Kronheim had a stall down on Maxwell Street, selling coats and furs that came from an unnamed, silent source. She referred to that as his "downtown office."

Every Sunday morning, Maxine would bundle up young Barbara and bring her down to the rollicking, smelly, loud, pushy world of Maxwell Street, two blocks south of Roosevelt Road and Halsted Street.

The peddlers from the small villages of Eastern Europe had pushed their carts across Western Europe, across the vast, blue seas of the Atlantic and across half of the New World onto Maxwell Street, where they traded their push-carts for wooden stalls, rickety card tables, boxes, booths and the backs of rusty delivery trucks.

Here the new Jews of Chicago with the occasional *goys* and their young *shiksas* came looking for the perfect bargain as the old peddlers looked for the perfect chump. The chorus of hawking sellers and dismissive buyers reached a feverish pitch before closing time

Young Babe hated these trips with her mother. She hated when her mother plied her head with feathered hats, wrapped her

79

arms in long, black crepe gloves, crammed her feet into small alligator pumps and sprayed her wild, black hair with nasty perfume.

Maxine refused to call her daughter anything but "Barbara". "Babe" sounded like a prostitute, a *kurveh, a nafka.* As she grew more and more into the woman she was to become, Babe would over-hear her mother on the phone to her sister Goldie, calling her ugly, a *schlumb,* a *pisher.*

Babe shamed her mother for refusing to go on dates with sons of the Nathansons' friends, for marriage with a young man of the Jewish elite would be the perfect ticket for Maxine to extend her influence and visibility.

When Babe realized that she would never get her mother's approval, she just had to settle for her understanding. Maxine never understood. The day came when they barely spoke. What was there to say? This broke the Judge's heart.

Maxine Nathanson was a "Hadassah" wife, a leader in the Jewish intellectual and social community. She served on fund-raising committees for the Jewish Family Services, the ACLU and Americans for Democratic Action, the Cook County Democratic Party. She was co-chairperson with Mayor Edward J. Kelly's wife for the Mayor's Committee on Human Rights.

Maxine had such little time for her tomboy daughter that when Babe had her first period, she ran screaming to Patsy, their Irish maid. Totally unprepared, she thought she was bleeding to death, until Patsy explained that she was now going to be woman and showed her how to care for herself during this time of the month. It was never mentioned to Maxine.

Shaken, Patsy called the Judge and told him, in cloaked language, about Babe's first period. He brought his only daughter a single red rose and told her that now she was a woman and that he was proud to have her for a daughter.

As the sun set in the west and the lake grew dark, Lizzie held and rocked Babe that evening of the loss of her first case when the young children were awarded to their abusive father. Lizzie remembered that beautiful early March morning when she was first allowed to go with her father to the hillside at lambing time. A young ewe had delivered a flat, lifeless lamb and her udders had leaked the rich, creamy colostrum that had to be taken from her and shared with the other new-born lambs.

The young ewe looked mournfully at young Lizzie and Lizzie held her and rocked her and sung her an old Irish lullaby. Just like holding Babe Nathanson who had failed so horribly in her first try at being a good lawyer and bringing justice into the world.

Lizzie closed her eyes and took herself back to the green hills of Clare and softly sung:

Oh, the summertime is coming and the trees are sweetly blooming
And the wild mountain thyme grows around the blooming heather.
Will you go, Lassie, go? And we'll all go together
To pluck wild mountain thyme, all around the blooming heather
Will you go, Lassie, go? Will you go, Lassie, go?

CHAPTER 15
And I'm Proud to be an American

Mammie and I spent our days walking to the lake, taking slightly different paths each day to get to know the neighborhood. Mammie's limp was getting worse and her cough deeper, but she tried to ignore them. Mammie knew she had to earn our keep but cringed at the thought of scrubbing floors and cleaning toilets for strangers.

Lizzie told her to wait until I was settled in at St. Liam's. I was the right age for 5th grade, but the nuns questioned my ability to fit in academically and socially. I was excellent at the Irish, but that did me little good in Chicago.

Sister Raphael Mary was my teacher. She was young and beautiful, with a heart-shaped face and large, twinkling chocolate eyes framed in her starched white linen gimp. Like a very little girleen, she never walked, but ran. She was a thoroughbred, alright, and I always felt, even at my tender age, that she was held down by the other nuns and by the church.

Her mother had come from Kilkee, a stone's throw down from Quilty and on some tribal level, she knew that the same blood flowed in our veins. We always know our own when we meet them.

She instantly recognized the brains that lay fallow in my head and the anger wrapped tightly in my own painful shyness. Like a good, protective mother, Sr. Raphael Mary took me under her wing and worked with me after school and on weekends. My mind was as hungry to learn as her own.

Sister asked a husky boy in the class, Tim Armstrong, to act as my "Guardian Angel." Anytime a crowd would gather around me, Tim would appear and the crowd would fly like snow-flakes in December.

When Tim mentioned his own father, I shrank. When I was asked about my own father, all I would say was, "He's dead", and a thick cloud would cover me and I would wonder if any of the other kids would know what a liar I was. I'd then get vague, change the subject and stick my head in the clouds.

After school, Auntie Nellie Sweeney had my tea and biscuits ready. She kept house for us and Lizzie when she was home. Lizzie spent most of her time with Babe and, if the truth be known, Babe was supporting Nellie and the rest of us. A certified check for rent arrived the first of each month and Josie Delaney tended no questions.

Sr. Raphael Mary got me up to speed to join the altar boys. I think she must have seen something of the priest in me, even at the early age of ten. Auntie Nellie would help me with the Latin responses, as if she were preparing me for the priesthood. We'd put the tea and biscuits away, sweep up the crumbs, and away we'd go.

After I became an altar-boy, a horrible thing happened. We were in 6th grade, getting ready for the 10:30 Mass that Msgr. Quinn always said. The servers from the 9:00 Mass had finished up. Suddenly, Billy McCarthy, a kid from next door, burst out of the locked room where the gold monstrance and chalices were stored. We called it the "Safe'.

Billy ran out the door, almost knocking over Msgr. Quinn. He threw up in the trimmed bushes along the sidewalk. Even though I had on my cassock and surplice, I ran out to see if Billy were o.k. He was crying and vomit covered his face. I asked him what had happened.

Between his coughing and vomiting, Billy tried to tell me. The early people were starting to arrive for Mass. "That priest! He forced me into that room and whipped out his long, hairy woop-de-doodle that stood up as straight as a flag-pole and wanted me to kiss it. He told me he loved me and this is how I could love him back. I hate that son of a bitch and I'm never coming back here! He's a creep!"

I felt like vomiting, too. I never heard of such a thing. He was what they called a "visiting" priest. I know Billy's father went to Msgr. Quinn, but he didn't believe him. Mr. McCarthy was just a milk-man. Then he said, "But, Jack, I can't do anything about it anyhow. We just must pray for sinners and good priests do sin on occasion. And to be brutally honest, why should we believe your kid?"

83

When I came home from school later that week, Mrs. McCarthy and Mammie were in our kitchen having tea. Mrs. McCarthy was crying and my mother's hand covered Mrs. McCarthy's. My mother looked up at me and said that they needed a little privacy and would I please go outdoors and play.

The McCarthys yanked Billy out of St.Liam, sent him to the public school and the whole family stopped going to church. It was sad, because Mrs. McCarthy's two sisters were nuns and I know they would not have told them the reason why.

I grabbed an apple from the ice-box and as I walked out the kitchen door, I turned and said, "I just want you to know that I know what you're talking about. I was there and Billy told me." Mammie bolted after me and I ran down the back stairs and out into a bright, windy November afternoon.

****

Sarah Ahern, from across the street, had become friends with my mother and invited her to St. Liam's Social. It was the second Saturday in October and the leaves on the maple tree that grew in front of the Delaney's apartment house at 1252 Castlewood were turning burnt orange and poppy red with streaks of gold.

On the second Saturday of every month, St. Liam's held a social in the gym. They served tea, brown bread, scones and orange marmalade. Msgr. Quinn, the pastor, was vehemently opposed to alcohol being brought within St. Liam's walls and anyone who defied him was barred from St. Liam's for life.

The neighborhood church was the life of our immigrant family. In Ireland, the church was the state and the state was the church. In America, the church was a parallel universe to the city. Its mayor was the Cardinal and bishops, the aldermen were the pastors and the city wards were frequently identified by parish boundaries.

Catholic schools, orphanages and hospitals took care of Catholic people. Parish identity afforded a strong personal, social identity – "I'm from St. Rita's…I'm from St. Sabina's…" It was at parish dances and social events that many Irish immigrants met, married and settled down to raise their own families.

Men in dark suits and women in flowered dresses were twirling and stamping as Tommy Moran's band shook the timbers of the old gym. Msgr. Quinn walked the perimeters with his massive hands behind his high, broad back and his thick, black eyebrows raised in alert, his black eyes squinting in the dark, lest he miss anything. No sin of the flesh would be committed on his watch.

As Kate and Sarah made their way to the tea table, a hand grabbed Kate's waist and pulled her out to the floor. He sang to her:

"Keep your hands off red-haired Mary
Her and I are to be wed,
We're seein' the priest this very mornin'
Tonight we'll lie in the marriage bed."

Despite Kate's tender ankle, he and Kate danced faster than the other couples on the floor, his rhythm and force lifting her into the air. Slowly the others stopped dancing and stepped aside, clapping and singing,

"Oh, 'twas goin' to the fair at Dingle
One fine morning last July
And walkin' down the road before me
A red-haired girl I chanced to spy.

Msgr. Quinn stopped Tommy Moran and the crowd grew silent. "We'll have none of this! People making a show of themselves! Not here at St. Liam's! Get your tea now and you'll all be off out of here in 20 minutes – by 11:00 p.m. sharp!"

Some of the women started to cry and the men, most of them policemen, firemen or other city workers, ground their teeth and swore under their breath.

The man asked if he might walk Kate home and she told him that she had come with Sarah Ahern. He said, "No harm, the three of us will go together." As they came to 1252 Castlewood, Sarah said good-night and crossed the street.

Stephen Flaherty and Kate sat on the front steps, holding hands. The clay, broken apart millions of years ago, had found its other half. They sat close, breathing in unison as the street lights softly broke through the leaves of the tree on Kate's auburn hair. They said little.

85

Neither Kate nor Steve trusted themselves to say anything. The moment was too charged to defuse with words – what was there to say? How different it was with Jeremiah Murphy who drove her out of her mind and finally attacked her and then left as quickly as he had come. The stillness between Kate and Steve was sacramental – the outward sign of the deep mysterious grace stirring within.

****

On Christmas Eve after Midnight Mass, Stephen Flaherty asked Kate Sweeney to marry him. She was 26 and he was 32. Steve had just passed the Chicago Police Sergeant's exam and would be able to provide for them. After they were married, he would move into the flat above the Delaney girls where Kate had been living with her sister Nellie and me.

Stephen Flaherty hated secrets and lies. That is why he had requested transfer into the Detective Bureau. The mystery surrounding the death of his father troubled him, as he always sensed there was something more than just Captain Joe Flaherty running bravely into the burning building to save the three little babies on the 3rd Floor in a sordid tenement house.

He had a need to know and a right to know, but his mother and the rest of the family felt he was too young and, "what harm", let little Stevie think old Joe was a hero. They felt a need to protect him, as if he were too callow to be told the truth.

Then the lies about Captain Joe Flaherty took on a life of their own and could not be refuted, even on his mother's deathbed. The reason Stephen did not go join his brothers and friends in the Fire Department is that the entire Department colluded with the family on the myth of his father.

Captain Joseph Flaherty was with his mistress on the night of the fire. There were three little children, but they were in the adjoining apartment. The Fire Department, the family and the church all tacitly agreed to make a martyr out of him, despite the fact then when he was drinking, he left his lighted cigar smoldering. He and his mistress were found wrapped in each other's charcoaled arms.

He hated the framed picture of the entire Flaherty family receiving the City of Chicago's Medal of Honor for his bravery from the Mayor and himself, a new-born, in the arms of his eldest sister, Fiona. Here he was, an infant, passively participating in the myth of Joe Flaherty.

Stephen became more and more troubled about who had fathered me. Whenever he asked Kate, she flashed her temper at him, angry that she had been caught off-guard. Then she would look far away, as if the hills of Clare were calling to her, the very cliffs that held the beginnings of my life that were not to be revealed to a single soul, including to the man who was soon to be her husband.

His entreaties of "Kate, I need to know," or "Just tell me one time," or "This isn't fair to me, Kate," all met with the same stone-walling, the same silence. He had finally worn her down, so much that she finally said, "Stephen Flaherty, I am going to tell you this, and only this, once and for all! All I can say is that it's in the Church! In the Church! Not the Church records, but it's just in the Church! Now, never again bring this up or I'm out the door and I mean it, sure as God is my witness!"

****

Sgt. Flaherty pulled the squad car up to St. Liam's one afternoon in early January. He knocked on the 5th grade door, introduced himself to Sr. Raphael Mary and asked that I be excused.

The class saw the sandy-haired giant in the Chicago Police Sergeant's uniform and gasped. What had I done wrong? I gathered my books, hat and coat and headed for the door with a big grin on my face. Sgt. Flaherty put his arm around my shoulders as we walked down the hall. The boys looked at each other and Tim Armstrong and Sr. Raphael Mary smiled at each other.

Steve took me to Buffalo's Ice Cream on Irving Park and Pulaski. We sat in a quiet booth. Steve asked me how I felt about his getting married to my mother.

"O.K., yeah, O.K." I replied as I dove into my banana split.

"That means I'll be your father."

"Not really. My real father is dead." My tooth throbbed at my lie.

"You know, Martin, there are different kinds of fathers. We call the priests 'Father' and they are good and kind men who give their lives to serve God."

"Right, I know that."

"Then a man can be a father of a child through love. A man can have his own blood kids, but he can also have a child just because he loves him and wants to be his father."

"O.K. So what?"

"I want to be your father, Martin. You know I love your mother and I'm going to marry her and I love you and want to be your father. And when your mother and I have kids, you will be the oldest kid and you'll be ours just as much as the others."

I felt like he cocked me in the heart. I looked down at the chocolate ice-cream pooling in the banana-split dish. Tears filled my eyes and I put my hands in front of my face to hide.

"Martin, you O.K.?"

"I want my real father. I never met him."

"I know how you feel, Martin. My father was killed in a fire before I was born. When I was a boy, I'd cry myself to sleep, I just missed him so, even though I never met him."

"Right, but you've got a picture of him. I saw it on your mother's mantle. He had on a white hat and a dark suit."

"Martin, Lad, take a good look at me. I want to be your father and I am going to be your father. And you're going to be my first and best son, you hear me?"

"What you want me to call you?"

"We'll figure that out on another day and it will be whatever you want, Martin, as long as it's not "Sergeant Flaherty".

****

Stephen and Mammie were married in St. Liam's on St. Patrick's Day, 1949. Our family, the Sweeneys and Delaneys were on the left side and the Flahertys and McGraths on the right. The back half of the church was filled with police and firemen. Msgr. Quinn said Mass in gold brocade vestments, despite it being the middle of Lent. Lizzie was Maid of Honor and Bill, Stephen's brother, was Best Man.

The wedding reception at the Blackthorn went on until dawn, but Mammie and Stephen slipped out at 2 a.m. for a few days in Niagara Falls.

There was a lovely quiet when Mammie and Stephen were together, as if everything had been said. Their hands or shoulders or knees were always touching in a peaceful way, as if they had searched over many life-times for each other and now they were made whole.

At first it made me mad, but I could hardly begrudge my mother a little human comfort, after all she had been through. And Stephen was hard to remain mad at.

When they returned home, I ran to my mother. She whispered, "*Bail o'Dhia ort*, Pet, God bless you again and again." Stephen tapped me on the shoulder. I wheeled around and jumped up in his arms and buried my face in Steve's hot neck.

The three of us climbed the steps to the second floor to begin our new lives together. Nellie, Lizzie and Brendan had all gone their separate ways so that our new family had the second floor to ourselves.

Sweet Aunt Nellie, at only 29, went into a cloistered community of nuns in Wisconsin. Despite having only one eye, she was welcomed into the community. Her new life would be hidden behind closed doors and when she would speak with us, it would be behind the grill, a small, wire-meshed window. We would never again see her nor would she see us. Her new life was one of constant prayer, mortification and fasting. She basked in her white Irish martyrdom with the strange German nuns.

Lizzie, now 30, had moved into Babe's large apartment by the lake. Babe was in practice in the family firm and Lizzie was in her second year at Mundelein. She was planning on being a social worker for Catholic Charities, maybe even getting her doctorate in psychology.

Brendan, at 31, was in his first year of law school at DePaul. He lived with a group of friends in Lincoln Park. Donnie Rizzo had introduced Brendan to his little sister Rosie. Brendan couldn't keep his eyes or his hands off her, until Donnie settled him down. If the truth be told, they were all getting the "marrying bug". Brendan was obsessed with Rosie, but felt out of his league with the family.

It was never clear how the Rizzos could afford their big home, cars and a pool in the ground with "hot and cold running maids," as Mr. Rizzo would laugh. He never seemed to work, but was frequently "in conference" over whispered calls and short men in black suits and white shirts were around him like a band of thieves. Mrs. Rizzo stayed in the kitchen.

As we entered into our second floor flat, it seemed so different from before. Now we were a family with just a mother and father and a kid. Steve had to report for work that evening and I had to go to school the next day. Mammie was five days pregnant, her rich womb was becoming a soft nest for two tiny, little eggs.

CHAPTER 16
I Will Arise and Go Now

Tim Armstrong and I genuflected and slid into the two last seats in the cold, Gothic chapel. There were hollows in the hard, wooden kneelers made by the thousands of young knees that had knelt in prayer over the years. It was September 8, 1952, the Feast of the Nativity of the Blessed Virgin, and the first day of high school at Quigley Preparatory Seminary.

I was in knots with excitement. I had wanted to be a priest ever since I could remember, trudging with the wind blasting and waves roaring at me as I held on to my mother's hand on the way to Mass at Our Lady Star of the Sea.

Every day I had offered my life to the Blessed Virgin Mary, as I wanted to remain pure and good and serve God. I wondered what Packy back at home would think of me now, really on my way to becoming a priest. Packy was the only one I had shared my dream with. He just wanted to be a farmer.

We were all 13 or 14, and all 173 of us bobbed and wiggled and scratched ourselves throughout the Mass. I towered over the other guys so I had a clear view of the altar. When we went to communion, we all looked so pious and humble, but we were checking each other out, like cops on a beat.

After the Mass, the priest turned to face us. "Young men, you have now begun your very first step to the priesthood. The journey will be long and hard, but the end is worth all the suffering and sacrifice.

"If the Good Lord, Jesus Christ Himself, has called you to be his prized servant, a priest in the Holy Roman Catholic Church, then you will indeed become that priest with the power to forgive sins and to change bread and wine into the very Body and Blood of Jesus Christ. Some of you will not make it. That is nothing to be ashamed of, but other vocations will be opened for you."

"So welcome to Quigley Preparatory Seminary. Now go quietly into the gym and arrange yourselves alphabetically starting with 'A' under the flagpole." The priest turned abruptly and headed toward the sacristy.

We sat like statues. The priest appeared again and shouted "MOVE!" We rose and marched quickly into the gym where the letters of the alphabet were posted on the walls. Tim muttered, "Like lambs to the slaughter," and I jabbed him with my elbow.

Tim went off to the small group of "A's" and I headed for the "S's" where nearly 20 guys gathered. A senior called off the names, "Slattery, Smith, Szymanski, Savio, Sullivan, Scott, Shield, Sweeney..." As us "S's lined up, the "H's" were brought alongside us. The senior explained that the person next to each of us would be part of a "Buddy System" to help and support each other throughout the year.

I extended my hand to my "H" partner, Harry Hogan. We were both nearly six feet tall with wavy black hair and violet-blue eyes. We could have been brothers, but Harry weighed a good 25 pounds more than me. He was impressive, but his nails had been chewed down to the quick.

"Welcome to Quigley, Martin!"

"Pleased to meet ya, Harry!"

An older classman dashed up to the small "H" group and called out, "Call for Harry Hogan... Important phone call for Harry Hogan! Judge Hogan's on the phone!"

His father was Judge Harry Hogan. I guess you'd call his son a V.I.P. Seems like the Hogans couldn't miss the opportunity to broadcast to these new class-mates and priests how important it was to be Harry Hogan, Jr. We nodded at each other and smiled, knowing that we'd have lots of fun with future mistaken identities.

****

My mother watched the two young ones, Liam and Clare, the two-year-old twins, playing in the sandbox. There was the slightest whiff of autumn on the wind, as the acorns started to bounce on the sidewalk and the air was charged with a hint of coal from the neighboring furnaces.

This was my first day in the seminary and I didn't know how she felt – of course she was proud to have a son even think about being a priest. Being the mother of a priest in those days would stand her in a very special place; but these things had little impact upon her, as she couldn't be bothered with such nonsense. There was an old knowing about my mother and it was hard to impress her.

It brought back to her all those ugly days with Jeremiah Murphy and his arrogance and cruelty. Her son was anything but arrogant and cruel, but was being a priest a hereditary thing? What if my father were a fisherman? Did Jeremiah Murphy fool all of them, heading off to a life of pretend celibacy and sleazy lies?

Kate opened the letter she had received earlier that day from her brother Tom. Kate dug her nails into the palm of her hands as she read it over again.

> *Kate, Love,*   *August 26, 1952*
>   *I hesitate to tell you this, but all the Devitts, including the Archbishop Ronan, were on their way to Rome and their plane crashed into the Alps. Ronan was going to be made a Cardinal and Fr. Jeremiah* <u>Murphy</u> *Devitt was waiting at the airport. Imagine.*
>   *They will probably make Jeremiah a Bishop for all his troubles. Hope they don't send him back here. He has caused enough trouble to last life-times for all of us. He's a weak and wily one, he is. They finally adopted him so he goes by "Devitt" now. Think it was for all their pretenses and probably a way to protect all their money.*
>   *I think them Pookas had something to do with it. The church people can be fooled, but not them dark spirits, them old Pookas. "What the Pooka writes, the Pooka can read", as they say. I do be wondering about all those old things, as I have so much time on me hands.*
>   *The wheat and oats are in and stowed away for the winter. It was a lovely crop this year. I think often of how you loved running and*

jumping in the fresh-mowed hay. And bringing
the hot tea with plenty of sugar and milk down to
the fields for us men. Them days are gone forever
and now we have to make do with our own ways.

Packy was thinking of going up to
University in Galway, but said no. He wants to
work the farm. He is bigger and stronger than
me, but for sure I'd never admit it to him.

Biddy's getting bigger than ever, just
rocking by the old fire and sipping cups of tea, as
usual. I wonder what's going on in that head of
hers. She's still goes on about the 'durty black
bog.''

Best to Martin and Stephen and all the wee
ones. Is it true that Martin is off to be a priest?
(Maybe it's in the blood.) He was always a pious,
wee lad. God help him! "What the Pooka
writes, the Pooka can read."

Hear monthly from Nellie – just a few
pious words, but she never had much on her
tongue as it was. Lizzie seems happy. Do she have
any men friends to marry?

We miss ye all here at home. Will ye be
over in the springtime?

Your brother,
Tom Sweeney.

Her hands started shaking as she put Tom's letter in her
apron pocket. Little Clare looked up at her mother as Kate felt a storm
rumbling in her chest. The remote nearness of Jeremiah Murphy felt
like a kick in the gut, a danger that was always pending. Yet he was
the father of her precious son Martin and nothing would ever change
that.

Josie pulled the curtains back and watched Kate. She put the
kettle on for tea and knew that she would need a nice visit with her
old Auntie Josie.

Even before we had left Ireland, I had wanted to be a priest. My mother was under the sweet, old pear tree, peeling the pears for a custard when I stole up to her and whispered in her ear, "Mammie, I'm going to be a priest when I grow up."

As my mother covered her face with her apron, the big, juicy pears rolled on the ground. I pulled her hands down so I could see how pleased she must be with me. When I saw her look of horror, I ran to Biddy and threw my arms around her neck and cried into her bosom.

"Oh, Biddy, Mammie doesn't want me to be a priest. Priests are holy and can help poor people."

Mammie walked into the house and gently lifted me to herself. "Come to me, Pet, come to me."

Hesitantly, I went to my mother and she held me in her lap. "Martin, if you want to be a priest, I would be the happiest mother in all the world. A priest is good and kind and holy and that is just the kind of priest you will be, Pet. I am sorry I didn't look happy, Love. You just took me by surprise, that's all!"

Mammie would watch me "say Mass" with Packy as the server. Even at 10 I had memorized much of the Latin and imitated the gestures of the priests. After the evening rosary, when the rest of the family finished up their chores, I would follow the winding paths and kneel in prayer as the sun dropped into the sea and the gulls made their last catch of the day.

"Do they have priests in America?" I'd ask her. "Do the Delany girls know any priests? Can I say Mass in Chicago?"

"Martin, Love, they have good and holy priests in America and if that's what God wants for you, a priest you will be, have no fear."

I guessed that my mother held some secret deep within her own heart and had promised, on the graves of her parents, Annie and Martin, that she would never again display her own pain to me. In silence she vowed again that she would never tell me who my father was – ignorance was better than the truth, for what good would come of it? A priest I will be, come hell or high water!!

CHAPTER 17
The Real Old Mountain Dew

Our life at Quigley Seminary was different from any other Boys'
Catholic High School in Chicago. We had daily Mass, silence in the
halls and Thursday was our "day-off," rather than Saturday. This was
to lessen contact with girls, except for female relatives.

As soon as the bell rang for dismissal, Tim and I raced to our
lockers and ran to the #156 bus. We had to wear a white shirt, tie,
jacket and dress pants, and we kept the tie and jacket in our lockers.
By the end of the year, ties and jackets were ripe for discard.

Lunch of steaming meat and potatoes was 30 cents, desert
another five cents. Fridays it was tuna casserole and jingly red Jello.
Those families who could not afford lunch money were quietly
subsidized.

I grew with every bite I ate and was soon a half-foot taller
than Tim Armstrong, but still shorter than my step-father Stephen. I
was frequently moved to tears in prayers as I thought of how very
blessed I was to be on my way to the priesthood. With all my heart
and mind and soul, I wanted to be a priest, a good and holy priest.

My relationship with Harry Hogan was like a mosquito bite
– irritating, pleasurable to scratch, but often bleeding. During our first
year, Harry would refer to me as 'Fartin' Martin.' Over and over I
told him to 'cut it out.' Finally, it was one time too many and I
punched Harry in the nose. Before long, we two big apes were on the
floor of the lunchroom, landing blow after blow.

We were brought before the Rector of Discipline to explain
ourselves. When we were asked to explain ourselves, Harry described
how I had been 'gunning' for him since we first met, and that Harry
was in a quandary to understand what he had done to anger me so. I
said nothing. We were then put on probation for 'losing decorum.'

I received a more severe punishment and had to report to
school every Thursday, our days off, until the end of the year. I had to
clean the lunchroom on my hands and knees. Harry received a mark
on his permanent record. We were both warned that another out-

break would result in immediate dismissal, regardless who our fathers were.

As we left the Rector's office and headed toward our lockers, Harry said to me, "They'd never let me go. My father is the Cardinal's attorney, my uncle is his doctor, my family's accounting firm does all the money for the Archdiocese and my Uncle Pat, you know, Msgr. Patrick Hogan from Holy Name Cathedral, is close to the Cardinal. They all think I'm going places in the church, so you'd be smart to stick by me and I'll take you with me, Martin, Fartin' Martin."

I told Harry that he could go to hell. I had no desire to "go places in the church." Harry smiled, nodded and whispered in Martin's ear, "We'll see about that, Big Boy, we'll just see." I gathered up my books, hung up my tie and jacket, slammed my locker and ran for the bus.

Later that year, I was standing on the bus next to a young woman with lavender cologne. I thought I was going to faint with desire. Swaying I held on to the bus straps, feeling out of control. I said to Tim, "I've got to get out of here!" At the next stop, I jumped off the bus and ran home the last four miles like I was being chased over the hills by the Conley's bull.

At home, Stephen was studying for the Police Lieutenant's exam, I was jumpy with my hormones, Clare had decided not to eat, Liam was pleasant and imperturbable, so much like his Uncle Tom at home. Mammie was coughing more than usual. Sometimes I'd see blood on the tissues she would be saving.

The Delaneys had asked the Morrisons on the third floor to move to make way for Stephen's brother, Billy, and his new wife, Sarah Ahern, from across the street. The house was like a three-layer cake: the Delaney sisters on the first floor: Stephen, Kate and us three kids on the second; Billy and Sarah on the third. Sarah was pregnant again after three miscarriages.

****

This was the First Friday in October and the Delaney girls would be at it tonight. All four would attend Mass in the morning at St. Liam's, making the nine First Fridays. In the 17th Century Jesus had

97

appeared to St. Margaret Mary and had promised to the Faithful who received Holy Communion on the First Friday of each month for nine consecutive months the grace of final repentance on their death beds and that His Sacred Heart "will be their secure refuge in that last hour."

Each of the Delaneys feared they would have a bad death, unrepentant of their sins and turn away from God at the last minute, so the Nine First Fridays had become a way of life for them. A spiritual insurance policy of sorts.

After Mass, Mayme, Norah and Kitty Delaney went off to work and Josie took care of the house and meals as usual. One by one they came home, and when the last of the Delaney girls was in the door, they locked the door, pulled the drapes and sat down to fish and chips with vinegar and coleslaw. Apple pie with cheddar cheese was served for desert.

For an hour, the first floor was quiet until it started, until the Jameson's Red Breast Irish whiskey kicked in. Jimmy Dalton at "Jimmy's Pub" ordered it by the case for the Delaneys.

Twice a year, when the case was down to a few bottles, Josie would knock like a little mouse on the back door of the pub. Jimmy would open it quietly, look around Josie Delaney with her little black purse and whisper to her, "Now is it more of the Pink Tit that you're after, Miss Delaney?" Josie would nod, hand over a roll of bills and fly home like she was being chased by a Banshee. The case would be delivered in the dark of night so as not to cause scandal.

Soon after their dinner settled, out would come the music - Mayme beating on the bodhra'n, (the Irish drum made from a goat-skin stretched over a round frame), Kitty on the uilleann pipes stuck under her arm, Norah on the fiddle and Josie on the accordion. The sweet and haunting sound from Kitty's pipes would start their tears flowing. Mayme beat the bodhra'n harder as Kitty sang:

"Father Murphy from old Kilcormack
Spurred up the rocks with a warning cry
'Arm, arm', he cried, 'For I've come to lead you,
For Ireland's freedom we fight or die."

"Oh, Jaysus, will we ever get our Freedom? Oh, Sweet Jesus, our Freedom!" shouted Mayme. "*Saoirse! Saoirse Freedom!*"

"Bugger the English!" shrieked Josie, "Bugger the whole damn lot of them!"

"Sweet Mother, remember Uncle Tadhg, and him up before the firing squad with James Connelly and Padraig Pearce at Kilmainham Jail after the Easter Rising!" wailed Kitty.

Then from Josie, "Ah, shut up, ya dirty bitch! Didn't old Tadhg croak in the gutter of Dublin without a stitch on, the dirty bollix!"

Then they would get personal: "You look like a harse's arse, ye do!" shouted Mayme. "And you, Norah, with that old black tooth in the middle of your head, ye look like a witch's tit!' yelled Kitty.

"But will we ever forget our own dear Rosie, her and that blasted old ship hurling her to the bottom of the sea and her with child! Jaysus, our own dear Rosie and breathing in all that old salty water," wailed Mayme, tears streaking down her wrinkled cheeks like a river streaming to the sea.

"Would you ever close your big yap, Mayme!" shrieked Josie. "It's something we're never to say, you know it well, Mayme. Jest shut yourself up!"

"Ye, bastard, ye filthy bastard, just shove it up your hairy arse altogether!" blasted Norah.

And so it continued until the posts and pans started to fly and Mayme attacked Josie and Kitty started to scream and Norah wept.

Stephen would go quietly down the stairs and knock on the door. "Chicago Police Department – We're getting calls from the station about you 'disturbing the peace.' Please quiet down in there. Please respect your neighbors."

There wasn't a sound after that. The four sisters turned out the lights, tip-toed to bed in silence. Their hangovers would shame a pregnant sow and the walls would shake like the wind in the barley with their moanings and groaning and beseeching prayers, "*Go sa'bha'la Dia sinn... God help us! God help us!*"

Toilets flushing at all hours of the night and day, the tea-kettle whistling every half-hour and unexpected crashes as one of the sisters fell into a chair or the china cabinet. The punishment fits the crime.

The shades remained down and the drapes closed until Sunday, as the four little Delaney sisters, like four little nuns, walked down Castlewood to St. Liam's without a word spoken, eyes downcast and black purses clutched tightly with both hands. They would each double their contribution to show God that they meant Him no harm by their episodes.

These monthly out-bursts were never mentioned or referred to in anger or in jest. Mammie tried to figure out if they were controlled by the moon. Stephen felt it was an ancient Druidic rite that only the Delaneys knew or made up. I figured that it related to the First Fridays and when a First Friday coincided with Good Friday, the Delaney Rampage was postponed for a month and then they made up for lost time.

Stephen discretely pulled the empty Jamison Red Breast bottles out of the refuse, wrapped them in newspaper and discarded them on his way to work. But not before I had emptied every last one of the bottles, in case there were a drop or two that the Delaneys had missed. And if I were lucky, I'd find a good mouthful waiting for me at the bottom of a bottle. I always had a packet of Good & Plenty to chew to get rid of the smell so my mother wouldn't detect anything.

"Ah, sure," wondered Mammie, "what little of the joys of life can they have? They deserve a bit of comfort as they are getting on in years. Ah, and we won't be judging our very own, now will we?"

"And sure if me own mother, dear Annie Delaney herself, had not met my father Martin and him carrying her off to Quilty and with all them kids and all that work and the walls weepin' with the damp and it going into her lungs, sure, wouldn't she be with her four sisters carryin' on like that until the wee hours."

Mammie started to cry and cough. Stephen held her closely and breathed softly as he tried to calm her down. This was always the aftermath of the hysteria down below. Her cough was getting deeper as she gasped for breath. She pushed him away and ran for the sink. She choked into the sink and spit up streaks of blood that she washed away before he could see.

"But none of us would be here to hear their lovely music and we'd all be up in the air, floating around somewhere with them stormy clouds."

Steve would lift Mammie, carry her into bed, place a soft, cool cloth on her forehead, and hum "Keep Your Hands off Red-haired Mary" as she drifted off into a fitful sleep.

And down below, the four sisters held to themselves and to each other, knowing that they had missed the horrible poverty and hardship, the judgment of the surly priests at home. They were each so delighted with themselves for their little piece of America that no one could take away from them. They felt safe with their lovely niece Kate and her husband above them, and even young Martin on his way to the priesthood. The Delaney sisters gloried in their little lives in America.

CHAPTER 18
Lace-Curtain Irish

The year was 1959. John Fitzgerald Kennedy was running for President against Richard Milhouse Nixon, the Republican Vice-President under President Eisenhower. This was the first time in the history of the United States that an Irish Catholic would be elected, bringing into legitimacy the experience of the millions of us who shared his heritage and religious identity. No longer would we be second-class citizens, now truly we would have arrived. It was great to be Irish! It was great to be Catholic!

We had finished high-school at Quigley and were now completing our four years of philosophy and would soon begin four more years of theology at St. Mary of the Lake Seminary in Mundelein, out in the green country of farmlands and lakes of Lake Co., far from the frenzy of Cook Co.

Our bucolic environment at the seminary included the Lecture Hall and Feehan Library, the dorms and the Grotto of Our Lady of Lourdes, the Chapel of St. Mary of the Lake. It was a beautiful, graceful campus where we young men were educated, disciplined and modeled into priests

We have an 18 - hole golf course. The golf course was originally just 9-hole, but the Cardinal's doctor told him he needed to take long walks, so he enlarged the course and could be seen walking the fairways alone in his top-coat and biretta. There'd never be a golf club in his hand or a friend by his side.

Harry Hogan had received permission to attend his parents' 40th Anniversary celebration in Lake Forest. Mass was to be at St. Mary's Church with dinner after at the Deer Path Inn. He asked me to accompany him. We were both in our black clerical suits with crisp, white collars and shiny, black shoes. We had to be back by 10 p.m.

The long, black Mercedes slowed as it passed through the seminary gates. We were met in front of the administration building where we signed out by the Hogan's' black chauffeur. Harry called the chauffeur "Sam" and Sam called him "Mr. Hogan". Harry introduced me as "Mr. Sweeney", but I told him please to call me

"Martin". I was getting bad feelings already. I tried to sit low in the plush, leathery back seat, but it was hard to demure in this setting.

As we headed east towards Lake Forest, Harry told the driver to circle around down by the lake to show me the area with the winding ravines, the silent, surly gray stone and red-brick mansions, the massive manicured grounds where weeping willows, towering oaks and Japanese maples stalked the night.

I sat beside Harry in the backseat, knowing that I should be in awe at such opulence and Harry's familiarity with it. We slowed as we passed the Hogan's residence on Mayflower. Their money had come from the Quinns' steel business, but Mrs. Hogan, Harry's mother, the former Cecilia Quinn, never mentioned it to anyone, as she would be shaming her husband.

Harry thought his exposure to this level of intimacy with the powerful men in both the church and city would endear him to me. Every man has his price, he thought. Instead I propped my head on my fist and leaned against the window. I was bored and revolted. My poor tooth throbbed, feeling the lies.

What does this have to do with me and my life in Quilty? Our little home by the sea with Tom and Packy eking out a living from the hard, salty soil and the fishermen dragging the sea for something to eat? I felt a betrayal to my own people, my own history - I didn't belong here. And the haunting refrain that pounded in my ears: Who and where was my own father?

The chauffer parked behind the church. We went into the sacristy, as we were the "altar boys" for the Anniversary Mass. The small room was filled with clergy – Msgr. Pat Hogan, the Judge's brother; Msgr. Robert Quinn from St. Liam's, Cecilia Quinn Hogan's brother; Msgr. Gallagher, the pastor of St. Mary's who was ordained with both Paddy Hogan and Bobby Quinn; and the Dunphys, their three Shanty Irish cousins whom they called the "Dumpy Dunphys," who were only poor parish priests. The Hogans were too "democratic" to leave out their scruffy cousins.

There was talk that the Cardinal might appear, but he had not been well and they didn't expect him.

Just as Msgr. Hogan was about to step out to the sacristy for Mass to begin, Msgr. Quinn grabbed his arm. The Cardinal had made it to St. Mary's! We withdrew until the Cardinal and his assistant were vested for Mass, then we all proceeded to the sanctuary with the Cardinal in the lead. The congregation gasped, for they had not expected His Eminence, James Cardinal Joyce, to get out of his sick bed and come to show his admiration for the Hogans.

So many eyes were on Harry and me, the tall, handsome seminarians serving the Mass. I wanted to disappear into the woodwork. This was not my idea of why I wanted to be a priest. I thought of my poor uncle Paul, stuck up in that God-forsaken place in Donegal, long forgotten by the Jesuits, but, God, didn't we all dearly love him and him delivering the baby for that poor woman.

I lowered my eyes. I noticed both the Cardinal and the other priests bypassing Harry to look at me. I think they could read my own judgment of them - their arrogance and superficiality, their spiritual superiority. They could feel that somehow I felt purer and holier that they were, fawning over the Cardinal and kissing his arse before God's holy altar. My reversed elitism. I breathed in humility and asked to be forgiven for my pride, the Queen of all Sins!

Harry bit his lower lip, as it was always me that drew the crowds. He looked down to his mother for reassurance, but she, as well as most of the Hogans and Quinns, were looking at me, the tall and handsome Irish Prince who strode from out the mists of County Clare at the stroke of midnight.

Well, if Harry couldn't be me, at least he could get credit for being my friend.   He had the drive that I was lacking. I just wanted to be a simple priest without all that folderol. It went against something deep inside – we had no time for the "lace curtain Irish" with all their airs.

At communion, Harry held the paten for Msgr. Hogan and I held it for Msgr. Quinn. Harry noticed that most of the communicants lined up with Msgr. Quinn. My concern was that no Host or particle of Host fall onto the floor or onto the clothes of anyone receiving communion. The bread was the true Body of Jesus and could only be touched by a priest.

104

I remember as a child cycling toward Lahinch with Packy. We stopped in a small chapel along the road to make a visit to the Blessed Sacrament. There was an old woman on her knees, bent over something in the aisle. We went up to see if she were well. She lifted her black shawl from off her head and whispered to us, "Quick, go get the priest! It is Jesus, Our Lord here on the floor!"

We ran for the priest who dashed to the small chapel, lifted the Host off the ground, and placed it back in the Tabernacle. He then cleansed the floor with Holy Water and thanked us for alerting him. The three of us looked around for the old woman but she was gone.

My own eyes filled with tears at the thought of that humble old woman kneeling on the stony floor in adoration of the Blessed Sacrament with the wind rattling the old wooden door and shaking the salty windows until the priest could come.

The Hogans knew that I was simply a poor kid from Ireland whose step-father was a Chicago cop. I'm sure they hoped that I was in awe at the many prelates honoring their exemplary Catholic life and their generosity to the Church, both in Lake Forest and to the Archdiocese of Chicago, as well as personally to the Holy Father in Rome.

Ah, "still waters run deep," whispered old Paddy Dunphy and he had to bite his lip so as not to laugh. The Dunphys knew me as one of their own. They resented how their rich cousins patronized them with fruit baskets and subscriptions to *America*. How when old Mrs. Dunphy, their mother, was dying, Judge Hogan and the Mrs. were too busy to pay her a visit.

As the Solemn High Mass concluded in billows of incense and showers of Holy Water, Judge Harry Hogan, a towering, burly figure, and Cecilia Hogan, his delicate, little wife, renewed their vows before the Cardinal and the three Monsignors. With their youngest son Harry on the altar, their nine other sons and two daughters knelt beside them and the slew of grandchildren stood behind their parents.

The Judge appeared irritated and whispered to his wife. She looked around and frowned back at the Judge. The photographer was a "no-show." The Judge would take care of him as soon as this was over, he nodded to Cecilia. She smiled back at him, knowing that she could always depend on the Judge to protect her and make her little world more than right.

The three poor Dunphy priest cousins had made their way to the sacristy, quickly changed out of their vestments and snuck out to the parking lot for a smoke and a good, loud laugh. I saw them through the green and gold-colored windows in the sacristy. I wanted to get out there with them, with real guys like myself, not with the red and purple fancy dresses of the powerful.

Harry was talking with the Cardinal, achieving a delicate balance of looking down at him from his six-foot, three-inches height and appearing obsequious at the same time. The three Monsignors stood apart, letting the young priest-to-be speak with the Cardinal. They all knew that Harry was well on his way to a place of power and authority in the Church.

Harry would flash his eyes quickly from the Cardinal over to see if I were watching him, but I was looking wistfully out at the rollicking Dunphys, slapping each other on the back as they let go of all the bottled-up laughter that had been building since they took a step into St. Mary's. Harry motioned for me to join him with the Cardinal. I looked over at Harry as if I were jolted out of a beautiful dream.

Harry introduced me to the Cardinal who had turned his hand, palm-down and bent his wrist for me to kneel and kiss his ring. Harry nudged me but I looked at him blankly. The three Monsignors hastened over to cover for their nephew who was obviously embarrassed by my ignorant behavior. Or was it arrogant behavior on my part?

I was taught long ago to bend my knee to no man. The Irish had been on their knees for 800 years and I did not come to this country to turn back the clock.

****

The Deer Path Inn was a spectacle that would shame the Old Guard Wasps. It was modeled after a 15th Century manor house in Chiddingstone, England, with its stone fireplaces, beamed ceilings and leaded glass windows. I half-expected Henry VIII to stroll out

106

from behind a door with one of his wives. The crowd was directed down the plum carpeted stairs to the large, elegant English Room which had been reserved for the Hogans.

Harry and I were placed with the priests, with Cardinal Joyce honored to be seated between Cecilia Hogan and the Judge. After the Cardinal had said Grace, the waiters came around for drink orders. Harry ordered Scotch on the Rocks for himself and for me.

Harry sipped his and I drank it like water. Harry motioned for a refill for me and continued to sip his with a smile. The Hogans lived by the motto, "If you learn to drink at home, you will never become an alcoholic". We had no alcohol at home, so I couldn't learn how not to become an alcoholic. That was my excuse.

My head began to swim as I thought of Graymour Manor up the mountain from Quilty and how we all hated that place, saying it was haunted and "nothin' but bad ever came out of it." This place started to feel like that. Sure, this house I was eating in was an English trap, not a place for me to be at all. I was a West Clare Irish rebel!

Not to be confused with the Republican Party in the United States, the folks in West Clare were Republican to the core. From 1918 – 1921, the Irish fought the British for their independence. In 1921 the Treaty was signed and the Irish Free State was established, breaking the country into the 26 free counties in the South and the six counties in the North that remained under British rule. The Free State was headquartered in Dublin and the six counties were North in Belfast.

A Civil War followed, as the Free Staters under Martin Collins agreed with the division of the country. They fought their own brothers, named the Republicans, who did not want Ireland to be divided, but to become "a nation once again." With a price on their heads, many of the Republicans had to flee Ireland and they sought refuge in the States.

My neck and face were turning red from the drink. I was thirsty for another drink and Harry, still nursing his first, obliged, waiting for me to make a bloody fool of myself. I began humming "Boulavogue," as the drink was shutting down my poor impulse controls and my blood ran greener. I started to sing:

"Then **Father Murphy** from old Kilcormack

Spurned up the rocks with a warning cry:
'Arm, arm' he cried, 'For I've come to lead you,
For Ireland's freedom we fight or die.'"

I felt a rough hand on my neck. "On yer' feet now, **Fr. Murphy**! On yer' feet!" Fr. Paddy Dunphy led me out of the English Room and around the corner to the White Hart Pub. He ordered two ice-cold waters and told me to get it down and chew up some crackers. He reached into his pocket and pulled out three battered aspirin and told me to get them down, fast!

"What the hell you doing, Lad? You want to make a spectacle of yourself? That's all your buddy Harry would love, you know that?? He's so jealous of you that he glows in the dark. Makin' a goddamn arse of yourself in this fancy setting is all he needs and he'll hold that over you for the rest of your life."

I breathed deeply as I gulped the water and chomped down the salty crackers. I hung my head and the sweat rolled out from under my arms. "Ah, Dear God, I'm so sorry, I'm so sorry!"

"Now, never mind with the sorry business, Lad. Just mind yourself and stay off the drink, it'll be the death of you. Are ye ready to go back to your seat and behave yourself? And never mind that Fr. Murphy business in a place like this. Sure, ye got to keep your mouth shut if you're going to be a priest. Just learn to keep your mouth shut, Lad, your eyes closed and stay off the drink!"

I nodded at Fr. Paddy and we made our way back to our place and sat together as the prime rib had already been served. A nine-year-old boy, Harry Smith, his sister's son, was sitting on Harry's lap and Harry was bouncing him up and down. As we returned to the table, Harry lifted the boy off his lap and told him to go back to his own seat. Harry secured his napkin on his lap while Fr. Paddy Dunphy lifted my knife and fork and told me to "eat up."

So all I could do was focus on the juicy red slab of meat and huge baked potato, topped with butter and sour cream. I lifted off the sour cream, put it to the side, shook the salt and pepper and dove into the potato. Fr. Paddy patted my shoulder and whispered, "Good Lad, now, good Lad, eat up and you'll be right as rain before the night is over." He had saved my life.

Harry Hogan smiled as he sipped his red wine and picked at the meat. He now had my number. The Hogans knew well the danger of drink and strictly forbade drunkenness of any kind. It was called the *Irish Virus*. "So our great Irish Achilles has a weak spot", Harry whispered to me. He knew before I did.

I sobered up quickly. The red had left my face and the melancholy lifted from my soul. I know that dreamy, far-off gaze I get came back as I tried to figure what had gone so terribly wrong. I closed his eyes and thanked God that Fr. Paddy had been the angel sent to protect me from making a bloody arse of myself.

"Oh, Angel of God, my guardian dear," I prayed, as the Hogans and the Cardinal climbed the plum carpeted stairs to that gray, stony foyer and a uniformed guard pushed open the dark, wooden doors as they made their way under the green canopy to their waiting black limousines.

The Dunphys piled into Paddy's brown Ford Falcon sedan that had seen better days. Fr. Paddy waved at me and made the Sign of the Cross in blessing to me as they turned north on Oakwood, a sticker for *Kennedy and Johnson* stuck to their bumper.

CHAPTER 19

O, My Dark Rosaleen

It was a wonderful day, December 10, 1959. I looked out my small, leaded-glass window as the snow fell quietly from the northern skies. The whole world was blanketed in snow, the softest and purest white where only angels could dance.   I was in my last year of Philosophy, anxious to start the last four years of theology. Then Priesthood!

John Kennedy was a long way from his grave and women were buying *The Feminine Mystique* for their daughters. A black Baptist minister in the south was beginning to stir thing up with the Montgomery bus boycott and whites were getting nervous. Just a year ago, a 76-year-old fat little Italian was elected as Pope John XXIII. He was the Patriarch of Venice and had bought a round-way ticket to Rome and back. He didn't return to Venice.

We, the seminarians of the Ordination Class of 1964, sat in our big maple-brown leather sofas and reclining chairs around the gray-stone fireplace in the Students' Lounge. We were anxious to get home for the holidays. We would assist at the Midnight Masses at our own parishes and be up on the altar for all the other Masses of Christmas Day. We were almost priests.

As we watched the logs hiss and crackle, we were like kids, excited about the new direction the church was taking. We were at the very cutting edge of the church - the New Frontiersmen as John Kennedy would say, young men with the vision and courage to hurry the Church into the modern world.

New priests, new liturgy, new theology. A melting of the frozen face of winter to make way for spring - the warm, new countenance of love and beauty on the face and in the soul of Holy Mother Church. We were giddy to be young, on our way to Priesthood, the Boundary-Spanners with one foot in the Old and another in the New.

We thought we were carefully poised not to lose our balance, but to be sure-footed in helping to negotiate change for all the People of God. We were almost like the young goats I'd see up on the cliffs of Clare, leading the way through the dangerous cracks and crevices of change - young, frisky goats we were indeed!

Garrett Lyons had transferred from the Jesuits to Mundelein, as he was impatient to be ordained a priest and the Jesuit process was lengthy. Their extended preparation of nearly 15 years would make him 35, and by then, he could have been a Chicago priest for 10 years.

He was all my six-foot, four-inches, as husky as Tim Armstrong, as street-smart as Harry Hogan. Garrett had straight dark brown hair that parted itself in the middle and swept back from his face and hazy, hazel eyes that were both dreamy and focused, depending on which way the wind blew that moment. He was innately lazy, moving as slow as a "three-legged donkey," as Uncle Tom would say.

I'd smile as I noticed that Garrett always had something of James Joyce tucked under his arm or buttoned into his cassock. With his ear to the ground, Harry Hogan had Garrett's number the minute he put his foot into Mundelein; if the truth be known, Garrett knew the price of Harry's soul without checking his own wallet. I'd see him looking at how Harry's little stump of nails disappeared into his fingers – Harry wasn't as cool as he thought.

I unwound my long legs and reached for more logs to keep the fire going. As this was officially the night before the start of our Christmas vacation, we were allowed the bottles of cognac that Judge Hogan had sent to the seminary. The note from the Judge to his cousin, Msgr. Clarke, the Rector, said: "If our fellows are to be Chicago priests, they must learn to drink like Chicago priests! Indulge! Please!"

From the public-address system, the Sistine Chapel Choir sang *Panis Angelicus, Bread of Angels*, in the sacred language of the church. I could feel tears start to well up in my eyes, but quickly cleared my throat. Tears were not a sign of priestly manhood.

Garrett puffed deeply on his brown briarwood pipe and Harry lit his fat Cuban cigar. Tim Armstrong tossed an imaginary basketball through the invisible hoop on the burled-walnut mantle, stroked his strong, cleft chin, and looked around like a defense lawyer about to address a sleepy jury.

"Hey, Guys, what do you *really* think about the church? I mean, what are we really doing here? Where are we going with the idea of renewal? The whole celibacy thing? No more fish on Friday and no more fasting from midnight – not that we ever see midnight? Maybe they'll throw out Mary and Joseph and the Popes? What about women saying Mass and not just cleaning up after us? Maybe we'll become obsolescent, strange anachronisms that they'll stick in the Field Museum."

His remarks hit a brick wall. We stared into the fire for answers, but remained speechless. I think we all felt threatened… with one quick flick of his wrist, had he tossed our vocations into the flames? Were our dreams of becoming priests just ashes and cinders? Did he just articulate what all of us had been thinking, but were unwilling to put out for public consumption?

Tim lowered his eyes and held his head in his hands, "Come on, Guys! Talk to me!! Don't let me hang out here to die!!"

Garrett cleared his throat, "to *dry*, not to die, to *dry*, Timmy. Got to keep these things straight, Timmy."

Tim Armstrong lunged for Garrett and began flailing at him. Being non-athletic, Garrett could only shout, "Down, Boy, down now, be a nice doggy, Timmy Boy, be a nice doggy." Harry and I lunged for Tim. Garrett straightened his cassock and refilled his pipe. The silence among them was thicker than the gray sheets of flagstone around the fire.

"Talk to me, Martin! Please talk to me!" Tim looked to me, but I remained focused on the fire and brandy. "Please, Martin…," he said quietly, as his voice faded in his throat. Courage was not my strong suit. I wish I had had a father to teach me how to be a man when I was young and wandering about for direction.

I remained silent. I could only think about the Mystical Body of Christ – the *Church Triumphant* (those in heaven), the *Church Suffering* (those still in Purgatory) and the *Church Militant* (those struggling here on earth, marching on to heaven). I knew if I said much, I'd be shot down by Garrett, whom we called "The Jesuit."

Scanning the group with his dark, roving eyes, Harry said that the Church was really two things: the spiritual thing about God and that stuff, but really was the biggest powerhouse in the world, bigger than General Motors, bigger than the US Government. He picked a shred of tobacco off his lower lip, spit it into the fire and rolled his tongue around the rim of the brandy glass.

Garrett leaned back against the soft leather head-rest, stuffed more sweet Abington tobacco into his brown, burled pipe, pulled his thick eyebrows down over his eyes and said nothing for a while. Tim cleared his throat, waiting for the Jesuit to speak. Garrett kept them waiting. "You know, Guys, would she not be 'the old sow that eats her farrow?' "

Harry spit again into the fire. Garrett yawned. Tim continued to hold his head in his hands, his elbows on his knees, supporting the weight of his thoughts like *The Thinker,* hoping to be able to reason through his turmoil.

I closed my eyes. I didn't like the way this was going - Garrett was too damn intellectual, Harry was too cynical, Tim was too argumentative. Was I just too soft, too stupid, too naïve? Were none of them there just because they loved the Church? Did they not want to be priests just because they wanted to be priests, pure and simple?

It was too hard for me to define my dream, that magnetic pull of Grace that had been placed in my heart long before I was born.

Suddenly jerking myself straight up as if a red-hot poker had been rammed up my arse, I began to speak in my oldest, deepest, dampest West Clare voice,

"I go to encounter for the millionth time the reality of experience and to forge in the smithy of my soul the uncreated conscience of my race." Sure, they got it right back at home:

"Oh, Ireland, my first and only love,
Where Christ and Caesar are hand in glove. "

I slapped my knees, out-Joyceing the Jesuit, out-foxing Tim who didn't know how to stop debating himself, out-cynicing Harry with the words of the greatest cynic, James Joyce, whom the Irish church had already known, but only too well.

We grew silent as the logs slowly lost their flame and grew into wise, old embers, the silent witness to our brandies and smokes and to our young thoughts and words already shaping our tender minds into the thoughts and words that we would profess as ordained priests.

In the background, the Choir of St. Martin's in the Fields sang, "Oh, Come, O Come, Emanuel!" Feeling slightly drunk after the brandy and smoke and edgy intellectual forays into the waiting storms of uncharted waters, they headed for their safe, lonely rooms.

****

I stayed behind. Stone sober. I sat before the silent, glowing embers, my fingers arched upon my long nose like the flying buttresses of a great Cathedral. The brandy bottles were far from empty. It was a shame to throw them out.

I moved the white-veined ashtray aside and lined the three bottles up on the dark oak table next to the arms of my smooth leather chair. The fat bottles morphed, shape-shifted as small, dark, voluptuous women, ready to serve. I reached for a bottle and caressed her, my own *Sheila na Gig*.

I lifted her to my lips and swallowed slowly, letting her burn my throat and quench my thirst. I closed my eyes and swallowed another perfect mouthful of rich, thick brandy. I rested her on my cheeks and lifted another woman off the table and rested her on my other cheek.

I was breathing hard and fast. I was lifted far away to a white tent in the middle of the hot white sands in the Arabian Desert. Camels and palm trees surround the luscious night oasis and Salome is dancing the dance of the Seven Veils at my feet, bongo drums are beating and cymbals are clashing from outside the tent. I gulped another huge mouthful of brandy, banging my front teeth in my rush.

Lying naked on scarlet pillows atop layers of red and orange and pink Persian rugs, I watch scantily clad women fan me and sing to me and massage my stiff body. Their full, brown breasts pillow my leathery cheeks and wild, wild hair. I groan and moan as the brandy spills on my cassock, on the leather chair and runs down to the dark blue Oriental rug beneath me.

114

I sit in a stupor, my eyes heavy with drink and release. A flat, contented smile plays on my lips. I slur, "I'm a rambler… I'm a gambler…I'm a long way from home…If you don't like me…Well, leave me alone…I'll eat when I'm hungry…I'll drink when I'm dry…And if moonshine won't kill me…I'll live till I die."

A strong arm lifted me to my feet and pointed me to my room. I tried to push him away, but belligerence wasn't in me and I went quietly to where I was directed. Harry opened my door, unbuttoned my cassock, pulled off my shoes and led me to bed. He covered me, closed the door and walked quietly to the lounge and cleaned up the remnants of my foray into the desert.

The following morning, I woke with my clothes on and my cassock balled up on the floor. I had no memory of the night before and Harry Hogan kept all this to himself. I later understood that he was ingratiating himself into my life; good old Harry could always be trusted to look out for me.

In January after the Christmas break, Tim Armstrong's room was empty. The sheets had been stripped from his bed and the curtains were drawn. Tim enrolled in the School of Law at DePaul University and soon began dating a young nurse.

PART THREE

Chapters 20 - 28

On Pembroke Road look out for my ghost
Disheveled with shoes untied,
Playing through the railings with little children
Whose children have long since died.

If Ever You Go to Dublin Town
Patrick Kavanaugh

Chapter 20
Fork in the River

On the way to the priesthood, there are many stepping stones. We can either jump to the next stone or jump out of the river altogether. I had no intention of jumping out of the river. I was winding down my four years of Philosophy, which would have been four years at a regular college. I was getting ready to graduate and to begin the final phase of my studies to the priesthood, the last four years of Theology.

It was the time of our annual eight-day retreat, a period of silence, prayer, meditation and discernment. They never hesitated to weed out any guy that they felt was not in for the long haul and would not make a good priest. I knew some guys had doubts, but they pushed through anyway. When the rector had his doubts about anyone, he was gone.

I was spared this torment. I knew before anything else that I would be a priest. I loved the Lord with my whole heart and soul and only wanted to please Him in everything I did. I wanted to be His servant and minister to His people, looking beyond my own comfort and pleasure. I wanted to be good and holy and faithful, and, with the help of His Blessed Mother Mary, I would someday be a priest.

It was during retreat, early in the afternoon. I was making my Holy Hour before the Blessed Sacrament, kneeling in silence to adore Christ. I felt a tap on my shoulder. Fr. Archibald motioned for me to come with him.

I left the pew, knelt on both knees, bowed my head, and followed Fr. Archibald out of the chapel. Hot sweat gathered under my arms and on my neck. I felt like throwing up. I was panicking inside, thinking they were going to send me home. Or my mother had died. Or someone had reported me for something.

As we left the chapel, I stuck my shaking fingers into the holy water, blessed myself, and looked back at the altar, a final glimpse at my fading priesthood. Like that final glimpse of the green hills of Kerry, ten years ago, as I watched my life disappear into the sad Irish mist, so full of grief and longing and loss.

Fr. Archibald led the way to the Rector's office. He whispered, "He wants to see you" and rapped softly on the Rector's big, wooden door. I knew my poor knees would not hold me up and prayed to the Mother of God, that above all else, let me be a man. The Rector motioned for me to take a seat and nodded for Fr. Archibald to leave.

I sat. The Rector continued signing papers. I sat. He got up and went into his bathroom. I couldn't move. He finally came out, looking for all the world as a hangman ready to curl his noose. He looked at me. I looked at him and then deflected my eyes, so as not to appear bold, but confident enough to look him in the eye.

"Martin, Martin Sweeney, I want to talk with you for a moment, despite the fact that you are on retreat."

"Yes, Monsignor."

"You're going to Rome in September. A place called the *North American College* and you'll study at the *Pontifical Gregorian University*. For your four years of Theology. Then you'll be ordained by the pope!"

"But I just got here!"

"What are you talking about? You've been here for four years already."

"I mean, Monsignor, I just got to this country. I'm sorry, I'm so sorry, I didn't mean to be disrespectful or disobedient, I'm sorry. I was thinking of Ireland."

"O.K, now, Martin. Calm down. I didn't realize that this would be such a surprise. It is really an honor, you need to know. The smartest and the best seminarians from all over the world are chosen to go the Gregorian Institute. It's called the cradle of bishops and theologians. We want you to go and represent the Archdiocese of Chicago. At this point, it doesn't look like anyone else will be going with you. You'll be able to go far in the church, Martin Sweeney."

"Yes, Monsignor. Thank you, but I've never thought about being a bishop. I don't even want to be a bishop. But now, what do I do? How do I get there?"

"Well, whether you become a bishop or not is not in your hands, Martin. As the Dominicans say, *'keep the rule and the rule will keep you.'* Fr. Archibald is in charge of all you need to know. He'll arrange for everything. Come in and say good-by when you leave, Martin. And make us all proud of you. Now, go back to your prayers and say one for me, Martin."

I knelt by the side of the Rector's desk and asked for his blessing, thanked him and ran to the *lavatoria*. Thank God I had to move along, quickly, or I would have asked him if he had attended the Gregorian. But he was neither a bishop nor a theologian, so I kept my place and did not inquire, nor pose such a personal question to my superior, even though it was not to challenge, but for the sake of conversation.

For years and years there was no questioning, just nodding compliance. Imagine if all us young guys challenged the authorities – what a church we would have had! But that all came later. Gertrude Stein wrote that the Germans had to learn how to disobey. I was older when I read that and it nearly blew me away. But before you can disobey, you must be able to discern the worthiness of an order. For now, I had my marching orders – I was off to Rome in the autumn.

****

It was the 5th of September, 1960. The die was cast and I was off to Rome, still with my old Irish passport, the small green document with the gold harp on the outside and with a picture of my scared 10-year-old mug on the inside. Just for luck!

"All Aboard! All Aboard!! All Aboard" rang through the dark platform of LaSalle Street Station. I knew it was time to say my final good-by. The whole family had come down, even the old aunties – Josie, Mayme, Norah and Kitty. Lizzie and Babe, Brendan, Mammie and Steve, the kids – Clare and Liam, even my old pals, Tim Armstong and Harry Hogan.

I hugged the old aunties, shook hands with the kids and the guys, half-hugged Steve. He softly punched me in the arm and told me to make them all proud, to let him know if I needed anything. Tim bowed before me, as he threw my suitcase into the belly of the train.

I threw my arms around my mother and felt her racking cough shake her thin body like the old water pipes rumbling down

120

the basement in the winter. She buried her boney face in my neck and her hot tears softened my stiff collar.

"*Dia leat...Dia leat,*" she whispered over and over. "My Martin, my Martin, I love you so much, Pet, just pray for all of us and we won't notice the time passing. God bless you, *Dia leat,* Martin." Mammie gasped for air and Steve pulled her into himself.

When I wasn't looking, Harry Hogan kissed me on the lips – I shoved him away, spit on the tracks, wiped my mouth against the sleeve of my jacket. Sure Harry was a wolf in sheep's clothing, coming on like that at this saddest time for us. He always knew when to move in.

I climbed those worn steps of the *20th Century Limited*, the very same that brought us here to Chicago 12 years ago. I found a seat by the window and pressed my face against the cold glass. I could still see them. My mother didn't look, but the others were waving.

I put my arms around the soft leather haversack that Babe and Lizzie had given me. In it I had: an apple; two boiled eggs and slices of my mother's lovely brown buttered bread in a little brown bag; my tickets to New York and to Naples; my American and Irish passports; health certification; letters of recommendation; family pictures; my prayer book and a Bible. My whole life of 21 years was packed into that plump brown bag.

The engines hissed, the bells clanged, the doors slammed shut. Ever so slowly we pulled away from the station, my family growing smaller by the second. Through the steam rolling out from under the wheels, I saw an old priest standing alone, a prophet descending the mountain, breaking the clouds. He raised his hand in blessing. Through my sudden tears, I waved back at Fr. Archibald.

CHAPTER 21
The Heart-Scalding Dreamings

Grand Central Station. I was over-whelmed. St. Mary of the Lake Seminary had turned me back into a country boy and here I was, all alone, trapped right in the middle of New York City. It was so beautiful, but oh, so scary. The sounds and smells and the simple elegance of this magnificent palace caught me off-guard. The knees are the first to go when I get to this point.

Following the directions from Fr. Archibald, I found a taxi stand out on 42nd Street and asked the cabbie to take me to Pier 88. He drove so fast, clipping corners, yelling at old ladies and kids who got in his way, spitting out the window and blowing his smoke back at me. I felt sick to my stomach and I grabbed Lizzie's haversack to steady my nerves.

We got down to the port on the Hudson River, on the west side of Manhattan. Ocean liners loomed large above the scruffy drive into the terminals - newspapers, dog crap, broken whiskey bottles, a few bums sitting on the curbs, skinny kids who should have been in school chasing each other. Not at all like Cobh on the bottom tip of Ireland that was dark and stony and full of grief. Pier 88 was exciting and hopeful, for we were Americans going east, not immigrants coming west.

The meter read $17.25. I handed the driver the exact amount and thanked him. He held his hand out to me. I didn't know if he wanted me to take the money back or what. I picked up my luggage and thanked him again. He smiled bitterly and shouted, "Thanks so much, Little Pussy! Nothing like a smart-ass faggot to drive around! Thanks, Pussy Boy!" He drove off hard and dirt flew in my eyes. I had no idea why I had made him so mad.

My directions said to find the North American College – NAC – group in the terminal and that we would go through customs together. I introduced myself to Msgr. Duffenbach, the rector from NAC who oversaw us. I heard a slight accent. He was balancing a clip board on his knee as he clicked his red ball-point pen. A long white pipe was held between his teeth. He had to get us future bishops and theologians to Rome and would brook no nonsense.

We had to arrange ourselves in alphabetical order for boarding and cabin assignment. I fell in next to John Sullivan from Cleveland. Msgr. Duffenbach was the first to board and waited for us to clear customs and get on the ship, the *Paul Revere*. He reminded me of Uncle Tom at home, herding the cattle to fresh fields, not wanting any to stray.

After John and I emptied our luggage and put the toiletries in the head, we went on deck. John was a red-head, short and stocky, built close to the earth, looking like he was about to clutch you into a tight head-lock if you got in his way. I was a half-foot taller, thin and more of the airy type, vague, more inclined to run than fight. The bishop and the theologian!

We came on deck just as the *Paul Revere* slipped anchor and began to sail. As we slid past the towering Statue of Liberty, I shuddered. All she had seen of our dreams and nightmares, our success and failure. Annie Moore, a little Irish girl of 15 with her two younger brothers, was the first to be admitted to Ellis Island. *Isle of Hope, Isle of Tears* was written for her, the brave little girl.

An old man was standing next to us, the tears rolling down his cheeks. His knobby fingers were like old white claws that grabbed the railing. I was afraid he was going to hurl himself over. I said a little prayer for him and moved away, coward that I was.

There must have been 30 or 40 of us, from all over the country. Lots of dioceses sent two, but I guess Chicago could afford only one. I know the Hogans wanted Harry to study in Rome and that Judge Hogan actually went to the Cardinal and offered to pay for both of us, but the Cardinal did not want Harry to go to Rome, despite the Hogans' involvement in the business of the church. He did not budge. I could never figure that out, but I was glad to have Harry in Chicago and me away in Rome.

All of us had nothing in common, just our burning desire to be priests. I'm not sure of anyone but myself and I could have done it just as well, staying at home. But the Will of God, as expressed by my legitimate superiors, said I was to go to Rome. The future "theologians" seem to cluster with the other intellectuals and the "bishops" found themselves before we were out of port.

I didn't fit with either group. That was the story of my life – I'm always on the outside, looking in. Irish passport, American clothes, Irish accent, American humor. Now I get to put *Italia* into the mix, and God only knows how I'll turn out. And without my flesh-and-blood father that tears at my heart with every beat.

So often I'd stand on the portside deck, straining to see if I could catch a glimpse of Cork or Kerry over the sea. I knew it was silly – a ship going from New York to Naples doesn't go to Cobh, but I'd wish that the Gulf Stream current would just shove us a bit north and bring me home. But where was home? My roots in Ireland? My mother in Chicago? My destiny in Rome?

I hate to admit this, but I was envious of the other guys. They were all sure of themselves, where they had come from, as it wasn't hard to distinguish some guy from Boston from someone from Kansas City or Denver, just by the tongue in their heads and the size of the chip on their shoulders. I had no edges, no definitions. Just vague.

Late one afternoon, a few days short of docking, I was standing portside in all my glorious melancholy and oozing self-pity, trying for the last time to catch a glimpse of *"that little bit of heaven that dropped from out the skies one day."* Msgr. Duffenbach approached. I nodded my head. We were both the same height, well over 6 feet. I tried to shrink myself a bit, so as not to seem too bold.

He said nothing but cracked his knuckles. I wasn't going to open my mouth. He lit his long white pipe. I was down-wind of him and the smoke that hit me smelled of the turf fire at home. The throat-lump was there again and it resisted my swallowing. He puffed on his pipe and I studied the empty horizon.

Without looking at me or taking the pipe out of his mouth, he growled, "Martin Sweeney, just cut it out! Cut it the Christ out! You're making me sick to my stomach and you're making all of us sick. If this moodiness and melancholy continues, you'll be sent home before your big feet touch Italy. And I'll see to it that you'll never be a priest. So just cut it out, here and now!"

124

As he walked away from me, he jabbed me with his sharp elbow. I never realized it until then, but I had never had a man talk like that to me, let alone the elbow. I think I kept myself safe by projecting a woundedness that women loved because they could mother me, and even Clare, my little sister, pretended to be my mother. But I think I turned men off, my woundedness perceived as weakness. A disclaimer to my manhood.

I always thought of myself as an orphan, and I know if Mammie ever knew how I felt, it would kill her, because all the Sweeneys were filled with love for me. I carried the name *Martin*, the proud name of their proud father, Martin Sweeney.

But my secret is that beneath my soft, black cloak of melancholy, beat a heart of rage at the Irish bastard that fathered me. I hated him with every cell in my body and if I ever met him, I would beat him to a bloody pulp. How dare that bastard just impregnate my young mother and head for the hills, not even wanting to stick around and see what he had done. The profound sadness that I guarded so tenderly kept me safe and those around me were spared the volcanic cauldron of my wrath.

****

There was a lot of bustle as the ship pulled into the Bay of Naples. There was no turning around at this point, so it was back in alphabetical order, get our luggage and pass through customs. The Italian chaos was in sharp contrast to the regimented, military ambience of Pier 88.

Msgr. Duffenbach, towering over most of us in his no-nonsense, authoritarian black suit, puffed on his white pipe and silently pointed us to the yellow bus with NAC painted on the side. He could not compete with the happy, crazy pandemonium that engulfed us, so he did not even try. We were on a "mission from God!"

The battered old bus left the port and headed to the town of Paestum, a small Greek town with temples and columns older than the church. The director there said it had been founded by the Dorians, followed by the Lucanians, the Christians, the Saracens. John and I walked among the ashy remains of the volcano of Mt. Vesuvius that erupted 79 years after Christ. I often thought that Ireland was the oldest spot on earth with our towers and crumbly castles – little did I know what was ahead for me.

We stayed the night in Sorrento, an old fishing village overlooking the Bay of Naples. We were all in a state of quiet excitement. There was nothing in the States that compared to the sights, sounds and fragrance of Italy and this was just the beginning.

After dinner we were allowed a glass of dusty yellow liqueur, *limoncello*. Lemon trees covered the hillsides and now every time I get a whiff of a lemon, I'm back to that first night in Sorrento. I picked a few and they are twice the size of our lemons, not bitter at all but sweet, and little pips you can swallow.

Then up the torturous, twisted Amalfi Coast in our rickety, little yellow bus. Cliffs over-hung the Tyrrhenian Sea with ancient villages tucked into its side. Trees and flowers sprouted everywhere like the whole place was on fire. Cars and trucks vied for space and the air was filled with honking, yelling and shouting. Right smack below us was the water with no guard-rail or anything to keep us from plunging right over.

It was scary, but fun. I'd love to be one of those guys who could just blast away to anyone who got in my way. I wonder what it would feel like, instead of having to be so guarded, controlled and obedient. I was nearly 22 but still felt like a boy, a very young boy. I had a long road ahead of me. I was glad to have John Sullivan beside me as my new pal. We were both scared but neither of us admitted it to each other.

CHAPTER 22
Rome: The Smithy of My Soul

The driver drove slowly along the *Fiume Tevere*, the Tiber River, with the glories of Rome splayed out before us. He crossed a bridge, the *Ponte Sant' Angelo*, and turned in front of the *Castel Sant' Angelo* onto the *Via della Concilliazione*, right smack up to the sweeping piazza in front of St. Peter's Basilica. We gasped. With every turn of the wheel of the bus, we were getting closer to priesthood. St. Peter's!!

Snaking our way along the Tiber River, our bus driver pointed out the Palatine Hill where Romulus founded the city of Rome. When they were first born, he and his twin brother, Remus, were thrown into the Tiber by their father. Rescued by a wolf that nursed them with her own milk and fed by a woodpecker that brought them seeds, Romulus killed his brother and established the great city and named it after himself.

We turned sharply up the *Gianicolo* and pulled in front of a large, yellow brick, six-storied building which was to be our home for the next four years. It looked like any other American high-school or small college, extremely modest by Roman standards. Like we Yanks knew our place in the great roll of time.

The driver was shouting to us in Italian to get our luggage and Msgr. Duffenbach had his clip-board ready. In alphabetical order we entered the North American College, knowing that we were in the big leagues now.

There was a terrible silence on us, except John Sullivan and I caught each other's eyes and broke out laughing. It's a nervous thing, an Irish thing, because our feelings are so strong, but we never know what to do with them. The laughing had gotten me in trouble many times, but I just couldn't contain myself and when people would ask me why I was laughing – at a funeral, at a graduation, when getting scolded – I never knew what to say. It's not that it was actually funny, but it was all I could do. Now I had an accomplice with my man Sullivan.

A little Italian nun took me up to my room. She actually tried to carry my luggage, but I asked her not to. I could just see Mammie smacking me for even thinking about it. My room was on the 4th floor, right across the hall from John's. It was bigger than my little alcove at home, with a bed, a desk and chair, and a wardrobe.

I thanked the nun and started to unpack. I opened the wardrobe and in it hung two cassocks, one plain black and the other one black with blue buttons and blue piping and a bright, red sash. That was the traditional colors of the North American College that we were to wear to the Gregorian and anywhere out of the college.

Every morning at 6 a.m. we were called to prayer, breakfast, and then we boarded the bus to take us to the *Pontifical Gregorian University,* commonly called the *Greg,* located within a few blocks of the *Fontana di Trevi,* the fountain where the 'three roads meet'. Seminarians came from all over the world for this First Class priestly education. All our classes here were held in Latin, the universal language of the Church.

The Greg was founded in 1551 by Ignatius of Loyola and run by his Jesuits, an order of priests and brothers who take a special vow of obedience to the Pope. Aware of its own importance, it was the only order to name itself, the *Society of Jesus,* after Jesus Christ Himself. Others were called after holy men such as Francis or Dominic or after the Blessed Mother, such as the Marists. By many vengeful critics, it was said that the Holy Father was the White Pope and the head of the Jesuits was the Black Pope.

James Joyce said that the Jesuits were the gentlemen of Catholic Education and the Christian Brothers the drones. Joyce, in a verbal combat with a critic, said that he himself ought to be referred to as a *Jesuit.* In true Jesuitical fashion, when asked if he were becoming a Protestant, he replied, "I may have lost my faith, but not my reason."

From 8 a.m. until noon we studied. Most of our classes were held in the large lecture halls called the *aula.* The Greg, named after Pope Gregory XIII, is impressive on the outside with its classic Ammannati-designed pale umber/white façade to reflect the grandeur of the Papacy and the critical work that was going on inside its arched doors.

The interior is plain and simple – just tables and chairs, black-boards and books, plain walls and doors and wooden floors. There was nothing to distract our young minds from the rigid and rigorous task of preparation for the priesthood. This was very serious business.

I think one of the big secrets is that the Franciscans are known for their *poverty,* but the Jesuits practice it. Poverty - not as a goal within itself, but to free the mind for spiritual and intellectual pursuits. Materialism was just not the Jesuit way and most of us really found that it was a strange juxtaposition to all the glory that surrounded us.

Our classes in Theology, Philosophy, Moral theology, Scripture, Church History, Sacraments, Doctrine and Spirituality were all without debate, without questioning, without research. It was all laid out before us and our job was to soak it up.

As we were going about our education, steeping ourselves in ancient and infallible church doctrine, teaching and thought, our dear little old man of a Pope, John XXIII, had called all the Bishops and theologians and scholars from all over the world to come to Rome to bring the Church into the 20th Century. He said, "Let's open the windows!! We need some fresh air!"

Pope John XXIII was elected to be the "care-taker" pope, until they could get someone more appropriate, but he ended up being just perfect for our time. He was a dumpy little man and at first, we could hardly take him seriously. He looked like any one of a dozen Italian laborers sweeping the streets below our windows. He had none of the solemnity of Pius XII or the intensity of Paul VI who would follow him.

This may seem unbelievable, but we were unaware of all the upheaval that was going on, as our eyes were holding fast to the unchangeable truths of the past. Perhaps it was just a universal get-together, just to be sure that everyone was on the same page, that no heresies were creeping into the one, true Church. Little did we know then that the Church would be stood right up on its own head, right on its own magnificent golden dome.

Fr. Vaughn from Glasgow had taught church doctrine for over 40 years. His toe-hold into his work had begun with the Church being the Rock of Christ, the impregnable boulder that Peter had used as the strong, timeless foundation of Christianity. Fr. Vaughn had written many books and was quoted world-wide for his vision of what the church meant.

He came into class one morning with his books, threw them in a basket and said, "All that stuff is obsolete. Now the Church is the *People of God!!*" Fr. Vaughn was a humble, obedient Jesuit and from there on, he taught *Lumen Gentium, (The Light to the Nations),* to his students. This was one of the central documents of Vatican II, the Constitution on the Church.

At noon, we returned to the NAC, ate our big dinner and were able to talk with each other, as we were on *Silence* for the most part of the morning. There was time built in for a long siesta, prayer, walking around Rome in our American cassocks and finally supper at 7:00. The little nuns did all the work, so we did nothing. We were bishops and theologians in the making, so we needed to learn to act like they did.

When we went out, we wore our American cassocks and a traditional hat, the *Cappello Romano*, with a wide, circular brim and a round crown. Ours were black and the pope's was red. At first it felt strange, foreign, but after a while it was rather comfortable, shading my eyes from the glaring Italian sun and signaling to the world that I was an authentic man of the church.

On Wednesdays, the Pope held his weekly address to those who gathered in St. Peter's Square. While we couldn't see the Vatican from the NAC, with our windows open, we could hear him. During our summer breaks, we went to Castle Gondolfo, the papal retreat about 15 miles south of Rome. I was blessed to have seen and heard the Holy Father on many occasions.

When I was in my third year of Theology, President Kennedy came to our college. It was the 2nd of July, a month after Pope John XXIII died and a few days after the coronation of the new pope, Paul VI. He shook every one of our hands. He looked too young and energetic to be our president. He was dead in four months.

****

We had no school twice a week and were able to take little junkets around Rome in our black American cassocks and *Cappello Romana*. During the day, we went in small groups to the Trevi Fountains, Spanish Steps, the Pantheon, from which they stole the gold to decorate the columns of St. Peter's, or so they said. We were meant to know these magnificent places if we had the privilege of studying in Rome. I loved every brick, every balustrade, every fountain and flower of Rome. I couldn't get enough.

Rome cracked me wide open. All my senses were assaulted with wildness, a fleshy violence that hurled me to my knees. I walked in the steps of Caesar, Michelangelo, Peter. I breathed their same air and drank their waters. My home was antiquity and I felt I could take my rightful place with the heroes of all time. And the wild Roman women nearly drove me crazy. Where was my vagueness when I needed it?

This life was so different from what I had lived at St. Mary, so different from my little alcove in our house in Chicago, so different from our humble little cottage in Quilty, with the larks making their homes in our grassy meadows. Although we were sheltered, clothed and fed, I felt more like a man of the world, almost bordering on the urbane. I often thought of Rome itself as my cloister.

Just off the *Piazza di Spagna* on the *Via della Croce* was the **Croce,** a wonderful restaurant that welcomed us at any time. It was dark and cozy with cats that sat on the tables. So here I was, sipping red wine by the Spanish Steps, balancing my *cappello romano* on my head, swatting the cats and laughing with Johnny Sullivan.

Croce means cross in English, but the restaurant was anything but a cross. John Sullivan and I made this our regular stop on any of our weekly junkets. Johnny hated the cats, but he loved the lusty red *Ribolla Gialla* that rolled down his throat like the waters of the Trevi Fountains.

At a small table in the corner, my eye would catch a lone figure, sipping wine with his eyes down-cast, the sights and sounds not a distraction. He was a solemn figure in his long, black cassock. Yet his luminous red hair and flaming beard reduced the solemnity of his person to the madness of the mad-man from West Clare, the

131

feared *Pooka*, the nasty goblin, hiding behind the rusty bins on the twisted alleys in dark Kilrush.

He never spoke to us but seemed to nod in our direction in a rigid priestly way. It was so subtle; I'd have missed if I blinked at the wrong time. I saw him frozen in time, a cool black marble statue of a tormented god. He read documents, not books, with thin wireless glasses perched low on his straight nose. Under his bushy, red brows, bright corn-flower blue eyes watched. One long, thin black foot flew back and forth at the end of one long, thin black leg.

After we had seen him a dozen times, he motioned with a nod of his head for us to join him in his corner table. His name was Graham Byrne. He was already a priest, studying Canon Law for the Primate of all Ireland, the Cardinal of Armagh. He was a good 15 years older than we were, but his body was charged with the restlessness of a much younger man.

The first thing he said to me was, "Now, you're really not a Yank at all, are you? I hear the West of Ireland bubbling somewhere down your throat."

I introduced John Sullivan and myself and told Graham that I was from the Archdiocese of Chicago, but that I had come from Quilty in West Clare. He smiled a big, toothy smile and said that his very self was from a small village in Donegal, one of the poorest and bleakest that ever rolled out of the Hand of God. Graham covered his eyes, as if he could not bear to see it again. He smelled like the fires of turf.

Then he grasped his beard and asked me, "You wouldn't have ever known a Fr. Sweeney, a Jesuit with a little problem with the drink? Got sent up to our village to get him out of their hair"

"Oh, my God! Yes! Oh, yes! He was my Uncle Paul. My grandfather's brother. He'd come down to visit now and then. We loved the dear man and hated to see him leave."

"Now, Martin Sweeney, we have a small world here. Your Uncle Paul delivered my little sister Molly. Doc Nolan was dead drunk and couldn't help Mammie when her time was come, so I ran for the priest and Fr. Sweeney got down on the floor and caught Molly when she came flying out. A wonderful priest he was."

"Was?"

"I went home for his funeral last May. He was a beautiful man, a holy priest. We Jesuits left him up there for years and years. I think we forgot about him. Paul Sweeney was a good priest, a fine Jesuit, but he couldn't stop drinking. If he could have thought himself sober, he would have been dry for life. It was not to be."

Slowly I stood up, hanging onto the edge of the thin table for dear life. John and Graham nodded as I left. I made for the eight blocks to Trevi Fountains to mix my tears for my dear Uncle Paul with the cascading waters where the Triton tries to tame the wild horses.

The Triton is having as much luck with the horse as Paul did with the bottle. The Triton holds a twisted conch shell, his trumpet to calm or stir up the waters. Paul held strong to his faith, an anchor for his troubled soul. God have mercy on his precious soul!

CHAPTER 23
Juicy Papal Secrets

Graham Byrne and I drew close. There was something strange and not strange about it all – what Graham called in that old Irish twist, *the seed and the breed*. We had no trouble understanding each other, despite the 15 or 20 years that spanned our ages. I guess I became the son he never had, and he was my father.

We sensed in each other a haunting loneliness for that black space where we both dwelt before we were born. Could it be our real selves were lost in *Tir na O'g*, the Celtic otherworld where the gods and fortunate mortals remain forever young and blissfully happy?

Maybe our Roman jaunt was all a hoax – me at the Gregorian and Graham with the Canon Law, trying to fool ourselves and the world that we were authentic priests, real "other Christs". God forgive us both!!

To this day I feel that the sweetest thing in the world is to be understood. Jesus said something to that effect: "How long have I been with ye and still ye know me not?" That pained Him. And all my life up to this point, different people got parts of me, but no one really got the whole of me, myself included, until Jesuit Fr. Graham Byrne fell into my life. And him with the smell of the turf glowing in the hearth.

I could tell that he loved me as much as I loved him. It is difficult for an Irishman to speak of loving another man, but we did love each other. I thought that I was becoming a homosexual, but I never had sexual feelings for Graham and I seriously doubt that he had any for me.

It was a strange mix of nostalgia, blood, early manhood, the Church. I hope this isn't sacrilegious, but our love for each other was almost *sacramental*, the outward sign of inner grace, the gift of two lost souls finding each other. John Sullivan slipped away a bit, but not too much. He knew that he was needed there among us. It is funny, but in those early days we knew what we knew, but we didn't know we knew it.

That very same dynamic came into play years later when we priests were in crisis and knew what we weren't supposed to know. It all got twisted around until we found ourselves bound in our own knots of lies and ignorance and culpability. More concretely, priestly lust and violence abounded and the bishops' cowardice and betrayal pretended that it didn't exist. We were all under an implicit 'gag-order' from the Holy Office to keep our mouths shut.

My own loss of innocence began quite harmlessly. We had a Monday off for the Feast of the Immaculate Conception. Graham invited us to the *Pontifical Council for Legislative Texts* where he studied and worked. It was located on the *Palazzo delle Congregazione* at the very entrance to St. Peter's Square. *Defensor Civitatis*, (The Defender of the City) is written immediately below the address, *Piazza Pio XII*. Many other Curial offices were in that ancient, pale parchment building.

On our very first journey to the North American College in 1956, the bus had turned back to the *Gianicolo* in front of this spot. Little did I know then what it held for me. It was difficult to get into such a deified place, but Graham had a key and said it would be good for our education to see where the ancient documents that went into the current making of Canon Law were stored.

I was curious about Graham's life and his path to the Jesuit priesthood, but it was bad form to ask directly. He did allow that he had read law at Oxford. He held J.C.D., a doctorate in Canon Law, with emphasis on the influence of the Irish monks on the formation of current church law. It was these Irish monks that gave us private confession, as it was previously banned.

His earlier studies for the priesthood were at the minor Jesuit Seminary in Mungret, outside of Limerick, and then to Stoneyhurst, the Jesuit Seminary in Lancashire, England. He allowed that our Uncle Paul Sweeney invited him to be a Jesuit.

Graham had a knack for explaining complex issues very simply and made that esoteric world of church law come alive. The word *canon* means *rule* and the current Canon Law was from 1917 and covered 777 pages, just really a small book. It was the text we now studied at the Greg with the Jesuits. Interestingly, for the first thousand years, all the different regions - like Spain, Germany, France, England – all had their own bishops who wrote the rules for their people.

In the 11th Century a Camadolese monk, Johannes Gratian, taught in a monastery at Bologna, which was the center for the study of Roman Law. He gathered all the various canons from the different regions and organized them according to the brilliant legal system laid out by the Romans. Our centralized system of church law is still modeled on the ancient Law of Rome.

Graham Byrne loved what he was doing. As a scholarly Jesuit, he loved breathing and touching those ancient texts and making them come alive under his fingertips, Pygmalion breathing life into Galatea, Henry Higgins teaching Eliza Doolittle to speak! He wanted only for John and me to catch fire as he had and become priests who loved and lived the precepts of the law!

The Irish were high on penance and their writings contained catalogues of sins and misdeeds and the appropriate penance for each. Graham spent his days in his office or in the Vatican Library with his head in the *Collectio Hibernensis,* a gathering of over 700 ancient texts, just the "bits and bobs" of the roots of the system that govern our religion to this day.

Graham then asked how we understood the Vatican, the Curia, how the whole thing worked. We stumbled a bit, then he explained that it was a big organization, just like General Motors, with each congregation or department responsible for specific missions of the church. The most important was the Congregation for the Holy Office of the Inquisition, just called the **Holy Office.** It oversees Catholic doctrine and takes great pains that heresy not creep into the purity of what we believe. No softies worked in the Holy Office!

"I see, Graham, I get it. Now, whatever about secrets?"

"Everything is a grave secret; it is what keeps this place rolling along. Secrecy opens and closes doors, hides and finds treasures, creates and destroys in the blink of an eye. Church careers are made and unmade by the knowledge of the secrets, the keeping of the secrets."

"I don't really get it, Graham. Jesus said, 'Know the truth and the truth will set you free.' It just doesn't seem right somehow."

"This has nothing to do with Jesus or Mary or Joseph. It is about how the Italians do business. How the Romans do business. You ever hear of the Mafia? *Omerta? - 'He who is deaf, blind and silent will live 100 years in peace'.*"

"A French philosopher wrote, 'What is man but a miserable little pile of secrets'. This whole place here is built on piles and piles of secrets. It crawls with secrets. Keep your eyes open but your mouth shut and you'll be a fine priest. You know I'm not referring to the secrets of the confessional – that's a matter of the Sacraments. Just the big picture and how we do business here. And in every diocese all over the world. We have our own *omerta!* We keep our holy mouths shut!"

****

We would go out in groups to explore Rome. Our Rome! Often I had already spent time at the Forum or at the *Piazza Sallustio* and wanted to spend what time I had with Graham; I know he relished the time we had together. He didn't seem to have friends, at least not what I could see. And if he was deep in thought or on a call, he'd kindly wave me off and I'd show up later. He was always pleased to see me, if I'm not flattering myself too much to admit. Besides, he was a priest, a Jesuit.

We had all been at the *Croce,* having a good time. The Roman spring came early. There was a pick-up in the number of tourists, walking around with their cameras and maps. I loved to be asked where something was, as these foreigners took me as a native.

We were anxious for classes to end, the summer to begin. We would be spending time at Castle Gandolfo where the Pope usually vacationed. We would be half-way through our studies, half-way to Ordination. The class two years ahead of us had already received the Diaconate and would be ordained in a few weeks. My own priesthood was becoming more and more real.

****

Graham had taught Canon Law at the Gregorian Institute and now he was back doing research and writing. I think he missed teaching, because he never missed an opportunity to explicate a tenet of law or throw light on the workings of the Curia. Sardonic, yes, even mordant, and he loved to be challenged by questions, but he never invited a question of his loyalty to the church or to the Jesuit Order.

One day he had called over to the NAC, asking for me to meet him at his office. He had never done that before. The Rector, when he delivered Graham's message, seemed pleased that a priest of such stature would be personally connected to one of his students.

"Oh, yes, Martin. By all means, go and see what Fr. Byrne wants. He called on my personal line for you." The Rector wanted me to know that he was also personally connected to Graham Byrne. He always kept score.

There was fire in Graham's eyes when I walked into his office. I had been there only a few times before. The old pipe was in his teeth and he blew the heavy smoke out of his mouth like a train engine about to scale a mountain.

The only thing on his walls, beside a crucifix, was the framed quote of Teilhard de Chardin, the French Jesuit: *"Someday, after mastering the winds, the waves, the tides and gravity, we shall harness for God the energies of Love, and then, for a second time in the history of the world, man will have discovered fire."*

"Martin, there is something I am going to share with you. I have thought long and hard about this, as this is not something you perhaps would ever come across. I've prayed and I probably should have spoken with my spiritual director. I don't have a logical explanation for wanting to share this with you, but I trust the Holy Spirit that moves us as it wills."

He sat under a cone of light suspended from the ceiling. Graham was usually serious, but I had never sensed such gravity as I saw that day - his shoulders were sharply squared under his black cassock, his voice was deep and rolling as the sea. The light shone brightly on his red beard, illuminating the new silken threads of white that were running freely through his bushy red whiskers.

"I'm holding a fresh document: *Crimen sollicitationis: Instruction of the Supreme* **Sacred** *Congregation of the Holy Office. To be kept carefully in the Secret Archive of the Curia for internal use; not to be published or augmented with commentaries.* This document is never to see the light of day. Contrarily it is being released at the end of the week and sent to every bishop in the world. It will sink the church to greater depths of secrecy, paranoia and lies - to cover-up what weak and sinful men in the priesthood can and will do to children. It will kill us!

"Right here in my hand lies the ultimate power to destroy the church. I've never seen anything this brutal in the 20th Century. Cardinal Ottaviani has now topped himself at the Holy Office of the Inquisition!! It **is** brutal – his latest foray into the business of us priests behaving ourselves!! He can't leave us well enough alone!"

"What's it say?"

"It basically is about priests not propositioning anyone <u>in the confessional</u> – man, woman or child. And if a person is propositioned, that person has the moral responsibility of reporting the priest to the bishop within one month or that person is excommunicated – not the priest who solicited the sex!! And all this business is all done with the utmost of secrecy of all parties concerned. It you speak of it to anyone, you are automatically excommunicated."

"But how can anyone report the solicitation if they are unaware of the obligation to report it? The priest in the confessional is certainly not going to inform them? A kid has to go to the bishop?"

"Now tucked in, right at the very last part, is the crux of this document. There are five separate sections, called Titles. The various items under each title are numbered. It's all written right here in the last and shortest section of this document, Title V, *crimen pessimum*: Item #73: having sex with a child (*impuberes*)or with a brute animal (*bestilitas*) is a *crimen pessimum*. Item #71. "the foulest crime" is having sex with another man. What kind of a perverted mind could even dream up such non-sense?"

Graham flipped through the printed document, reading phrases such **as: 'reasons of confidentiality'; 'strictest confidentiality; 'by permanent silence'; 'secret of the Holy Office';**

'administered the oath to maintain confidentiality'; 'ordered the acts to be put in the secret archive'; 'they will be able to transfer him to another place'.

"I dunno, Graham. I'm getting scared."

"You damn well better be, Lad. I think the Holy Office has reached a new level of depravity. The essence of this document is the protection of the Sacrament of Penance. And so it should be protected. The focus is on the priest and not the victim. And even after this issue is settled, everyone's lips are sealed.

"A priest can fool around with a child or a goddamn sheep and we will protect him. It is all to be hush-hush and anything of this nature will be handled in Rome. And by 'handled in Rome' means to be lost in Rome. The catacombs are long and deep and many a cleric's sins have been buried with the dry, old bones.

"All the bishops in every diocese throughout the world are getting this thing right now, 16 March 1962, and they are not even allowed to keep it in their diocesan files. It has to go below into their vaults and never to see the light of day.

"How come?"

"Just because it is about sex and celibacy and the power of secrets and money. There's nothing anyone can do about it, because the church is so powerful. It is our Holy Roman Mafia!! Look at your own country and the pride Americans take in the separation of church and state. John Kennedy said that he does not take orders from the Pope –that's all well and good – for now."

Graham refilled his pipe, lit it and puffed away to have the crumpled shreds of tobacco catch fire. He reflected that there was an issue even deeper, the basic issue that elicited these smothering layers of secrecy.

The ordained priesthood was at the core of the organizational, political and legal underpinnings of the founding and continuation of the church. Many, many priests and bishops abuse children, but because they are priests, they have always been protected by the Canonical process. If their sins are so evil, they are tried in a church court.

Historically, this has always been the case. Let a few priests be charged in a criminal or civil court and be sent to prison, and then the whole system of protection and secrecy comes tumbling down.

By his ordination, a man received the unspeakable power to change bread and wine into the Body and Blood of Jesus. He received the power to forgive sins and with that, the sacred responsibility to maintain the Seal of the Confessional, even if that meant his death. He was a man no longer, but "a priest forever, according to the order of Melchizedek."

Without the sacred, consecrated hands of the priest, there would be no Mass, no Eucharist, no Confession. Even our Baptism and Marriage are usually performed by a priest. This is the crux of the matter. And when the priest commits a crime, it cannot be perceived as a crime to be punished by civil society. It is a sin, to be forgiven.

With ordination, a man is immediately lifted up and he now dwells in a lofty sphere. No human rule or law applies to him. If he commits a crime, it is not a crime, but a sin. All the forces of the power of the church, localized here but spread throughout the world, go immediately into action to preclude the secular powers from even touching a priest.

"Graham, I think I'd better get going. This stuff is making me nervous…"

"Now you just wait a minute, Martin. Part of the hold on us is the powerful part that *mystery* plays in the church. The confessional is dark, curtained, and full of whispers. Our Mass is said with our backs to the people and all they see is us weaving and bobbing, heads bowed, elbows and hands moving around under the chasuble. And all the language is in the glorious cadences of ancient Latin as that is the only language God Himself understands.

"Mystery and secrecy are the two ingredients that allow Roman Catholicism to maintain its hoary hold on all of us. They've got us by the neck and the grip only gets tighter, with Ottavani and his boys over at the Holy Office pulling the ropes.

"I just can't believe that our dear old Pope, John XXIII, signed off on this. He is all about opening the windows while Ottavani is bolting them closed. In six months the bishops will be coming from all over the world to pull the church into the 20th century, while those working against the Holy Father are pulling us back into the Dark Ages with censure, punishment, secrets hidden away in moldy, dead vaults. They are trying to kill the very spirit of Jesus Christ who told us to be open and free with knowing the truth."

"Well, Lad, I probably shouldn't have showed you this thing. Mark my words, Martin, now you know of it - ***Crimen sollicitationis*** - and you can't pull it out of your head. And someday when life batters you around a bit and your scars are glowing like diamonds at the bottom of the sea, you'll remember old Graham Byrne in his little office at the Vatican telling you the truth about the church and its secrets and lies that could close us down forever.

"There will come a day when the people will not put up with it. And we will need brave priests who will speak up for the truth, for hurt and broken children, men who are not afraid to walk in the footsteps of Jesus Christ. You, my friend, Martin Sweeney, will be one of those men."

CHAPTER 24
The Vatican – Chicago Rhapsody

October, 1963. Deep within the recesses of the Roman Curia in the Vatican, Carlo Cardinal Confalonierei, Head of the Sacred Consistorial Congregation, was meeting with his top staff. They were concerned that the fury that had been raised by the Vatican Council had stirred up the American church to the point of frenzy and they feared they would lose control.

The Church was *Roman* Catholic, not American Catholic or new Catholic or Do-Whatever-You-Damn-Well- Please Catholic. Some of the American Bishops and Cardinals were leading the Faithful astray, interpreting the Documents of Vatican II as they saw them, not slowly, carefully, and judiciously in a manner that the Church historically preferred.

Cardinal Joyce in Chicago was not well. It would be only a matter of time before that position would be open. As this was the Congregation that placed the names of potential Bishops and Cardinals before the Holy Father, they needed to be wise. If they chose someone with Leftist leanings, there would be disaster for the institutional church in the second largest Archdiocese in America.

The Bishop from Dublin knew the perfect man. The late Archbishop of Dublin, Ronan Devitt, "God rest his soul," had a nephew, Fr. Jeremiah Murphy Devitt, an expert in Canon Law, who was just as right and tough as his late uncle. He could be made a bishop and within a short time, Fr. Jeremiah Murphy Devitt would be elevated to the level of Cardinal and Chicago would remain faithful to the Church of Rome.

Archbishop Ronan Devitt had been killed in the plane crash with his brother and sister-in-law, Lord and Lady Devitt, when they were on their way to Rome for their adopted son's ordination by Pope Pius XII. The Devitts had legally adopted Jeremiah after his parents, Molly and Peter Murphy, had died tragically in a fire in their little white cottage tucked into the windy hills of Clare.

The poor Murphys had toiled away many years for the Devitts with a loyalty that knew no bounds. When the Devitts made an indecent offer of payment to adopt their only son, Jeremiah, the Murphys abruptly terminated their employment. If the truth be known, the Murphys had lost Jeremiah long before to the powerful Devitts. Molly and Peter Murphy, advancing in years, maintained their dignity and refused the Devitt's offer to *purchase* their son.

Fr. Jeremiah Murphy Devitt was presently working in the Vatican archives on the legal and moral position of Pope Pius XII *vis-a-vis* Hitler during World War II. He would certainly be available to lead the Church in Chicago. Besides, there were many Irish in Chicago who could use a good "sorting out" from a man from home.

Fr. Jeremiah Murphy Devitt was made a Bishop by the Holy Father, Paul VI, and sent as the Co-Adjutor Bishop to the ailing Cardinal Joyce. With that title came the right of succession. It would be just a matter of time before 45-year-old Jeremiah Murphy Devitt became the Cardinal of Chicago, as all major Archdioceses required a Cardinal in the highest position of authority. And he would drop the "Murphy" part of his name to honor the Devitts.

Little did Bishop Jeremiah Devitt know that the vast and mysterious ways of the Good Lord were playing out on his behalf and that every single detail had been put in place - perfectly, flawlessly, joyously. For all his importance, he was aware of none of it.

The old Cardinal had a peaceful death in his sleep on January 6, the Feast of the Epiphany. Holy Name Cathedral was filled with Cardinals, Bishops, priests and lay people as Bishop Devitt assisted the Papal Nuncio and other Cardinals at the Funeral Mass.

A kindly old man, Cardinal Joyce was deeply loved by everyone who ever had contact with him. His soft brown eyes were in sharp contrast to the steely blue of his successor. The Church in Chicago would no longer be cared for by a kindly shepherd, beloved of his flock, but it would be ruled with a firm hand and any who did not fall in line would be dealt with most severely.

Chicago was the central pivot point for the Church in America and Cardinal Devitt was the perfect man to protect the one, true church against the forces of change that threatened to destroy it. Bishop Jeremiah Murphy Devitt was now simply Cardinal Devitt, dropping the *Murphy* surname as insignificant to his new position. His new title was clean, clear, and crisp.

Even though the practice of wearing them had been discontinued, Cardinal Joyce's scarlet red, wide brimmed hat, the *galero,* was fastened to the high, arched ceiling, 150 feet above the nave of the massive cathedral, joining the *galeros* of the Cardinals who came before him. After his death, Cardinal Devitt's *galero* would swing from the ceiling, joining Cardinal Joyce's and all the other Cardinals of Chicago who had gone before him.

****

I was an ocean away from all that was going on at home. I remained removed and ignorant of my mother's deteriorating health. Everyone felt that I should not be bothered by trivial family affairs in Chicago; my life and studies were in Rome.

My mother's conditioned worsened. They watched as she wasted away and the grooves in Stephen's face grew deeper and darker. She refused to go to the hospital, so Dr. Corrigan came to her. Stephen had gone to Loyola University with Mike Corrigan and Mike wanted to take care of Kate as long as he could. As he left her bedside, his voice sounded graver and more cautious.

Stephen and Mike Corrigan sat in the kitchen, drinking tea as Kate was sleeping longer and longer. Dr. Corrigan thought that she might have six to eight weeks left. Maybe less, maybe more – it was all in the Hands of God, as they all knew so well. Steve was distraught that Mammie would never see me ordained a priest.

Nellie, now Sr. Mary Bridget, had the nuns praying around the clock for Kate. Stephen made an appointment with the newly appointed head of the church in Chicago, Cardinal Jeremiah Devitt, to see if anything could be done to hurry up my ordination. The Cardinal stated that his hands were tied because Canon Law was clear on the matter. There was nothing he could do, but he would pray for Mrs. Flaherty.

Stephen had never been told the whole, unadulterated truth about my paternity, but he started to find the missing pieces hiding in strange places. As detectives have been given the gift of smell,

145

Stephen was sniffing in exactly the right places. He called Lizzie and she and Babe met him at the law firm.

Stephen and Lizzie had always liked each other but had never really had any time alone. When he walked into the Nathanson's Law Office, they hugged each other tightly. Neither of them could hug Kate any longer.

He shared with Lizzie and Babe his thoughts about the Cardinal and Martin. Lizzie's face grew red, as she was not proud of her behavior toward Kate in those days of her pregnancy and delivery. Lizzie affirmed that his hunch was correct. But he was in a quandary – was there anything he could do?

Babe frowned and asked Lizzie, "Where is that older brother of yours? Tom, is that it? Why isn't he here to take care of this mess? Let's get him and the younger one over here right now!"

Babe wanted to know directly if Tom and Packy were aware of how serious Kate's condition was. Lizzie nodded her head, but added that they know and they don't know. They only know what they want to know. Babe frowned – she didn't get it. Stephen understood only too well.

Stephen and Lizzie looked at each other and shrugged their shoulders. What was Babe up to now? Why hadn't they thought of this? Babe got Tom's number from Lizzie and had her secretary call Tom Sweeney. Over in Ireland it was 7:00 at night, so Tom and Packy would be in for their tea.

After Babe had made a few well-placed phone calls, Lizzie called her brothers. Their Irish passports had never been used, but they had them just in case such a crisis would evolve. The *Aer Lingus* flight #77 was leaving the following day at 10: 00 a.m. and their tickets were at the counter. He could ask the neighbors to take care of the farm while they were gone. There were resources here to pay them. He said that it was not necessary, they had the money.

Tom and Packy had never been to America and as they started their descent into O'Hare, both had a good shot of Paddy's whiskey from a stewardess whom Packy had charmed across the Atlantic Ocean. They wondered if they smelled "like pig shite" or if

146

they'd just be two Clare culchies, fresh out of the bog - they'd give the Yanks a good laugh, so they would.

Lizzie, Babe and Stephen met them as they exited customs without being checked. Babe had forgotten nothing. It was 4:00 in the afternoon in Chicago and 10:00 p.m. in Ireland, and they were exhausted. A Chicago squad car drove them to Babe and Lizzie's apartment. All agreed that Tom and Packy not see Kate until everything was in its place. A rehearsal was in order.

****

At the Chancery offices near Holy Name Cathedral, an old Irish priest in a rumpled black clerical suit with a stained Roman collar and a dirty, brown tweed cap walked into the Cardinal's offices and stood leaning on his blackthorn stick. He insisted on seeing the Cardinal. The Cardinal's secretary, Fr. Stackmann, a thin, wispy priest with a seasoned clerical frown, began wringing his hands as he was having trouble getting rid of this nuisance.

"Now Father, ah, Nunan, is it? The Cardinal has meetings scheduled all day and if you really want to see him, I could schedule something perhaps at the end of the month, if that would meet your fancy."

"Please, you tell the Cardinal that I have a message from home for His Eminence. I have been personally 'encrusted' with it and need to see him now."

"Ah, Fr. Nunan, your voice is being raised now and we execute things with proper protocol as befits the office of the Cardinal. You don't have an appointment and I have to ask you to leave or I'll be forced to contact the police to escort you out."

"Sure, the Chicago Garda are already here! Steve, we need your help!!"

Lt. Flaherty, in full dress uniform - Navy with gold buttons and his gold detective shield with a sharp, starched white shirt and Navy tie - came from around the corner, grabbed Fr. Stackmann's boney arm and told him that he was to open the Cardinal's door, graciously announce Fr. Nunan's arrival and respectfully escort Fr. Nunan into his office. "And if that doesn't happen, you'll have all hell to pay. Now move it, Squirt!"

147

Fr. Stackmann slithered into the Cardinal's office, ran to his desk and whispered in his ear. He was mortified that he could not control the situation but the cop had bullied him and there was nothing he could do and he was 'oh, so sorry.'

With his best pulpit voice, Cardinal Devitt told Fr. Stackmann to let Fr. Nunan in, as a priest from home needs no appointment with a fellow countryman.

As Fr. Stackmann escorted the old priest into the Cardinal's office, the Cardinal raised his hand for the old one to get on his knees and kiss his ruby-red ring that he had personally received from the pope. The Cardinal was tall and proud, his scarlet cassock with 33 buttons up and down the front and five on each cuff, stood like a mountain in red, unafraid of the power of his office. His wavy black hair was sprinkled white, like perfect snow fallen on the mighty.

The old priest, his whiskery face shaded by his tweedy cap, motioned with his shoulder for the Cardinal to excuse Fr. Stackmann. After Fr. Stackmann left, Cardinal Devitt again raised his fine, manicured hand to Fr. Nunan.

The old priest threw his cap on the floor, pulled off the Roman collar and threw the black suit jacket on a chair. Tom Sweeney stood militantly before Jeremiah Devitt, Cardinal of the Archdiocese of Chicago.

The Cardinal gasped and the blood drained from his face. He saw a ghost, as he thought that now the old Sweeney business was long gone. They both knew that the old business had never been resolved and this was the time for old scores to be settled. Once and for all, the old issues had to be forever reckoned with.

Tom Sweeney felt a surge of old, old rage soar through his veins. "Now, Jeremiah, you know what you can do with your big, old, girly ring. Ah, sure, old Peter Murphy would be ashamed of you, but it's what you always wanted, isn't it?

"You were always the better of us. And your old folks and the royal Archbishop Devitt, crashing into them big Alpy mountains in the fog, while you're off in Rome, hob-knobbing with the Pope and them bishops in their sissy pink dresses. And you left with everything, with all that money coming from us poor Irish farmers with not enough food on our tables to feed our babes. Good job, Jeremiah!"

"Some tea, Tom? Anything at all you want? What can I do for you, Tom? It's been so long…"

"Sure, you know my sister, Kate, the youngest of all the girls. You feckin' well know her, don't you, Jeremiah? And sure the little pet is almost dead and her son Martin can't even say her funeral, because he isn't a priest yet."

The Cardinal scowled his best professional frown. "I don't understand, Tom. What are you talking about?" Jeremiah was telling the truth.

"You fuckin' well know what I'm talking about, smart arse that you are and always have been. You just fuck off, Jeremiah! Jeremiah Fuckin' Devitt and you and your lyin' ways! Turnin' your yellow back on all us poor creatures from Clare!"

Tom knew that he was getting ready to punch the living daylights out of Jeremiah, 'sure, red-hot ashes are easily rekindled,' he thought to himself. Lest he explode, Tom walked quickly to the door and motioned for Stephen to join them. The Cardinal began to raise his hand for the obligatory finger kiss. Tom shot him a quick look and the Cardinal thought better of it. He quickly locked his hands behind his back in the old Irish fashion.

"I believe I have met you, ah… Lieutenant Flaherty. And you know my old friend from home, Tom here. Is there anything I can get you, Lieutenant?"

"As you have most probably figured, Cardinal, I'm married to Kate Sweeney and Martin Sweeney is my step-son. He never knew who his father was…"

Stephen stared right into the face of the Cardinal and saw my own dark eyes with the full, arched brows, my nervous habit of tugging on my right earlobe, my straight white teeth and full red lips. He felt light-headed for a moment – this is who Kate meant when she told Stephen that my father was "in the church."

Stephen was three inches taller than the man in the long, red dress with all his glorious buttons and knew he could take him out

149

with one shove and crush him under his shoe. He caught himself quickly and banished his angry, violent thoughts. He had a job to do.

Tom Sweeney continued, "And our dear Kate is dying. The consumption is in her lungs and she hasn't long to live. Martin needs to be ordained now. I hate to say this, but you, you fuckin' bastard, are the only one who can make it happen." Steve Flaherty moved closer to Tom Sweeney, warning him not to lose it.

"Sure, it's your job for all the pain you caused everyone. You should never have been born…but then we'd never have our Martin, would we? Dear Martin and he after comin' out of such wormy seeds - out of your ugly seeds, Jeremiah!" He moved to choke him, but Stephen grabbed Tom's shoulder.

"I never knew Kate had a son…" His voice trailed off and he closed his eyes and lowered his head. He sat down silently in the chair behind his desk.

Tom and Stephen allowed time for Jeremiah to absorb what he had just heard. He gathered himself together and cleared his throat. "Now, now, Tom, as I explained to the Lieutenant here, my hands are tied. Canon Law says that…"

"Just stick it, Jeremiah. We've had enough of your Canon Law crap. You never had the balls when all was said and done. Run and hide is the way you done it. First with the Devitts and now with the holy rules of whatever the Pope says. Run and hide…run and hide, you coward!"

Stephen went to the door and asked Babe Nathanson to join them. He introduced her as their attorney. Cardinal Devitt didn't know what was going on. He tugged hard on his ear and twirled his ruby-red ring. Fr. Stackmann was hiding in the kitchen.

Uninvited, Babe sat down heavily in a large deep blue leather chair by the Cardinal's smoldering fireplace. Tom Sweeney and Stephen joined her. She reached into her stiff, black leather briefcase and held before him a 10-page affidavit. She motioned for the Cardinal to sit down on one of his own small straight black leather chairs by the fireplace.

Cardinal Devitt was numb, gob-smacked with a cold, dead fish. Perspiration was gathering in his arm-pits. He knew that he had been "had" and there was no worming his way out of this. Ordinarily, he would have stood tall and inhibited anyone who got in his way. What was this strange Jewish woman even doing in his office? She had the upper-hand for now…

Very slowly she stated to the Cardinal that unless Martin be ordained with "all deliberate speed" before his mother dies, they were prepared to go immediately to the editorial board of the Chicago Tribune and deliver this affidavit, given by Thomas Sweeney of Quilty, Ireland, Martin Sweeney's uncle and Kate Sweeney Flaherty's brother, to the fact of Martin Sweeney's paternity.

If Kate Sweeney died before her son returned from Rome in time for his ordination, the editors of the Daily News would also be informed of Martin's paternity. Babe Nathanson would leave no stone unturned and had no doubt as to the moral and legal rightness of their position.

It was up to the Cardinal. Babe needed an answer immediately. There was a limo waiting to take them down Michigan Avenue to the Chicago Tribune. There had been precious time lost because of his lack of moral courage and his cowardly legalisms.

"The ball is in your court, Jeremiah. We need an answer right now."

The Cardinal nodded to Babe and said that he would get back to her within 24 hours. He shouted into the kitchen for Fr. Stackmann and told him to cancel the rest of his appointments as he needed to get back to his rectory on N. State Parkway.

151

CHAPTER 25
Getting Out the Door

Hanging the "Do Not Disturb" sign on his doorknob, Cardinal Jeremiah Devitt went into his quarters in the dark red brick castle that was his home. He tore off his red cassock and black pants, climbed into his old, blue sweats, poured a stiff drink in a Waterford tumbler and stiffly rested himself in his black leather recliner.

Jeremiah was gripped with a fear he had never felt. All that he had worked for, studied for, groomed himself for - was now over. He would soon be exposed for the man he really was. He would be the laughing stock of all the priests and bishops, of all the people in Chicago, of the Vatican and the Irish church. The papers would have a hey-day with him.

And the irony of it all is that there was nothing in Canon Law that addressed the issue of a priest fathering a child. Quite simply, priests were to be celibate, unmarried; they were to be chaste, to refrain from sexual activity. They took no vow; the meaning was implicit. Perhaps even a "gentleman's agreement" regarding the activity of their genitals.

The early Apostles and Disciples were married men, as was the custom in the early days of the church. Not to be married was to render a man suspect – what was the matter with him? A eunuch? A faggot? A woman?

However, issues of land and church wealth being inherited by the children of priests were of major concern as early as the Council of Elvira in Spain in 310. The celibacy issue was finalized in 1139 at the Second Lateran Council when mandatory celibacy, the rule forbidding priests to marry, was imposed on all priests. There was no mention in Canon Law regarding the children of priests. They weren't supposed to exist.

Celibacy does not equate with chastity. All Christians are to be chaste, pure, faithful regarding sexuality, as was Jesus. Technically, Jeremiah had relations with Kate before he was ordained, so he knew that he hadn't exactly broken the rule, despite the fact that he was in the seminary. Church Sophistry. Another lie garbed in a bit of truth, so no one was guilty.

Jeremiah had heard whispers about the Bishop of Galway, Eamon Casey, having a son in New York. Casey had supported the boy and his mother with church money and the entire incident was kept quiet. The Bishop was popular and even was the principle greeter of the Pope when he went to Ireland. If that ever got out, the Irish church would crash like a house of cards.

Images of himself with Kate on the wind-swept cliffs of Clare flew up in his mind from a place deep within that he had buried for years. He didn't feel like himself, the wooden celibate, self-contained, alone in the world, living forever in his head, denying his emotional self, denying his soul-self.

Now he had a son, his own flesh and blood. He was really a man, not a "eunuch" for the Kingdom. The entire world felt different in the space of a minute – it had taken on a third dimension – before it had only height and breadth, now there was depth. Profound depth, as he was now officially a member of the human race, a real man.

If the truth be told, Jeremiah had frequently felt that there was more to his life than what he presented to the church and to the public. He had a foggy feeling that he had a child, a son. He would scan the faces in crowds to see if any looked like him. At the Masses at Holy Name Cathedral, visiting parishes, administering the Sacrament of Confirmation, walking down the street.

As a young priest on a lonely night in Dublin, a boy crossing the Haypenny Bridge over the black waters of the River Liffey. The boy, 11 or 12, looked at him as if he had always known him, as if he was his father. Jeremiah grabbed the rails of the bridge, as the breath was knocked out of him. The boy ran away.

He knew well that various dioceses supported the children of priests and they remained active priests. It was top-secret information, as privileged as the identity of the diocesan exorcist. And if the priest-father were a pastor, he could siphon off parish money to support his family. All of this was known, but not known. Sophistry at it most practical.

As Jeremiah did not belong to a religious order, like the Jesuits or Franciscans, he did not have a vow of poverty. He still had most of the Devitt money that he had inherited at the time of their deaths and he easily could have supported his son. The Devitts had placed all their money in a London financial house. He had never even bothered to look at their monthly statements or letters from the bankers. He had no idea how much there was. His guilt was untouchable.

Jeremiah began to laugh and his laughter turned into a roar and the roar into tears that began to melt the lump of hardness that had grown within him over the years. He felt Kate's body turning with his body and how lovely and beautiful and wonderful it was to be with her. Yet he would hold her apart, some lowly thing he could use, abuse and discard at will.

Now he had his very own son, his very own flesh and blood. Having been set apart from the world with his celibacy had made him feel less than a real man, almost like a freak of nature who had to deny his whole sexual self and pretend that he was an earth-angel without a body, without a soul, without desires and needs and urges of his own body and soul.

Now he had his very own son. Martin Sweeney was his child and he, Jeremiah Devitt, was his father. He closed his eyes, rested his head back and smiled at this greatest of gifts.

Jeremiah slipped on a thin, blue wind-breaker and a black ski-cap, stole out the side door of the rectory and made his way down North Avenue to the lake. He began jogging along the bike path up north past Fullerton and into Belmont Harbor. Boats were bobbing in the water and bumping against the wooden piers. The air was crisp and the sky was black. A pale, crescent moon was emerging from behind the John Hancock Building.

Jeremiah looped around the harbor and headed back south. He had never felt so free in his entire life. He threw his arms out and above his head. He could fly! The fear of losing his position, his power and prestige was gone. He was who he was and "the truth had set him free". The secret of his son's very existence had been kept from him and now he knew the truth. He was a man.

CHAPTER 26
My Grave Will Warmer, Sweeter Be

It was the middle of April, 1964. Rome was beautiful, vibrant, sensual all at once. As Fourth Year Theologians, we had received the Diaconate in January and would be ordained later in the Spring. We were rounding 3rd and coming home!

The bus from the Gregorian had returned us to the North American College for our mid-day meal. We had just settled into our places, said grace in Latin, and the little Italian nuns were running out from the kitchen into the refectory with our food. I had certainly gotten used to the service rendered, the deference paid, the respect showered on us. I had gained 28 lbs.

The Rector's secretary came into the refectory, anxiously looked around, and spotted me about to dig into a bowl of penne pasta with hot tomato sauce, covered with fresh, smelly Parmesan cheese, streaming into my face. He motioned for me to come with him. My mouth was watering. Hesitantly, I placed my napkin on my chair and followed him up the back stairs.

He led me to the Rector's office and left me alone with him. I stood at the doorway and he motioned for me to come in. I simply stood before his desk as he put his cigarette out in a white marble ashtray and blew his smoke toward the floor. He did not ask me to sit.

"Martin, you're going home tonight. Your mother is not well, not well at all. I just received a telegram from Cardinal Devitt and he wants you in Chicago immediately. He's going to ordain you Saturday morning before she…"

I froze. I know he could hear my heart beat. I could say nothing, but simply nodded. "The nuns are working on your clothes. Just wear your black suit and collar. Leave your cassocks here. Tomasco will take you to the airport, leaving here at 4:00 this afternoon. Your plane to New York leaves at 6:35 this evening. You'll have to change planes in New York for Chicago. I trust your passport is in order."

"Yes, Monsignor. Yes, of course, Monsignor."

"Now I don't want you to get your bowels in an uproar...nor this entire place in an uproar. I know you will need to say good-by to some of your class-mates, but we just can't stand a lot of commotion around here."

"Yes, Monsignor, I understand."

"I'm sorry about your mother, Martin. I've enjoyed having you here at the North American College. Tell your new Cardinal over there that you have been a credit to all of them. All of them out at your seminary there, your seminary with the golf course. "

"Yes, Monsignor.

I went to the chapel and knelt on the left side before the pure, white Carrara marble statue of the Blessed Mother. The candle in the red-glass vigil stand beside the altar glowed, quietly signaling that the Blessed Sacrament was in the tabernacle.

One of the old Franciscan nuns (who provided the housekeeping for the priests and seminarians) knelt in rapt adoration. Peace and quiet. The old nun prostrated herself on the cold terrazzo floor before the Blessed Sacrament. She lay in abject surrender. I watched her rise from the floor. The pop and crackle of her old knee joints echoed around the chapel.

My mother would never live for her knees to fill with arthritis and crunch beneath her weight. As the old folks back home would say when a young person would die: "And we thought she'd live to comb gray hair." Not my mother.

I know my mother was never well. Even Uncle Tom used to get after her before we left Ireland. "Katie, dear, you're always after achin' and painin' and moanin' and groanin' about your poor, wee health." He'd go on, unmercifully, "Sure, Katie, I afraid that you'll die goin' over and they'd have to wrap you in the Irish flag and slide you into the sea as a feast for the sharks."

I'd hear him going on about her and she would be sitting by the fire, heart breaking that she had to leave, as there was no future for us there in Ireland. Her whole body would wrack with the cough and, even before it would stop, she'd be out the door to spit up the blood so no one would see.

156

They used to call it "consumption" and so many Irish were dying of it. Now it was "tuberculosis". I've often wondered how Mammie got into America with her illness, but I guess Doc O'Boyle gave her a clean bill of health before we came over.

I burst into tears. How horrible for her to be dying and have a son so far away. I sobbed and sobbed and my anguish rang out around the empty chapel like a raging black storm that would shake the rafters back home in Ireland.

I had never had a father and now me poor, sick mother would lie cold in that foreign soil so far from home. Far from Grandpa and Grannie and the bell at our small church, Our Lady Star of the Sea, that they promised would ring out across the hills and valleys of Clare when we got back home again.

I sobbed more deeply and felt my breast bone would snap in my chest. I thought of my mother's beautiful red hair and Stephen singing that old song about "keep your hands off red-haired Mary."

The old nun got off her knees, knelt behind me, placed her gnarled and twisted fingers on my shoulders, leaned over and kissed me softly on my shaking red neck. Her breath smelled of parsley and God.

****

It was hard. We all thought that we would be ordained together by early summer, and even then, we knew we would never see each other again, as we were from all over the States. The guys on the East Coast could easily get together, but not the rest of us. Once we were ordained, it was all over.

There was none of the jubilation that would come with ordination. Just grief that my mother was dying, that I was saying a final good-by to each of my pals, that I'd probably never see Rome again. I'd never be young again. I'd be no one's son.

Tomasco pulled his red car up to the front. The entire North American College was out to wish me off. The Rector was the last to descend the steps and the crowd of seminarians parted to let Moses through. Johnny Sullivan was wiping away his tears and the old nuns held tight to their rosaries.

157

I just nodded and waved to everyone. Tomasco placed my suitcase in the trunk and slowly pulled away, heading to the new Leonardo da Vinci Airport, southwest of the city by 16 miles. I was numb. I'd never see any of those guys again. My mother was dying. I was truly more alone than I had ever been in my life.

The statues, fountains and hotels flew past me. I knew that in 24 hours this would all be a dream. Right now Quilty is not real and Chicago is not real. My mother is still breathing. I have not set my eyes on her in over three years. *God builds the back to suit the burden.*

Tomasco pushes the little car harder to get us out onto the narrow highway, I swing and sway like a reed in the wind. My head is bumping the roof and I'm getting sick to my stomach. In the heat of a sunny Roman day, I'm in the blackest of nights, without a moon or a star to guide me. Tomasco chuckles to himself as he looks down at laminated pictures of his children and lights another cigarette.

As we approach the airport, he drives over the curb, racing another driver in the second lane. My head hits the window frame and he shouts, "Scusa ! Scusa, Padre!" I pat him on the arm and he smiles back. I look at his family and his smile broadens. Everything is forgiven.

Like a nervous zombie, I make it through customs, check in, get my boarding pass, and direct myself to the TWA gates. A happy, excited crowd pushes in on me. I've never flown before. The Rector handed me my ticket just as I got into the car – the thought of a ticket never passed my mind.

I don't know what I'm doing. I don't know who I am. Martin always the Vague. I don't know where I'm going. I'm the man without a country. Without a mother. Without a friend in the world. What have I ever done to be rewarded with such horror? Is my Mammie dead already, or will she wait for me?

I can feel the tears welling up and know they think I'm a priest and I can't cry in public. Men, women and children are all crying as friends and family get ready to leave the old country again.

Someone sits next to me and hands me a clean, white handkerchief. He's all in black, just like me. His firm hand goes on my knee to steady me. I look up through my pity. Graham Byrne smiles at me and I rest my eyes on his bushy red beard.

Suddenly, I remember how Grannie used to begin her stories by the fire with, "Long ago and long ago it was when blue birds made their nests in old men's whiskers…" I start to laugh in that crazy way I have when my emotions are too much and I don't know what to do with them.

People are starting to board. Graham stands and motions for me to get up off my seat. He smiles down at me, "Come on, Lad, we'll make a priest out of you yet!"

CHAPTER 27
I Will Go Unto the Altar of God

I had left Rome April 22, arrived at O'Hare on the 23rd and was meeting with the Cardinal at St. Liam's Rectory on the 24th of April, a warm and windy Friday. I had slept at home, to spend every minute with my mother. I met with him at 10:00 a.m. in Msgr. Quinn's office. The housekeeper, Marge Quinn, his other sister, brought us coffee and Danish on a silver tray.

Cardinal Devitt himself had come out to St. Liam's to meet me and to see for himself if he thought me sufficiently mature for my age, intellectually developed and amply robust in my spirituality to take on the awesome responsibilities of priesthood.

The Cardinal, dressed in a simple black suit, was taken to Msgr. Quinn's large office in the front of the Rectory. Fr. Archibald had already told the Cardinal that I was ready. The Cardinal quoted him verbatim: "Now, if there were a choice between Martin and any of the rest of them here, Martin Sweeney would be my man. He's ready for ordination right now." Fr. Archibald hadn't seen me in over three years.

Both the Rector and Fr. Archibald admired the Cardinal for his attention to one single seminarian out of 98 in my old class at St. Mary's in Mundelein. They both knew how highly irregular it was to ordain someone early, but didn't they do that in time of war? Didn't they even ordain a Polish woman back then? My mother was dying and she would never see me a priest.

But the Cardinal was a prominent Canon Lawyer and they both knew that he had probably found a loop-hole and was not afraid to make a bold decision when needed. And this was Chicago where "the end always justified the means" and that every loop-hole had another loop-hole. I knew nothing of the underground railroad that had been running on my behalf.

The Cardinal sat behind his desk as I was ushered in. Rather than going around the desk and kneeling beside the Cardinal, I went over to the desk, put out my hand to receive the Cardinal's hand and still standing, bent over the desk to kiss his ring. I kept my eyes down-cast as a mark of respect.

"Martin, I've called you home from Rome. I know this must be a shock to you. I've come out to St. Liam's to meet with you personally before I ordain you tomorrow. I understand your mother is ill."

"Yes, Father."

"Address me as *'Your Eminence,'* Martin".

"Yes, Father."

"Did ye not hear me?? I'm' *'Your Eminence'* to you, Lad!"

A wave of adrenalin shot through me! I yanked my eyes from off the floor. I knew a West Clare accent if I knew anything. Boldly I looked the Cardinal in the eyes. It was like looking in the mirror, seeing what I would look like in 25 years.

The Cardinal stared at me. I stared back. We knew. We both *knew.* The Cardinal's eyes flitted to the window. He blinked several times. I continued to stare. A rush of power soared through my veins! I didn't know if I should slug him or kiss him.

I had found him after all these years! And he had come all this way to meet me on my own turf! I breathed deeply and dropped my eyes for a second to see if he was exhaling fire, but I couldn't take my eyes off Jeremiah Devitt, my own Son of a Bitch father!

I smiled and, without his invitation, sat down in the deep purple leather chair before the Msgr. Quinn's desk that the Cardinal was using. I coughed to dispel the mix of rage and love that soared through me. I didn't know if I should laugh or cry or shout to the rafters that I had finally found my very own father! My own Son of a Bitch father who had been hiding from me in the church before I was even born.

Breathing deeply, the Cardinal stared into his lap and twirled his big, gold ring he had received from the Pope. Gathering himself together, he softly told me that he wanted to ordain me earlier than my class because of my mother's illness.

I stared at him. Yes, my mother was dying – how could she ever see me be ordained? Who would say her funeral Mass? Who was this guy? I was without words. I couldn't stop the tears rolling down my cheeks.

"Martin…"

"I'm sorry, Father. I just can't think. What about everything? I'm not ready. My mother is dying…You know my mother, don't you? You know her from home, don't you? You know her…You do…You do know her…"

The Cardinal said nothing. I looked at him. He could say nothing. He pulled on his collar, as if the words were wedged down deep in his throat and he could not free them loose. He nodded to me and got up from his desk. I didn't move.

****

The bright red Chicago Fire Department ambulance crept ever so slowly down Castlewood. Inside, strapped on a gurney, was my dying mother, Kate Flaherty, my step-father, Stephen, Dr. Mike Corrigan and Fr. Paddy Dunphy, the Chicago Fire Department chaplain.

As the sleek ambulance negotiated the curb, Mammie gasped with pain. Dr. Corrigan pulled his stethoscope from out his pocket, warmed it in his hands and listened to Mammie's heart. He avoided looking at Steve.

St. Liam's was filled to over-flowing with family, friends, seminarians, members of the Police and Fire Departments, priests and monsignors and Mayor Daley with three of his sons. Some were deep in prayer, others were waving to each other, straining "to see and be seen."

In the sacristy, I knelt on a rickety old wooden *prie dieu*, vested in an amice, alb, stole and maniple. The white chasuble, the outermost garment that only a priest would wear for saying Mass, was neatly folded over the *prie dieu*; I would carry it over my left arm. In my right hand, I would carry a white candle and a white linen band that would be wrapped around my hands. Traditionally this was given to the mother of the priest and placed in her coffin and buried with her.

A few days ago I was just a student in Rome, wandering like a native along the Tiber River, speculating about my ordination later

162

in the spring. A glass of wine with Graham, avoiding the rector, enjoying my friends from all over the country, finishing up my studies at the Greg.

This is the moment my whole life had prepared me for. I was not ready. I prayed to be open and humble and gracious as I was lifted into the priesthood. I was distracted by finding that the Cardinal was my father and my mother was dying. I asked the Lord to take those worries from me for this most sacred hour. I just wanted to be a good priest.

I watched out the window for the silent ambulance. I tried to pray. I strained to see if the ambulance was coming. I could not bear to look at my father vesting for Mass, vesting for my ordination, vesting like a regular Cardinal with no personal relationship to the *ordinandus*.

Jeremiah Devitt thought of his own ordination at St. Mary Pro-Cathedral on Marlborough Street in Dublin back during the war years in 1941. Bishop Ronan Devitt had placed his hands on Jeremiah's head and prayed, *"Da, quaesumus, omnipotens Pater, in hos famulos tuos..."* just the way he would place his hands on Martin Sweeney's head, today, 24 years later.

Back then in Dublin, the front rows were filled with Devitts - aunts, uncles and cousins had come from Australia, America and Canada. Peter and Molly Murphy were not there and there was no one else from West Clare – no priests, no cousins, no friends or neighbors or classmates or even an old lover from Quilty.

Twenty-five years old at that time, Jeremiah Murphy Devitt he had been proud that he had divested himself of all those third-class folks. He had never made any friends. He didn't know how to extend himself, as he thought he had no need of any people except the Devitts. He was sheltered under their wings, and there was room for only him.

He had begun to realize, late one night in the Vatican as he struggled with the Pius XII documents, that the Pope might have sold himself out to the Nazis, not being man enough to confront Hitler about the Jews.

That night he first thought of those words as applied to the Pope. And as a young tenor sang out the aria from Madame Butterfly in St. Peter's Square, he realized that the Irish poet Patrick Kavanaugh had written about what his life could have been: *I looked into the heart of this life and saw that it was good.*

What if he had stayed at home and married Kate Sweeney and had a slew of children and taught up in Galway or down in Limerick and was just Jeremiah Murphy? What if he had never heard of the Devitts? What if he had been content with a normal life? What if Peter and Molly Murphy were still alive?

Because his ascendancy to the head of the Chicago Archdiocese had been so rapid, the Cardinal had never ordained any priests. Although his associates were responsible for directing him through the words and rubric, he was nervous. And Fr. Stackmann made him more nervous, running like a scared old goat when the bull was loose.

Not that the Ordination would not be proper, but that all the Sweeneys – Tom, Brendan, Lizzie, Nellie, Packy – would all be in the front. He had given special permission for Nellie Sweeney, now known as Sr. Mary Bridget, to leave the Wisconsin cloister for these days and to stay with the Adrian Dominicans at St. Liam's.

And Kate Sweeney, their sister, his old love, dying right in front of them all. She really was his old love, if Jeremiah Devitt was capable of love at all. Before the Church had him lock, stock and barrel? I looked over and saw a fleeting wave of disgust pass over him. I think it was for himself, not for me.

And how many nights, in the depth of the Vatican or socializing with church dignitaries from all over the world, did he not think of Kate Sweeney and his heart raced under his clerical garb and did he not long to lay his eyes on her, racing to meet him on the windy cliffs of Clare and to touch her soft auburn hair as it blew in his face and wrapped itself around his white neck.

The Cardinal felt light-headed as the flashing lights from the silent ambulance drew up to the front of St. Liam's. He had not seen Kate in 25 years, when she tore her ankle in the rabbit hole, running away from him and he carried her to Dr. O'Boyle to tape it for her.

164

His flesh-and-blood mother, Molly the house-keeper, shooed him away with her wet tea towel.

Kate Sweeney – the most beautiful woman he had ever laid his eyes upon. She must have been two or three months pregnant with her baby. With his baby. He looked over at me, still as a statue, my warm face buried in my cold, quivering hands.

I watched as Msgr. Quinn, still the Pastor at St. Liam's, looked out at all who had gathered in his church. A tidal wave of pride washed over him. If he ever knew the real story, the tidal wave would have knocked him on his old arse and he would be carried far out to sea with the backwash. What Robert Quinn didn't know - didn't hurt him one bit.

The driver and his assistants opened the rear doors and ever so gently, lowered the gurney onto the street. Stephen, in full Chicago Police Department Lieutenant's dress-uniform, and Dr. Mike Corrigan, in his blue pin-striped suit with a pale green tie, exited the ambulance quickly. When they got to the church doors, Stephen lifted Mam off the gurney, placed her weak arms around his neck and carried her into the church like a rag-doll.

They went up the green marble steps and into the sanctuary where two, young Irish nurses with soft, white blankets and a reclining wheel-chair were waiting for her. Ever so gently, Stephen placed Mam in the chair like he would put a sick baby in a crib.

The Cardinal went over to me and motioned that it was time for my ordination to begin. "Wait, Father, is my mother here yet? We can't start before she gets here. Is she here?" The Cardinal nodded and pointed to where my poor, sick mother waited. Her lovely ginger hair was now thin and white and her poor skin carried a tinge of yellow and green.

With giant strides, I crossed the sanctuary, knelt before my darling mother and buried my head in her thin lap. She leaned over and kissed the top of my head, right at the spot that my father would place his hands and make me a priest. The people gasped and Uncle Tom Sweeney thought his heart was going to explode.

I returned to the sacristy, composed myself, received directions from the Cardinal's assistants and followed Fr. Archibald

165

back out to our places before the altar. Fr. Archibald was the keeper of my secrets and I trusted him with my life. He was a good man and I needed him there.

I saw Fr. Archibald take a good look at the Cardinal and a good look at me - there was no denying the same face on the both of us, although one a bit more battle-worn, as I hadn't a wrinkle, groove, mole or scar on my young, unseasoned face.

I continued to watch Fr. Archibald. He was the only one on the altar who knew the real story and here he was, pretending that I was just another young man about to be ordained by just another pompous Cardinal. I wondered if he wanted to run to the pulpit and shout at the top of his lungs, "Hey, Jeremiah Devitt is the father of Martin Sweeney and the Cardinal's life is a lie!" He adjusted his cincture and kept quiet.

I looked at my three friends serving the Mass – Garrett Lyons, Harry Hogan, and Tim Armstrong, even though he had left the seminary. Harry pulled me aside and said that although he had not been feeling well that morning, he knew that I would want him there.

Somehow, everything was always about Harry Hogan, not about me. I nodded and told Harry I was glad he could make it. I noticed that Harry's fingernails were again chewed down to the stub, with small, flesh-colored adhesives covering the nail-beds.

I broke into a big, nervous grin when I saw Tim who quickly shot his thumb up in victory, our private code since 5th grade. I started to laugh, as I always did when I was nervous. Fr. Archibald gave me a sharp elbow. I frowned so I could stop laughing and look serious.

Tim's fiancé was with the rest of the Armstrongs. Patty Chernoff was studying to be a nurse at St. Francis in Evanston. Although they weren't married yet, Patty looked like the Armstrongs. I wondered if Tim and Patty were having sex. I closed my eyes and banished that thought – this was not the time.

The Four Delaney sisters, sitting in order of age – Josie, Mayme, Norah, and Kitty - were all in brand new blue and purple hats from Marshall Fields. They went to the same hair-dresser and the same dentist. They each had her own memory of the first day

Mammie and I arrived in Chicago and "him after fallin' sound asleep at the table, the little Pet."

Sr. Raphael Mary had snuck into the sacristy so she could see everything. I saw her and smiled. Fr. Paddy Dunphy and his brothers were vesting for the Mass. Paddy irreverently made a sign of the cross in the air and I nodded at him, remembering the Dunphy rescue squad at the Deer Path Inn.

Harry Hogan went over and made a dutiful greeting to his three Dunphy cousins but distanced himself as quickly as possible. He didn't want to be identified with them in anyone's mind, much less the Cardinal's. You're known by the company you keep and blood is thicker than water and birds of a feather…

We all stood immobilized, facing the altar, while the St. Mary Seminary Choir sang *Veni, Creator Spiritus*, - "Come, Holy Spirit, Creator Blest, and in our hearts, take up Thy rest." Chills ran up my spine at the intonation of this ancient hymn calling for the very Spirit of God to come upon us.

I prayed, "Lord, fill my heart with your grace and your presence and help me to be a good priest. Let me never betray You. I love You so very much." I was overwhelmed that all these people were here to honor me, to honor the priesthood, to honor my dying mother.

Stephen took Mam's frail hand in his. Cardinal Devitt, vested in gold vestments, watched her turn slightly toward Stephen and kiss his hand that rested on her arm. Jeremiah Devitt bit his lower lip.

There was standing–room only in this mammoth Gothic church, built by the sweat and blood of Irish immigrants, needing a spiritual place to call home after centuries of persecution, poverty, famine. Over half the seating was with fire and police officers, nuns from the parish, families of my class-mates at St. Mary's.

Msgr. Quinn was bursting with pride. The Cardinal, other bishops and priests were on his altar and there wasn't a sound from any of the faithful, kneeling in the pews. Most of their eyes were on my mother, then off to me, then back to Mammie.

With his aides, the Cardinal had seated himself at the foot of the altar and on his head they placed his gold and white miter, that triangular hat that rose 12' over his brow. The pre-ordination excitement had subsided and silence filled the sanctuary and the pews. The younger nurse whispered a blessing to my mother, "*Go sa'bha'la Dias inn,*" and the older one repeated it after her.

As the ordination ceremony began, the Cardinal turned and faced me, the young man about to be ordained and he addressed me in Latin: "Dearly beloved Son, as you are now about to be consecrated to the office of the Priesthood..."

Suddenly, the sacristy door flew open and into the crowded sanctuary burst a wild man in a flowing white chasuble, his long red beard and bushy red hair creating gasps among the faithful, as his fearsome-like had never been seen before on the North Side of Chicago.

Graham Byrne ignored the Cardinal, nodded to me, and fell on his knees in front of my mother. He bowed his head for my mother's blessing and as Stephen lifted her little hand to Graham's head, the nurse again whispered, "*Go sa'bha'la Dias inn, Athair, God bless you, Father.*"

While my uncle Tom Sweeney did not understand Latin, I watched him follow the translation in the small leaflet prepared for the ceremony. I thought he'd turn himself inside-out. I knew the anger that raced through his tough farmer body, as he had always hated Jeremiah and now he had the gall to stand up there and call me "Son."

Then Tom started to snicker as he thought of himself, only a few days ago, as the foxy old Irish priest, black-mailing Jeremiah with public exposure of his story. His laugh was gaining momentum as Lizzie, a big grin on her face, shoved an elbow into his side, which only made him laugh louder.

Then Brendan and Packy picked it up and started to laugh and Nellie, Sr. Mary Bridget, glowed red with embarrassment. Stephen heard the Sweeneys rocking in the pew and started to smile. He knew what was going on and was afraid if he'd start to laugh, there'd be no stopping him.

Mammie looked at him questioningly, but he just reached over and softly kissed the top of her head, her once beautiful, thick red-hair now thin and white. The doctor and nurses were not sure what was going on down there, but Steve just shook his head and they went back to monitoring Mam. The taller nurse with the strawberry-blond hair glanced at Stephen, knowing that this was taking its toll on him. She didn't want two patients.

I took my directions from the assistant to the Cardinal, then prostrated myself on the cold, hard marble floor before the altar.

In Latin, the Cardinal asked me if I were prepared to take on the responsibilities of the priesthood. I replied, *"Ad sum."*

The Cardinal asked me if I were prepared to celebrate the mysteries of Christ faithfully. I replied, *"Ad sum."*

The Cardinal asked me if I would preach the Gospel and consecrate my life to God. To both I replied, *"Ad sum."*

The Cardinal then silently placed his hands on my bowed head. With this simple action, I became a priest.

My hands now had the power to change bread and wine into the Body and Blood of Christ. The Cardinal then anointed them with oil and bound them together with a long, white linen cloth as he prayed, "whatever these hands bless, be blessed and whatever these hands consecrate, be consecrated." This linen cloth would soon be placed in Mammie's coffin and would be buried with her.

Mammie smiled, as she knew how I had kept my hands special for the time when they would be consecrated. Then she slipped back into a light sleep. The Irish nurses looked at each other. Her time was not long.

As the Mass and the Ordination ceremony concluded, the Seminary choir sang *Salve Regina - Hail, Holy Queen, Mother of Mercy,* the same hymn that all the other priests sing at a priest's funeral. I went directly over to my mother for her to receive my first priestly blessing.

I held her frail, little face in my priestly hands and kissed the top of her warm head. With her eyes closed, Mammie smiled at me and reached for my hands. She brought them to her dry, parched lips and held them there. I wanted to stay here forever. I didn't want her to die. I was gone for so long and I should have been here with her.

I caught my breath. *Vita, Delcedo, et Spes nostra, Salve* – Our life, our sweetness and our hope. I still couldn't breathe. I couldn't move. Suddenly, a strong arm was around me and the Cardinal stood close by my side. He leaned in even closer. I bent over and listened to the Cardinal.

"Son, you are a priest now. You must go on with this, for all these people need your first blessing. Put your dear mother in the hands of God, straighten up and I'll be by your side. The doctor and nurses are with her. She needs to leave now, so you go down to the communion railing with me and the folks can have a double blessing if they want. I won't leave you. You have to do this."

For the briefest moment, I leaned against the Cardinal. As I thought of it after, I almost swayed into him. In a flash, Graham Byrne grabbed my other arm and propped me up. There was a huge gasp from the people in the pews, but I just smiled at everyone and headed down to impart my first blessing. I could smell the old turf smoke clinging to Graham's beard.

I faced the packed church, smiled and quickly walked down the three marble steps to the communion railing where my family was already waiting for my blessing. The Irish nurses helped Stephen lift Mammie's feathery little body into his arms.

****

Kate Sweeney Flaherty, my mother, died early the next morning, just as the sun was coming up in pink and mauve over the lake. She was surrounded by our family, the nurses and Dr. Corrigan. I had given her the Last Rites in the middle of the night. I sat alone with her warm body until Mahon & Murphy Funeral Directors came for her. I had gone to St. Liam's with Dudley Murphy so we knew her body would be treated with great reverence.

My First Mass was the funeral Mass for my mother at St. Liam's. Again, the church was filled. I placed the thin white linen cloth that had bound my anointed hands at my Ordination on top of her heart as she lay still in her pearl-gray coffin.

170

All three of the Dunphy brothers were on the altar with me and the monsignors. Tim Armstrong announced that he was going to serve the Mass along with Garrett Lyons. Harry was too sick. The pall bearers were Mam's three brothers – Tom, Brendan and Packy – and Stephen's three brothers – Billy, Joe and Sean.

Msgr. Quinn held the silver water bucket as I sprinkled her coffin with holy water. Cardinal Devitt swung the thurible and thick white incense curled over her coffin like the breath of angels. In their fine, young male voices, the St. Mary Seminary Choir sang *In Paradisium Deducat Angeli* – May the Angels Lead You into Paradise.

I was in another world as I followed my mother's casket down the long aisle. I looked out through the open doors and saw her, my own mother, standing there, smiling.

My own mother Kate – without the limping and suffering and early aging. Mam - young, a baby on her hips, walking the open green fields of Clare down to the sea. Mam - covering her face in horror when I told her I wanted to be a priest. Mam– impatient when I insisted on knowing about my father. Mam - telling me to hush up, the babies were sleeping and my father getting ready for work.

Mam – polishing my shoes, ironing my white shirts for Quigley and slipping 35 cents into my pocket and an extra dime "for some poor cra'thur who had nothing." Mam – beaming on her monthly visits to the "Farm", what she called Mundelein, and watching me beginning to take on the shape of a priest. Mammie – kissing my consecrated hands the day before she died.

My mother stood as bright as an angel as they lifted her lovely coffin and placed it in the black limo to take her body to Cavalry Cemetery. She kissed me on the neck and nodded to the Cardinal, to my father Jeremiah Devitt. Ah, sure, but no harm, he was long ago forgiven. And hadn't they produced but a glorious son!!

171

CHAPTER 28
We Had Dreams to Dream and Songs to Sing

There must have been over 50 cars that followed the hearse and Mahon & Murphy's black limousines from St. Liam's up north to Calvary Cemetery. All traffic up Sheridan Road stopped respectfully, as squad cars from the Chicago Police Department were at every traffic light, the officers giving us the right of way.

I was in the limousine directly behind my mother with Steve Flaherty, Mayor Daley, Bishop Teddie Szymanski, Msgr. Quinn and the Cardinal. This is how things are done in Chicago. Everyone keeps score.

The empty grave was a deep hole in the ground waiting for my mother. A green indoor/outdoor carpet draped the fresh earth, playing games with our denial of death. Out of a corner of my eye I saw the old grave-diggers propped against their shovels up on a little hill, ready to heap the old dirt on top of my mother's casket. They were smoking and laughing, taking a quick nip from their silver flasks - just another day's work. I wanted to hit them.

After everyone was in place, the six pall-bearers put my mother's coffin on their shoulders and, following David Murphy's directions, made their way to the grave-site. They suspended her on a frame with straps over the empty hole. These straps would be used to lower her to the bottom.

The hymn, *"**In Paradisum Deducant Te Angeli**: May the angels lead you into paradise: may the martyrs receive thee at thy coming, and lead thee into the holy city of Jerusalem"* was sung in Latin as we removed my mother from the church. I loved it and found myself humming it as I saw the men coming over the little rise with my mother on their shoulders.

As I was the celebrant at the Mass, I was the official at this burial. I stood tall, so proud to be the son of Kate Sweeney Flaherty. I know that my sweet mother cast me off and blew a strong wind into my sails. I intoned with a newly-found authority: *Benedictus Dominus Deus Israel...In sanctitate et justitia...Kyrie eleison...Requiescat in pace".*

172

My voice did not falter, my hands did not shake, my eyes did not fill. I sprinkled her pearly gray coffin with the hyssop, Tim Armstrong standing close to me with the holy water bucket. Tim was leaning on me; I was a support to him. I know that this strength and clarity I was feeling came with the Sacrament of Holy Orders, my ordination. I couldn't have done this a week ago.

Dennis Murphy announced that everyone was invited back to St. Liam's for lunch. He cleared the way for the Cardinal, Bishop Teddie Syzmanski, the Mayor, Msgr. Quinn to get to the limousine. I told Dennis to go on without me, I needed to stay a little longer.

I stood with Tim at the foot of Mammie's coffin. Priests, seminarians, families, friends of the twins, cops and fire-fighters, Dr. Corrigan and his family, the nurses, St. Liam's parishioners - all passed by, nodding, touching my arm, blowing me a kiss. Tim did not move away from me.

The sweet irony of the Good Lord not allowing Mammie to take her secret to her grave. This dark secret had made her sick all these years, and now she could release it. Yet it was through her dying that everything fell into place and that Jeremiah Murphy Devitt had to stand and to account for his sins and lies and compromises. We all had to make peace with the past.

When everyone left, and we were finally alone, Tim wrapped his arm around my waist and I threw my arm over his shoulder. The memories held us together, and no matter where our separate lives would lead us, it would always be just Tim and Martin.

"God Almighty, Martin, I loved her so," Tim choked, "I loved her from the first day we met. She was another mother to me, I don't know if you know. Before I left the seminary, it was to Kate Sweeney, now Mrs. Flaherty that I went. She told me to listen to the still, quiet voice of the Holy Spirit in my heart and to follow where that was leading me. 'Sure, Timmy, you know what is in your heart. Just follow it and you won't be wrong'."

I knelt over my mother's casket and kissed it. My hands gripped the top of the casket. I could see her sick, little body in that cold, hard box and before my raging sorrow could take hold, I began to hum, "*May the angels lead you into paradise and may the martyrs receive thee at thy coming."* I kissed the box again and Tim helped me up. She was now with the angels in paradise.

Tim and I got into his little yellow bug. I set the bucket and hyssop on the floor in the back, next to dirty jogging shoes, law books and candy wrappers. He drove ever so slowly, dragging out our last good-by until we got back out onto Sheridan Road. The grave-diggers were already covering up my mother with big clumps of earth. They'd then throw a few handfuls of grass seed to make it look like she'd been there forever.

As we headed south on Sheridan Road, Tim slowed and pulled right in front of a pub, *Mollie McGuire's.* Without a word between us, we headed into the bar. Tim ordered each of us a shot of Bushmills. I wanted mine doubled...I was taller than Tim. I couldn't go in and face that crowd without something under my belt. I could feel the thirst coming on me stronger and stronger. I'd stay in control, I knew I could.

****

The gym was decorated in white bunting by the Knights of Columbus and the women of St. Liam's Guild had prepared a magnificent luncheon for the Cardinal, clergy, my Sweeney and Flaherty families and our neighbors and friends.

This was the first time in the history of the parish that Msgr. Quinn allowed alcohol to be served. Robert Quinn would never want it to be said that he was ungenerous, especially as he was honored to be the pastor as such a critical time - Kate Sweeney Flaherty's funeral and the ordination of her son by the Cardinal. Msgr. Quinn's sister, Cecilia Hogan, had provided the drinks, although it was officially given by Judge Hogan and his family, all of whom were there.

There were clusters of Sweeneys, Flahertys, Hogans, Delaneys, priests and monsignors, people from the parish, all with their tongues hanging out until the bar was opened. They acted as if the appetizers hit the spot, but stole furtive glances to see what was the trouble – where's the booze? When the bartenders finally appeared from Jimmy Dalton's Pub, the sigh of relief was audible.

After the Cardinal was served, I was offered the next drink. I refused a drink to honor my mother. I had promised her that I would

174

forego liquor for the rest of my life. It was at the end of my three years of Philosophy. A party had been held in the student lounge, booze and food supplied by the Hogans. I had gotten very drunk. The following afternoon, my family had driven out to Mundelein for our monthly visit.

As I put my arms around my mother, she pushed me away. "Martin, you've been drinking! I can smell it on you right now, so don't lie to me!" I told them about the party the previous night and admitted to "having the drop taken." The twins snickered, and Stephen looked out toward St. Mary's lake.

Mam did not take her eyes from me. "Sure, Martin, you go to that priest you know so well and have the Pledge taken! Ahh, we have suffered so much, all of us Irish, because of the drink. And I won't have a drunken son, and you, a drunken priest, on my hands!! You get on your knees, Martin, and promise the Good Lord that you will never again raise a glass! You get on those knees, Martin, you hear!"

I did not go to Fr. Archibald, I did not take the Pledge and I did not stop drinking. Only around her did I refrain from drinking, like a game we played – she knew that I was drinking, but I made sure she had no proof; I knew that she knew I was drinking, but had no proof. I could continue to drink with impunity, at least for now.

As the wake began, I watched Msgr. Quinn, once a ferocious man, well over six feet, now beginning to shrink with age. With his sister Cecilia on one arm, he lay hold of Cardinal Devitt's arm and steered him toward the Hogan's entourage. After introducing him to his brother-in-law, Judge Harry Hogan, he called over the Judge's son, another Harry Hogan, my old pal, who had been playing in the corner with his much younger nephew, Harry Smith.

The Cardinal stated that he had met Harry in the sacristy as they prepared for Martin's ordination. "Now, don't you have those three Dunphy brothers that are priests? Nice fellows. Are they not your cousins? Grand priests the Dunphys are"

We looked around, as the Hogans certainly had not invited the Dunphys to my mother's funeral. They knew that they were more than welcome, with Fr. Paddy the Chaplain of the Chicago Police

Department and my step-father, Steve is a Lieutenant. The three Dunphy brothers were laughing with Stephen Flaherty and his brother Billy. It became obvious that the Dunphys wanted to keep their distance from the Hogans as well – *water seeks its own level.*

As the various Hogans approached Msgr. Quinn, "Uncle Bob", to be introduced before the crowd got to him, the Cardinal extended his arm to shake hands, but each of the many Hogans fell to his knees to kiss the ring. It was clear that the Cardinal was growing uncomfortable with all the fawning, especially as he saw the long line waiting to meet him. I caught his eye and nodded to Uncle Tom.

Tom Sweeney assumed his old man role, quivering and shaking as he stumbled across the floor of the gym, grabbed the Cardinal by the arm and muttered something about meeting the Sweeneys before he had to go back to Ireland.

Tom kicked open the door to the coach's office. White T-shirts with the team's logo, a sailing ship with "Liam's' Sailors" printed in black, lay neatly folded in piles on a chair. Tom tossed them on the floor and motioned for the Cardinal to sit. "Sure, take a load off, Jeremiah." Tom sat on the desk.

Tom pulled a bottle and two plastic glasses out of his coat pocket and poured the Cardinal a small glass of Irish whiskey. The two knocked them back in no time. Tom Sweeney began to laugh, "Sure, Jeremiah, it was much easier to have ye an enemy than a friend. Now I've got to be nice to you while them Yanks are looking"

"Sure, Tom, a few good looks from your Yank cousins would never change a strand of hair on your bloody thick head."

"Ah, some more Pink Tit, Jeremiah?" The Cardinal raised his empty glass and Tom gave a shout to Packy to get some more Red Breast Irish whisky.

"You know, Tom, I have a lot to answer for. Never in a thousand years did I ever think I would get to this place, but meeting all of you over here – it just takes me back to so long ago. I was a right bloody bastard, the way I treated everyone. Who did I think myself to be, Tom, better than all of you Sweeneys and so proud to be a Devitt."

The Cardinal continued, "Everything I touched turned against me. Like I poisoned all of them. Peter and Molly in that goddamn fire, the Devitts in that fiery crash on the mountainside the day I was ordained. Now poor Kate in her grave."

"Sure, but you're the only one I can think of to tell this to, Tom Sweeney, but just knowing that I have a real, 'flesh and blood' son changes everything. The way I treated your lovely sister Kate put a heavy curse on me for years and years. Sure, I carried it on my shoulders for years, like a soaking, bloody horse blanket, weighing me down, making me a bloody bastard of a man, I hated myself as much as the devil himself!"

Tom Sweeney scratched his chin and smiled, "Now, Jeremiah, do ye think you're as powerful as Almighty God, Himself? That ye can cause planes to crash, that ye can give me very own sister her consumption? Sure, ye may be a big man with the church and the pope, but ye don't have power over life and death. Sure, ye don't."

"You don't think I caused all of this? It was that horrible fear in me that turned me all black inside and out. Like I was going to be found out for the bloody bastard that I really am. Jesus, Tom, I hate myself, every bone in my body, every drop of blood in my veins, every hair on my head!"

Tom reached for the top of Jeremiah's head, lifted off his little red skullcap, the *zucchetto,* and patted it, the wandering cur come back home, wagging his tail, with a dead squirrel in his mouth. The door was opened for the old mutt and he found his place by the fire.

"Sure, what were ye afraid of, Jeremiah? What was it that made ye turn your back on all of us? There wasn't a soul in all of West Clare that would harm a hair on your head. Was it not maybe ye were afraid of yourself? I dunno….I dunno. Maybe ye needed to hide in that big, old scary place up the mountains so ye couldn't catch yourself. Was it yourself ye been running from, Jeremiah?"

"If I could only turn back the hands of the clock…"

"And maybe our man here, Martin, would never even have seen the light of day."

"God, I have a son!! I never, never knew, Tom, so help me God!"

Msgr. Quinn turned the handle of the coach's office but the door was locked. He knocked on the locked door. Tom opened it a crack and Quinn stared at the two old countrymen sipping on their Jameson's Red Breast. The Cardinal nodded to Msgr. Quinn. He'd be right out.

Tom closed the door again. Without a word, Tom and Jeremiah stood, spit into their right palms, rubbed them together and shook hands with all the solemnity of two old Kerry horse-traders completing a treacherous deal.

Brendan Sweeney brought Mr. and Mrs. Rizzo and Rosie up to Martin for his blessing. The Rizzos were accompanied by four thick men in black suits, white shirts and black ties. They expressed their condolences to the family. Mrs. Rizzo and Rosie knelt for the blessing. Mr. Rizzo handed Martin an envelope. Martin tried to hand it back, but Brendan graciously took it and said something about "safe-keeping."

Mr. Rizzo, scanning the gym like a submarine in hostile waters, spotted Judge Hogan. He grabbed Brendan's arm, "You guys related to that stinkin' bastard over there?" The family knew to stay clear of any member of the judiciary.

Brendan shook his head and told him that Harry Hogan was in my class at the seminary and that Harry was almost a priest. The Hogans were **not** related to the Sweeneys. Young Harry Hogan in his black clerical suit was the one playing with the kid. The kid was again sitting on Harry's lap and Harry was showing him a trick with a deck of cards. Harry's cheeks were red.

Sammy Rizzo snorted. "What the hell's the matter wid' that guy? Playing with the kid like that? He some kinda' fairy?"

Mrs. Rizzo reached for his elbow. She knew how he acted around priests, as they wouldn't bury his father in a Catholic cemetery. He pushed her away. Scowling, Sammy lit up a cigar, spit out another piece of tobacco and blew the smoke toward Judge Hogan.

The Judge spotted Sammy Rizzo and the Cardinal. The Judge's frown deepened and his pale, pink cheeks redden. Brendan Sweeney knew that he was observing a world-class chess tournament and he didn't miss a move. Sammy wanted him to do just that.

Brendan saw his brother Tom coming out of the coach's office with the Cardinal. Brendan asked Sammy if he'd like to meet Cardinal Devitt. Sammy said something in Italian and Mrs. Rizzo whispered, "Maybe next time, Brendan."

Sammy punched Brendan playfully on his arm. "Blood flows both ways, Brendan, and this blood is bad, bad, bad." Brendan didn't know what he meant. Sammy held his soggy cigar up and pointed toward the Judge. He spit again, winked at Brendan and whisked his wife and daughter out the door to the waiting limousine.

I noticed wispy Fr. Stackmann, who could not figure out what was going on but knew better than to ask, trying to gather up the Cardinal as he was due down at the Chancery in a manner of minutes. The Cardinal saw Lizzie and Babe in the corner and motioned for them. Lizzie dreaded that Jeremiah would stick out his hand for them to kiss his ring.

The Cardinal leaned over to kiss Lizzie on the cheek. She whispered a "thank you" in his ear. He looked at Babe. "Nice job, Counselor. Nice job altogether." Babe smiled and nodded her head. She wasn't about to give him too much. No freebies for the church.

"Nice job. Next time, Miss Nathanson, use a newer affidavit. That one was over a year old and the wrong names were employed. You ought to come and work for me!" They all burst out in peals of nervous laughter. Was everything fixed or was there another battle waiting in the wings?

This was the first time that anyone found out the mysterious workings of Babe Nathanson. Judge Harry Hogan took note of the familiarity of the Cardinal with the Sweeneys and especially with the likes of Babe Nathanson. The bad blood flowed back and forth, with so much history in and out of the court-room. Babe Nathanson took it all in and relished the fact that she could hob-knob with the Cardinal. The Judge could not afford to forget what he saw.

We all gathered at the door as the Cardinal was preparing to leave. Stephen Flaherty offered his hand and told Jeremiah not to be a stranger. Tom told him that he was more than welcome to be with them next time in Quilty. Frail Nellie, Sr. Mary Bridget, grasped his hand and thanked him for letting her out of the cloister to bury her sister Kate.

The Cardinal reached into his breast pocket and handed me a small folded sheet of paper. He had copied it in his own handwriting the night before and had read it that morning at the cemetery, his voice breaking as he looked up from the prayer to the pearl-gray coffin suspended over the open hole, waiting for Mam to be lowered six feet into the open ground.

I moved over to the hedge that surrounded the gym and unfolded the white sheet of paper. Not a sound was heard as I began to read to myself:

"Death is nothing at all.
I have only slipped away into the next room.
Whatever we were to each other,
that we are still.
Call me by my old familiar name.
Speak to me in the easy way
which you always used to.
Laugh as we always used to.
Play, smile, think of me,
pray for me.
Let my name be the household word
that it always was.
Let it be spoken without effort.
Life means all that it ever meant.
It is the same as it ever was;
There is absolutely unbroken continuity.
Why should I be out of your mind
Because I am out of your sight?
I am but waiting for you, for an interval,
Somewhere very near just around the corner.
All is well.
Nothing is past; nothing is lost.
One brief moment and all will be
As it was before,
Only better, infinitely happier and forever.

180

We will all be one together with Christ".

The Cardinal's eyes grew misty as he looked at the faces of all these beautiful people, his very own folks from home in West Clare. Fr. Stackmann cleared his throat. Tom Sweeney stared at him with a clenched jaw. Fr. Stackmann walked deliberately to the waiting limo and opened the door for the Cardinal.

I put my arm through the Cardinal's and pulled him aside. "Thanks, Da, for all you did. You made it all possible. We're grateful and every one of us knows what you did for us. Sure, if me mother were here, she'd thank you, too!"

The Cardinal bit the inside of his cheek. Quiet tears ran down his face as he looked into the deep, blue eyes of his son, "Martin, no one ever called me 'Da'."

He waved to everyone, slid into the back of his car as Fr. Stackmann gently closed the door, hopped into the driver's seat and sped off toward the expressway. The Cardinal was going to be late for his meeting in the Chancery.

Off to the side, observing the tribal rites of the Sweeney's, Fr. Graham Byrne stood and waited for me. He told me that he was leaving, that he was holding a seminar for the Jesuits at Loyola on changes coming from Vatican II. He bent low so no one would hear.

"Martin, you be careful of that Hogan character. I know you guys are friends and that he looks up to you. I don't like the smell of him one little bit. He's got his own agenda and I wouldn't be surprised if he didn't pull you into it. You're terribly innocent, Martin, and he's 'a spoon ye'll sup sorrow with yet'."

"I hear you, Graham, I know. They've got so damn much money, nothing can touch him."

"Oh, that guy will have his comeuppance, alright, regardless of the money. I just see you getting caught in his web, Martin. Harry Hogan will 'build a nest in your ear', and you won't know where the bird's song comes from. Just tread softly with that guy."

I thought of the time I was leaving for Rome and he kissed me on the lips. I thought of his nephew bouncing on his knee and the

181

cluster of young men who gathered around Harry Hogan, the Pied Piper of Lake Forest.

Graham shook my hand. My eyes filled with tears as I hated the thought of his going back to Rome. He smiled, "Now Lad, our paths will cross many times, whether in Rome or in Chicago. Probably here, as they like me down at Loyola. I'm as far as a piece of paper or the telephone. I'm proud of you, Martin, and now let me go..."

****

The day after Kate's funeral, Rosie called Brendan. She was crying. "Brendan, I'm so sorry, I could kill myself. My father's standing right here with me. I can't see you anymore. Never again!"

Brendan gasped, "What, Rosie, what are you saying?"

"It's those people at your mother's funeral. They're all friends of yours, like that judge and all those cops. They're our enemies and I can't see you anymore, Brendan!" Rosie choked on the words.

Sammy Rizzo grabbed the phone. "You little bastard. Comin' in here like ya' did, all sweet and humble and charmin' Rosie and her mother. If you come within 200 miles of my daughter, you're dead and that priest of yours is chopped liver, you sonoffa' bitch!"

"Sir, Sir, I...."

"Listen, ya dirty Mick, I dunno who ya working' for, but you're dead meat, ya' get it? Ya' get it? And I'll beat Rosie to a pulp if you come sniffin' around her. Just stay the fuck away from all of us, ya dirty Mick!"

The phone slammed down. Like a mortally wounded lion, Brendan roared and roared and roared. His hair turned white overnight.

182

PART FOUR

Chapters 29 – 42

Child, do not go
Into the dark places of soul,
For there the grey wolves whine
The lean grey wolves.

I have been down
Among the unholy ones who tear
Beauty's white robe and clothe her
In rags of prayer.

Child, there is light somewhere
Under a star,
Sometime it will be for you
A window that looks
Inward to God.

To a Child
Patrick Kavanaugh

Chapter 29
Corned Beef on Rye

1971. The Ship of State was careening on the rocks, with Richard Nixon, Robert McNamara and Henry Kissinger heating up the Vietnam War. Cambodia had been secretly bombed in 1969, the same year that John Kerry, leading Veterans against the War, said, "Who wants to be the last man to die because of someone else's mistake?"

Black body bags were piling up faster than they could be shipped home. Martin Luther King and Bobby Kennedy had been dead for three years and John Kennedy for eight.

It was hip not to trust anyone over 30. Harvard Professor Timothy Leary led the initiation into psychedelic drugs - "tune in, turn on and drop out." Student sit-ins were being held across the nation. Young men were burning their draft notices and young women were burning their bras.

Within the church, discontent was rampant. Leadership was trying to stay ahead of the typhoon. Nuns and priests were leaving in droves, either falling in love with each other or reasoning that they could do just as much or better out in the world. The people in the pew said that the church had gone too far or not far enough. Masses in English delighted many, betrayed others.

The crowded deli up on Dempster in Skokie smelled of chicken matzo ball soup, corned beef, dill pickles, mustard and other foreign odors. The two tall Irishmen were crowded into the booth in the back. They saw only each other. The loud waitress, Sheila, with her blond bee-hive, stood silently with her hand on her hip, knowing that the men would notice her sooner or later and order.

A large golden *Chi*, the Jewish symbol for "life", danced on a chain above her bouncing bosom. "O.K., *Buhbelah*, what's your *nosh* today?"

Besides our decidedly Gentile appearance, Jeremiah and my bewildered look gave us away as *"goyem."*

"Oy," sighed Sheila with a wink, "It means 'What'll ya have?' Bubelah!" We were taken aback by this "dish" who would "dish" and we laugh and were put at ease.

184

We always met on a Wednesday, my day off. First it was up to Wisconsin to the cloistered nuns to say Mass. With her superior's permission, Auntie Nellie, Sr. Mary Bridget, had asked me if I would come up to celebrate Mass. Although the nuns were tucked behind the grill and I could not see her, I never missed a Wednesday and my chance to breathe the same air as she did.

There was something about a cloistered life that appealed to me. Down in County Kerry, the ancient monks each lived in their own little 'beehive' cells, stones piled up in a circle that came together on the top. This life of solitude and prayer appealed to the introverted part of me, but the extroverted part couldn't abide the isolation. Nellie was a consummate introvert, so her choice was just fine.

The other nuns knew that I was Nellie's nephew and secretly begrudged her this honor. In her lax moments, Nellie whispered to me "Irish begrudgery", but stopped herself, knowing that the German nuns wouldn't understand, but the small-heartedness was the same.

She simply annoyed them because she was so different. She had only one eye and they all had two; she spoke with an Irish accent and they spoke with a German accent.

Nellie's life was one of complete renunciation of the things that the "world" holds dear: money, sex and self-will. She had taken permanent vows of poverty, chastity and obedience. She became a non-person, her own will being subsumed into the will of her superior. Nellie's life was spent in prayer - both private and communal, and in work - cleaning, cooking, gardening, sewing.

The nuns did not speak, except for the hour of "recreation" each evening. Their long, black habits were worn every day of the year and a second habit was given to a younger nun when one of them died. Her clothes, shoes and all, were recycled through the community, regardless of the fit. When a sister needed to bathe or take medicine or receive communication from her family, she knelt down before the superior to request permission.

Under the vow of obedience, each sister relegated her own will to that of her superior's. To even *think* of questioning a superior's judgment or orders was a violation of her vows. Nellie viewed this relinquishment of her will to be the perfect White Martyrdom, for her will and sense of herself were her dearest right as a human being and the most precious gift from God.

Nuns were considered to be "Brides of Christ," and any other relationship - romantic, sexual, friendship – was against the vow of Chastity. The very first day that Nellie entered the convent, she was warned against "Particular Friendships," although no one chose to define exactly what that meant. When a nun would brush up against another nun, she quickly beat her breast, the sign of forgiveness, lest the inadvertent touching be misconstrued as something else.

If the truth be known, her life as a cloistered nun was not so very different from her life at home. Some of the nuns were cruel, but perhaps their feet hurt. Some were strange, but perhaps they were not well. Some were overly friendly, but perhaps they were lonely.

The real grind was the small, irritating personal habits that would annoy Nellie – someone constantly clearing her throat during meditation or moaning as she climbed the stairs or slamming down her coffee cup or standing too close or humming as she waxed the long, white marble corridors.

Nellie loved the silence, especially because so many of the nuns were German, and their harsh words and loud delivery offended her. She knew that they didn't like her and when she tried to be accommodating, they took that as weakness. At home, her mother frequently reminded all of them, "The less said - the better." That applied to her life now.

She didn't mind taking orders, for hadn't Lizzie taught her how to bow and scrape to a Higher Power? She loved the long hours of prayer and meditation, for she was just doing what came naturally. Nellie loved being the "Bride of Christ," for hadn't she loved the Lord and Him alone from the moment she drew her first breath?

Nellie, Sr. Mary Bridget, took pride in my priesthood. She once confessed such pride and the priest, waiting to give her absolution, told her never again to confess such nonsense. I smiled as I remembered the words of Bishop Fulton J. Sheen on hearing nuns' confessions as "being stoned to death with popcorn".

186

My father and I had a special deli ritual - first we talked in hurried, hushed tones over refills of coffee and then tried to order off the menu, asking Sheila ("Mam") to explain in detail braised brisket, challah, kugels, pastrami, chopped liver, lox and bagels, stuffed cabbage and the difference between Kosher pickles out of the barrel and just regular pickles, to which Sheila would reply, "Pickles out of the barrel are regular pickles, but Kosher are Kosher…"

"Kugel's fresh this morning, guys. How 'bout a 'bissel'?" Sheila had a slew of regulars, all craving her humor and mothering touch. "*Mazel Tov,*" she'd shout to Mr. Shulman on the birth of his new grandson, Jacob. "How're the *mishpuchah?*" she'd inquire about someone's in-laws.

Sheila's customers were like a family to her and they tipped her well, appreciative of her care to them as friends. We loved all that Jewish life, so different from ours.

"What can I say," Sheila would shrug, "I gotta' good schtick here!" She'd laugh and schlep another tray of fresh cherry blintzes from the kitchen.

Then we'd proceed to order our regular corned beef on rye with seeds and a chocolate phosphate, as Sam Silverman, the owner and Babe Nathanson's cousin, had told us what to order. The first time we ordered, we wanted "corned beef on white." Sheila threw her hand over her eyes, leaned over and whispered, "Whenever someone goes into a deli and orders corned beef on *white,* somewhere on earth, a real Jew dies!"

Then it was more coffee, sugary rugelaches, a big tip and we were off, but not without a golden loaf of sliced challah bread, slipped under Jeremiah's arms, with Sheila again whispering, "Never leave a restaurant empty-handed!"

Our conversations were hushed, almost confessional. We both felt safe, as not many would expect Cardinal Devitt to be at Sam & Hy's and my parish was farther south, so I wouldn't be up in Skokie for lunch. An invisible curtain hung beside us and only Sheila had the strength to pull it aside.

"Funny, Jeremiah, but I had to lose my mother before I could find you. Sure, she'd be on about you being a fisherman that rescued the French sailors, a hero at the time of the Black and Tans who died for old Ireland, whatever she could think of at the moment. I didn't give her a minute's peace. And even when I wasn't saying it, she could read my mind..."

"Christ, Martin, if I had ever known you were alive..."

"What would you have done? Tell the Pope on yourself?" I joked, a bit harder than warranted, for in a deep smoggy blur within myself, I wanted to smack my father straight across his sharp, handsome face for hiding from me for so long.

For all the pain I carried every day of my life, from the first moment I realized that I was different because I had no father. Oh, my longing and tears and dreams. I never tried to get professional help for my pain, as that was just not done. Besides, Sigmund Freud said "The Irish are the only race of people for whom psychoanalysis is of no use whatsoever."

Shaw wrote about the Irish, "Oh, the dreaming! The dreaming! The dreaming! The torturing, heart-scalding, never satisfying dreaming, dreaming, dreaming!" Those words described me to a T.

For as long as I could remember, I had tormented my mother for the truth. She won. Her lips were sealed as tight as a wick in wax and I hated her for keeping this secret from me. I felt I had a right to light that wick. I had a *right* to know and a *need* to know who my dirty, fuckin' father was and I alone had the right to judge if he was a saint or a sinner.

But Mam kept this right from me. And how could I really hate my dear, saintly mother who had given her life for me? Every day when I revisited this mystery, this conundrum, I went crazy all over again and the only thing that would bring me a touch of sanity was a good, stiff drink.

We both laughed as we chomped on the big, juicy corned beef sandwiches and slurped down our rich, bubbly chocolate phosphates. It was nice to be together, out of our priestly roles and with priestly clothes, with people who didn't know us, with strange food, our own personal, guilty pleasure.

As we took turns going to the men's room, Sheila would bring more hot coffee, trying to figure out who we were, with a hunger different from any of her other customers, so hungry that we could never get enough of each other.

Not much slipped by Sheila, but she was stumped. We used only cash, never a check or credit card. We looked and acted so much alike, yet we couldn't be brothers or cousins - it was closer than that, but without the static of a father and son, yet the age difference fit that.

The day came when I asked my father about my grandparents, Philip and Mary Devitt. He put down his corned beef, closed his eyes and held his head in his hands. "I knew this day would come...Christ, God Almighty! Lord, help me!"

I was determined not to rescue him. I had a right to the truth. My mother, "God rest her soul," had kept the truth from me for nearly 25 years and I could wait no longer. I had to hear this from my father, however it made me feel.

"I was not a good son, Martin. I was a bad son, a foolish bastard that broke their hearts, and them not deserving a bit of it. It would have been better had I not even been born, for I rode the devil's back into places I had no right to be."

I looked Jeremiah Devitt dead in the eye. There'd be no more sliding away from the truth. He shed his new American accent and continued, "I had it in me head that I was better than all the folks in West Clare, something like the Golden Calf that felt it should be honored on bended knee."

"In reality, I was the three-legged black ass that should have been hurled over the cliff. God Almighty, if the Pope had ever known the blackness in my heart, I wouldn't be here, Martin. I wouldn't be here..."

"Jeremiah...What were they like? Tell me something about them."

The Cardinal choked on his corned beef. He took a deep breath, wiped his eyes and began. "First of all Martin, the Devitts

189

were not your grandparents – I was a sitting duck for all their wealth and power or as they say, *'The doorstep of a great house is slippery'*. Dear, old Peter and Molly Murphy were my real parents. They ran the house-hold at Graymour Manor for the Devitts. I was Jeremiah Murphy for 20 years.

I closed my eyes. One lie on top of another. Devitts and Murphys and Sweeneys – who did that make me? I felt like a mongrel. What would happen if I ever got to the bottom of all their fiction? I plain do not understand the need for all the lies. I do not understand their lies.

"Your grandmother, Molly, sometimes thought I was a changeling - that her own dear son had been swapped for an evil fairy child. Peter, my father, your grandfather, longed for a son who was more like himself, a solid man of the earth, of the tides of the sea, of the winds that beat at his back as he'd muck the Devitt's stables."

As he wiped his eyes with his large, white monogrammed handkerchief, he told me of turning his back on the lowly Murphys and cozying up to the Devitts, until they all fell in love with him and wanted to adopt him.

He continued in a whisper, "Lord Philip Devitt had a powerful brother, Bishop Ronan Devitt, who would 'be kissin' the arse off the pope' just to get ahead. And I would 'kiss the arse off Bishop Ronan," just to be like him. Philip Devitt was too meek for me; Bishop Ronan Devitt was a man of pride and action and I wanted to be like him."

"But what about your real parents, Molly and Peter?"I begged to know. They were my real grandparents and this was the first time that I had heard that they even existed. Who were they? Who was he? My heart was breaking in two.

"Your Aunt Lizzie could fill you in about my mother Molly – Kate Sweeney loved her and the two of them would sit in the big kitchen, having a nice spot of tea and a few Boland's biscuits. My Da Peter Murphy and Tom Sweeney, your old uncle, were cut from the same cloth and they loved the horses more than people. They both could whisper to a stompin' black horse and he'd eat out of your hand."

Jeremiah shook his head and put his hand up to stop himself. "A fire...they had a fire and died together in the fire. I didn't even know...I was in Rome. They loved me. And how they would have loved you, Martin." Jeremiah began to cough and choke. He couldn't continue. I felt numb.

Lizzie had already told me something of the Devitts' death in the air crash on the way to his ordination in Rome. All three of them – Lady Mary, Lord Philip and Bishop Ronan. I couldn't understand how they all fitted in, but I knew if I kept asking questions, it would all assemble itself in good time.

The Murphys died together in a fire and all the Devitts died together in a mountain crash. Kate Sweeney dead at 39, leaving us all to ourselves. Does Jeremiah carry a black karma that can only be avenged by death? *There'll be many a dry eye at his funeral,* so the saying goes. And will I be the next to go?

Sheila turned from the counter to her "boys in the corner," as she called us two Irishmen. She could hear his quiet moans and gasps for air. I did nothing but wait until my father got control of himself. Jeremiah still hadn't told me enough about his parents. I couldn't console him.

"Lad, I can't talk anymore just now...God, how I hate myself when I think of it all. I need to make a good confession of all of this. You know, your uncle Tom Sweeney and some of the girls could give you a better picture of Peter and Molly.

"Jeremiah, you know I'm a priest. I could hear your confession." I smiled at him.

"Right, Fr. Martin Sweeney, sure don't I know you're a priest!"

The Cardinal looked for Sheila to bring him another phosphate. "Make it extra sweet," she told the soda jerk. "That one's really *farblunget* today," Sheila said as she cocked her head toward Jeremiah.

When she came back to the table, she commented, "Don't your wives feed you? I never seen such hungry men as you two! What your wives do all day?" We laughed, both of our faces turning red, both of us thinking of our absent wives who never feed us.

191

As Sheila cleared our dishes and brought us rugelach and more coffee, Jeremiah looked out the window. Both of us were quiet. I poured cream into my coffee. Jeremiah got up to go to the men's for the second time. When he returned, he bit his lip. I left her a nice tip and Jeremiah paid.

CHAPTER 30
The Bubbeleh at the Deli

Jeremiah and I were feeling at home at Sam & Hy's. We were more like 'orphan-men' with Sheila's care and feeding. She seemed to balance us out, like all of our pale clerical energy took on color with her earthy scarlet, blues and blacks.

There was also something about Sheila that demanded honesty. I felt that every bone in her body was true and when I looked her in the eye, I knew that she would brook no lies. I had no idea what her life was like, but I did know that she took her life seriously and she was a survivor. Of what, I knew not.

Over and over, I had asked Jeremiah about all the bizarre stuff that was going on in the rectories and with the priests going off to Maryland and St. Louis for treatment. Then back on the job and off to another parish, until they got sent back for treatment and then to another place.

Every single time I brought this up, he would give me a blank stare. He knew absolutely nothing about all these goings-on, and if I had anything to report, I should call the Priests Advisory Board. He would even put me on it, if that would make me any happier.

I wanted to smack him. Make me happier? What about the kids? Then in my mind, I saw young Harry Smith, bouncing on Harry Hogan's lap. Young Harry up in Door County and the younger priests in their bright red and blue Speedos, the tighter the better.

I knew he was sitting on all of this. He was the top guy in the church and I'm sure that nothing got by him. But the energy had changed, as Sheila, a woman honest to the tip of her red polished toes was watching over us like an angel from God, and in her presence, lies, dissembling and obfuscations had no place.

On one of our Wednesdays, just as we had started in on our corned beef sandwiches, Jeremiah looked up with yellow mustard on the tip of his nose, "I need to ask you something, Martin. A little delicate, but it is the stuff I must deal with. The chickens come home to roost, I guess."

193

"Shoot, Jeremiah."

"Although I have always denied this, Martin, information on the priests who step out of order comes down to the Chancery. I've been hearing more and more about priests with kids. Boys...boys of all ages. Some girls, too. It makes me so sick I could throw up."

"I dunno, Jeremiah. Whadda' mean, whadda' ya' mean, Jeremiah?"

"Christ, Martin! What do you think I mean? These guys are fooling around with kids! Taking them up to the rectory or off to cottages or boats or what the hell else, I don't know! They're fuckin' around with kids, that's all! You know stuff about this and you have been trying to tell me."

"Jeremiah, you mean me?"

"Christ, Martin! Of course not! I'd ask you directly!"

I bit the side of my mouth, thinking that maybe he'd heard about the nun. The young nun I might be falling in love with, God help me. Her face came into my mind and I banished her as quickly as she had appeared. She avoided me and I avoided her, but we'd bump into each other in the sacristy or the gym. The feelings between us were like bolts of blue lightening as all our sexual energy had been bottled up for years. Did the Cardinal somehow know?

"Martin? Where did you go? I know you hear of these things with the priests? This is what you have been trying to tell me for the past five years. I have to make decisions about what to do with them. But we don't even know if it's true."

"Who's telling you these things?"

"It's coming from their parents, from the pastors, from some doctors and social workers. I heard about this with the Irish Christian Brothers at home or some of the priests with their dirty hands down the front of some young lad's pants. Right before saying Mass. You'd tell me if you'd heard, Martin?"

"Well, Jeremiah, it depends on how I heard it."

"I know, I know, don't go getting sacramental on me. I know the rules better than you do, Lad. Not to be pulling rank, but I do know. Do any of the priests go to confession to you?"

I smiled at my father, knowing that even this question was somewhat out-of-bounds, for I would never be able to tell him. Best not to ask.

We fumbled around between ourselves for enough change for a nice tip for Sheila. She placed our bill on the table, leaned over, her deep cleavage on display, and said in a lowered tone, "You guys tell the wives to feed you, for God's sake. Nothin' worse than a hungry husband to send him on the prowl!"

Sheila winked at my father as she took her hand off the bill. Heat rose to his face. "Sure, I'm not dead yet," Jeremiah Devitt chuckled to himself as he cleared his throat to batten down the rising tide within.

I walked my father to his car, a 1971 powder blue Cadillac with automatic shift. As Jeremiah opened the car door, we hugged each other and, a bit embarrassed, quickly pulled away and the Cardinal slid into his seat. "I ought to assign you to be my driver, Martin. You'd be a hell of a lot better than meself, trying to find me way home on these dangerous streets."

I closed my father's door and watched him shoot out onto Dempster, narrowly missing a bus pulling away from the curb. The bus driver honked and gave the Cardinal the finger. Jeremiah Devitt waved at him as he tore down into Evanston, the bus left far behind.

I walked slowly toward my car, Stephen's old white Chevy Nova with dents in every fender. These deli meetings with my father were both wonderful but unsettling. I wonder what he really knows about this business with kids being molested.

We all know about some priests getting changed every few years after they come back from treatment for sex problems. What does Jeremiah Devitt really know about all this? He seems to be so innocent. Why is he asking me?

I really didn't know how I felt about my father. How could he have not known that I existed? Did he think he could just walk into my life and all would be forgiven? What was there to forgive? Part of me hates his guts. He makes me sick – just plopping down into my life as if he had just been away on a little trip. But if I get mad at him, he'll just disappear again.

I remembered the feel of my father's hands on my head to make me a priest. But now we have to keep all of this a secret. My dirty little secret – my father is the Cardinal and he ordained me and he never even knew I existed and I've been looking for him all my life. Now I found him and I can't tell anyone. My secret is making me sick. Is this what killed Mammie?

I hated my father for putting me in this straight-jacket. If word of this got out, the scandal would be tremendous. I love my father for finally turning up and for being in my life. My terrible search to find him is finally over, but now I'm left with nothing but turmoil. Would my life be better now if he had never turned up?

This guy, my own flesh and blood father, feels too slippery, like a greased eel. Too smooth. Too polished. And dear Steve Flaherty, my step-father, who's been here for me for 20 years. Through thick and thin and teaching me what it means to be family. What is means to be a man, let alone a priest.

The skies clouded up quickly. Sheila went to the large picture-window and blew on the dry and dusty leaves of the palm plant on the window-sill. She looked into the parking lot and saw me looking up to the darkening sky and she wondered if my wife knew I was meeting this older man every week.

What was the nature of our relationship? For a woman who was made privy to everyone else's life, this was a mystery indeed. It kept her on edge and if anything, Sheila was a woman with a finely honed edge. She'd find a way to figure us out.

She reached into her pocket and drew out the $50 bill we left for her. It would go right into her *bootle* for Joel, her Down's Syndrome son. She wouldn't even tell Sammy Silverman about us guys. She'd keep her mouth closed. Besides being better tippers than most, we were never a bother and were awfully handsome, to boot.

As I stood by my car and watched the traffic on Dempster, I thought about Harry Hogan and that strange day at the table at the Deer Path Inn with his young cousin, Harry Smith, sitting in his lap. When Paddy Dunphy sobered me up and brought me back to the table, Harry quickly sent the little guy back to his parents.

And of all the times that Harry was going on one of the Hogans' grand cruises, courtesy of the mother, Mimmie, and the father, Pippie, Harry Hogan would share a room with young Harry Smith. "An outside state-room for both my Harrys," as Cecilia "Mimmie" Hogan put it, despite the fact that neither Judge "Pippie" Hogan nor Msgr. Robert Quinn, Cecilia's brother, particularly liked the idea, but they would never say *why*. The less said, the better.

The Hogans owned property right on the bay in Egg Harbor, Door County, Wisconsin, a favorite vacation spot for Chicago and Milwaukee families. Apart from the Judge and Mrs. Hogan's large home, there were four separate large cottages so that the Hogan boys' families could have one with room for extra friends and relatives.

The Judge and Mrs. Hogan saw themselves as the Kennedys of the Midwest, robust, wealthy, fun-loving Irish Americans. The rest of us could only envy them. Part of that scene, I did envy, but the other part gave me the creeps.

Most of the priests of Harry Hogan's ordination class of 1964 loved to spend their summer vacations up in Door County at "Mimmie and Pippie's pad," as Harry referred to it. Harry would ask me and Garrett Lyons to come earlier than the rest, just to have some time to ourselves.

Young cousin Harry Smith and some other young boys, 12 or 14 years old, always seemed to be lurking around, even after the rest had gone home. Last summer, when Garrett Lyons and I arrived at the time Harry had asked us to come, dozens of young boys and a few of the newly ordained priests, friends of Harry, were milling about the place, smiling and some were drunk. Some wore only a towel or low tight Speedos.

I was uncomfortable and wanted to leave. Garrett told me to "cool it," as Harry was "just being Harry" and the other guys would be up in a few hours and they had the whole week to themselves.

I frequently wondered how I had gotten myself caught up in this relationship with Harry, but then I'd chide myself for judging Harry so harshly. "Harry is as Harry does," Garrett would say, meditatively puffing his pipe. Then we'd both shake our heads and change the subject. Usually about innocent gossip that was going around.

     I had never come clean with Garrett about who Cardinal Devitt was to me. Garrett was smart and I'm pretty sure that he has us figured out. I should have told him at the time of my ordination, but I wasn't at that point yet, so I let it slide and now it was too late. In one way, it gave him the upper-hand between us and I had the role of the *secret-keeper*.

     They say in Ireland, *A secret is a weapon and a friend.* The fact that I had not brought my secret out in the open to Garrett served as some sort of a blunt weapon that hung over our heads. Not like the sharp Sword of Damocles, but for me a pressure to be constantly alert not to refer to the Cardinal as "Da".

CHAPTER 31
The Silver Apples of the Moon, the Golden Apples of the Sun

I absolutely love being a priest. I fit into the daily life of a priest like a hand in a glove. I love celebrating Mass, administering the Sacraments, visiting the sick and burying the dead. I was an instrument of God's love and mercy and in my daily meditation, my heart filled with gratitude that I was so happy with my calling and was chosen to serve the People of God.

I loved playing baseball and basketball with the kids on the school playground. I was so lucky to know what I wanted to be since I was a kid in Ireland and that dream never left, but only became more real with the passing years. Some of the guys were growing discontented, but my soul was finally at rest.

We continued our lunches at Sam and Hy's. My ambivalence toward my father was unrelenting: feelings of love and hate mixing together like fire and water - wild hot fire and rushing icy water. When I was together with him, I was always mindful of a revenging karma that he had heaped upon himself, the karma that required punishment for his sins. My little sister Clare was teaching me about *karma*, wanting me to be a priest who was "with it'.

A change was happening between us, like a balmy zephyr from the west disturbing the balance of power. At first it was so subtle that I didn't notice, but then I could feel his quiet yielding of outside layers of himself, almost a sharing of the burden of what it meant to be Jeremiah Devitt. He had always worn a coat of armor and it was growing heavy with the years.

Although years beyond what was stylish, Sheila continued to wear her bee-hive, snap her gum, and know when to approach our table and when to wait. After all the years of her waiting on us, we never spoke to her with any intimacy, never addressed her by name, nor, like most men, did we flirt with her. Now my lower left molar, my *faicail,* the old Delaney curse that made it throb in the presence of a lie, is hurting. I'm lying. We did learn to flirt with her. She taught us.

Sheila never let her schtick drop. She knew well enough how I enjoyed the cinnamon raisin rugelach, always slipping me an extra piece just to put some meat on me. Just like Mrs. Armstrong.

Late in December, Jeremiah and I met at the deli. A different woman waited on us. We both looked around for Sheila, but we hesitated to ask for her. An older waitress surmised our discomfort and said, "If you guys are lookin' for Sheila, she's not here."

We were visibly alarmed. Neither of us realized how much we had come to crave her caring winks and warm touches and outrageous banter. We inquired as to her whereabouts and she said Sheila was in the hospital with her arthritis. We both looked dumbfounded – she belonged here.

"What? You guys comin' in here all these years and didn't notice her ankles like watermelons? She could hardly walk sometimes and carryin' these heavy trays almost killed her. She won't be comin' back and I don't know what she's gonna' do with that retarded kid and all. That bastard of a husband has never lifted a finger to help! Wadda' ya' guys want for lunch?"

We ordered our regular lunch, but found it hard to eat. Of all the food Sheila had served and of all the coffee she had poured over the years, we had never once inquired about her. Our main concern was for our own anonymity, our own agendas, our own lives. Our priestly narcissism precluded her.

Through all of our distant fascination with her, could it be that she had become but one of many women – mothers, nuns, housekeepers - paid to take care of our needs? We remained helpless boys, not grown men. We noticed her cleavage, not her swollen ankles.

We ate in silence, ashamed of ourselves for whom we had become. I thought of the nun that I had once loved when we were just kids in our early 20's, I was just a very young priest and she was an even younger nun, back at St. Joseph's, my first parish on the far South Side.

When for the last time we ran into each other on the playground, she looked me right in the eye and said, "I can't take this crap anymore." I really didn't know if she meant our bizarre relationship or the convent.

She left in June when school was out. She walked out of her classroom with her brown habit on, dumped her books in the trash and jumped into her father's green station-wagon and went home. She got in touch with me and we went out for dinner a few times.

Our relationship evolved quickly into a heated, physical involvement. We never fully consummated it —we just flirted around the margins. I think I really wanted to have sex and told her that I would marry her if she got pregnant; she slapped me in the face and told me to go to hell.

What a coward I was, shifting the responsibility for my priesthood onto her. She was right. How I needed to maintain my innocence at all costs! I'm sure that turned her off – who wants a chicken for a husband? I'm glad she was so clear because I needed to stay in the priesthood and my vagueness obliquely saved it.

The waitress brought our chocolate phosphates, waterier than Sheila would have allowed. We sipped our thin drinks and picked at the corned beef. The waitress hovered over us and wanted to know if anything was wrong with the food.

I picked up my paper napkin and wiped off my bright yellow mustard mustache. A wave of the old ambivalence toward my father washed over me again. I wish he would have taken charge.

Jeremiah reached into his breast pocket, drew out his pen and a small pad of paper and asked for Sheila's name and the hospital she was in. She wrote: Sheila Levy, Ravenswood Hospital, Lawrence and Broadway. She squinted her black eyes in a "don't you dare hurt Sheila" look.

Sheila Levy was the Queen Bee and Mother Superior of Sam and Hy's Deli. Her absence was palpable. The coffee was weak, the fries were cold, the rugulach skimpy. If the truth be told, both of us felt like out-casts, like the sign for unwanted animals: "Orphans of the Storm."

The following day he told me that on his way back to the Chancery, he stopped at the bank, withdrew cash, stuffed it in an envelope and made his way down Sheridan Road to Ravenswood Hospital. With his cap drawn down over his eyes, he inquired as to Mrs. Levy's room. He went in.

Sheila was asleep. Her ankles were raised on pillows. Jeremiah left this note with the money he had withdrawn:

> *Dear Sheila,*
> *We were sorry to have missed you today at*
> *Sam & Hy. Please accept this for all the good*
> *food and great service you have given us. We*
> *hope you get well. We pray for your health.*
>
> *The Monks in the Corner Booth*

Our secret was finally out. Every dimension of my life involves secrecy and in that dark, moldy place within my soul, the truth could hardly breathe. A little shaft of light finally pierced that dark, moldy place.

Following my father's example, I withdrew cash from my skimpy account and brought it down to Ravenswood Hospital. I went up to Sheila's room and as I popped my head in, I saw a bald, fat sweaty guy standing next to her bed, arms folded, feet tapping.

As I took one look at the situation, I excused myself and made for the nurses' station. The nurse looked up from her paperwork, wanting to know if she could help me. Something about her looked familiar, but I dismissed it. I handed her the envelope and asked if she would give it to Sheila Levy after her guest left.

The nurse, tipping her head toward Sheila Levy's room, rolled her eyes and stuck the envelope in a drawer by her knees. Her name, *Patsy McGrath, R.N.*, was clipped to the front of her starched, white uniform, so I stared at her round breast. Her sharply chiseled features were softened by her soft, strawberry-blond hair, twisted in a French braid.

Nurse McGrath said, "I know who you are. I took care of your mother when you were ordained. I always wondered what happened to you. Your father was so sweet to her, so caring. I never saw a man like him. Was it Flatley? Fleming? Flaherty? Yes, of course, Lt. Flaherty."

I stood and stared at the nurse. I had taken no notice of her at the time. She was with my mother when she died, in the house throughout the night when I gave her the Last Rites. She was right there on the altar when I was ordained. I hadn't paid any attention to

202

the woman who was making my mother safe and comfortable as she drew her last breath.

"Father, are you all right? I didn't mean to bring up anything that was still so painful to you. I'll see that Mrs. Levy gets this envelope. Do you want your name on it, Father? Father Sweeney, are you alright?"

I shook my head and stared at the nurse. It was always just about me and what was best for poor me. What I wanted and what I didn't want. What I needed and what I didn't need.

Poor Martin didn't have a father. Poor Martin, his mother died so young. Poor, poor Martin. That was what Mary Pat Casey, the young nun, was trying to tell me, but I didn't have the heart to hear her.

I had become turned in upon myself, while Tim Armstrong, now with five kids, was turned out. Brendan was turned out from himself, as he worked hard for Maggie and their six kids. The women I knew, even the old Delaney girls, were turned out. The nurse knew who I was, but I couldn't be bothered with her. She was just someone to provide service to me.

I turned quickly and headed for the old elevator. I pushed the down button and stopped. I went back to the nurse's desk. Her head was down, charting the conditions of her patients.

"Pardon me. I don't think that I ever really thanked you for taking care of my mother. I should have thanked you. I'm sorry."

"Oh, now, Father. With all that you had on your mind...we just never expected you to take any notice of us. We were just doing our duty. Your father, the lieutenant, was very generous and wrote a note to our supervisor. We were honored to be there at that sad time for your family."

"I should have thanked you myself. I'm sorry. I hope you can accept it...ten years later." I noticed she was not wearing a wedding ring.

"I don't mean to be rude, Miss McGrath, but I don't see a ring on your ringer. Are you married?"

"Ah, sure I was, Father. Didn't he get himself killed one night, chasing the drug fiends over the fences on the West Side?

Tommy was a right, good soul and a good police officer, one of the very best, don't you know, but he took chances he shouldn't have. We were only married less than a year and I without a child. I just thank God I had my nursing and friends."

"You never remarried, did you, Miss McGrath? You're still single?"

Patsy looked at me with the typical mix of candid Irish and blackguardin' Irish. I knew that Patsy knew that I was getting the message. "Sure, I've no time for the dating and all those games. My Tommy was the love of my life and always will be. I've my nursing and the church and my friends. Sure I'm busier than a one-armed paper-hanger!"

"Miss McGrath, can I have the Lieutenant give you a call?"

Patsy McGrath looked around and saw that all her patients were quiet, the neurologist was busy with his notes and the custodian was mopping the floor. She tore off a small piece of paper and scribbled down her phone number.

CHAPTER 32
The Bold Fenian Man

Tonight was the monthly poker party at the Armstrong's. We were a motley crew – some were priests, some had been seminarians but left before ordination, some were priests that had left and gotten married, some were ex-priests with either a girl-friend or a boy-friend. It didn't matter.

The bonds of friendship that were laid down when we were just boys were solid. Where we stood on the church, what our marital or social relations, who we knew or didn't know, money or family connections all paled in the light of our bonds of friendship, so fluid, so open when we were just kids.

Tim was my oldest friend in the world. It hurt me so when Tim left the seminary and I would frequently feel envious of Tim's wife and family, of his home and private law practice.

And when Tim was overwhelmed with responsibilities and his wife and daughters 'PMS'ing, sons acting out and clients lying, he'd be envious of my solitude and freedom to read and pray and just be myself, not someone's father or neighbor or partner.

When Tim's mother died, I had the Mass down at St. Liam's. I had almost as much trouble getting through it as I did with my own mother's funeral, my First Mass. Mrs. Armstrong always took me seriously, which gave me great confidence. She saw something in me that she liked and she let me know it.

Back in 5th grade when Tim brought me home after school, Mrs. Armstrong would sit us down at the kitchen table and give me twice what she gave Tim, "I've got to fatten up this lad. He looks like a refugee from the Second World War." And she'd plop an extra dollop of whipping cream on my Jello or applesauce and spread the butter thicker on my bread than Tim's.

When our motley crew got together, talk inevitably turned to the church, the Pope and the Cardinal. Whenever the Cardinal was mentioned, Tim would look surreptitiously at me and I would stare back at him with a look that could have stopped a herd of buffalo.

There was some gossip about priests in the south, New Orleans, and what they were doing to children, mostly boys. There were huge lawsuits and the dioceses had to pay out "a pretty penny." There were a few guys a year or two ahead of us who were going away to St. Louis or New Mexico for treatment for unspecified sexual issues.

There were several priests who got changed every 12 or 18 months, but the regular time anyone would spend at a parish would be about five to seven years. This was bothersome. No jokes were made about them, but neither were there any explanations. We just thought they couldn't get along with their pastor or were restless or something.

We were feeling the first, slight tremors of the quake that was to soon shake the church to its foundation. In a few years we would look back and wonder how naïve we were. *There is none so blind as he who will not see.* Like those on the *Titanic* who knew that even God could not sink their mighty ship.

Garrett Lyons, our classmate, had an older sister who was a nun. Her name was Sr. Felix and we all called her "Happy" or just plain, "Hap". She had known me from our early seminary years, so we were comfortable with each other that we could talk in a short-hand that was fun for both of us. She was small and round, like a mini canon-ball, making people nervous that she would "go off" when you least expected it. This helped Hap to stay in control of a school of 2,200 kids and 26 nuns.

When I was an assistant at St. Rose's, she was the superior and principal. I'd go over to the school to see if I could help out and she would talk to me about what was going on around her. Right before Halloween, I went over and she was sitting at her desk with her lips quivering. Her ruddy cheeks were colorless.

"Martin, I just have to tell this to someone. The pastor comes over twice a week and pulls the Furst boy, Thomas, out of class, 7th grade, and the kid comes back an hour later looking like hell...I know he is up to something...not the kid, the priest. I can't exactly question the kid. I'm not sure what to do – if there is *anything* I can do. You

206

don't question Msgr. Arthur Crofton as you will find out soon enough!"

I shrugged my shoulders. I wasn't sure I knew what she was talking about, but I knew damn well what she was talking about. I couldn't lie to Hap, but neither could I collude with her against the pastor. I shrugged again.

Sr. Felix continued, "And it's always when your house-keeper, Mrs. Lopez, is out of the house. Tuesday mornings and Friday afternoons. What in the name of God is he doing to that poor child? I don't know what to do!!"

She stared at me. I looked out the window. "Martin Sweeney, what shall we do?"

"We?"

"Yes, Fr. Sweeney, you are in this as deep as I am, now that I've told you. Are you completely oblivious to what is going on in your own home?"

"Home?"

"Where you damn well live, Martin, the *priests' house* and don't be playing word games with me. Thomas Furst's safety, both physical and spiritual, is on the line. You live there. I don't!"

I told the little nun that I would keep an eye out for anything that seemed off, especially if I saw Thomas Furst over there. She knew damn well that I would never confront the pastor. I was not a man of clarity, preferring the vague state so I didn't have to make a statement, put myself on the line, so I could just coast along. Hap could sense this about me and I shamed myself.

I turned to walk to the 5th grade class-room. Sr. Felix called after me, "Martin, I'm going to tell you something and I never want you to forget. Someday you will have to deal with this, maybe not right at this time, but I feel deeply that you will have to deal with this abuse of a child on a very personal level. There will be no escaping for you, Martin. You'll have to deal!"

For the first time in a long time, I thought of Graham Byrne and the document *Crimen Sollicitionis* ordering silence for every and all sins of this nature. *See no evil, hear no evil, speak no evil.* That's what

Rome had decided. Msgr. Crofton was a treasure and Thomas Furst was expendable.

Vague was no longer working for me. It had kept me safe, so far. I wouldn't have to speak up, to take a side, to stand on my own two feet. When the pressure started to build, I could always hide behind the church. No longer – and I knew Hap's prophesy was going to be fulfilled.

****

Harry Hogan wasn't turning up at our monthly meetings as frequently as he used to. He told me that nobody ever liked him anyway, so what did it matter? When members of the group gathered to play golf at the Hogan's Windmore Country Club, Harry insisted on a ride there, so he could sort out those who were really his friends. Being chauffeured around had become a habit for Harry.

Since I had to pass St. Dymphna's Rectory on the way to the club, it usually fell to me to chauffeur Harry, despite the fact that Harry had a brand-new silver Beemer and I drove my father's old Chevy. St. Dymphna was the patron saint of the mentally ill.

It was noon in early April. Harry had asked me to pick him up at 12:30, as we had a 1:20 tee time. "And don't be late, Martin, like you usually are!"

With my clubs rattling in the trunk, I drove up to the rectory at 12:20 and waited for Harry. Another car, a large champagne colored woody station-wagon with a young mother and two younger children, was also parked and waiting. I waved to the little kids in the back and nodded to the mother.

The time was 12:35 and still no Harry. I got out of my car, tucked my cream-colored golf-shirt into my black pants, let myself in the side-door of the rectory which was always opened and stood in the hall outside of Harry's room. I heard loud music and muffled screams.

Thinking that there was a robbery in progress and Harry was being accosted, I kicked in the door. Harry's black pants and shorts were in a heap on the floor. He was on his hands and knees on the bed, his big, pink arse bouncing up and down over a naked child.

The young boy was crying and sobbing, "You're hurtin' me, Father, you're hurtin' me, Father, please don't do this, Father."

I saw stars! I pulled Harry off the boy and hurled him against the closet door, the buttons on Harry's yellow shirt flying in the air. Harry was stark naked, sweating and hysterically laughing and shouting to the kid to come back, he wasn't finished.

I shouted to the boy to get his clothes on and get out of there fast. I slammed Harry's head against the wall repeatedly and shoved my knee into Harry's crotch. I threw Harry on the floor, kicked him in the groin and walked away. Then I went back and spit on him. The bed was wet with blood, tears and semen. Harry Hogan's lust.

I ran out of the room and out of St. Dymphna's. I threw up in the bushes, my face beet-red and my clothes a mess. My knuckles were raw. I tucked in my shirt, straightened my pants, and headed for my car. I looked around for the boy. He was in the station-wagon with his mother's arms around him. The little kids had stopped playing and were looking with great concern at their big brother.

The mother looked out her window at me. I wanted to talk to her, but I was shaking so, I just got in my car, slammed the door and shot the hell out of the parking lot. I needed a drink.

The subtle rumble was subtle no more; I felt it loud and clear. The firm foundation of Holy Mother Church that I had built my life upon was cracking open and I was falling in. My safe world was no longer safe, but full of danger and death. I could no longer retreat into my vagueness as I had already tumbled into the abyss. I needed to see clearly.

CHAPTER 33
Guilty until Proven Innocent

I had spent the last few days shaken to my core. What had happened to that little boy? What about his parents? *'Father, don't hurt me, please, Father, let me go!'* was ringing in my ears like a bizarre monastic chant that grew higher and higher, faster and faster.

I had murder in my heart and I wanted to shoot Harry Hogan right off the face of the earth. If he had done this to our twins, Liam or Clare, I'd choke him with my bare hands.

I could tell no one: my need to protect the kid, my loyalty to the priesthood, Sr. Felix's prophesy that I could no longer bob and weave, Jeremiah Devitt's feigning ignorance of what bad priests were up to, my long-time relationship with Harry and the Hogans – this all had me in a bind. The Irish hate informers, squealers.

If I were to call my step-father, he'd have eight squad cars, sirens blaring, up to St. Dymphna's within 20 minutes. Sr. Felix would tell me to do the right thing. Graham Byrne would puff on his pipe and tell me that I was a priest and in my heart, the Holy Spirit was guiding everything. Fr. Archibald had had a stroke and couldn't talk. Graham Lyons would laugh, wondering why I would have expected less than this from Harry Hogan, priest or not.

We priests get to say Mass and administer the Sacraments, regardless of the condition of our souls. *Ex opera operato* is the term used to describe this right – that a sinful priest could administer the Sacraments and the Sacraments would still be valid.

So there was Harry Hogan and thousands of other priests who were molesting kids – it simply does not interfere with the actual function of their ministry. And the Bishops don't really care about the poor kids- they just need someone up there to say Mass, administer the sacraments and collect the money. And if a priest is putting the church in potential legal danger with his bad behavior, there were places he could go for treatment, doctors to sign off on his recovery, and other parishes that would take him, without question. The bishop's hands remained clean.

More importantly, they were doing what they promised to do when they became bishops – to protect the church at all costs. The bishops are not "aiding and abetting", because this is all a matter of the internal working of the church. And the state has to keep its nose out of our business, so says the First Amendment.

So I don't have to be holy and I can actually be quite sinful. I have been ordained and that is the end of it. The condition of my soul has nothing to do with the validity of the Sacrament. If I commit sins, I go to confession just like any other Catholic, say that I am sorry and make a firm purpose of amendment; my sin is forgiven, removed from the pallet of my soul.

And if I abuse kids, I, an ordained priest, commit a sin, not a crime. Over the long course of 2,000 years, historically from early days, up through medieval times and right up to today, the courts have no jurisdiction over a criminal priest. Priests do not commit crimes; they commit sins.

Church documents, as recently as our 1962 *Crimen Sollictionis* , papal encyclicals, church councils and proceedings, church courts and Canon Law all direct the mechanical, inner workings of the church. And so far, it has all worked as elegantly as a fine, platinum Cartier watch, moving time forward, silently on firm, steady masculine hands.

Other churches and religions expect their ministers to be good and holy. The term _ex opera operandi_ means that the personal sanctity of the minister is the key to the validity of the Sacraments. Basing the validity of the Sacraments on the personal holiness of the priest was rejected in the 5th Century by the Roman Catholic Church as the Donastist Heresy. It cleared the way for us to be purely Sacramental functionaries, priestly robots. And it was a comfort to the laity that the Sacraments were valid, despite the state of the priest.

The phone rang at Our Lady of Hope Rectory. The pastor, Msgr. Schmitz, and the housekeeper were gone for the day. I had eaten the cold dinner she had left for me in the refrigerator and was watching the news alone. Nancy Reagan was turning cart-wheels every time she laid her eyes on her Ronnie. The phone rang again.

"Our Lady of Hope, Fr. Sweeney here."

"Martin…I need to go to confession."

"Why are you calling me?"

"I want to go to you. You can't refuse me, Martin." He was right. The only time I could refuse to hear a confession is if I had actively participated in the sin, such as committing a robbery with someone or holding a person being murdered.

"I'm closing up the church at 8:00. I'll be in my box at 7:45."

"Can't I just come to the rectory? I hate going into the church. Someone might recognize me."

"I'll be in my box at 7:45."

I put on my cassock and went into the sacristy for a stole. I kissed the stole, put it around my neck and walked quickly to my confessional. I sat down, flipped the switch, lighting the red bulb over my name above the door. How different it was to be a Catholic priest than a Protestant minister. Those guys were judged on the quality of their sermons and their sermons were an extension of who they were.

Within a very few minutes, the penitent lowered his full weight onto the small wooden kneeler on the other side of the curtain. I thought of Harry, kneeling on his bed, over the small screaming boy. I slowly parted the dark red velvet curtain.

"Bless me, Father, for I have sinned. It has been nine years since my last confession. I have sexually abused boys. I have used my powers as a priest to worm my way into their families. I have said Mass and administered the Sacraments while continuing to abuse them."

I breathed heavily. I thought of the small, naked boy under naked Harry, *"Please, Father, this hurts, let me go, Father!'* Who was speaking for him? Who was he?

I closed my eyes so I would not look at him. He was using me, putting me in a bind to keep my mouth closed. The Holy Seal of Confession was one of the most serious, sacred vows we make. My lips were locked. "Do you have a firm purpose of amendment? Are you going to continue abusing boys? Are you going to get help for this problem?"

"I firmly resolve never to do this again. I will speak to the Cardinal this week about getting help for my problem." Harry was lying to me through his teeth. My own tooth rocked, as it registered his lies. I could not tell him I knew he was lying and deny him the Sacrament.

I leaned toward the penitent and told him to make a good Act of Contrition and as he did so, I lowered my head, made the sign of the cross, and said in Latin, "*I absolve you in the name of the Father, and of the Son and of the Holy Spirit, Amen. For your penance say the Rosary. Go in peace and God bless you.*" I banged the sliding screen closed and waited for the penitent to leave.

Harry didn't leave. He knocked on the screen. I opened it.

"Martin, you know last Monday... I forgot to move my clock up. I thought it was only 11:30. 'Spring ahead, Fall back', you know. I forgot to *Spring ahead*. I thought I had another hour until the mother came for him. Until you came. Just thought you'd like to know. If my clock had been right...and I know that some of these kids really enjoyed it..."

I slammed the screen shut and waited for the penitent to leave. When he left, I snapped off the light, returned the stole to the sacristy, locked up the church and went back to the rectory. I went up to my bathroom and vomited again.

Then I pulled the bottle of Jameson's Irish whiskey out from under my bed and drank right from the bottle until I passed out.

Mary DeMarco took her ten-year-old son, Ryan, to their pediatrician. He had been bleeding from the rectum and his small anus had been torn to shreds. He would not stop crying and hadn't slept in 24 hours. He would not tell his mother what had happened, except that he had "sat on something big."

Dr. Stern took one look at Ryan's bottom and told Mary that her son had been raped. He would have to report it. The child was also suffering from *traumatic aphasia*. This was a result of the rape. Ryan was no longer able to speak, ask questions or answer them. He could look at pictures and point to what was asked. Dr. Stern told his nurse that "the kid is a dishrag". Ryan's mother heard the remark.

Ryan's father, Buddy, had died of pancreatic cancer two years previously. Fr. Hogan had become friendly with Mary and had become almost a surrogate father to her three children – Ryan, Sarah

213

and Kylie. Mary loved to put in a pot roast with carrots and onions when Fr. Hogan was coming to dinner. He would take all three to get ice-cream cones but paid special attention to her only son who needed so much more attention from a man.

Ryan, a young altar-boy, was having trouble with his responses at Mass, so every week Ryan was getting special training from Fr. Hogan. While waiting for Ryan outside of St. Dymphna's Rectory, Mary had noticed a strange man waiting in another car. He had gotten out of the car at 12:35 and had gone right into the side door of the priests' house. He was driving an old white Chevy Nova with Illinois license number 93-428.

Mary's father had been a Chicago detective and had told her to always get the license number if she suspected anything wrong. Mary had compulsively memorized numbers on cars while waiting for a light, in a parking lot, in a line to pick up the kids at school.

In her fantasies, she would imagine that she would help solve a horrible crime by providing the license number of the get-away car or of someone with a dead body in his trunk. Anything to help her to focus on her children and away from the unbearable grief of Buddy De Marco's death at only 36 years old.

She had watched a big man run out of the rectory and vomit in the bushes. His face was red and his yellow shirt was hanging out of his pants. He had black hair, heavy eye-brows and a sharp chin. He looked a lot like Fr. Hogan, but it wasn't him. He jumped in his car and drove off in a hurry.

Mary didn't know what to do. She was frantic. She had sent Ryan into Fr. Hogan for tutoring to be an altar boy and he came out sobbing, bleeding and holding his bottom. As soon as she left the doctor's office, Mary called her brother Mike Brennan who was with the Cook Co. State's Attorney office.

Mary told him about young Ryan's condition and that she had gotten the license number of the man who came running out of the rectory right after Ryan. She had already taken Ryan to Dr. Stern. Her son had been raped…inside a priest's house…No, she hadn't talked to Fr. Hogan.

She was sure Fr. Hogan did not know anything about it. Fr. Hogan was such a good and kind man and she didn't want to upset him about this. It must have been that other man and only God knows where he came from.

Mike Brennan had the number traced. The title of the car was under the name of "Martin Sweeney" who lived at 16814 Kenyon Rd., Our Lady of Hope Rectory. He quickly brought to his supervisor the preliminary evidence of his nephew's medical condition, his sister's statement of observation of the man running from the rectory and the license number, traced to a Martin Sweeney. A warrant for my arrest was issued.

CHAPTER 34
The Sacred Seal of Confession

All the papers were alerted. Photographers and television cameras were ready when the red, white and blue Chicago Police Department squad car, emblazoned with the motto, "We Serve and Protect," pulled up to Our Lady of Hope rectory.

Within minutes, they brought me out in my black suit, my hands cuffed behind my back. I was read my Miranda rights and hustled to a squad car. A fat, young officer threw me into the backseat and smiled at the rolling cameras. I couldn't get my bearings and rolled around the back seat, bumping my head on the windows and doors. The siren wailed as the squad car sped onto the Kennedy expressway and down to 26th and California – Cook County Jail.

I was thrown into a jail cell with other men, arrested for drugs, drunkenness, domestic violence, robbery, car-jacking, stabbings. Their acrid stench and violent sounds assaulted me on every side. Like the old garbage trucks swinging back and forth on our narrow street, orange peels and egg shells and dirty diapers flying into the air.

I was immediately the center of attention. They spit at me and shouted blasphemous words about the church and the Pope and queer priests, dirty faggots just like me who would get taken care of by the brothers once I was inside.

To be spit upon is the ultimate sign of pure contempt. I was getting what was due Harry and there was absolutely nothing I could do but to take it. I wonder how many times Jesus was spit upon on His way to Calvary. There was no Veronica to wipe my face, so their hot tobacco juice and sticky phlegm ran down my cheeks.

I thought of the many times I had said the Stations of the Cross and had contemplated the suffering of Jesus. Kneeling on a clean, marble-floor in a church, sitting in a soft leather chair in my room, at retreats with 50 or 80 other priests and thinking of my golf clubs. Little did I know.

Lieutenant Commander Stephen Flaherty was enraged at my treatment. Since he was in the 7th District, he was unaware of my arrest until after I had been brought to the jail. The desk sergeant had knocked on the Commander's door and told him that a priest, Fr. Martin Sweeney, had just been arrested. Stephen shouted for his driver and flew down to 26th and California, sirens blaring.

I was there to await the Bond Hearing before a judge to determine my flight risk and, if none, to release me on my own recognizance. I was allowed one phone call to my attorney.

Brendan Sweeney and Tim Armstrong were there within the hour. They showed up just as Commandeer Flaherty's car pulled up. The Bond Hearing was held and I was released on own recognizance, an I-Bond. I guess they figured I wasn't going to run away.

Stephen put his arms around me. "Come home, now, Son. Come on home." He directed his driver to Our Lady of Hope on Kenyon. No siren was needed.

****

Shaken, I returned to the rectory. My pastor, Msgr. Schmitz, stormed around his office. He told me to pack my shit and get the hell out. He never wanted to lay eyes on me again. He wished that I had never come to Our Lady of Hope in the first place and if I had abused any of his parishioners, he would kill me. Right then and there. I had to get my filthy self the hell out of there, leave the keys and never put a foot onto his property again.

The housekeeper hid in her room and sobbed as she rocked herself in the soft chair that I had bought for her. She was a close friend of Kitty Delaney and of all the Delaney sisters and had been to my ordination and my poor mother's funeral. She knew there was something wrong, but since the police had arrested me, they must be right.

She found nine empty bottles of Jameson's Irish whiskey and one bottle half-empty under my bed when she cleaned my room. She said nothing to Msgr. Schmitz.

******

My uncle, Brendan Sweeney, a senior partner in the law firm, turned the preparation for my defense over to Tim Armstrong, a junior partner who had joined Brendan's firm right out of law school.

217

Brendan couldn't stand watching me being pulled through this meat-grinder and he would be the senior counsel if the case went to trial.

He sat with his wife Maggie and cried that I was being subjected to such humiliation. "I hate to say this, Maggie, but I'm glad that poor Kate is gone and doesn't have to watch Martin get beat up for something he never would have done."

I know that Maggie and Brendan tried to shield their six kids from what was happening to their cousin, but my face was all over the television and newspapers. Their name was "Sweeney" and they had even bragged about their uncle the priest. The neighbors and classmates taunted the Sweeney kids and Maggie told them they had to hold their heads high, that we were all flesh-and-blood and we always stick together.

Cardinal Devitt was enraged. He called Our Lady of Hope for Martin. Msgr. Schmitz told the Cardinal that he had no idea where I was, but that he had kicked "that dirty bastard" as far as he could see him. I had brought nothing but shame to the whole parish and it would have been better if "he had kept his sorry ass back in Ireland, where he belonged with the pigs and the shit and the fairies!"

The Cardinal got in touch with Commander Flaherty and Stephen told him that I was back home on Castlewood. I was working with Brendan and Tim Armstrong on my defense, but I wasn't of much help to them. Stephen had to station a police unit outside of our home, as a rock had come through the windows at the Delaneys and "bags of dog stuff" were thrown on our lawn.

After talking with Steve, Jeremiah called me and told me that Sheila was back at work and that he'd meet me at Sam and Hy's at noon. Sheila would take care of us. I was surprised that she was able to go back to work.

******

At the cloister up in Wisconsin, Aunt Nellie, called Sr. Mary Bridget, was told that I was no longer needed to say Mass for the nuns. The superior had found a replacement. As the nuns did not know what was going on in the world, much less in Chicago, Nellie was ignorant of the charges being flung at me.

Nellie was directed simply to tell me that I had been replaced when I came for Mass the following week. The Superior, Mother Rosarita, had a sister, Betty Jane, who lived within blocks of the convent and would bring the Tribune or Newsweek to her, as the nuns did not subscribe to media of any kind.

My picture was all over the front pages of the Chicago papers. Betty Jane circled me in red and slipped the paper through the old milk-shoot at the side door of the convent. When Mother Rosarita read about me, she informed Sr. Mary Bridget of the change without telling her why. Nellie had been trained not to ask, not to even think of questioning the superior's decision.

When I showed up to say Mass, Nellie whispered to me through the grill that I had been replaced. She told me that she was coming through the door that enclosed the nuns from the public and that she wanted me to take her out of there. She pushed the heavy door open and walked through it like someone climbing out of her coffin, knocking over the grave-stone on her way to a new life.

I put my arm around her little back and hustled her out of the cloister, through the sacristy, down the back steps and out into the world. Nellie threw her head back and breathed.

I hadn't seen my aunt's face in many years. Despite the heat, Nellie was wrapped in a heavy black shawl that covered her dark brown habit. On her little white feet she wore large, brown, men's sandals. Her little toes were curled under like cashew nuts. Her face was pale and lined and her blind eye seemed to be turned more inward than I remembered.

I told Nellie of the charges against me and that I had been kicked out of the rectory by Msgr. Schmitz. Brendan and Tim Armstrong were defending me and that I was back home on Castlewood with Steve. That was why the superior didn't want me to say Mass.

"Just get me out of here, Martin. I can't believe what she did, after all these years of you coming up here to say Mass for us on your days off and the funerals and the holy days and everything. I can't stay here if they are going to treat you that way."

219

How much easier it was for Nellie to take a stand on behalf of me, yet she was defenseless to protect herself. She knew that she really didn't fit in with all the German nuns and how they would make their sneaky gestures about her one eye and her Irish cooking. One time she overheard some nun referring to her as a "one-eyed Mick". Nellie couldn't take a stand for herself, but she had no trouble taking a stand for me. She would do anything for me and I knew that.

Nellie started to cry and I held her close. She hadn't felt another body next to hers in over 30 years. I know she smelled liquor on my breath, despite my mints, but she ignored it. What did she know? Who was she? Where did she want to go?

"Just bring me home, Love. I want to see the Delaney girls. I miss everyone so much, so much. It's been so long since…dear Mayme and Norah and Josie and Kitty. And my own rough sister Lizzie who blinded me in the cabbage patch back home in Quilty…"

"Nellie, Norah and Josie are gone. They've been gone for a long time. Kitty's not well and Mayme tries to take care of her. Stephen's still on Castlewood, but the twins are gone and married. Brendan's married with six kids out in Oak Park."

Nellie held her face in her hands. She couldn't believe how the world and how her family had changed. I held her tighter. Nellie buried her head in my chest and cried her heart out. She told me that she wanted to go back to Castlewood and that she would be with Kitty and Mayme and take care of them.

She had taken care of the old German nuns before they died and she'd like to do that now, "for my own flesh and blood as long as I still have a breath in my body. *Go sa'bha'la Dias inn*, Oh, God help us all, Martin, Love!"

******

Before my appointment with Tim, I had lunch with the Cardinal at Sam and Hy's. Sheila met us with a smile and escorted us to our booth like a mother hen shooing her chicks into their coop. Same lunch of corned beef on rye with seeds and a chocolate phosphate. I kept my sun-glasses on, even though the day was dark.

Jeremiah told me that there was plenty of money for my defense, that the Archdiocese would pay the lawyers and court costs.

220

I'd stay on salary, plus a little more if I needed it. I could not say Mass in public, as it might lead to a scandal. I wanted to ask him what the hell I was involved with anyhow but held my peace.

As we were getting ready to leave, Sheila bent over and whispered into my ear, "Fuck 'em all!! Just fuck 'em!" I reached for her hand and squeezed it. As they left, Jeremiah slipped $100 under the edge of the paper place-mat.

My father never once asked me if I were guilty as charged. I pondered as I drove down to LaSalle Street to meet Tim that no one had asked me if I did what I was accused of. The cops, Msgr.Schmitz, the German superior, and the papers all presumed I was guilty, but no one near me even asked.

I was escorted into Tim's office. His secretary brought us coffee. Tim closed the door and motioned for me to sit at the small conference table next to him.

"Just for the record, my dear friend, I need to ask you if you touched Ryan DeMarco. Just for the record, Martin."

"No, Tim, I did not. And I never touched a kid or anybody. I did not touch Ryan DeMarco."

"Do you know who did?"

"I did not touch Ryan DeMarco."

"You know, Buddy, I'm in a hell of a position here. I know you did nothing and I know damn well who did this to the kid. How the hell am I going to defend you if I have no evidence? Juries don't give a damn what the defense feels happens. We are in the realm of gathering evidence, Marty. Cold hard evidence and I need help!

There was a firm knock on the door. Babe came into Tim's office. I hadn't seen her in a while and she was aging. Babe must have been well into her 60's, yet her hair was still mostly black, with white around her temple. She was wearing heavy Navaho turquoise and silver clip-on earrings and a heavy silver necklace. No make-up.

I'd hear her knees crunch and her breathing deepen. She grabbed a few biscuits and kissed me on top of my head. As her knees couldn't bend, Babe tilted straight-back into the deep leather cream colored chair with a large plop.

"Who just farted?" shouted. Babe and she looked around.

221

"Please, Auntie Babe, stop that! This is a law office," Julie Nathanson, just out of law school, yelled across the room.

"Julie, Sweetheart, whose law office is this?

"Please, Auntie Babe, try to behave yourself…just for once!"

"And by the way, while I have all you guys here, I have to report that one of my spies over at Mercy Hospital, told me that Dr. Richard Hogan, fondly called "Dick" by his friends, and admitted his nephew, under a false name, for bruised and lacerated genitals. He had to wear a catheter for a week. I guess he ran into a post outside the church or something like that. Who knows?"

None of us said a word; Tim got up and poured more coffee.

Babe looked at Tim and she looked at me. "Strange, guys, here we are at Nathanson and Nathanson, dealing with all you Catholics and your sacraments and secrets. Lizzie has been trying to educate me for all these years, but so much I just don't get. Remember, Martin, taking you into St. Patrick's Cathedral in New York? And you got lost? And Auntie Babe rescued you?"

I smiled at Babe. She has been such a part of our entire family for years and years. I'd never doubt her for a second. Today she was our Apache mother, settling us with her powerful energy.

"Look, Martin, we all know what the real story is and that schmuch should be in your place right now. He always gave me the creeps and I avoid his father's court-room like the plague. I'd never ask you to go against your teachings, Marty, you mentsh, but there must be some wiggle-room, so we can defend you."

"Babe, dear Auntie Babe, I can say nothing. If it means swinging from a hang-man's noose, so be it. I understand the position you're in – ech mir…"

Tim could keep quiet no longer. "Hmmmm….it seems that I remember crusty old Fr. White, the brilliant Jebbie who taught us Sacramental Theology. The HOLY SEAL OF CONFESSION …NOTHING, NO WHERE, NO TIME, NO PLACE, NADA, NOTHING, UNDER NO CIRCUMSTANCES WHATSOEVER, ABSOLUTELY NOTHING can allow you to break the Holy Seal of Confession. And if you are not prepared to take on this awesome

222

responsibility, then walk right out of here now. NADA, NADA, NADA."

I looked out the window. "Yes, I remember Fr. White. I remember him."

Tim continued, "And St. John Nupomucene who was drowned by King Wenceslaus in the river because he would not reveal the Queen's confession. And there have been priests who have had their tongues cut out and their heads smashed on rocks rather than break the HOLY SEAL OF CONFESSION."

Behind her round dark glasses, Babe's eyes widened. "You guys putting me on? Tim? Martin?

We both nodded and stared at the floor. I look out the window. "Yes, I remember."

"Goddamn it, Martin, how the hell can we defend you? "

I continued to stare down LaSalle Street.

"Look, Martin, I know who did this to the kid. And you know that I know...What if I brought in Brendan? Would you at least send us in the right direction so that we can mount a decent defense of you? Otherwise, you're going to swim with the sharks!"

"Tim, I did nothing to the boy or to any other child. I am innocent of the charges against me. I did nothing."

"I know that, Old Buddy! I have no doubts absolutely. I just need some help from you! I'm frustrated as hell. Babe and Lou and Brendan and all of us. This is serious stuff, Martin. You could go to prison and you know what the Brothers do to child rapists! I don't want that to happen to you, for God's sake!"

CHAPTER 35
All Shall Be Well

There was nothing in my life that prepared me for this humiliation. All the hours upon hours that I had prayed for surrender and for the grace simply to do God's Will with every breath I drew – is this what I had set myself up for?

I couldn't say Mass, hear confessions, play with kids on the playground, attend parish meetings, bring the Eucharist to the sick, and anoint the dying. I couldn't even wear my Roman collar. Blue button-downs and khaki pants, brown loafers, sweat pants and sweat shirts and gym shoes. I was 'a priest without a church'.

I was living at home in the little loft on the third floor. The two old Delaneys and Nellie were still on the first floor, Steve and Patsy were on the second floor, as the twins were now in college. At loose ends, I called Sr. Mary Felix, dear Happy Lyons, Garrett's sister. She said that she had been waiting to hear from me and to come over for lunch.

So many of these old convents looked alike - sterile, virginal, impersonal. The nuns got changed from one school to another so often, it didn't matter who they really were as women, just bodies to fit into teaching slots: first grade, second grade, third grade, etc.

Mary Pat Casey, who had slapped me in the face when I told her I'd marry her if she got pregnant, told me that when all the provincials got together at the end of the school year to change assignments, they called it *Horse Trading*. "I'll give you two seventh-grade teachers for two first-grade teachers…"

The nuns had all gone back to school after their lunch-break, so we had the convent to ourselves. We went into their dull yellow kitchen and Sr. Felix fixed me a ham and cheese sandwich, potato chips and lemonade. She got herself a cup of coffee and we headed to the refectory and sat at the end of the long gray Formica table.

"Martin, I've spoken to my brother as soon as this happened. Garrett told me who did this to that boy and that all the priests in your class knew immediately. The only reason that I can think of for you not defending yourself is that your lips have been sealed through the confessional."

I took a big bite of my sandwich and swallowed hard. The phone rang and she told me to ignore it. I was not even free to tell Happy that she was right - the confessional seal was the issue for my silence.

It was making me crazy: part of me felt proud to be such an orthodox, strong priest with my lips sealed; the other part made me feel weak and passive with all my silence, like I was too stupid to realize that my life was on the line.

"You must know that I'm so sorry that it has to be you that takes the fall, but as we learned in the Novitiate, "*God is not mocked!*'. Despite Vatican II and all the wonderful changes we are experiencing, the volcano is rumbling with all the horrible things that priests are doing to kids, both girls and boys. It is going to erupt, sooner than later, and these flames of lava will destroy everything in its path.

"Martin, this is just the beginning, and as sorry as I am that you are the target, I'm almost glad it is you. Actually, Martin, there is none better than you to crack this open. All our papal and clerical secrets are making us sick, or as they say, "*We're as sick as the secrets we keep*".

"Hap, I just don't know if I can do it..."

"Nonsense, Martin! You're the best of the best and the truth 'will all come out in the wash'. You're tough in the fiber, you come from good, Irish peasant stock and you're not going to be blown over by this. You are being a good, faithful priest, Martin, and radical changes are on the horizon."

"The humiliation of not being able to be a priest and having to live with my father, like a bad boy expelled from school..."

"I know this is all so ugly, Martin. I'm glad that your dear mother is not around to see what you are going through. This would kill her!"

We both broke out in rather undignified laughter. Happy refilled her coffee and brought us a plate of chocolate-chip cookies. We were silent, letting all the emotional debris settle a bit.

Sr. Felix began again, "Now I'm new here at St. Dominic's parish with all these 22 nuns and five priests over in the rectory. That new young guy, David Somers, he will never make eye-contact with me. He surrounds himself with the 6th and 7th grade girls. Every time I turn around, he has his arms around the girls' shoulders and they're bumping into him, all in the name of good, clean fun."

"Martin, I went to the pastor and he just laughed, 'Well at least the guy isn't a faggot, Sister Felix. We're getting plenty of them, and Fr. Somers is over at the school and not sitting around here waiting for an assignment.' "

Part of me felt shocked. So many of these guys thought they were flying below the radar, like Harry Hogan, going after kids who could be silenced so easily. What were they doing to the very heart of the church? I could hear the volcano reverberating as clearly as Happy could, as Sr. Felix in her position.

What was the church doing to her priests? How much of this could be blamed on the demand for our celibacy? For us to deny the vital force of life roaring in our veins? They asked for our balls right at the door, and if we refused to hand them over, that was the end for us, both gay and straight. The greater irony is that it was as impossible to cut off our balls as it was to rip out our hearts. It's who we are and always will be.

Sr. Felix handed me a little holy card. Nuns loved holy cards. It was a prayer from the English mystic, Julian of Norwich:
"All shall be well, and all shall be well and all manner of
things shall be well."

"I've got to get back over to the school, Martin. Trust the Good Lord and I know that your good name will be cleared in a way that none of would expect. I believe so in the power of prayer, Martin, and miracles happen when we least expect. God bless you, dear Fr. Martin Sweeney. Don't forget: *All shall be well..."*

******

Evidence against me was presented to the Grand Jury by the State's attorney David Kincaid. These 18 people, having deliberated in secret, delivered an Indictment of Probable Cause against me for having sexually raped a minor, Ryan DeMarco. This was a class X

Felony, punishable by a minimum 30 years in prison, possibly 60 years.

My case was assigned by the Chief Justice of the Cook County Circuit Court to Judge Marie Kopec, a young judge about the age of Ryan's mother. The charge against me of having sexually abused a child was read aloud.

The document was presented to my attorney, Timothy J. Armstrong. At this time, a plea of 'not guilty' was entered in open court. Everyone avoided looking at me. I hated that expression: no good deed ever goes unpunished. I am not inclined toward cynicism, but today it fits.

Back up in the office, Tim and I again sat at the conference table. This was the time of Discovery, of garnering evidence for the case. Tim was frustrated in his attempts to defend me, as I was unwilling to provide any evidence which would exonerate myself. Tim's secretary was plying us with pots of coffee and plates of sugar cookies.

"Martin, Old Buddy, I've got to hit the head. Too much coffee."

"I'm coming with you."

We stood at the urinals, peeing together as we had done so many times in the past. Tim, not wanting to look at me, modestly stared at the ceiling. Suddenly, Tim gasped and pointed at my penis.

"Oh, my God, Martin! You've never been circumcised! Oh, my God!! This is our case. The kid pointed out circumcised penises! Oh, my God!!"

When we returned to the office, Tim again explained to me that the state had to prove me guilty, "beyond a reasonable doubt." They now possibly had a classic defense of "Mistaken Identity" and that the abuser most probably was Harry Hogan, in whose rectory the abuse occurred. Harry, like most American boys, most certainly had been circumcised. I was uncircumcised – I was born in Ireland where they did not cut off the baby boy's foreskin.

As Tim thought of Harry Hogan, he looked at my smooth hands and nicely clipped nails. Harry Hogan bit his nails to the quick and he frequently had them covered. If the penis distinction failed,

Tim always had the nails. Ryan said that the guy that hurt him had no nails.

Harry and I had been taken for each other since our first day at Quigley some 30 years ago. We were both big men with dark hair, dark eyes, a cleft chin and long strides. At Mundelein, we were frequently referred to as "the twins", although I thought I was by far the better looking. At times a slight sneer played out across Harry's face that scared me and set us apart.

The evidence had been stacked against me with the child, Ryan DeMarco, and his mother both identifying me as the abuser with the black pants and yellow shirt. The mother had my license number and saw the condition I was in when I ran out of the rectory.

Both Ryan and his mother identified my face from a police mug book. There was some confusion as to the "yellow shirt," as I did not own a yellow shirt. I hate yellow. I wore cream-colored shirts.

Tim subpoenaed Rita Clifford, the housekeeper at St. Dymphna's, for "probable cause" to see if she had ever laundered a yellow shirt for Fr. Hogan. She stated that Fr. Hogan had many yellow shirts that she washed and ironed every week. He had no cream shirt, as Mrs. DeMarco identified the priest leaving the rectory as wearing a "creamy light shirt".

I liked cream-colored golf shirts and had a number in my closet. They go better with black pants…cream and black, just like a glass of Guinness. Some would even say 'black and tans'. Yellow and black were the color of bees and hornets, just like Harry Hogan, ready to sting.

Tim advised me that he was going to subpoena Harry Hogan to be seen by Dr. Silverman, a urologist, to determine if he had been circumcised or not and if there were any other unusual characteristics on his genitalia. Harry was the only other male in the rectory at the time of Ryan's rape.

I would have to go through this process as well. He would likewise request that photos be taken of our genitals and presented to Ryan for identification. Was his abuser circumcised or not? If not, I would be found non-guilty. I couldn't see how dropping my pants would be breaking the Seal of Confession.

Ryan DeMarco was able to distinguish his circumcised abuser from me, by the cut of our male organs. He identified his abuser as having been circumcised. He had never seen "a guy like that," referring to a picture of my foreskin being intact on my genitalia.

Tim filed a motion to dismiss the charges against me. State's Attorney Kincaid agreed and sought an arrest warrant for Fr. Harry Hogan. Judge Marie Kopec dismissed my case. Lt. Steve Flaherty hugged me hard, slapped me on the back and tears ran down his face.

Tim felt victorious, wanting to call together the old gang to celebrate my acquittal. I asked him not to, as the victory was bittersweet. I knew that Harry would feel that I had broken the SEAL OF CONFESSION and flashes of Fr. White's "Nada, Nada, Nada" rang in my ears.

Sr. Felix was the first one I called. She picked up the phone in her office at St. Dominic's and all I could say to her was *"All shall be well, and all shall be well and all manner of things shall be well"!!*

She gasped for air and I could hear her holding back her tears. "Good work, Martin, great work and God bless you, dear priest, dear, dear Martin!"

CHAPTER 36
Soul Retrieval

It was the last Saturday in September and the stars were in perfect alignment. The *Dungarven Grill* was emblazoned in gold above the Irish pub on Addison. The crowd from Wrigley Field had thinned out and the chant of "Just wait until next year" had grown dim. The tables were filled with police and firemen and their families, some lonely souls drank alone at the bar.

Stephen Flaherty held the heavy, oaken door for Patsy. As the owner, Pat Murray, spotted Steve, he led him to a small booth in a hushed part of the pub. Some of the police officers stood as the lieutenant and his date made their way through the crowd. Steve nodded and waved and motioned for them not to rise.

Pat took their coats and snapped his fingers for the waiter to attend to them. He sent over a bottle of chilled white Bordeaux for the couple and a plate of steamy onion rings and potato skins. As officers past their booth, they would hesitate, not knowing if they should speak or leave the lieutenant alone.

"Well, Lieutenant, I see you're quite the celebrity," Patsy began to break the ice.

"Ah, we all have authority issues, don't we?" Steve mused.

Steve began to thank Patsy for what she and the other nurse had done for their family when Kate was dying. Patsy graciously accepted the compliment and grew quiet as she swiveled her wine and picked on a long, cheesy potato skin.

"I've never told anyone about this, Steve... but I feel that I've never quite been the same since I was in your house on Castlewood nursing your wife. Something happened to me in that house that I can't explain and that was over ten years ago."
Steve sat silently, looking alternately from his white wine to Patsy's wild blue eyes. He knew how to be quiet when someone was struggling with words.

"Go on, Patsy. I'm listening, I'm listening."

"I don't know if I left something there or took something that wasn't mine."

Steve raised his eye-brows. Was Patsy a thief? He looked up to the Bears, so as not to reveal his thoughts and raised his wine to his lips, Father Flaherty at Mass.

"Don't think that of me, Stephen. If you're going to be that way, I'll not tell you another thing. You know I'm not a thief and if I can't share these feelings with you, then I'm away."

"Forgive me, Patsy. I guess it's just one of the hazards of the job. You didn't deserve that and I'm sorry. Pick up where we left off now…"

"I don't know about all this reincarnation stuff. But back in Ireland they'd say, 'Sure that one's been here before.' And someone else had 'an old soul' and there'd be some of the old folks that knew of things to come, like old Biddy Early back in Clare 100 years ago who said that big machines would fly in the sky like birds on the wing."

"Steve began rubbing his jaw. "Patsy, do you think that you would ever like to come back over and have a look around? I'd be more than happy to have you come over."

Patsy gulped her drink a little harder than she wished she had. "Oh, dear God, I don't know what we'll be getting in for! I have something inside me that I can't name. Sometimes it even drives me out of my mind. I can't sleep sometimes, and I feel if I could only figure this out, I'd be at peace."

Steve laughed, and Patsy reddened at what she had said.

"Ah, sure me and my big mouth!"

"If you are free after the 10:00 Mass at St. Liam's…that's when I usher…we could get a bite to eat and then come over. I'm sure the Delaneys below will be in good form."

As they finished their dinner, Stephen asked the waiter for his check. Pat Murray came back to the table and told them that their dinner was 'on the house.'

"Pat Murray, if you don't give me the bill, I'll never put my foot back in here. And neither will Patsy McGrath, if I have anything to do with it. Gimme the damn bill, Pat, if you know what's good for you!"

"Right! Right, Lieutenant! But would you kindly accept the wine?"

"What wine, Pat?"

As Stephen pulled up to Patsy's apartment on Briar, the lights were dim. He reached over and kissed her. She reached for the back of his neck and pulled him closer. They both began to breathe faster, faster than they had breathed in years. In an instant, they pulled apart.

Steve went around, opened Patsy's door and walked her to the door. He bent down and kissed her on top of her wild buttercup hair. "See you after Mass, Patsy. Bring your old soul and we'll get to the bottom of it all."

******

It was the Seventeenth Sunday after Pentecost, October 2, the Feast of the Holy Angels. Msgr. Quinn tore through St. Matthew's Gospel: "Master, which is the greatest …thou shalt love the Lord thy God with…What you think of Christ…And no man was able to answer…"

Msgr. Quinn had box seats to the Bears – Green Bay Game which started at 1:00, so the sermon was short. After the sermon, Steve and the other ushers took up the collection. He stretched the long-handled basket to Patsy and she reached in her purse for a dollar. As she was ready to toss in her dollar, he pulled the basket away from her then returned it in front of her. She tried again and he lifted the basket above her head.

Patsy started laughing and couldn't stop. People were looking at her. She bounced with hilarity on the hard, wooden pew, making it squeak, and then she laughed even harder. Knowing she had to get out, Patsy excused herself as she disturbed those praying.

An usher opened the heavy oak door and Patsy rushed out, feigning illness. She rested her head against the cold Doric pillar and tried to get herself together. "Patsy, get a grip! Get a grip, Girl!" she scolded, knowing that she would soon be flying out of herself, never to return. She was scared.

Steve poked his head around the column, sporting a sanctimonious look of holiness, of having been scandalized. He extended his hand to Patsy. She took his hand and held it for a moment too long. Whatever that was about, neither of them knew for sure.

After a somewhat awkward breakfast at the *Steak n' Egger* on Broadway, Steve brought her back to Castlewood. Mayme Delaney pull aside the fine lace curtain that hung over their front window to sneak a glimpse of Steve's new girl-friend.

He only told the Delaneys enough about his life so they knew how to reach him if there was a problem, but not enough that they knew his every move, which they would have liked. Not nearly enough information to satisfy their curiosity, but they always felt safe with a Chicago Police Lieutenant right above, so they really couldn't complain.

Patsy McGrath didn't know why she was there. She stood like an orphan on the street in front of the Delaneys' apartment house. But deep in the marrow of her bones, she knew something was waiting for her inside.

Patsy was still, almost like a red sanctuary lamp, announcing that there was a presence inside her that was as mysterious as the Blessed Sacrament. She had the both sides of her – the quick and wild, and the still and deep. A quiet grace stole over her, for now she knew that she was about to cross that threshold that would change her life forever.

Patsy was thin, but in a subtle way, she was stronger than those twice her size. Adopted at birth, as her poor unmarried mother had been sent to the Madelene laundry in Cork, Patsy's face revealed a vagueness that conflicted with the clear, strong image she projected with her body. She ached to learn of her flesh-and-blood parents, of the source of the blood that flowed through her veins like the small streams that sourced the great waters of Niagara Falls.

If there was no beginning, how could there be a middle? How could there be an ending? On some primal level, Patsy knew the minute she stepped foot into that red brick apartment house on Castlewood and nursed Kate Sweeney Flaherty in her last days on earth that the keys to unlocking the mystery of who she really was and how she had come to be were within that house.

They climbed the narrow stairs to the second floor. Steve opened the door, stood back for her to enter the small hall-way and then showed Patsy around his tidy apartment. It was a typical Chicago configuration with the living and dining rooms in the front overlooking the street, the kitchen in the back with a small attached deck, three bedrooms and a large bath between them. It had hardly been changed since Kate's death, ten years before.

Patsy shook her head. She was disappointed that it didn't seem quite right. Steve put on the kettle for some tea. There was a rap on the kitchen door. Steve knew that it was Kitty, sent up by Josie to see who this woman was. Kitty was the official spy, pretending to be on some "errand of mercy", what Steve referred to as an "errand of curiosity."

Steve opened the door. Kitty stepped gingerly into the kitchen and handed him a jar of tomatoes to open, as the top was on too tight. She took one look at Patsy McGrath and bolted down the back stairs, shrieking, "A ghost! Sweet Jesus, a ghost!! I've seen a ghost!"

Hearing the screams, Josie opened their kitchen door and Kitty flew past her, shrieking, "Oh, Rosie! It's our Kate herself! It's Katie Sweeney, come back from the dead! Sure, she's alive and standin' right up there with Stephen and the other one! She's like that new one up there with Stephen!!"

Mayme and Norah came running from the back of the house and Josie turned on the kettle and Kitty jumped up and down with the fright of it all. All three of the other sisters held on to Kitty, trying to calm her and make sense out of her hysteria.

"Hush, now hush, Love. Tell us what's the matter, Pet. Please calm yourself, Kitty. Just calm yourself, Love, so we can understand," crooned Josie. Norah poured a splash of rich cream into a cup and then poured Kitty a 'nice cup of tea.'

Steve came down the back steps and knocked on the back door to see what the matter with Kitty was. As he came into the kitchen, the Delaney sisters were relieved, knowing that Stephen would sort it all out for them.

Josie placed her wrinkled hand on Kitty's thin shoulder and told her to tell Stephen why she was so upset. She stuttered and stammered that the "lady upstairs with the wild, strawberry blond hair" looked like someone they used to know, and they thought she would probably be dead by now or very old and how could she look so young.

Steve sipped at the strong tea in the thin China cup. The detective in him was trying to put together Patsy's feelings of having been there before and Kitty in her state of shock. He asked Kitty who Patsy reminded her of. Kitty slapped her hand across her face and Josie squeezed her shoulder. Norah ran to the bathroom and Mayme busied herself, scrubbing the clean sink.

"Sure, now Stephen, we're not at liberty to disclose everything," Josie disclosed.

Steve felt a surge of anger soar through his body, the way he did when they were called to a domestic violence situation and the wife would not press charges against a drunken, abusive husband.

"Josie," Steve began, "I can't help you if you hide this from me. I've known you all for years and we have been through so much together and now you want to keep this from me? I think this is a very serious situation and we all need to work together to figure out what's wrong. I can't help if I don't know what's wrong."

"Who is that woman upstairs?" asked Mayme, squeezing dry the thin, blue sponge.

"Her name is Patsy McGrath and she is a friend of mine. She was one of the nurses who took care of Kate at the end. None better, I'd say."

Nodding, the Delaney girls started to settle down and they turned to Steve and he continued. "Patsy felt sure that something had happened to her when she was here taking care of Kate and that she's never been the same ever since. I invited her to come over here after Mass to see how she felt or if she was just dreaming of something that was not the least bit true.

"Why would she need to know that, Stephen? Is it not just better to let the 'sleeping dogs lie'?" asked Norah, suddenly asserting herself, wanting to be a part of this crisis. Kitty, Josie and Mayme all stared at her, scowling, shaking their heads that she had already said too much. Norah stormed out of the kitchen and slammed the bathroom door.

"I think all of you are hiding something and I have no idea what all this is about. I have a right to know and I also know that all of you are champions at keeping secrets and hiding stuff that others need to know."

No one uttered a word. Let it not be said that the Delaneys couldn't keep a secret. Norah sneaked back into the kitchen and the four sisters joined ranks against Steve's inquiry. Four pairs of pale, blue eyes burrowed into him. He leaned against the sink and met their fixed gazes with his own pale, blue eyes.

"Well, girls, I know that 'loose lips sink ships', so I'd better get upstairs," Steve began, but was interrupted by another shriek from Kitty, "God help us! *Go sa'bha'la Dias inn!* God help us!!"

Josie slapped her hand across Kitty's lips, squeezed them tight and nodded for Steve to leave. Norah ran back to the bathroom and Mayme hung her head over the sink.

Steve returned to his apartment and apologized for his absence. Another pot of tea had been brewing, the Irish elixir to heal all wounds, solve all problems, fix all broken hearts.

Steve sat with her at his small, white wicker kitchen table. The wicker chair crunched beneath his weight and as Patsy got herself comfortable, their chairs squeaked. Patsy started to laugh - the way to cope when you don't know how to cope.

"Patsy, I don't know if I can be of much help to you," Steve began, ignoring her laughter. "I do know that they are sitting tight on some information that might concern you. We'd have to load them up with sodium pentothal to get the truth out of them."

"Sure, Steve," added Patsy, "you know there is a great Irish tradition of how hated is the informer, the one who betrays his own people."

Patsy pinched her lips. Steve looked out the window. Patsy poured more tea. "Ah, Patsy, you may have just said it, '*his own people*'. I think there is someone who belongs to them that they can't betray. I know well what happens to the traitor. God, don't I see it every day on the streets of Chicago?"

"If you don't mind my asking, Patsy, how old would you be? When is your birthday?" asked Steve, not knowing exactly why he had to know.

Patsy whispered, "I'm 39. I was born the day after Christmas, December 26, 1934. And I hate water, if you want to talk about ships. I just hate it and sometimes I must close my eyes if I'm on the Outer Drive and can see the lake flying up in front of my face. I'm 39, Steve."

Again Steve apologized that he had to get to work and that he would drive her home. As he readied himself, Patsy tidied up the kitchen and sat back down on the white, wicker chairs. For the first time in her life, Patsy felt slightly less empty, less a mistake even to have been born.

CHAPTER 37
Monday, Monday, So Good to Me

Monday morning before the sun was up, Norah stole quietly up the stairs and knocked softly on Steve's back door. He opened the door and Norah deflected her eyes to the clock, not wanting to behold a man in his night-clothes. He motioned for her to be seated and he went off to change.

Smiling in spite of herself, Norah sat at his small kitchen table looking out through the old curtains with the yellow daisies and orange butterflies that Kate made six months before she died. Steve came into the kitchen and put the kettle on.

"A penny for your thoughts, Norah, for your early morning thoughts..."

"Sure it's lovely being up before everyone else, isn't it, Stephen?"

"This will be between just the two of us, Norah. You must have something up your sleeve, now don't you?"

Norah fingered the old curtains, touching where her dear niece, Kate, had so lovingly held when she made the curtains for her little family. Now dear Kate was gone from us for ten long years.

She closed her eyes and began to tell Stephen of the old bonesetter in Killaloo, the 7th son of the 7th son, who had knowledge of the soul's migration, the journey of *loss and found* even on this earth. How the soul that was soft on its edges would lose parts of itself to someone in need or take on parts of another's suffering soul, all with the intention of goodness, to do no harm whatsoever.

But then that soft soul would suffer the loss of herself and end up carrying parts of someone else's soul, like switching an arm or leg, a throat or an eye. So the soft soul would have to give back what it had taken and retrieve what it had given.

Norah smiled at Steve. His mouth dropped open. Norah pulled back Kate's curtain and looked back out the window. She nodded her head and reached for Steve's hand. "You just bring Patsy back to me, Stephen, and all will be well, bring her to me and we'll sort this out. She'll be right as rain in no time."

238

When Steve told Patsy what Norah had revealed about the bone-setter from Killaloo, Patsy shivered. She agreed to meet Norah, but she couldn't tell any of the Delaney sisters apart. They all looked alike to her, "with their little mousey buns sitting on top of their little mousey heads."

"Be kind, Patsy, be kind to those wonderful old women. We'll never see their like again, you know. They're a rare race of women and they hold great secrets that they'll take to their graves. They keep it all to themselves, but now Norah wants to share this with you, Patsy, and you'll be making a grave error not to take her up on this."

******

It was mid-morning, the priests, servers and other Mass-goers were gone from St. Liam's. Patsy sat in the last pew, waiting for Steve to bring Norah Delaney to meet with her. Patsy felt foolish, trusting this crazy old lady to bring her a modicum of peace, anything that would stop the throbbing ache for something she knew not what.

Norah dipped her two little knobby fingers into the holy water font, blessed herself, genuflected into the pew, knelt silently in prayer, and sat back into the hard, wooden pew next to Patsy. Neither of them talked. Norah reached for her hand and held it gently.

Norah spoke ever so softly, sharing with Patsy what she had understood about the softness of her soul and how she had lost part of herself to Kate as she lay dying and how she had taken a part of Kate's soul, just to keep, perhaps for Martin or for Stephen.

Those actions had thrown Patsy out of her own equilibrium, out of her own serenity and to restore her balance, she had to return Kate's soul to her and to ask for her own soul parts to be returned from Kate. Patsy nodded in agreement. The old lady knew what she knew and none of it was a lie.

Patsy raised her brows, questioning how she would do this. How do you get your soul back from someone who is gone? How do you give back what you have taken?

Norah smiled at the young nurse. She understood the quandary she was in, but it was all so simple and Norah knew the way. "You've known all along, Patsy, where your soul has been waiting for you. Right there at our place on Castlewood. You just have to bring a little gift – a flower, a piece of bread for the birds, a medal of the Blessed Mother – you'll know."

In the dark of night, Patsy McGrath walked by herself down to 1252 Castlewood and stood under the street-light. It was well after mid-night, but Patsy was not afraid. She well understood old Norah's directions to give back what she had taken and to get back what she had given away.

Into the dirt of the parkway beside the sidewalk, Patsy buried the strange square black stone she had picked from the strand at Kilkee the morning after the storm that had thrown it up beside the Pollock holes under the cliffs. A fresh breeze came up from the lake, freeing Kate's soul from Patsy and bringing back her own lost soul.

Norah Delaney moved away from the curtains and blessed herself in thanksgiving to the old bone-setter from Killaloo and the tender mercy of Almighty God. For the gift of freedom for dear Kate Sweeney and for wholeness for dear, dear Patsy McGrath.

CHAPTER 38
"May His Great Name Grow Exulted"

Babe hung up the phone and stood looking out at the lake. Dark clouds hung low over the water, with breaks of brilliant light where the sun broke through, like a flashlight piercing the dark. She prayed, *"Baruch dayan emet,"* - Blessed is the one true Judge.

Drying a glass, Lizzie came in from the kitchen and said gently, "Who died?"

"That was Sammy Silverman. Sheila Levy, his best waitress, it's her son, Joel. The one with Down's Syndrome. He was 28, but her only kid. She was married to that *gonnif,* that bastard Lenny Levy. I got that devil sent away for 20 years…imagine that thick thug beating his wife and that poor little Joel and after all that her mother and aunt went through over in Poland during the war."

"Are we going to the *Shiva* house?"

"Of course, Lizzie! She's been good to Sammy and he's been good to her. Dear Sheila, a real *mensch,* she made that deli what it was! Sheila was the heart of that place, otherwise Sammy would have just been *schleppin'* matzo balls and kreplach up and down Devon Avenue."

"She's had a hard life – took care of her mother and her aunt, both survivors of the Holocaust. All the rest of her family is gone. Her mother and the aunt came to Skokie right after the war and they left her mother a *meshuggener,* crazy in the head as well as the aunt. And then that *schmuck* she was married to.

"Left her with that boy and no money, but that Sheila, she's a *mensch* if there ever was one! She could have been anything she wanted to be, but she didn't have the chance! *Oy vey!"*

Lizzie put on the kettle for tea and dished up some raisin kugel from the frig. She knew when to hold her tongue and to let Babe talk. Babe sat smiling to herself. Something was cooking and Lizzie knew that she would come out with it in her own time. If Babe were pressed, it would only take longer.

When the tea was steeped, Lizzie poured the first of the tea into the sink, as the ancient Celts gifted the earth with the first of their

241

fruits. As they sipped their tea, Babe went for more kugel. Lizzie poured more tea.

"And....Sammy said that Sheila wanted those priests to know about Joel, especially the older one. Jeremiah is just a priest to her...I can't believe she hasn't put 'two and two together'. She has no idea, Lizzie!"

"Sure," smiled Lizzie, "'When the sky falls, we'll all catch larks!'"

"What are you on about, now, Lizzie? What does this have to do with Joel?"

It was now Lizzie's turn to be mysterious. "Sure, it's nothing about Joel, God rest his soul! Oh, that Jeremiah Murphy or Devitt, whatever his name is. But just the same, 'The older the fiddle, the sweeter the tune, Babe'."

Babe called Jeremiah's private line. Babe prided herself as being the only one in the city of Chicago who could or would speak to him fearlessly, as he didn't really hold anything she needed or wanted. Besides, she knew that he liked her and if the truth be told, she had liked him, for all his scarlet red dresses and red beanies.

Babe told Jeremiah about Sheila's son and her wanting him to know. They were going to her house to sit *Shiva* the following evening and wouldn't mind meeting him there if he would like to go. Babe would direct him so he'd know what to do, him being a "*goy*" and all that.

******

It was an early, summer evening, with the pink and plumy sky free of clouds. Lizzie stood in front of the square, yellow brick apartment house with her Irish soda bread and fresh, whipped butter, watching for Jeremiah. He pulled the car up to the curb and got out. He was dressed in khaki slacks and a blue shirt with a Navy sport-coat. Lizzie raised her eye-brows.

"*Dia duit*, Lizzie!"

"Good day, yourself, Jeremiah Devitt or Jeremiah Murphy or whatever ye are today!"

"Now go aisey, Lizzie. Where's your girl-friend?"

"She's not my 'girl-friend,' Jeremiah. In polite society we say 'partner,' if it's all the same to you."

"I'm sorry, Lizzie… I really am. Do you know what we're supposed to do? I don't want to make a fool of myself."

"Not anymore than you already have. Here comes Babe now. Oh, she's with her cousin Shelly. She'll fill us in."

The four walked up to the second floor. On the right side of the door-jamb a small, brass *mezuzah* was glued to the wood. Shelly and Babe kissed their fingers and touched the *mezuzah,* expressing their love for God and promising to keep His commandments. Lizzie touched the *mezuzah* and then blessed herself. Jeremiah nodded.

The four walked into Sheila's small apartment. The front room was filled with those who had come to grieve with Sheila and to remember Joel. The mourners sat in their stocking-feet on milk crates or on the floor - they had been brought low by the loss of Joel.

On the window sill a tall, white candle burned to remember Joel in keeping with the words from the Book of Proverbs, "The flame of God is the soul of man." The dining room table was lavished with food and in the kitchen, women were preparing more food. Sheila would not have to cook in this time of mourning.

The mirrors were covered in black - this was not a time of personal vanity and looking at yourself in the mirror to shave or to fix your make-up. The focus was on the loss of Joel and on Sheila's grief.

On the walls of Sheila's home were framed Joel's art, dark with swirls of purple and inky blue and green, black with splashes of red. They were forbidding and intensely beautiful, yet screaming for something. Jeremiah's breath left him as he stared at Joel's soul on display. He knew that Joel had been abused.

Lizzie, remembering that it was her job to cover the mirrors with black cloth at the time of her father and mother's death, wondered how the old Irish and the Jews could be so much alike. She was also the one who stopped the clock at the exact moment they died and when their bodies were taken out of the house, she reset it.

Sure, it wasn't so much to prevent vanity that the mirrors were covered, but so that the soul of the departing one not be trapped within that second dimension, that portal to the spirit world. And if

243

you looked in the mirror after a departing soul was trapped in there, it could grab you and you would be trapped in there forever.

Babe guided Lizzie and Jeremiah to Sheila. They all held her hand and said that they were sorry for her loss. Sheila's cousin, sitting next to her, made his way to the food. She patted his empty spot for Jeremiah to sit next to her. Lizzie quietly began to fill her plate – at least she knew how to do that.

The room was filled with pictures of Joel at every age. Sheila turned to Jeremiah and spoke softly, "Did you know that Joel was a mongoloid?" Jeremiah nodded and moved closer to Sheila.

"The doctors said, right when he was born, that he couldn't learn and wouldn't live a full life. Well, they were right about the last, but my boy could draw and paint and he loved colors and would never wear a white shirt, it had to be colored. He could read, not too much, but he could read. And a heart of gold, my little Joel had, a heart of gold…my little *boychick,* my little *boychick* now with his Bubbie and with God, wherever God is!"

Jeremiah moved even closer to Sheila. Babe and Lizzie were enjoying how Sheila was so intimately turning to Jeremiah for nurturing, after all the years he had been fed by her. She and Babe stood close together. Here she was at a Jewish wake and Lizzie remembered how Babe acted at Kate's wake and funeral and how she helped her navigate the strange rites and rituals. The roles were now reversed. Gracefully.

As it was after sundown, it was time again for the men to say *Kaddish,* the ancient Jewish prayer in memory of the deceased. They were to comprise a *minyan,* a quorum of ten men, necessary for the holding of a public worship service. Only nine adult men were there. Everyone looked around nervously, hoping that a man would appear, from the bathroom, hallway, anywhere. *Kaddish* was to be said for Joel.

One, lone *yarmulke,* the thin, round skull-cap worn to show reverence, sat on the small table next to the white candle. Sheila leaned over to Jeremiah and told him that they needed another man, they had to have ten and there were only nine. Jeremiah nudged

Sheila's arm, stood and placed the *yarmulke* on his own head. Just like his own little red silk *zucchetto* that he wore for Mass.

The ten men stood together and began, "*Yitgaddal v'yitqaddash sh'men rabba…*" Sheila looked at the tall, handsome Irishman, a priest, for God's sake, praying in Hebrew as if it were his own language. He had learned Hebrew in Rome as part of his Old Testament Scripture studies. Jeremiah's eyes were closed and he recited the sacred hymn from memory, from the depth of his own heart. "*Exalted and sanctified is God's great name in the world which He has created according to His will.*"

Dr. Schwartz, one of the minyan, knew who the number ten man was. He had seen Cardinal Devitt's picture on television, in the papers hundreds of times. He smiled, knowing that everything ends up even. One hand washes the other.

The old doctor remembered long ago. He was a young cardiologist and his patient was dying, but struggling, raging, desperately crying out for a priest to come and hear his confession. He could not die without a priest and no priest came.

Wise beyond his years, he whispered into his patient's ear, "My son, I have come now. I am your priest. Let me hear your confession." And as the dying man shared his sins, Dr. Schwartz recited *Kaddish* at his bedside and when he finished, the old man had closed his eyes and was gone.

Lizzie leaned against Babe as the prayer for Joel ended. Both of their eyes were filled. Lizzie whispered, "Sure, does the Good Lord not take with one hand, but He gives with another?"

******

After the seven days of *Shiva* were over, Jeremiah called Sheila. He wanted to meet her. She was getting back to work, but Sammy said he only wanted her to work half-days for the first two weeks and he would pay her for whole days. She'd be finished after the lunch crowd left, so he could pick her up at 2:00.

Jeremiah drove to Harms Woods in Glenview, parked and walked around to open the door for Sheila. She sat and waited. As she got out of the car, Sheila looked at Jeremiah with tears in her eyes, smiled and said, "No one ever opened a car door for me. Thank you."

245

Jeremiah smiled, bent down to her and said, "I've never opened a car door for anyone. Thank you, Sheila, for giving me this opportunity." He was neither courtly nor sarcastic. He was beginning to feel safe with her and could begin to toss away all his old defenses.

Jeremiah drew his brown tweed cap down over his eyes as they began to walk the trail into the woods. Glenview was Catholic country. There was a small space between them as they began their walk, for they had never been together in a public place, beyond Sam and Hy's. Neither of them was sure what was going on and how they should act.

Jeremiah stopped Sheila as they stood under an old weeping willow. There was no one in sight. "Sheila, I'm not sure how to ask you this, but I want to know if you're alright for money. I know your life has been hard and…"

"Jeremiah! Come on!! I have my boodle! My mother left me $5,000 and it's in a bank and Sammy has paid me O.K., but it's been my customers, especially the one I'm with right now and…"

She smiled up at him. His face fell. Sheila knew immediately that she had crushed him. He readjusted his cap and tried to smile down at her. Before he knew what hit him, Sheila threw her arms around his neck and kissed him on the lips. He moved closer and kissed her ever so tenderly.

The last person he had kissed had been Archbishop Ronan Devitt. Their bizarre, confusing relationship had extended over many years. It was not a real relationship, because it was predicated upon the Archbishop's power over him, from the time Jeremiah was a child until he was ordained.

Ironically, the Archbishop and Lord and Lady Devitt were precluded from attending Jeremiah's ordination in Rome, as their plane had crashed in the Swiss Alps the week before. They had finally been able to adopt Jeremiah after his own poor old parents died in the fire in their little cottage by the Sacred Well of St. Bridget.

Jeremiah's father, Peter Murphy, had visited that shrine as soon as Jeremiah was born, paying special tribute to the pagan goddess of fertility, *Sheila na Gig*, who's statue above the entrance to

246

the Sacred Well depicted the goddess with her legs splayed open, to receive life and to give life.

Sheila na Gig shared the altar with the Blessed Mother Mary and with Bridget, patron saint of cows, the hearth, butter and sailors. Bridget was also ordained a bishop, but church authorities denied that.

Jeremiah was confused about his sexuality. Sometimes men and sometimes women looked at him and, while he enjoyed the sexual attraction, he didn't know which way to go. He was grateful for his Roman collar that fastened him to the church like a dog chained to a fence. He just didn't know.

Under the shade of the weeping willow, Jeremiah and Sheila melted into each other. And over the seas in a cave tucked into the side of the great mountain cliffs, the sacred waters splashed on the smooth black stones and *Sheila ni Gig* smiled at Bridget and Mary and together they knew that all would be well.

****

Jeremiah and Sheila grew to love each other and as their love grew, they shared who they were and who they were created to be.

From the death-trap of Archbishop Devitt's purple bedroom at Graymour Manor through the ancient vaults and libraries at the Vatican to the Episcopacy in Chicago and finally, into Sheila's bed with their twisting limbs and hot and simple and beautiful human passion, Jeremiah finally became the man he had always aspired to be.

From the smoldering embers of the death camps of Poland to the small apartment in Skokie, Illinois, Sheila's damaged mother and aunt grew older and returned to the horrors of Birkenau as if the forty years of silence in America were a pressure-cooker for all that they had seen and heard and experienced. Sheila nursed them patiently and with as much humor as they would allow. She honored them as living saints.

Sheila narrowly escaped the thick, abusive hands of her evil husband to care for her handicapped, abused and so much loved son. And from the hundreds of breakfasts and lunches and dinners she served until her back was nearly broken, and finally, into the arms of a man who had been waiting for her all his life.

For those who had eyes to see, Joel had been abused. When Jeremiah shared his thoughts with Sheila that her son might have been sexually abused, she told him that he was right. His father abused him for years. Despite his handicap, Joel had been a lovely, loving child until he was nine. As he aged, he became angry and Sheila grew to fear him.

The wise, young counselor at the Jewish Youth Center saw this anger in Joel and encouraged him to draw. She soon sensed that he was being abused. Reluctantly, he told her that his father was "hurting" him and he told him not to, but his father "just keeps it up!"

When Lenny was confronted, his physical abuse of Sheila escalated. Sometimes she couldn't go to work for the bruises and broken bones. The first time Jeremiah came to see her at Edgebrook Hospital, Lenny had lacerated her liver. If it were not for Babe Nathanson, Lenny Levy would have killed her. She got him out of their lives and locked up for the next twenty years.

Jeremiah was still a priest and he was still the Cardinal of Chicago. But more importantly, he was in love with Sheila Levy. In the depth of his conscience, he had made the decision to resign the Cardinalate and to ask for his papers releasing him from the priesthood. Many men would have taken care of the legal aspects of his relationship with the church before he began an affair, but Jeremiah had followed the rules for many, many years and finally he had decided to follow his heart.

How sweet it was for Sheila to rest in Jeremiah's arms after they had made love and to know for the first time in her life, she was truly safe. She knew he would protect her and keep her from harm, as long as there was a beat left in his heart.

Jeremiah never tried to control her. He knew better. He just had to stay out of her way and let her be herself, her glorious, salty, earthy woman self. With Joel's charcoals and paints, Jeremiah would sketch her full, voluptuous figure as if he couldn't get enough of her, despite her protesting her fat, *zahftig* self, and begging him to make her 20 pounds thinner.

"Ah, Love, why reduce yourself to nothing? Don't you know, 'Only a dog goes after a bone?' "

"Oh, you're just a sweet, old *Mensch,* aren't you, my very own love?"

Often Jeremiah thought of the French sailors clinging to the Quilty fishermen who rescued them as their ship was smashed on the rocks. He wondered if they had clung to the fishermen as tightly as he would cling to Sheila, her full breasts in his mouth and her hand around his old head and himself finally safe and loved and at home in her body, in her soul.

Although he did not know why, on the nights he would stay with her, he would drift off to sleep with his Sheila in his arms, and he would remember the sweet words to an old Irish poem and slowly say to himself,

O my Dark Rosaleen! Do not sigh, do not weep!
The priests are on the ocean green, they march along the deep.
There's wine from the royal Pope, upon the ocean green.
My Dark Rosaleen! My own Rosaleen!
Shall glad your heart, shall give you hope!
Shall give you health, and help, and hope! My Dark Rosaleen!

And all the old nightmares and ugly dreams were lifted from his sleep like a thick fog lifted by the warm rays of the sun and he learned to sleep like a baby in the arms of his own Dark Rosaleen.

Often Sheila thought of the wasted Jews who only stood and looked at the American soldiers who opened the gates of the prison camps and finally fell at their feet, no energy or faith to even begin to walk away. As she grasped Jeremiah's smooth back when he entered into her, she sailed to a place of freedom she had never known on this earth and wanted nothing else but to return to it over and over.

And Sheila would lie lightly next to her own sleeping Jeremiah and she would relish these moments absent of the old, blazing fear that racked her every night since before she was born. She would turn to Scripture and remember the loving words of King Solomon to his bride:

"Rise up, my Love, my fair one, and come away. For, lo, winter is past, the rain is over and gone. The flowers appear on the earth; the

time of the singing of birds is come, and the voice of the turtle is heard in our land."

Sheila would lean over and kiss the red lips of her lover and fall into the sweetest sleep that the hands of God could ever yield, the sleep of the angels.

CHAPTER 39
We Admit that We are Powerless over Alcohol

It was a blistering cold morning in February. The winds tore in off the Lake Michigan like the crack of a razor strap. The once lovely snow was hard and dirty. All the cars looked alike – gray and black from the salt sprayed across the icy streets for melting and better traction, but meanwhile chomping great pot-holes in the concrete.

I opened my eyes and, blinded by the brightness of the morning sun, covered my head with a pillow. I was in the same yellow single bed I had when I was a kid. My feet hung over the end of the bed and in the night I had spilled a glass of water I always took to bed with me.

My old books and games were still stacked in the closet and an old red robe from Quigley hung silently in the closet. It was after ten in the morning.

I had not yet been assigned to another parish and was still living with Steve on Castlewood. The Cardinal thought I needed more time to recuperate from the trauma of the accusation and the bad press. I would have to be assigned to a sensitive pastor and with a sophisticated community

Stephen knocked on my door sharply, waited a moment, and then came into my room. "Get up, Martin! There are some people here to see you! Get yourself presentable! And do it quick!! We haven't all day!"

My poor head was pounding like the drums of hell. My room was spinning as I crashed into the closet door. I went into the bathroom and looked at myself in the mirror. I couldn't even see myself. Stephen again pounded, "Let's go in there!! Shake a leg, Martin! We're waiting for you!"

I threw my old red robe on over the shorts I had slept in. There were no buttons on it, just a big safety-pin held the front together. I put my fist in the pocket and it shot right through. I hadn't shaved in three days and couldn't find a brush for my hair. I never owned slippers, so I put on my black loafers.

In the front room ten people, a *minyan*, waited for me. The Cardinal, Tim Armstrong, my uncle Brendan Sweeney, my aunts Nellie and Lizzie with Babe Nathanson, Garrett Lyons, Stephen, Bishop Teddy Szymanski, and a small, red-haired woman named Marguerite Gunning from Lake Forest.

Lt. Flaherty introduced Marguerite to me. She shook my trembling hand, directing me to a hard kitchen chair between Tim Armstrong and Garrett Lyons. Bishop Szymanski began, "Martin, we're gathered here this morning because we all love you. Every one of us. We have some things to say to you and I'm going to ask you not to interrupt. After we're finished, you can speak. Is that alright?"

"Ah, sure, a wink is as great as a nod to a blind horse, isn't it now?" I mumbled to no one in particular.

His voice breaking, Stephen read his letter to me. "Martin, I can't stand by and watch you drink yourself to death. Our entire place smells like a brewery. I recently discovered that my father had been drinking when he was killed in that fire before I was born. I'm not going to lose you, too!

"I hate it when I talk to you and you're slurring your words and can't remember what we've said. Every time I speak to you about your drinking, you shrug your shoulders and act like you don't know what I'm talking about, but you damn well better listen, or you're out on your ass today!"

In my disheveled condition, I could feel a chill run through the room. No one there had seen that part of mild Stephen, but they knew that he was at the end of his rope with me. He hadn't risen to be a police lieutenant if he was a push-over, but he carefully hid this side of himself from his family. Over the years Stephen and Jeremiah had spoken together about my drinking. They were both frustrated with me and with each other – who's place was it to make me stop drinking?

Finally, Stephen had revealed this "family secret" to Patsy McGrath. She had a friend, a brilliant, feisty nurse who was working in a treatment center. Jeremiah had called Marguerite to get the Intervention going and within 24 hours, the wheels of my recovery were already turning, unbeknownst to me.

Tim Armstrong began to speak, louder than he had planned. "Hey, Buddy, this has got to stop. You're not fooling anyone. I knew you were snitching that Irish stuff from your aunts when you were in 7th grade. I had to cover for you over and over again at Quigley and then out at Mundelein."

"If we had to go to trial, I was worried that you'd be hung-over and shoot yourself in the foot. Enough! Old Boy!" Tim Armstrong crumpled his letter and stuck it in his pocket. "And this is not the first time you've heard about this from me, Martin."

"That day you got me out of there," Nellie's voice quivered as she read her letter, "I smelled whiskey on you, Love. I've prayed so hard. It made me feel even worse than Mother Superior not letting you say Mass for us. I know if your mother, our sister, dear, dear Kate were here, she'd want you to get help. She once wrote to me for prayers that she knew you had a problem way back then. *Bial o'Dhia ort,* Ah, Pet, the good Lord is with you every step of the way!"

Garrett Lyons leaned back, stretched, cleared his throat and positioned his typed letter carefully on his carefully creased pants. Like the rest, he avoided looking directly at me. "I've been in recovery for over 20 years. It's been that long since I had my last drink. The Jesuits kicked me out; they saw that I had a major problem early on. That's why I transferred to Mundelein. I had to hide it from the rector and all of you guys."

"That's how I knew you were walking on the same path as I was; only I was a few steps ahead of you. My first pastor had me in treatment before the sun went down. I go to AA. I'd have been dead long ago without it. I want you to get sober, Martin. A piss-ass priest is an ugly man."

Babe would not write a letter, but she had plenty to say. "From that gorgeous Irish *boychick* that I saw when you and your mother got off that boat back in 1948 right up until now, you've become a first-class *yutz,* drinking, reeking of it, *schnickered* out of your head. That's why you were not invited to Joel Levy's *Shiva!*" Babe's voice was booming and as she raised her arm, a thick silver and turquoise bracelet caught the light and her finger point at me, the prosecutor shouting for a good conviction. I did not respond. I was out of it.

Marguerite said sternly, "Alright, Babe, you've made your point. We don't need to get all *meshuga*, not now, Babe." Marguerite was an Irish Catholic, but had worked with Jewish alcoholics for over 35 years and her Yiddish was superb!

Brendan and Lizzie began at the same time. He deferred to his sister and Lizzie started in on me. "Sure, Martin, the day has come for you to stop this insanity. I know that you've had pain in your life, but so have all of us. You've been sitting around for years in your old self-pity, bemoanin' the fact of no father."

Lizzie continued, her breath coming faster and faster. As Babe was so blunt, Lizzie had become softer, not usually speaking so bluntly to another - but she knew that my life was on the line.

"Well, Love, right now you've got your two fathers sitting right here in front of you and you're after breakin' their hearts! You gotta' get your life together, or it'll be more crooked than the old ram's horn!"

Brendan continued in the same vein, beginning to enumerate the times I had come out to his home and how he had to cover for me in front of Maggie and their kids. And this was the reason they didn't invite me out any more.

No one spoke. A fire siren wailed in the distance. They were waiting for the Cardinal. No one looked at him.

Jeremiah cleared his throat,, but didn't trust himself to speak. "It took me 25 years to find you, Martin, and I'll be goddamned if I'm going to let the booze take you away from me. You're going into treatment and you're going right now and you're going to get yourself sober and you're going to stay that way, Son."

My old class-mate, now-Bishop Teddy Szymanski, told me that they had a place waiting for me at Guest House in Michigan. It was a residential treatment place for priests and that I was to stay there as long as it took to get sober. They had a ticket on an American Airlines flight that left at 1:20, Garrett Lyons would drive me to the airport and I was to be on it. Someone would meet me at the gate in Detroit and drive me to Guest House.

I held my head in my hands. No one moved. I barely nodded my head. Picking up on that first, tender acquiescence, Marguerite Gunning instantly motioned to the team to say good-by. One by one, they approached me, hugging me and shaking my hand, wishing me luck, promising prayers.

When Tim Armstrong came to me to wish me well, I looked down at him, leaned over and whispered, "Fink," and tried to hit him. Tim ducked. Babe caught my arm and twisted it behind my back. She looked over at Lizzie and Lizzie nodded 'Yeah, this is what we're like when we've the drink taken!'

Stephen pulled out a suitcase and packed it, concerned that he not forget anything. Marguerite told him there were stores around there and they had plenty of supplies at Guest House.

I showered, shaved and dressed. My hands were shaking for a drink. Marguerite asked Stephen if he had any alcohol. "Nothing, just what's in his room." I shook my head and said that I was "out."

Nellie remembered the bottles of Jameson's Red Breast hidden in the big roaster oven in their pantry. She ran down and returned with an unopened bottle of Irish whiskey. Stephen opened it and Marguerite told him to give me "a good slug" of it, as she didn't want me going into withdrawal.

Stephen asked Garrett if he would give me another good drink when he got me out to the airport. Garrett told him that he really didn't feel comfortable driving out there with an open bottle in the car. "You know, Steve, put an Irishman in a room with a naked woman and a bottle of booze, we're going to reach for the bottle! I'd be playing with fire myself, sorry."

Marguerite turned to Brendan and asked him if he would go out there with me and walk me to the gate and give me a good drink to last me until I got to Detroit and they could take over.

Marguerite waited until Garrett had his car in front of the building. She and Stephen then walked me down the front stairs and placed me beside Garrett in the front seat and Stephen threw my bag in the trunk. Brendan was in the back-seat.

Marguerite and Stephen stood in the cold, their breaths visible before them. We drove down the icy street, sliding and swerving until we hit Western Avenue. Stephen took Marguerite's arm and they went back up to the apartment. Nellie had the tea on and fat slices of Irish soda bread and fresh butter ready for them.

Stephen began tapping his fingers on the table. "Oh, God, Marguerite...do you think we did the right thing? It seems so severe. I hope we did the right thing and that he won't hate us," sighed Stephen.

Marguerite sipped her hot tea, closed her eyes for a moment, smiled, and said, "Stephen, sure, don't you know that he was waiting for us? He would have been disappointed if we hadn't shown up! Now eat up your bread and drink your tea. It was a job well done! None better!"

****

The lives of Stephen Flaherty and Patsy McGrath fit together like a hand in glove. Steve was in his early 60's and getting ready to retire. Patsy thought she'd work until she drew her last breath, even though she had received a considerable sum from her husband's death. Neither of them had traveled and both had lives circumscribed by the church, their families and their work.

Patsy suffered waves of guilt for helping to blow the whistle on me. It was me who got them together, long, long ago. If I had not been ordained before my mother died, Patsy McGrath would not have been there on Castlewood to take care of Kate.

If I had not come to the hospital to see Sheila Levy and if Patsy were not on duty that night, I never would have gotten her number and Steve would never have met up with her. And poor Patsy would never have had the opportunity to retrieve those parts of her soul she lost taking care of my mother on her death-bed.

Patsy and Stephen were like kids, so delighted with themselves that they had another crack at life and that all the burdens placed so heavily on their shoulders were lifted. I was a mixed blessing to both of them, but my drinking was making Stephen irritable and Patsy needing to pull away.

Everyone was affected, even Patsy's patients, as she was preoccupied with me and Stephen, but not wanting to get too involved, not wanting to "bite the hand that feeds you."

There had always been an element about me that both men and women found seductive. My huge, violet-blue eyes bespoke a vulnerability, a deep, pervasive woundedness that pulled people to myself, like a huge canyon, beckoning others to jump across, inviting others to hurl themselves against the thin skin of myself to discover the mystery within.

It was this very sadness and solitude that Msgr. Duffenbach knocked me for on the ship to Rome. He could see right through me, but didn't know what to do but demand that I be responsible for this heavy cloud I carried for all to see.

The force of my psyche was irresistible, and it did not take long before I became aware of it and knew how to use it for my very survival. While others of my size and being without a father would choose brute force to protect themselves, I learned early that I could usually get what I wanted by being the wounded orphan, naked, hungry and buffeted in the raging storm.

With my dark eyes and heavy brows, me, the orphan-boy, mesmerized unsuspecting people. They gave me what I wanted, and I survived.

At home in Ireland with Packy and Tom and Biddy and all that was going on all the time, I felt safe, yet only half a person as I had no father. Uncle Tom was close to me, but he was not my father. Packy had a father, even though he was dead.

There was only the one time, when I was nearing 12, my mother told me to "get that look off your face!" I snapped at her, telling her I didn't know what she was talking about.

Mammie slapped me right across my face, screaming, "And don't ye go lying to me, Martin Sweeney! Ye know damn well what I'm saying to ye! You're like a stupid waif, waiting for someone to rescue ye!"

When I was a lad of only ten and getting off the boat that first, fateful day, I knew that Babe Nathanson was taken by me. Then it was the Delaney sisters, Sr. Raphael Mary, Mrs. Armstrong and then the women down in the kitchen at Quigley who'd always give me an extra plop of mashed potatoes, the choice cut of cake, a full scoop of ice-cream.

Out at Mundelein Seminary, some of the professors, some of the nuns, some of the clerks and custodians – they wanted to rescue me, help me. I knew that some even fell in love with me. That was what drew that young nun to me, but also what repelled her, as she wanted to be with a man, not a little boy.

Stephen and Jeremiah, the Lieutenant and the Cardinal had fallen under my sway. As both were powerful men in their own spheres, they were brought low by needy me. And I was revolted by this power I had.

Neither of them had been my real and full and right-from-the-beginning father, as I so well deserved, so the rivers of guilt ran deep and fast within both. As sure as a screaming infant demands to be fed, guilt demands punishment. And all of this is worked out in the depths of each man's psyche, where he is his own judge and jury, his own hangman.

To punish himself, Stephen Flaherty lived a strict, celibate life, depriving himself of the joys of life, spending his days at the station and his nights above the poor, old Delaney sisters. His occasional forays out to Arlington Park Race Track assured that he would place his meager bets on sure losers.

The Cardinal had an exquisite punishment for himself – he never spoke the truth to me, his son of whom he was ignorant for 25 years. When he wanted to nestle up to the truth of anything at all, he'd cloak it in a joke, a prayer, an old Irish proverb, or even in Gaelic or Latin. Although he didn't deserve to speak the truth to me, he demanded it from others and this made him crazy.

****

As the American Airlines lifted into the cold February skies, they all breathed deeply and with profound relief. All of them – Garrett, Nellie, Tim, Jeremiah, Stephen, Babe and Lizzie, Brendan – had spoken the "truth to power." Me, with my alcoholism and orphan energy, had controlled them for years and now I was invited to get clean and sober and be a real man. And they were free, for they never again had to return to their lies, to their half-truths for poor old me.

Initially, Stephen and Patsy had planned to wait until I returned from Guest House to get married. They decided it was unnecessary and they would just be continuing their old ways of putting everyone else's agenda before theirs. On Valentine's Day, Steve and Patsy were married in the hospital chapel by the old Franciscan priest from Poland.

Only Lizzie and Brendan Sweeney witnessed the marriage. Stephen finally moved out of his place on Castlewood, telling the Delaneys that he was still just around the corner. He and Patsy bought a condo at the newly converted Edgewater Beach Hotel.

I came home after three months. I did a lot of work on 'my family of origin' issues, my orphan tendencies or archetype, as they called it, and the trauma of the false accusation. I was beginning to live my life as a sober, honest man. It wasn't easy, but I had a good sponsor, an old Methodist minister with four kids, and he taught me 'to live one day at a time'. Not a bad beginning.

CHAPTER 40
House of 19 Chimneys.

The cardinal had ordered all the boxes, files, folders, crates and plastic bags of material on the priests who were accused of abusing children moved to his rectory, an impressive red-brick mansion on North State Parkway. To himself, he called this material the *detritus* of celibacy.

He had grown increasingly uncomfortable with his luxurious surroundings. The mammoth three-story, red brick rectory dominated the cluster of mansions in the Astor Street Division. It supported 19 chimneys, as perhaps the builders considered the heat that was going to be generated by these men of power. Chicagoans called it the *House of 19 Chimneys.*

The Cardinal occupied the second and third floors. The legal, medical and pastoral material regarding these priests was taking over his office in the Chancery, so he wanted it in a safe, secure place, away from the regular running of the Archdiocese.

The material was becoming so mountainous that it began to take over his office in the rectory. He then decided to move to a larger unused, open space on the third floor and asked his assistant for tables, so he could keep each priest's documentation separate. The original six long tables expanded to 12, and now there were more than 28 tables, covered with material he wished he had never seen.

Jeremiah thought of that children's story of the old woman who made the porridge that overflowed the pot and ran through the little house, out the door and down the road to the river. But for the hallowed, pontifical secrecy of the church that primarily protects priests, all these offenders would be in prison. His tables would be clean.

And if he had not vowed to operate within the deepest, darkest secrecy, he would not be in a position to send these priests away for treatment that could not and would not work, despite the thousands of dollars invested in their cure. Pedophilia was an intractable addiction that could not be cured. The only remedy was social – forever to preclude these men from access to children and adolescents.

The vast majority of his time was spent attending to this matter that was flowing right out of the pot, through the archdiocese, across the sea and right into the Tiber River and up to the Vatican. While in the public eye he was immune from the charge that he was protecting these abusers, few knew that he was hiding behind the Priests Advisory Board, letting them take the rap for these ugly men. This Board consisted of twelve members, mostly priests, but one lay woman and three male lawyers.

The pattern of abuse was the same: befriending a lonesome, fatherless boy or girl; earning the trust of the mother, which was simple, as these guys were priests and no one would question their motives or actions; taking the special kid aside for grooming with gifts and treats, over-nights at the rectory and vacations by a lake; molesting the child by kissing, touching their young genitals and soon penetrating their bodies; having the children return the favors; demanding a vow of secrecy from them and reminding the children that no one would believe that a holy priest would ever act in such a manner.

It worked every time. Some of the bolder priests would sexualize young boys in clusters, by families or age groups. The M.O. was that they were all guys, and this is what guys do to each other and with each other. One of the priests would have the 8th grade boys get in a circle with him and masturbate, calling it the "jerk off club". Many of the priests told the boys that every guy had to have this experience, so he would be more experienced with a girl.

Girls had to be abused individually, more secretly. There had to be an element of romance or a sense of detachment or dissociation, so the priest could claim innocence and purity, as the allure of the girl had somehow been beyond his poor human powers to resist.

And when the families received no hearing from their own pastor, they got a lawyer. If they received no hearing from the Cardinal, their lawyer was ready to pursue a criminal indictment. This got everyone's attention, so quickly came the pay-off money, with the obligation of perfect silence from all concerned parties. And if the perfect silence were to be broken, the penalty was excommunication. They would no longer be Catholic.

261

Jeremiah had been made a bishop in 1960 when he was only 44. They needed him to have the rank of bishop, as he was working with Cardinal Octavianni at the Holy Office, the most powerful place in the Vatican. With his background in Canon Law and church history, young, ambitious Bishop Jeremiah Devitt was one of the primary writers of *Crimen Sollicitationis.* The chickens had come home to roost in Chicago.

Jeremiah felt caught in a snare of his own doing. Never did he imagine that he would be in a position to negotiate, to represent the Holy Roman Catholic Church in the swelling rapids of real-life priests and sex and addictions and families and hush money and lawyers and damaged children.

Sitting so pompously with Cardinal Octavanni at the Holy Office, over-seeing that the obligation to procedural secrecy was observed on every item of their proud, explicit, self-serving document about priests and sex, *Crimen Sollicitationis,* Bishop Jeremiah Devitt was a naïve, ignorant, arrogant man. Standing in the attic of the *House of 19 Chimneys* in jeans and a white tee-shirt, with the piles of evidence against the priests choking him, Cardinal Jeremiah Devitt was a humbler, uncertain, wiser man.

How naïve was Jeremiah as he robed to begin the ceremony of his consecration to become a bishop. How ignorant to think he could resolve the paradox of protecting the church at all costs, yet be a good shepherd to his flock. How arrogant to think that the rest of his life would be as easy, as effortless, as his coasting through the first half of his time on earth had been.

Jeremiah knelt before the altar during his solemn consecration to the bishopric. His head had been anointed with the oil "of mystical anointing" and the Book of the Gospels had been handed to him "to preach the word of God". It was all so beautiful, so filled with grace and history. So simple and fit for a man of Jeremiah Devitt's strong vocation to live and love and work within the walls of Holy Mother Church. He had always been destined for leadership and this was the first step.

During the consecration ceremony, the deacon removed the Book of Gospels and on his finger was placed the new bishop's ring,

262

with the consecrating bishop saying, "Take this ring, the seal of your fidelity. With faith and love, protect the bride of Christ, his holy church".

The tall white miter was silently placed upon Jeremiah's head and then he was given his pastoral staff, with the words, "Take this staff as a sign of your pastoral office: keep watch over the whole flock in which the Holy Spirit has appointed you to shepherd the Church of God."

Wiser and tired, Jeremiah smiled to himself, surrendering the arrogance of his young ignorance, the pride of a young man who thought he knew what he could not possibly know, the secrets and sins of ordained ministers happening across an ocean even as he knelt before an altar, becoming a bishop to dance on the twin high-wires of protecting the bride of Christ and keeping watch over his flock.

He didn't even know what those words meant. He could define them, write eruditely about them, deliver a brilliant sermon, even use those words to ordain another bishop. Jeremiah thought he knew, but he was as mindless as a little lamb smiling at the hungry wolf, as trusting as a fatherless little boy going out to the Dairy Queen with the nice, new priest.

The new Cardinal's red, ruby ring meant he had to protect the church. Protecting the church meant to protect her priests at any cost. Priests were the bricks and mortar of the church. Without priests, there would be no church, no sacraments, no mass, no baptisms, no Eucharist, no forgiveness. The holy, consecrated hands of the priest literally held up the structure of the church, regardless of what other unholy things the priest did with his hands on his own time.

The Cardinal's shepherd's staff meant he had to protect his flock, climbing up rocky mountains and down deep valleys to rescue the abandoned new-born lamb, the ravaged ewe, the blind, old ruminant, ready for mutton. But if the lamb, the ewe, the ruminant had all been damaged by his own priests, how could he do both? How could he protect the bride of Christ, the church, and at the same time, protect his sheep from the ravages of the priests who are the bedrock of the church?

Jeremiah sat in the old, wooden teacher's chair rescued from an inner-city Catholic school that he had just closed. It rocked back and forth, squeaked when he tried to move it, and moved when he wanted it to be still. The long gray lunch-room tables came from that same little school and they were covered with the documentation of the sins of the priests or crimes of the priests, depending upon which high-wire he was balancing on. He often thought he could smell kids' food on them.

He popped the tab on a can of beer that he had brought with him to his lonely garret in the sky. He rested his head against one of the red brick chimney stacks and looked out beyond the other wealthy mansions to the lake. Who had designed this evil conundrum he was caught in? Had St. Peter or St. Paul? The Early Fathers? Augustine or Jerome? Venerable Bede? Who thought up such nonsense?

This whole mess was lying right at the feet of the bishops and cardinals. They were all caught in this trap, trying to do what was expected of them, what they had promised to do. They were all taking the right course to protect the bride of Christ, as they agreed upon as the sacred ruby red ring was placed on their fingers.

The simple fall-out for that obedience was that they were disobedient to the vow they had taken as they received the shepherd's staff. They became bad shepherds and no amount of money was going to make them faithful shepherds. Maybe the comparison with shepherds didn't sit well, for the old farmers said of the sheep: *We shear 'em, we fuck em', we eat 'em.* Maybe it said it all!

Jeremiah thought of the many times he had played ignorant to Martin when he asked what was really happening. He had deferred to the Priests Advisory Board, even offered Martin a spot on that board if he would like, as they were the ones who were in charge of the abusing priests. Then he would really get a nose-full of all the complexities that he had to deal with. There seemed no answer. Jeremiah knew that Martin knew his father was playing dumb, protecting his innocence by lying to his own son.

Then that little nun, Sr. Felix, was becoming a real pain in the ass. The letters, the phone calls, that morning she showed up at the

Chancery, demanding to be heard by the Cardinal. Her brother, Garrett Lyons, was a priest in the same class as Martin, so she probably thought she was entitled to be heard.

Sr. Felix was speaking the truth about these priests hurting kids, but he didn't have the ears to hear her. He tried to sooth her, to quiet her down, but she was inconsolable with her fury. Like a fiery angel, like a wounded mother, *"In Rama there was a voice heard, lamentation and weeping and great mourning, Rachel weeping for her children and would not be comforted..."*

Jeremiah found himself growing more and more angry that he had been placed to lead in such an unwinnable war. Yes, he certainly had participated, with all his ambition, good looks, and Vatican connections. He wanted to be a leader in the church, to be looked up to, to wield power over the lives of many. Was this his Karma come full circle?

He thought of his flesh-and-blood father, old Peter Murphy, saying, "A man has often cut a rod to beat himself." At the time, Jeremiah had no idea what his father was talking about, but the old man was telling his son that he was treading on dangerous ground, climbing too high. What seems good at one stage of life can back-fire in the next.

Jeremiah felt that he had been tricked – by himself, by the church that could spot a bishop in the little red bud long before he started to bloom, by the Devitts who had used him for their own glory, by the people who cried out for a handsome, powerful Cardinal to shower more attention on the city of Chicago.

By his brother priests, so confident in his sheltering arms that they could do whatever they damned pleased with a child of God and his poor family. By his brother bishops, walking lock-step with the decrees of secrecy, together turning their backs against the truth, all blocking their ears in unison against the voice in Rama, *lest they hear Rachel weeping for her children.*

CHAPTER 41
Bless Me, Father, for I Have Sinned

The Cardinal was largely absent from my life through all this ugly business. I spent most of my time alone, chasing ghosts and reading my "fan mail". Many times I had asked him about priests and kids sleeping in the rectory, boys going up to Wisconsin or Michigan to family cottages, two or three 12 year-olds on camping trips of a priest.

Jeremiah feigned ignorance of the entire thing. I'd ask him about various priests going for continual treatment in St. Louis or Maryland and how many of them were transferred from parish to parish within a year.

He'd comment that some priests are just restless, but he really didn't know. The Priests Advisory Board was canonically responsible for all of that and they rarely bothered him with the details. He asked me if I'd like to be on that board and I quickly denied any desire. He presented himself as basically ignorant of what I was telling him and innocent of any culpability in putting children in harm's way.

My lips were sealed regarding the fact that I had actually read *Crimen Sollicitionis*, had held it in my hands, and fully understood the primal, papal order of secrecy. I was then deep into the secrecy mire and on some level, I felt important to be a real insider. But sometimes I felt like the little gingerbread boy, riding on the nose of the fox. Graham wasn't the fox; the church was.

I wondered often whether the secrecy energy created the entire mystery of the church. Did it then get translated into *holiness?* There is something basically wrong with that syllogism: if $a = b$ and $b = c$, then $a = c$. The secrecy issue may have started out of necessity for protection of the innocent, but it became a monster in its own house and now it threatens to eat us up, like the little gingerbread boy on the nose of the fox.

Graham Byrne had asked me to protect him from showing it to me and I had whole-heartedly agreed. I have often wondered why Graham Byrne had shown this to me in the first place. He had made me study it and we discussed much of it. It was becoming clearer as this was his gift to me. It was both my anchor and my sail: I could sail right through my father's lies, yet be firmly anchored in the truth of what I knew. And he knew that I knew.

After my acquittal, I met with my father at Sam and Hy's. We had finished our meal and were sipping coffee. There was a comfortable silence between us, as if we had made peace with all that had happened. Jeremiah was proud of me, as he knew that I had protected the Holy Seal of Confession and had been willing to go to prison, if that was what was needed.

The Cardinal was stroking his chin. He was slowly growing a beard and the prickly white stubble was irritating to him. His eyebrows remained black, but his thick, wavy hair was as white as bleached bones. He raised his eyebrows and said in a low voice, "Martin, do you have your stole with you?"

I nodded and we rose to leave. Jeremiah again shoved a $100 dollar bill under the rolls and looked to see if Sheila was watching. She reached for the money, blew off the bread crumbs and stuck the big bill down her bosom with a wink.

"Come on, Son, you're going to hear the Cardinal's confession. A general confession. There are some benches down on the boulevard where we can sit for a while. You ok?"

"Right as rain, Jeremiah. My stole is in the glove compartment. I'll meet you down there."

We sat on the newly painted green bench, overlooking the north branch of the Chicago River. I kissed my purple stole, placed it around my neck and tipped my head closer to better hear what my father had to say. He was breathing quickly and holding his hands over his chest. I put my hand on his knee to stop it from bouncing. I slowly made the Sign of the Cross and ignored the traffic.

"Bless me, Father, for I have sinned. I have sinned grievously against my responsibilities to care for my flock. I have put the reputation of the church before children and their families. I have knowingly transferred priests who I knew for certain have abused children. I have caused 'religious duress' to my flock by manipulating the truth about these priest-predators and have set them loose upon the most vulnerable of my people."

He was catching his breath. I told him to slow down, that we were alone and that he was safe with me. I asked him to breathe more deeply and slowly.

He continued, "I have sinned as I have sought to cause no scandal to the church at the expense of caring for the victims of these men, thereby causing far greater scandal. I have turned a blind eye and a deaf ear to what I should have been seeing and hearing."

The Cardinal went on, "I have a misplaced sense of loyalty. I have succumbed to the glory of my position and have used my position to protect evil people from the consequences of their actions. I have endangered the faith of many and have betrayed my conscience, my vocation, my vows of fidelity to my flock."

"I have known better. I confess my sins of pride, of arrogance, of cruelty. I have been mortally aggressive in a passive way, thereby slipping away from any apparent guilt. I have caused great harm."

"For these and all the sins of my life, I am heartily sorry."

I lowered my head and making the sign of the cross, said, *"I absolve you, in the name of the Father, and of the Son and of the Holy Spirit, Amen."* I removed my stole, kissed it and slipped it into my pocket.

"There was a young Dominican priest, a Tom Doyle, a Canon lawyer. He met with all of us bishops years ago and told us that this nonsense was going on and we could either take steps to stop it or we would have a lot to answer for. We laughed at him – who did he think he was, ordering us around?

"Right about that same time, a nun - I think she was a psychologist or a psychiatrist – told us that this stuff was rampant and that changing priests from one parish to another was criminal. She warned all of us at our annual meeting that this was going to cost the church billions of dollars in civil suites, that priests and bishops would be going to prison, that we would lose millions and millions of good Catholics over this issue. Again, we laughed at the ludicrous nun."

I thought of Sr. Felix, 'Happy' we called her, ringing the alarm bell against the ignored sins and crimes of the clergy, low and high. Centuries ago, the Greeks honored the prophetess Cassandra who had received the gift of prophesy; her punishment for such an illustrious gift was that no one believed her.

My father continued, "It is all wrong for me now and I have to get my life together. I have to go back home and retrieve my soul. I want you to come with me, Martin. I'm not sure exactly when, but there are many things that you need to know and maybe it will help you understand your own life."

I said nothing. Jeremiah continued, "There are secrets that have been kept from you and you need to know all of them, for you can't be whole without understanding your past, Martin. Will you come?"

The throbbing ambivalence I felt for this man grabbed me in the gut. It was like the old Chinese handcuffs, the finger traps that tightened the harder the pull for release.

I hated my father and I loved him. Could I stand to be with him for so long? What if I said "no"? Would Jeremiah leave again like he did even before I was born? But he really didn't leave because he didn't even know I existed. How could he not have known about me?

I held my head in my hands and felt a blast of adrenalin soar through my veins. I just wanted to hit my father for putting me in such a bind. The harder I pull to get out of the handcuffs, the tighter they grip me.

"I'll let you know, Da. Everything isn't just so simple for me as it is for you now. Give me a few days and I'll let you know."

"Lad, things aren't simple for me either. Neither of us knew about the other for 25 years and now we're supposed to have a relationship. And our secret that I'm your father...we can't sit on that forever or it will kill us. I've got to get right – with myself, with God, with you."

"Finding out that you really exist and that was kept from me for all these years makes me crazy. I had a *need* to know this and I certainly had a *right* to know. I wonder if this is what killed your mother...she sat on this secret for all these years. Yeah, it would have been very messy if she had let us know, but she might even be alive today. Our secrets kill us."

269

I started to choke, trying to hold down my tears. "You know, Da, every night of my life I'd get down on my knees and pray, 'Dear Lord, help me find my Da, help me find my Da, help me find my Da' over and over and over. Mammie would get so upset and tell me to hush and to 'leave the poor man in peace.'"

"Martin, I know that we have both been guarded against each other. I don't want you to leave and you don't want me to leave, so if we don't get too close, we can keep a nice, safe distance and not get hurt. We're both afraid to get angry at your mother who made the decision to keep us apart. I completely understand why she did that, but she was wrong. "

"Don't talk about my mother! I love her and she brought me over here for a fresh start and to get away from you!"

"She wanted to get the hell out of Ireland, she did, just like the rest of us! Kate Sweeney and I were in love – you were our love child, sure, you were…I loved your mother and she loved me, but there were just too many things going against us back then. I loved Kate Sweeney."

"Why did you become a priest?"

"I really had no choice, Martin, I had no choice. I was a hostage to the Devitts and it was where I had to go".

"Why did you become a priest, Martin?"

"To be like my father!"

"Smart arse!!"

"I'll think this through, Da, and call you in a few days, OK?"

"Don't keep me waiting too long Martin. Sure, the green hills and black valleys are calling to me! To the both of us, Lad!"

CHAPTER 42
For Peace Comes Dropping Slowly

It was an early morning, bright, in the middle of May. I filled my car, vacuumed and dusted the inside, shined the windows and mirrors and went back inside for another cup of coffee. I changed into my light blue sport shirt and wondered if I had shaved. I knew I was stalling. I had to go to the toilet again.

Harry was waiting for me at the John A. Graham Correctional Center in Hillsboro, Illinois, deep in Montgomery County, south of Springfield and on the way to St. Louis. He was incarcerated at the residential sex-offender section at the down-state medium security state prison. We hadn't spoken in over two years.

I looked in the rear-view mirror as the proud, elegant city of Chicago began to fade into factories, residential areas and sprawling, indifferent suburbs. Finally, there were sweeping farms and lands as far and flat as I could see. Early corn and soybeans, wheat and oats were poking through the soil and a soft sheen of green covered the land.

I made my way through the small towns and large farms, passing through Springfield, the state's capitol, down into Hillsboro. The sign, *John A. Graham Correctional Center*, stood before the large buildings near the intersection of 9th Avenue and Rt. 185.

I pulled into the long drive and parked in the visitor lot. My stomach was in knots. I hadn't seen Harry in two years. Only Garrett Lyons, the "Jesuit", was a regular visitor, almost as if he had taken Harry on as a special project. And I'm sure that Sr. Felix was dunning on Garrett about priests' abusing kids.

Harry Hogan was the pariah in our class – he had gone from the rich, spoiled kid in Lake Forest to a sexual pervert, Class IV felon. Even though I had spent my four years of theology in Rome and was ordained early, my Mundelein class was my class and the guys never made a distinction. Harry was my classmate and I had known him from our first day at Quigley.

I don't really know why it had taken me so long to come here to see Harry. If the truth be known, I never really liked him, but I certainly availed myself of the generosity of the Hogans, with their Door County summer home, open to me all the time, and the big Lake Forest parties. I always felt that Harry wanted more from me than I was prepared to give him. There was a chilly lonesome place inside of him that I was afraid of.

I made my way to the formidable brown-brick Administration Building and approached the window. A hefty officer dragged herself from behind her desk and asked me why I was there.

As unemotionally as I could manage, I told her "Harry Hogan" and stopped myself from repeating, "Fr. Harry Hogan". Her short-sleeved green shirt cut into her thick, pink biceps.

A sneering black snake, tattooed from around her shoulder to the back of her fat hand, curled his red tongue at me. I wonder if she knew that the serpent is the symbol of the Resurrection, as it sheds its skin and enters a newer life. I didn't think I'd share that with her.

Behind the mesh wiring, she looked at my driver's license with a scowl. She asked for my keys, wallet, watch, knives or anything made of metal or strong plastic. I emptied my pockets and placed them directly into the black plastic container she shoved at me. Then she called over the loud-speaker for a male officer to search me. That was unpleasant. Then I had to sit for my photo.

When I was found to be somewhat acceptable, I was ushered into a small, cinder-blocked room with mirrored windows, a small table and two chairs to wait for Harry. For Fr. Harry Hogan, my old pal.

A short, bulky officer opened the door and Harry entered the room. He had lost about 40 pounds and his black hair was snow white with a little, round bald patch on the crown. Harry's deep blue eyes had begun to fade, and age-lines ran across his thin cheeks. His teeth had taken on a yellowish cast brought about by too many cigarettes, too much coffee.

He looked at me quickly then looked down. I could see he was taking in what aging was doing to me. I really don't think I was any different, just about ten pounds heavier and a little gray at the temples. I wonder what Harry saw in me. His gray-striped shirt hung down around his wrists.

We shook hands and slowly began to look at each other. Suddenly I felt shy, like I had caught him again at something very bad. There was so much history between us - some good, much bad. A fatal heaviness encompassed us and I always felt it was my responsibility to shoulder it. He was not able for it – I had always thought of Harry as a weak man and I treated him that way.

"Harry...how've ya been?"

"I thought I'd never see you again, Martin."

"I'm sorry, Harry...I'm really sorry..."

"I know that you didn't break the Holy Seal."

"No, Harry, I never would do that. I've missed you."

We sat together, two priests no longer young, not yet old. I picked at my cuticles. Harry tugged at his ears.

"Why did you come now, Martin? What do you want?"

"I just wanted to see you, Harry. I wanted to know how you are getting on."

"We both know that's not true. Do you want to know how I got here?"

"If you want to tell me, Harry."

Harry told me that he was getting individual and group therapy and was beginning to understand what had happened to him as a child that made him abuse children. I drew a deep breath and finally looked straight at Harry. I thought at first that there was a new clarity and maturity in Harry's faded blue eyes, but he was gone. I wonder if he ever was really here.

With a voice that was clear, but flat, almost clinical, Harry told me what had really happened to him.

"Us Hogans were not that big, happy family that we pretended to be, Martin. It was insane. We pretended to be sort of French-Irish, a little higher class than regular Irish-Americans. Where in the hell did "Mimmie" and "Pippie" come from? Who made those names up? In that huge, ugly black mansion by the lake, all hell was let loose."

"Mimmie was in the bag by noon, sipping her damn Bloody Marys and muttering her Hail Marys all morning and then gin and

273

tonic after lunch. After her nap, she started on the white wine until Pippie came home, if he came home."

Harry stared at the floor and continued a monologue of his childhood. "He usually went over to the Blackstone Hotel for a roll in the hay with one of his fat chicks for a few hours. He'd call and say he wouldn't be home, that 'the case was running over', but my brother Bobby had set up the phones so we'd know where he really was calling from."

"You know that there were a dozen of us: Ellen, Tom, Brendan, Bobby, Sean, Patrick, Danny, Joseph, Brian, James, Mary Kay, and finally me after five years. I was the mistake on that St. Patrick's Day in 1938 when they were both drunk. She was 46 and he was 50. I was born December 17, 1938. Surprise!! Now they're all doctors and lawyers, FBI agents, professors, pilots, even a fuckin' Congressman."

"Well, all the boys practiced on me since I was old enough to walk. Mary Kay tried to protect me, but now I'm sure they abused her, too. I'd run to Mimmie but she was so drunk she didn't know what was going on. I think she just couldn't cope with all the insanity, but she created more."

Harry continued, but with no emotion, no inflection, "Up in the attic, down the basement, in the bathrooms and bedrooms, down by the lake, up on the boat. Little Harry Hogan was theirs for the taking. They'd literally just snap their fingers and I knew I'd have to bend over and take it up my rear-end again and again."

"If it weren't for Haddie, our cook, and her husband, Sammy, our gardener, I would have killed myself. I could always run to her and she'd hold me and rock me and I'd cry myself to sleep."

"But they'd grab me and tell me they would kill me if I told anyone. Mary Kay and I would cry together and the nuns at St. Mary's said that I wasn't concentrating and wasn't working up to my potential, whatever that was. Christ, I was concentrating, alright. I was concentrating on how to get away, but I was trapped!"

"I couldn't think straight and my ass ached all the time. I'd bleed and the boys would tell me I was a sissy and that I had 'to take it like a man'. I took it and took it and took it and took it… I felt like a piece of shit all the time, just an old rag that all of them could use for their jollies. I hated them and I hated Mimmie and Pippie, but most of all, I hated myself. I still do."

My head was swimming. I didn't want to hear this stuff. "Harry, you don't have to go on. I get the picture, Harry. God, I never knew."

"I want to tell you all about this, Martin. Who else can I tell but you? We've been together from the start, back at Quigley. I hate what I did to you. I hate myself for that. You, of all people, didn't deserve it"

I reached for Harry's hand, but Harry pulled away from me. His eyes looked glassy. His voice held no inflection and his face showed nothing.

"I became like an ice-berg and never had any feelings. Everything was just shut-down and vague. I never knew when it was appropriate to laugh or cry. When life called for me to be present, I'd just split off – my body stayed here, but my mind would be off in another realm, and I could go up to the ceiling when they were abusing me so I didn't have to feel it. I could just look down on it all and then it didn't really matter, after all."

Harry continued, "I still do that. I did that when I first came in here today. It was too emotional to see you, Martin. My therapist calls it 'dissociating'. I still split-off like I did when I was a kid. That's how I survive in here."

"How I survived in the Seminary, in the parishes, when I was with our guys so you didn't know what a creep I am. I dissociate all the time here so I don't feel how much these guys hate me. Sometimes I think they'll kill me and then it won't be so bad. Actually, I know they will kill me. It won't be too long from now."

"So, Martin, I thought if I became a priest, I'd be holy, clean, washed down to my undies. I'd be able to get over all that crap and be better than those old brother fuckers. But instead, I became just like them, but only worse, because I'm a priest."

"My therapist says that I 'internalized my aggressors', like Patty Hearst internalized her kidnappers, she became just like them and robbed a bank. Some of the Jews became worse than the Nazis,

275

turned on their own people and were the *Capos*. They just swallowed the Nazis, digested them and killed their own people."

"I picture myself swallowing them and then I say a litany of their names – 'Tom, Brendan, Bobby, Sean, Patrick, Danny, Joey, Brian, James' – Sean was the worse and Joey would always cry and say he was sorry and I had to forgive him, but then it would start again and Joey got rougher and rougher. Danny was the quickest…Do you want me to continue, Martin?"

I looked at Harry, a man I never knew. Harry was sweating and his fists were clenched. I found myself compulsively looking at Harry's hands, at his nubby, bleeding fingernails. I nodded and said, "Go on, Harry, go on."

"I can never, never be around young boys. I'm just hard-wired to be sexually attracted to them and I know that I will act that out again. I'm not attracted to women or men, just kids. Ain't that sick, Martin? But that's my story."

Harry waited for me to say something. I said nothing, I couldn't talk. What was there to say? It was like a movie of a ship-wreck on a cold, black sea, but the film was running backwards and he could watch the ice-berg waiting patiently for the big ship to smash to smithereens.

"I know you've always looked at my fingers. My therapist tells me that I rip my nails just to feel the pain and to see the blood. Then I know that I exist. You should see my ravaged feet, Martin. Sounds goofy, I know, but it it's true. Otherwise, I'm just some floatin' fuck…"

I held my head in my hands. "Harry, Harry, Harry…I never knew any of this…I never knew…I'm so sorry you had to go through that…I'm so sorry, Harry…"

"They never would have ordained me if they had known all this. But I was protected by all the Quinn's money and all the Hogan's power with the city and the church."

"That was what that hot call from the Judge was about on our first day at Quigley. Just to remind everyone who I was and who my family was. Imagine who I would be today if His Horny Honor, Judge

Harry Hogan, had been as careful to protect me when I was little, as he was to protect his fuckin' family and his fuckin' name."

We sat silently in the small cinder-block room with the mirrored windows. We knew we were being monitored by the guards. What else was there to say? The small room was hot and airless. Harry began to dissociate, and I could feel him leave me.

"You've left already, haven't you, Harry?"

Harry closed his eyes and nodded. "Time for me to go, Martin. Thanks for coming down." He gave me a limp hand-shake and knocked on the door. A guard opened it, snapped handcuffs on Harry wrists and led him away.

I was taken out by another guard and my personal articles were returned. I walked quickly to my car and pulled out onto Rt. 185 without looking, barely missing a milk truck. The driver gave me the finger.

As I caught Rt. 16 out of Hillsboro, I saw a Dairy Queen and jammed on my brakes. I was sweating and my blue sport shirt was wet under my arms and on my back. I staggered to the small open window. A blond teen-age girl stood cracking her gum and staring defiantly, daring me to order. I forgot what I wanted.

I stepped aside as three 10-year olds jumped off their bikes and ran to the window. When they were finished, I ordered a double chocolate soda.

"I don't know what you're talkin' about, Mister. We don't have them here." The owner pushed her aside and asked if he could help.

I got my double chocolate soda and sat on a picnic table under the shade of a yellow-green weeping willow tree. I looked at the three boys and wondered what Harry was like at that age. They looked back at me and the biggest one shouted, "Hey, Mister, somethin' wrong?" and they reared their bikes up in the air, hit the ground and roared off in the opposite direction.

I sipped my soda slowly. It was a long drive back to Chicago and I would never again be the man I was early that morning when I left to see Harry Hogan. I had never really known Harry. He was not who I thought he was. Who was there to answer to the terrible travesty of Harry Hogan's tragic life?

PART FIVE
Chapters 43 – 53

But today
It is my father who keeps stumbling
Behind me, and will not go away.
"Follower"
Seamus Heaney

CHAPTER 43
The Green, Green Hills of Clare

The blue-green *Aer Lingus* jet cut through the morning clouds over the Shannon Estuary. It had been many years since either of us had been home. As I strained out the window to see Quilty, the sun blinded me. Jeremiah scratched his fresh beard to see if it were still there. He didn't want to be recognized.

The plane bumped down on the runway with a thud and taxied to the gate. Objects in the over-head compartments rolled around like thunder and our seats squeaked and strained on the floor of the plane, the old bolts faithfully holding their grip. The stewardesses in their crisp teal uniforms quickly composed themselves and stood at the doors like nuns dismissing their classes.

As we made our way down the shaky stairway to the black tarmac, I waited for my father. I had left Ireland with my mother and now I had come home with my father. I could not identify my feelings - it was all so strange. Should I laugh? Cry? I just wanted to lie on the earth and feel safe. I was finally back home, deep in my own land where I could finally breathe.

Men were scurrying to grab suitcases from the belly of the plane and were tossing them onto the waiting truck. The pilot and co-pilot in their teal blue uniforms bounced down the stairs at the front of the plane, mystery men under their caps and sun-glasses. Students with their back-packs and mothers with children in tow crowded around the large, steel door into the airport.

Suddenly, we all cleared the way for three stiff priests in Roman collars who carried only thin, black briefcases. We nodded to them, knowing that they would not acknowledge our membership in the same club. The priests ignored us, as we had expected. My father nodded gravely to me; I nodded back with even more gravity.

After getting our American passports stamped, we grabbed our bags from the carousel and tipped our caps to the customs officers pretending to check the luggage.

At the car-hire, the young man behind the counter took Jeremiah's credit card and looked at him, "Archdiocese of Chicago?

You're not a priest now, are you?" Jeremiah smiled at him and told him to "run the damn thing through fast because the Cardinal was hot on his trail". The young man began to remind us to drive on the left, but we were already gone.

We picked up a little blue Renault, folded in our long legs and I drove out of Shannon and on up through the villages of Newmarket-on-Fergus and Clare Castle. It was then into the first small town, Ennis, with crooked streets so narrow only a man with a few cows could have negotiated it. It is on the River Fergus just north of where it flows into the Shannon Estuary.

We stopped for coffee at the Old Ground Hotel and watched the fat Franciscan Friars strolling up and down O'Connell Street. When they'd see a young Tinker woman with her bundle of baby begging outside the cathedral, they'd give her their hurried blessing and run back to the monastery. The Tinkers curse was formidable and not to be taken lightly.

We turned west to get to the sea as soon as possible. I wondered if Jeremiah's heart was pounding as fast as mine. As we drove through Lissycasey, I started to laugh. As a boy, I thought there an important girl lived and the town was named for her. We sped through Knockalough and quickly into Kilrush. I knew we'd be there in 10 minutes or less.

We went through Moyasta and finally the wild sweep of Cook's Bay was spread out before us as a great feast for our hungry souls. I could hardly breathe, and my eyes were full of tears. The great white waves of the Atlantic Ocean, like blue horses with their white manes blowing over their eyes, rolled and crashed upon the sand. The tide was coming in.

It was early summer and the beautiful village of Kilkee right on the Atlantic Ocean was ringed with homes of bright Mediterranean colors - yellow, blue, pink, and green – the only place in Ireland to have such colors. Although I had been to Kilkee many times as a boy, I never knew how much I missed it.

There were men sunning their pale white skins on the rocks; children making castles and fishing in the scattered Pollock holes; mothers trying to read, with one eye on a magazine and another on

281

their children; teenagers jumping through the waves like young dolphins fleeing their mothers.

Three old men carried their tar-black *currach* over their heads like a giant black beetle on its way to the sea. In the distance, a ship was sailing westward, perhaps carrying another young boy to fulfill his destiny in another land.

Along the promenade were the local folks selling periwinkles, the bluish gray sea snails that we'd eat with a pin. They had been boiled in their own sea water and the folks would reach into their buckets with a tin cup and pour them into our little funnels made of newspaper.

The two old Flynn sisters, who were ancient when I was a boy, still sat by the band-stand selling dried leafs of dillisk, chewy and bitter. Every time I bit off one of those red leafs, I spit it out. My uncle Tom told me it was good for me and would put hair on my chest, but not at that cost. Tom would call both of them "Biddie" and they would both answer to it.

Tired and hungry, we stopped at the *Stella Maris* in Kilkee before going on to Quilty. The elegant old hotel at the end of O'Curry Street, stood like a salty Queen, like that fierce woman, Captain Grace O'Malley, watching over her strand and her wind and her wild, blue horses.

I was weak with hunger, yet almost too excited to eat. I was back in dear County Clare with my very own father. The missing father who had taken whatever shape my mother was feeling like conjuring up any day I would ask her. I had left with my mother who was now dead and buried in the cold, deep ground, thousands of miles away. Did she know I had come back? Did she know I had solved the greatest mystery of my life? Was she waiting for me to forgive her lies?

Jeremiah felt strangely frightened, a feeling he had not felt in years. This is where he was brought by the Devitts, or sometimes just by Bishop Ronan Devitt, when they were out for Sunday drives and Peter and Maude Murphy had the day off.

Neither of us shared with the other what we were feeling. We stood silently, honoring each other's silence and each other's separate history which we would soon share. They say that when you cross the ocean, it takes a week before your soul comes in. I think we may have been waiting for our souls' arrival.

We sat at the round glass window overlooking the sea. A pot of ferns kept tangling itself in Jeremiah's white beard until he shoved his chair closer to me. Ever so discretely, I edged my chair away from him; I couldn't stand to be too close.

We both ordered a second bowl of thick, creamy leek soup, another helping of brown bread and soft butter, a fresh pot of tea. Then a warm apple tart with fresh whipped cream and another pot of tea.

When we finished, I started up the car, transferring my watch to my left wrist to remind myself to stay on the left side of the road. I had never driven in Ireland and was afraid of floating over to the right side. Then it was up to Doonmore, Doonbeg, Kilmurrry and finally into Quilty.

As neither Tom nor Packy used a phone, they did not know that we were coming. They had heard about phones that would soon be coming to individual homes in the West of Ireland. There was only one in Quilty and everyone would go down to the post office when a call would come through. I drove on past the Sweeney property and, realizing that I had gone too far, circled back around.

It was in shambles. The fields were overgrown in places, barren in others. There were no cattle or sheep. "Not fish, nor fowl, nor good, red herring," I whispered under my breath. An old dog raised her matted white head, too tired and hungry to either welcome us or chase us off. Rocks from the stone walls had tumbled onto the drive and out onto the main road. The old apple tree was dead.

My face burned with embarrassment as I was about to welcome my father into our home for the first time. Unlike the old Irish custom of the open door, the door was closed and for the first time in my life, I had to open it from the outside. It was stuck, so I gave it a push and went flying into the front room.

Cups were piled high in the sink, chickens flew at us from below the table, the dog's dish hadn't been cleaned in days, newspapers were askew on the remaining chairs, the floor crunched with dirt below our feet. I had been a priest for 21 years and had never seen a place like this.

The old brown radio on the windowsill crackled with static and Packy sat mumbling to himself by the hearth. There was no fire, just an empty bottle between his legs. From the room behind the hearth, an old voice quivered like a wounded cat.

I avoided looking at my father. I went to the back room and saw a very sick and a very old man wrapped in dirty brown blankets. The room smelled of urine and dust and stale tobacco and putrid rags that lay under the bed. I scooped my dear Uncle Tom into my arms and carried him past my father and out into the iron bench in the yard.

Jeremiah walked around outside the cabin and found some old sods and small firewood. He set the fire, put fresh water in the kettle and swung it over the hearth, located a box of unopened tea and woke Packy who shot his finger in the air, stabbing at some invisible *Pooka* that was coming to get him.

Both Tom and Packy told us not to bother, to leave them alone, for who the hell were we to come and take over their lives, like bloody Cromwell and the "fookin' English." We stepped out back, careful not to splash ourselves with waste from 'who-knows-where.' The irony of once having our every want handled by a retinue of house-keepers was not lost on us.

Before we got any deeper into the cleaning, we went over to Kitty Whelan's nice B&B to check in. There was no room at the Sweeneys and we wouldn't stay in that mess as it was. Kitty asked of the Sweeney brothers and said that everyone was worried about them, but if anyone even approached them, Tom yelled and cursed and threw something at them.

I knew I had nothing to lose, so I told her what the situation was like. I could see her wheels spinning. Kitty scratched her head, drew the long pencil from behind her ears and said, "Now, Martin, a few of us will get in there, right this afternoon and will have those old boys sorted out before the sun sets! It will be 'right as rain', so it will be! There is no reason in this day and age for anyone to have to live the way they are. We couldn't do anything before you've come here.

284

Get them out of there and we'll come in and you won't know the old place!"

I knew that no Irish woman would have let a place go to hell like my uncles had. "Kitty, you are an answer to our prayers. I'm so sorry you and the others will have to see the placed in the condition it's in. Grannie is rolling around in her grave, as she kept it spotless. And Grandpa would be roaring if he ever saw the fields and the barn gone to hell."

We got Tom and Packy out of the house in minutes and down to the benches in the strand, yet only five minutes from the house. Within a few hours, they had the little place beginning to look like a home again. They swept and washed and scrubbed and filled the larder with fresh food. They burned the smelly sheets and blankets and Tom's old clothes that clung to him like a second skin.

The four women from the village worked like the Furies, avenging the wrongs that had fallen on the Sweeney home. I imagined that they had been dying to get in there for years, each of them 'house proud' about their own homes and the little village of Quilty, wanted the Sweeney's home to be clean and safe. This cleaning episode will be the talk of the village for years to come.

When Jeremiah and I went into the village for supplies, I bought Packy a bottle of wine, afraid that he would go into convulsions if he were taken off alcohol too suddenly. My father asked me how I knew to get Packy a bottle, I reminded him that Guest House had taught me many things.

I added that Packy needed to be in hospital, but since they would probably not admit him for alcoholism, we would both go the following night to an AA meeting in Lahinch, as I had a schedule. Packy was too far gone to fight me. He was too sick. We smiled at each other, remembering that horrible cold morning eight years ago when I was so strongly invited to get the hell sober.

Packy was my mother's youngest brother, so he was also my uncle, but Packy and I were the same age and had spent our young years together. We had been like brothers, but our paths had diverted when we were 10, and we hadn't seen each other since my ordination, 21 years ago.

For the next few weeks, my father cooked until Tom Sweeney was strong enough to kick him out of the kitchen. I was out in the fields, turning over the soil and digging up forgotten parsnips and carrots and the lone spud until Packy was sober enough to begin to help me take care of our land.

After Packy and I returned from our evening AA meetings in Kilrush or Lahinch, we would have our tea and sit around the hearth, carefully sharing our memories of the days gone by. We were still careful, very careful as there had been so much bad blood between the Sweeneys, the Murphys and the Devitts and so much that had never been shared around my mother Kate and her death and my ordination.

When either Tom or my father or I would refer to anything around that time or about any of the relatives, like Lizzie or Nellie or the Delaneys or the Flahertys, Packy would frown and scratch his head, as if we were speaking a foreign language. How stupid could he be?

I grew exasperated at Packy's obtuseness. "God, Packy, where the hell were you? My mother was dying and my father, Steve…my stepfather Steve Flaherty and the Chicago Police Department and Lizzie and her girl-friend and Liam and Clare, the twins!"

"I'll tell ye Goddamn well, Martin, ye ol' prick of a thing! I had me fuckin' head in a bottle, from morning to night and no one even noticed. That old bastard Jimmy Dalton from down your very own street, would take me few Quid and give me his cheap stuff that wouldn't sell, 'Oh, yeah, boys, here comes that stupid Packy Sweeney, let's pull out the royal shite for him, for that poor, bloody eejit Packy Sweeney.' "

"I was pissed out of me head from morning to night and not one of ye, not a Goddamn one of ye, even had a drop of love in yer hearts for old Packy what was drunk and never even a moment sober. I never ever got to shed a tear for poor Kate and her there dying away and leaving us all alone without her."

Packy continued his rage, "I missed me own sister Kate's funeral and you being a priest and all them old Delaney girls just wantin' a poke outta' me. And it took you here to get clean and sober and I don't know what will ever happen to me when ye leaves! God, but I hate yees all!"

I stood, straightened my trousers, tapped Packy on the top of his head, "Off, now, Man, to another meeting. The next thing after all this self-pity is a drink. No one poured it down your drain, you poured it down yourself, Pack. You poured it down yourself, just like I did. We have no one to blame. We just did it and we just don't do it any longer. No one can save us except ourselves, so grab your arse, Man, we're off!"

****

There was a knock on the door. Mr. McNally, the postman in the small village, had received a special delivery for Jeremiah Devitt, c/o Sweeney. He thought that it might be important, so he didn't want it to wait until Tom Sweeney came to collect the mail. It might be weeks and weeks.

It was a letter from Sheila. Jeremiah tore it open and a clipping from the Chicago Daily News, September 13, 1992, fell onto the floor. He read it:

Rev. Harry Hogan, 47, of the Archdiocese of Chicago, was murdered at the *John A. Graham Correctional Center* in downstate Hillsboro in Montgomery Co. At the time of his death, Father Hogan was serving a term of 30 – 60 years for the rape of a minor, a Class IV felony. While many of the inmates are being questioned, there have been no arrests made. His body has been returned to his family. Services pending.

Jeremiah handed me the clipping. I read it quickly, balled the paper and hurled it into the fire. "I knew it was comin'! I just knew this would happen to him! And he knew it was going to happen!"

I headed down to the sea. My heart was wrecked, broken into a million pieces of glass, ripping and tearing me apart. I stood like a statue and watched the tide go out. All I could think of was Harry ripping his fingernails and bleeding so he could feel something. Did he feel them kill him? Was he already gone? Dissociated, above and looking down on his own death?

I knelt on the wet, teary sand by a sharp, black boulder. There was no sun or moon, only the heavy clouds and the nasty wind. I pulled out my grandfather Martin Sweeney's old rosary and said the five sorrowful mysteries for the repose of Fr. Harry Hogan's dark and wounded soul. And for all the young boys who had been damaged by him and their poor families. I wept for the unfathomable sorrow of it all.

CHAPTER 44
Up the Mournful Mountain

The following morning Jeremiah rose later than the rest. We had long been out working in the fields and had come in for a break. Jeremiah poured himself a nice cup of tea and commented that he had been all over the world, but there was no tea like the Irish tea. His remarks were met with our silence.

Things were growing testy between Jeremiah and me. Once I had called him "Cardinal" when we were alone, Jeremiah spun around and growled in my face, "Don't ever do that to me again, ye hear!!"

I began to feel like a middle child, waiting for Tom and Jeremiah to begin fighting and was slightly disappointed when they didn't. I waited for Packy to start to drink again, but was relieved when he didn't. There was something in the air that didn't feel just right.

In the Irish family way, both Tom and Packy sensed that Jeremiah and I needed to talk, so they excused themselves to go take a look at their new calf. Jeremiah and I looked at each other, ready for a duel.

"Martin, I'm going up to Mayo today. Croagh Patrick is calling me." Jeremiah smiled at me. I wasn't charmed.

"Martin, I need to go up the mountain. I have a lot of penance before me, and what better place to begin than up in that rocky place?"

I looked blankly at my father. Fr. White's "Nada, Nada, Nada" back at Mundelein rang in my ears. I could not let a single nerve on my face betray to my father the fact that I had heard his confession.

"Christ, but you're a better priest than I ever dreamed of! If you'd like to come with me, Martin, I'd love to have you along. I'm not as young as I used to be and we can talk in the car. I'm going out to tell the boys, so you take your time to decide…Now don't be fussing over Packy. I can see it on your face. If he's going to drink, he's going to drink and neither you nor me, only God Almighty is going to keep him sober. It's not your job."

****

The wind rocked our small car sideways and the rain blinded us as we negotiated the narrow roads and sharp turns on our way through Clare and Galway and on into Mayo.

The weather changed from treacherous to gentle in minutes and we often found the windshield wipers slapping on a dry window or my shoulders still hunched for danger when the breeze turned soft and the sky was blue. A residue of fine salt gathered around the edges of the windows, as we hung close to the sea.

Finally entering County Mayo over the Partry Mountains, the winds seemed sharper and the air cooler. We stopped in Westport for lunch and drove the five miles along Clew Bay to Croagh Patrick, the cone-shaped mountain where the missionary Patrick, like Jesus Himself, fasted for 40 days and 40 nights and then cast the snakes out of Ireland for good. It was long revered as a place of penance. Pilgrims came from all over Ireland and Europe and the States to work off punishment for their sins.

When we reached Lecanvey, the mountain of harsh penance looked more like a simple desert mesa, a cut-off plateau of insignificant height. Everything was gray – the air, the clouds, the breeze, the stones, the mountain, even the rain. My mood was getting grayer by the minute and I felt immature, unseasoned for a man of 47 years, 47 untested, protected, 47 green years.

"It is traditional to walk the mountain without shoes, Martin," explained my father as he was bending over to unlace his boots. "But not all do…it is not required, at all. Not at all." I yanked my shoes off and threw them into the boot of the car and waited impatiently for my father. Jeremiah smiled to himself.

We began our assent, walking quickly over the low, rather friendly terrain. Our sins must be few as our penance was so easy. We soon met the large statue of St. Patrick, looking out over Clew Bay. The sun broke through the clouds, revealing the small islands of the bay like so many shimmering emeralds in a sea of deep blue velvet.

290

Jeremiah motioned for me to sit. I was impatient, as I had already slowed down to accommodate my father's slower pace. Again, I was caught unawares – I felt protective of my own father, as he was in his late 60's and had begun to slow down; yet I was still so choked with anger at his absence from my life, at Harry Hogan's murder, at all the predators in the priesthood that he could stop if he had only put his mind to it.

I had a great reserve of strength that I had just begun to use…I was a strong, angry stallion cooped up in a stable while the mares and colts frolicked in the soft, green grass. I looked further up the mountain, anxious to scale it like a frisky young goat.

"Son, I want to tell you about parts of my life that no one else knows. I'm not seeking your absolution, just your ear. And maybe your heart."

"Da?"

"This is what you need to know about me, Son, about your mother and mostly, about yourself and how you came to be."

"Da, please don't! I don't like hearing this stuff."

"You're going to listen to me, Martin, like it or not. You've been walking around with half or even quarter truths, and that hurts you more than you'll ever know. We don't really possess own our own lives until we can understand our own story in light of the story of our parents, God rest their souls."

Jeremiah began by telling me that he had been born the same year as Uncle Tom Sweeney, 1916, but Peter and Molly Murphy had lost twin girls before he was born. They found work at the Devitt's Graystone Manor, as those were times of such horrible poverty in Ireland. They were grateful for the work. But for fear of losing another child, they would bring Jeremiah up to the Devitts every day, as they could protect him.

The Devitts were childless and loved the sounds of a child around the house. Lord Devitt's brother, Ronan, was a bishop and when he would visit, he became so enamored with young Jeremiah that he'd ask Molly and Peter if they would allow their son to stay overnight at the big house. The large room at the top of the stairs had two beds and Jeremiah could share the room with the bishop.

Molly would tuck young Jeremiah into bed and Peter would come in and kiss him good-night and then they would leave him and trundle back to their little cottage. The nights were so black and cold and the sounds so scary that Jeremiah would cry and then the bishop would pat the red velvet quilt like you would for a dog. Then Jeremiah would crawl into bed with the bishop and the bishop would hold him until he stopped shaking and Jeremiah would drift off to sleep.

Before long, young Jeremiah would awaken with the bishop's hands on his little penis and he would make Jeremiah hold his penis with his little hand until it got hard and then more and more things would happen.

Jeremiah could never tell his mother or father; he thought they would never believe him and if they did, they would take him away from the Devitts and they would lose their job and they wouldn't have any money for food and they would all starve to death like in the Famine.

So Jeremiah kept his mouth shut. He grew angrier with his parents because he was doing this for them and they didn't understand the situation at all. They could have stopped it but they didn't even know what to stop and he was angry at them for not knowing, but how could they know if he didn't tell them? He thought he'd go crazy every day of his young life.

The Devitts owned him. They were making him in their own image and likeness. They gave him everything and expected everything in return. Then he was off to be a priest and the abuse continued up in Dublin and in Rome and even at the Stella Maris in Kilkee when he and the Bishop would go off for a drive on a Sunday.

When Jeremiah met Kate Sweeney, he knew that he had to be with her. And he could get revenge on her brother because Tom could live a natural life and not be kissing the bishop and other things. If he had never met my mother, Jeremiah would still be rolling around at the Vatican and there'd be no Martin Sweeney.

The happiest day of Jeremiah's life was when the Devitt's plane crashed into *La Grande Ruine* in the Dauphine Alps. Gratefully, they were all aboard – Lord Philip, Lady Mary and Bishop Ronan. He had prayed every day of his life that something would happen to break open the hell he had been locked in for nearly 40 years. He felt absolutely no guilt at their deaths, as his prayers were finally answered.

He didn't want his own parents, Peter and Molly Murphy, to come to his ordination because he couldn't face all his secrets and lies that he made his parents live with. They were simple people, good Catholics, and they would never be able to imagine what he had to endure. Jeremiah knew his parents would be hurt, but it was better than their being made fools of by the Devitts, especially that filthy bishop.

One day his mother Molly told him that if she ever needed to die, she would have one big drink and then just take a few sods of glowing, red turf and place them quietly under their bed and go to sleep. When he heard of the fire, Jeremiah knew that she did just that.

****

We found a small wooden bench off the path. Jeremiah held his face in his hands. I moved closer to my father but did not touch him. We sat in silence. Other pilgrims passed us with a nod. Jeremiah rose to continue our assent.

I let him go before me, as the path was becoming steeper and a harsh rain began to cover the slippery black rocks. Clouds came down to meet us and at times, I lost sight of my old wizened father.

Sharp stones tore at our bare feet as we continued up the steep incline. Jeremiah lost his footing, but caught himself before he went down the mountain. He lowered himself to crawl over the slippery rocks and stones on his hands and knees with the wind and rain lashing his stubborn face.

On his bare and bloody feet, I couldn't keep up with the renewed ferocity of my father, embracing the Purgatory into which he had cast himself. We crawled over the slippery boulders like two ancient Druids impelled to reach the summit to atone for the sins of our people.

With one last burst of energy, we reached the top on our feet. We had broken through the heavy black clouds below us and looked down on Clew Bay and out across Clare Island and Achill Island to the whole expanse of the Atlantic Ocean.

Behind us was Westport Quay where the Coffin Ships sailed from during the Famine on their way to New York and Boston. Those who stayed behind built bonfires on the hillside so those leaving could see County Mayo longer. Oh, Ireland is a sad old country, so it is!

Like a helpless old sheep with muddy, matted fur, Jeremiah's white beard was clumped with thick, heavy mud. His pale blue eyes filled with big, salty tears that streamed down his ruddy cheeks. He looked down on his tender feet and could see only mud and blood.

He gasped and started to cry. The tears turned to a roaring laughter and then he sobbed and wailed and pounded the earth with a fury that frightened the other pilgrims.

I tried to shield him from their eyes, but my father roared away, from deep, deep within, howling and weeping and weeping and howling. He needed witnesses to all that pain he had stored in his old wine skins that had turned into a nasty, angry vinegar and had poisoned his soul altogether. And mine with it.

Jeremiah gathered himself together and sat on the summit quietly. He breathed softly and looked toward me. I looked back to my father and nodded, smiling gently. This was the gift of the mountain which the Ancients believed was the Mount of the Eagle, of the Female who generously gave birth and rebirth to her children.

I lifted my father to his feet, embraced him and whispered in his waiting ear, "Da, I love you, I love you, I love you." He held me. His relief was complete.

We descended the mountain together through the gray cover of cloud and emerging into the clear light of day as the waters of Clew Bay bore our pain out with the tide, like the Coffin Ships that brought out the starving millions to a new life in the New World.

CHAPTER 45
The Mass Rock in the Glen

As the sun slowly sank into the western seas, the West of Ireland – round-towers, skeletons of Norman castles, hills, shrubs and lonesome trees, twisted roads, white sheep and black sheep and Connemara ponies – was suddenly rose and mauve and pink.

Jeremiah directed me into the heart of Connemara, following the signs to Clifden. We pulled in front of a lovely B&B off the main street. The sign read *Vacancy.* We checked in, again using the Archdiocese of Chicago credit card. We were taken to our rooms, freshened up and followed the landlady's directions to Barry's, "the best restaurant in town," most probably her son's.

Jeremiah invited me to have something to drink. I just wanted a large glass of ice water. I knew that there still was something unfinished between us. I checked out my father's beard and scratched my own itchy stubble.

"So, now, Lad, the last chapter is about to unfold...I'm leaving the priesthood after all these many years... are you surprised?"

I spilled my water. It rolled across the table and onto my pants. "Go on..."

"Your first Mass was your mother's funeral. My last Mass is going to be for my folks. On my walks, I've been over to the cabin and all that's left is the hearth stone. Did you ever hear the song, 'The Mass Rock in the Glen?' During the Penal Times Queen Elizabeth destroyed our churches and Mass was celebrated by priests on the run."

"The altars were flat hidden rocks so that everyone could disperse and there'd be no trace of the Mass. The ballad goes:
> *Our priests like wolves were hunted down,*
> *O God 'twas surely hard*
> *That from the right to worship Thee*
> *Thy children were debarred.*

"I have my own Mass Rock in the Glen, Martin, and surely, it's yours too. Molly and Peter Murphy were your grandparents and they were martyrs to the abuse that happened to me and to all the deceit that I thrust upon them. I need to honor them and say 'good-bye' and free them to go on, as I can feel them trapped, walking around in circles. They knew I'd be back someday, but surely not with the likes of you, Son…"

We both sat in silence. I didn't know how to feel, what to say, where to look. Jeremiah continued, "I love my faith, Martin, but it is no longer right for me to be a priest. Maybe it never was. I watch you…I've watched you and the priesthood fits you like a hand in glove. For me it was more like manacles on my hands. I was going through the motions and saying what needed to be said and writing what needed to be written. And thinking what needed to be thought. Ah, the manacles were in my mind…"

"How come? I didn't know this about you! Were you planning this all the time?" I stood up abruptly, knocking the water again.

Jeremiah caught the glass. I went back to the bar and got a glass of orange soda. I stood at the bar, looking at my father through the tinted glass of the mirror. Jeremiah suddenly looked fragile, older. I wanted to hurl a bottle of Scotch at him.

"Let's order, Da. I'm getting hungry. Imagine you are too with your 'Mass Rock in the Glen' and climbing that old mountain with our feet bloody and the rocks pelting down from above." We ordered the poached salmon and 'three veg.' Plus boiled spuds. And a nice pot of tea.

"Are you still a priest? Can you say Mass still?"

"Yes, Son. I've spoken to Bishop Szymanski and told him that I was going to the Pope and hand in my resignation. Teddie is a great guy, a bit too hungry to be the first Polish cardinal of Chicago. I'm sure that the Pope would like that, too. I told Teddie that I had asked you to come with me…that's all he knows. I had to confide in Teddie, because he has taken over right now that I'm gone. God, I really think he's glad to see me go!"

I was shaking inside. All these secrets now dumped on me and my head was crazed. I didn't know what to say to him. "Teddie Szymanski was in my class. Smart guy. Stood too close to me…"

"Oh, yeah, we all have to give Martin Sweeney a wide berth or he'll disappear." I bit my lips. I wanted to hit my father. "Martin, I'm the same damn way, so don't get too uppity on me now."

The brown bread and whipped butter arrived and within minutes, we were served our dinner. We ate in silence, each taking turns looking at the other. "What else? What else do you have to tell me?"

"I'm going to Rome on Sunday. I'm flying out of Shannon directly to Rome. I have an appointment with the Holy Father on Monday afternoon. Martin, I want you to come with me."

"You son of a bitch!!! You dirty son of a bitch, Da!"

I jumped up from the table, knocking over the salt. Jeremiah reached for it, throwing a pinch over his left shoulder. "Just sit the hell down, Martin. We're not finished, not by a long shot."

"You're fuckin' crazy, you know?? Fuckin' out of your mind, Man!!"

I shot out the high white door, bumping into an older couple coming into Barry's for their tea. The smoky green glass rattled in its frame. The waitress appeared from nowhere, so Jeremiah paid her and told her we would be back for the apple tarts and more tea.

I marched around the quaint village overlooking the Atlantic, a man with a storm in my legs, rage in my belly, and revenge in my head. The father I had sought all my life was disappearing. Up the mountain, down the mountain, a pot of tea and then it's over!! Fuck you, my dear son, Martin!"

I ripped off my shoes and threw them into the bushes. My feet were throbbing, cut and bleeding. I found a nice, flat rock beside a statue of three Irish heroes from the War of Independence. I locked my old mug in my hands and let the tears roll. The old couple from Barry's crossed the street to give me privacy.

Jeremiah watched his son from Barry's window. He had never had this chance with his own father. They say you must have a fight with your father before you can leave home. Jeremiah had never had a fight with Peter Murphy so it was just a nasty pick, pick, pick – not just one, big thunder clap and lightening strike to get the job done.

I wiped my tears. My rage and revenge had worn themselves out. I looked up and saw my father in the window. Jeremiah waved at me. I gathered my battered shoes, held them up for my father to see, and went back in the restaurant. Jeremiah had moved to the little snug off the bar, the little room formerly used by ladies who didn't want to be seen in a public house.

The waitress brought us another pot of strong tea and apple tarts with whipping cream. Neither of us said anything. I started to snicker. Within seconds, we were splitting our sides with hysteria, punching each other's arms, wiping away old, old tears.

We staggered back to the old B&B as Mrs. Barry was looking through her lacy yellow curtain. "Ah, now, have you boys the drink taken? Are you drunk at all?"

We assured her that we were stone sober, went to our rooms and slept the sleep of the dead.

****

Neither of us woke before 9:00. We bumped into each other going into her dining room. Mrs. Barry brought us a nice Irish breakfast of eggs and rashers, oatmeal, strong tea, brown bread, whipped butter and marmalade.

When she came around with a fresh pot of tea, she said, "Now, Fathers, wouldn't you like some more tea? Coffee?" We started laughing again and said that we were on our way home, we had had enough of her good Irish cooking, and we needed to settle up with her.

When she left us alone, I said, "Da, I'm not going back, at least not yet. When you were up there yesterday, rolling around that old mountain, getting crazy with the tears and laughter, it was like you were my *Sheela na Gig,* giving birth to me after all these years."

"For the first time in my life, I feel like a person, not a Zombie. I never felt like I was in my skin. I was in my head and just lookin' and lookin' and lookin' for you. I love Steve Flaherty to death, but I needed me flesh and blood Da! I'm staying and helping the boys with the land. I'm getting fat and flabby and soft and I need to toughen up and get in my real flesh and blood.

298

"Tom is slowing down, and so he should. The farm is too much for Packy. I never got a callous in my life or sweated or cut down a tree or got behind a plow. I need to be with the cows and pigs and shite. I don't know if I'll ever go back. I just don't know…"

Jeremiah felt he was going to burst with pride at his son. "I know there won't be any problem with the Archdiocese. Teddie told me to tell you to take as long as you need. I know there's no problem there. Take as long as you want, Martin. We've never been taught to honor ourselves…we let others honor us, but that's easy."

Jeremiah took two pieces of bread, wrapped them in a soft paper napkin, and stuck them in his pocket. We drove slowly through Connemara, around the town of Galway and back into Clare. We both sighed, how sweet it was to be back home again.

****

As we entered Quilty township, Jeremiah directed me to park in from the road. We made our way down an over-grown boreen to the shell of a cottage in a lonely glen. The thatch roof was long gone. Two broken windows still stood in their rotting frames.

Squirrels and chipmunks skirted out of our way. A faint smell of fire and ashes greeted us as we dusted off the hearth with branches of an evergreen tree. A wire mattress frame stood in the far corner.

We kissed our stoles and placed them over our necks, then we both blessed ourselves. Jeremiah pulled a booklet from his pocket and began the Mass:

"I will go unto the altar of God."

I responded:

"Unto God who giveth joy to my youth."

I read the Epistle:

"In those days, I heard a voice from heaven, saying to me, Write: 'Blessed are the dead who die in the Lord…they may rest from their labors, for their works follow them.'"

We held the fresh bread from Mrs. Barry's B&B and opened a small bottle of wine that Jeremiah had saved from the plane. Together we consecrated the bread and wine into the Body and Blood of Jesus and we both ate the bread and Jeremiah drank the wine.

Before we prayed the Our Father, Jeremiah read the Secret of the Mass:

"Receive, O Lord, the sacrifice for my father and mother; grant them ever lasting joy in the land of the living and in company with them, let us share in the happiness of the saints."

As we concluded the Mass, Jeremiah removed his black stole and lit it on the old hearth. Sacred objects need to be burned, not tossed in the trash. I kissed my stole and put it back in my pocket.

No longer trapped ghosts, Molly and Peter Murphy had become brilliant, shimmering spirits. They rose from their rusty bed frame and kissed their son and grandson, smiled, waved and followed the twisted boreen on out toward the sea and into the embrace of all their people who had waited so long.

There was beautiful Kate, no longer ravaged by her limp, illness and death, her arms out-stretched to greet old Peter and Molly, their young twin daughters by Kate's side.

Martin and Annie Sweeney and their daughter Biddy, just like our Aunt Jane, who finally found her freedom that dark night as she flew off the mountain. Whatever it was that made the two of them seek peace in a running leap off the mountain into the sea was deep in the blood. And all of Martin and Annie Sweeney's infants, born yet who never took a breath of air, wrapped in canvas and slipped into the night sea by their very own father.

There were Annie Sweeney's sisters, the four Delaney girls – Mayme, keeping time with the beat of the earth on her bodhra'n, Josie swinging to the ins and outs of her accordion, Norah with the pipes blowing from under her arm, and Kitty on the flute, piping her sweetest melody to welcome Peter and Molly up and beyond the tangled web of earth.

And Martin Sweeney's two brothers - Liam, who slipped out of Martin's reach and drowned, Paul, the priest who delivered little Molly Byrne one stormy night in a cabin on the cliffs of Donegal. He drank and the Jesuits sent him away and forgot about him. His hands were outstretched in blessings, welcoming his old neighbors and friends.

300

Grandpa's sister Rosie with Malachy Moran. They were both on the Titanic, but Rosie was rescued from the cold Atlantic and had a baby, then became a nun in gratitude for her life. Her family back in Ireland never knew.

And farther in the distance waiting were the Devitts – Lord Philip and Lady Mary and Bishop James. They asked Molly and Peter for forgiveness, for over the years they had been locked in a vague vaporous netherworld, in need of clarity, of forgiveness and of absolution for their sins. And as the Devitts received Molly and Peter's blessing, they all understood that it all had worked out perfectly.

We stood beside the hearth stone, their Mass rock in the glen. We breathed the breath of freedom - Oh, so deeply did we fill our lungs with that fresh, pure air that only freedom can bring. Above in their unchanging spirit place, we knew of the dance of their own spirit folk encircling them and they heard the piper piping away.

"Well, Son, we'll be with them in our own time and they'll all be there to greet us. For now, I've me own Sheila waiting for me in Chicago and you've got the lonely, lovely Sweeney land waiting for you right here."

We still stood by the hearth, not wanting the moment to pass. Jeremiah looked down at his feet. There was a little burnt ring, perhaps something from an old pot, some old piece of jewelry long forgotten. He picked it up and slipped it into his pocket.

We pulled away the bramble and made our way back through the narrow boreen. Reeds from the small lake beyond the boreen rustled in the gentle wind up from the sea. I, the dream boy, turned to my father and smiled. Jeremiah smiled at me and together, arm-in-arm, we looked out over the perfect blue-green sea.

CHAPTER 46
Rome: The City of White Marble

It didn't feel right to let Jeremiah go off to Rome by himself. The last time a cardinal of the church resigned was in 1927. It was now 1985 and I was anxious to catch up with Graham Byrne. I was learning Jeremiah's ways and when he was nervous, he grew quiet, but bit the inside of his cheeks.

We checked our small bags and stood in line to board *Aer Lingus* Flight 47 to Rome. The head stewardess motioned for us to get at the head of the line. My father was in his clerical suit and I was wearing only my black slacks and tan Donegal tweed sport coat over a white shirt. He told me I looked like a glass of Guiness, black at the bottom and tan on top.

He pulled the stewardess aside and told her that we wanted to be treated like the rest of the passengers and did not want to sit in First Class. If she had ever known that he was the Cardinal of Chicago, she would have had him flying the plane. Miss McDuff, or so it said on her name tag, told him that it was the principle of *Aer Lingus* to put the clergy in First Class, out of respect for the church.

He asked her what would happen if we refused to go up front. She stood on her tip-toes and whispered in his ear, "Father, now I'll catch hell from all of them. Please, just do what you're supposed to, Father, and I'll be able to keep my job!"

Jeremiah grabbed my arm and as we got to the front of the line, the pilot and co-pilot met with us and took us up their stairs to the cock-pit. The bright blue and green plane was dedicated to St. Brendan the Navigator, as that was freshly painted on the front side of the plane. St. Brendan was the first to discover America, a thousand years before Columbus even thought of it. Leave it to us Irish to get there first!

With a fresh rush of guilt, I looked back at the line and many were smiling at us. I guess it was our job to help them feel secure, that everything was in its place and was going to stay in its place. The Roman Catholic Church was the ballast, buried deep in the Irish Ship of State.

Although it was slightly after 10:00 a.m., the stewardess, smiling that she had won her victory over us two priests, offered us a full bar of Irish whiskeys. Jeremiah told her we "kill for a cup of tea" and she almost curtsied as she bolted for her little kitchenette.

With a kick from Almighty God, we sped down the runway and lifted off above the Shannon Estuary. We were soon over the Cork and Kerry mountains and out over the sea. It was soon into France. I tried to make out the Normandy beaches where thousands lost their lives, but they stopped the German Army. I could see only clouds. .

The great white Alps seemed to appear out of nowhere. Jeremiah's eyes were closed, but a somewhat revengeful smile was on his lips – all the Devitts were gone. He was nodding, not in sleep, but as if what he had long awaited was now complete. I had the window seat. He whispered to me, "Ah, the wondrous Alps, the wonderful Alps".

I nodded, but I could not enter into the peace or justice that he experienced over these mountains. "You know, Martin, they never found a single piece of any of them, just a few pieces of wings and rudders. It was like they were vaporized out of my life and off the earth. Fair play to them all!"

Like a magnet pulling me where I did not want to go, my father's life with the Devitts was his business, not mine. But they did shape him in and for the church, so they had a hand in my being a priest, however obliquely. I couldn't rejoice in their deaths, but I'm damn glad they are not around any longer.

"Martin, we're told to 'put justice before generosity'. All the Devitts were extremely generous to me, but horribly unjust. The irony is that I am a rich man with all of their money and their name that I carry on me like an old turtle's shell. I want to go back to being just *Jeremiah Murphy*...I'm no more a *Devitt* than that little nun here serving us our tea."

I thought to myself that then I'd be a *Murphy*, but *Sweeney* fits me just right. Thank God I didn't end up with that *Devitt* name stamped on me. *Sweeney*, the Irish name, is *Suibhne*, meaning the 'little hero'. God only knows of my cowardice, but being a hero is something good for a man to aspire to. I'm too quiet to be a hero. For now.

Soon we were descending into Rome, at what felt like a 90° angle. We had to buckle up, get the trays put away, and the little nun did everything for us except brush our teeth. St. Brendan landed with a few nasty thumps and the people in the back shouted and screamed with the fright of it.

Rome was a madness next to the tranquility of Quilty. I had never been back, but it felt like a pair of old shoes I had misplaced but slipped into with great relief and comfort. The sounds, the smells, the scenes were as familiar as yesterday. Here it was, June of 1985 and I had left so abruptly that January in 1964. Twenty-one years that had rolled by like the sand going out with the tide.

Jeremiah had booked us into two single rooms in the *Hotel Il Gattopardo Relais* on the *Viale Guilio Cesare,* just a five-minute walk to the Vatican. I could see the dome of St. Peter's from my balcony. He needed to rest and I needed to get out and find my way – back to the North American College and the Pontifical Gregorian Institute, my old "Greg". I was the hunter, getting a sniff of my prey, knowing right where to go! We would meet back there at the hotel at seven for supper.

I did not go into the NAC, but rather stood outside, remembering that first day when the rickety old yellow bus dropped us here to begin our ascent to the priesthood. Johnny Sullivan from Cleveland and me, just ready to jump out of our skins with the excitement of it all. Johnny made it to bishop and his family was so proud. Glad it wasn't me.

Then the last day, throwing my life of four years into a bag and flying back to Chicago for my mother's death. To find my real father. To become a priest. To say her funeral Mass. To reconnect with Harry Hogan and all that was ahead of us. To learn the real life of Jeremiah Cardinal Devitt, of Jeremiah Murphy, my father and friend.

Jeremiah was getting nervous about meeting with the Pope. He had come over here rather frequently, being on various boards, keeping the Pope apprised of what was going on in the States, for the installation of bishops and cardinals, financial concerns with the Vatican bank.

I wonder if the issue of priests abusing kids ever came up or was the entire thing literally buried so deeply "in the vaults" by *Crimen Sollicitationis* that it was just a 'done deal', that there was absolutely nothing to be said. That certainly was one way to deal with it. I wonder if Jeremiah was going to tell the Pope about Harry Hogan. Fr. Harry Hogan, RIP. I wonder if the Pope ever thinks about the kids.

I stayed away from the *Croce* as long as I could, but I knew that when I saw Graham, that would be the end of my wandering around the Eternal City. I headed for the Spanish Steps, called by the Romans - *Scalinata della Trinita Monti* - and he would be waiting for me right around the corner in the *Croce*.

My stomach was in knots. I hadn't seen Graham in over five years. He would make the occasional trip to Loyola in Chicago and we would get together, or in D.C. when he would be teaching at the Catholic Canon Law Society. These were always special times for me. Graham had been another man I used to fill the empty *father-space* in my life and he did it so well.

An old man was sitting at Graham's table in the darkened corner. My eyes swept the room, thinking that he was at another table. I looked back at the old man and Graham nodded at me. My hand began to shake. His wild red hair and beard had gone white, with a stubborn strand of pale red now and then. He had lost some height and gained a little weight, but so had I. His dark blue eyes were smaller and deeper. His shaggy eye-brows were snow white.

"So what brings you to my little town, Lad?"

"I'm here with the Cardinal. He's got some business with the Holy Father tomorrow. He just dragged me along. We were home in Ireland these past few weeks, trying to work out some old stuff that sat between us."

Graham raised his eyebrows, inviting me to tell him more if I chose. What was there to say? A waitress brought me a glass of red wine, but I apologized and asked for just a bottle of San Pellegrino, that light Italian mineral spring water. We sat without talking. There was always this transition time when we had to get used to each other again.

"Any chance that Jeremiah would resign? I've been hearing that there is a lot of stuff going on in Chicago. Must be a tough job. I wouldn't want it for anything."

"I've been thinking the same thing, Graham. Some of these priests are running wild with the kids and he has to pay tens of thousands of dollars for their treatment, then they come back, make a good confession, get sent to another poor, unsuspecting parish, play around with these new kids, then it's back for treatment. The Cardinal ends up writing the family a huge check to be quiet and sends the priest to be a chaplain at nursing home or hospital, away from kids."

"Aren't there kids in hospitals?"

"Of course, Graham, there are kids in hospitals. One of the parts that have me so concerned is that these pedophiles go to confession and state that they have a 'firm purpose of amendment'. Then they receive absolution, a clean slate, but it is far from over. It is impossible with someone so diseased; the compulsion is so deeply imbedded in the neurons of their brains, that it is literally impossible for them to control their proclivities."

Graham put his long feet back up on a chair and puffed long and hard on his new pipe. He held it up for my admiration. "Got this back in Chicago, last time I was there. Fancy little shop down in the Loop, under the EL tracks." He blew the smoke up to the darkened ceiling. I wondered what his lungs looked like.

"And so the conundrum is that if we perceive child sexual abuse as a *sin*, it can be taken care of in *confession*; but by the very definition of the pedophile, he is unable to make a 'firm purpose of amendment', therefore the confession is invalid. Interesting dilemma we've gotten ourselves into. Wonder what Thomas Aquinas would have to say."

This was not an intellectual problem that could be resolved by a dialectical approach. Or perhaps it should be: *thesis, antithesis, synthesis.* Something at the fundamental core of the church was not working. Like the brakes had been stripped clean and we wondered why we weren't stopping as we headed for the cliffs.

Apart from the theological and sacramental issues, there were the very political ones about power and denial of responsibility. About the tired ploy of setting up a *Commission* to study the problem. I was getting restless with Graham's staid, unemotional, cerebral approach. What if he had walked in and saw Harry Hogan raping that child?

"Christ, Graham, it's not my responsibility! They have this Priests Advisory Board and they make all the decisions. It is still held pretty much under wraps, but I think it is going to explode one day soon. There are small articles in the *National Catholic Reporter,* but the big papers haven't picked it up yet."

Graham sipped his wine carefully. He lifted his glass and asked me if his drinking bothered me. I shook my head. Right now the thought of alcohol made me rather ill. The cats were still on the tables. Sneaky little bastards.

"Imagine where we would be now, Graham, if it weren't for that document you showed me when I was a student. You remember, *Crimen Sollicitationis,* to be kept buried in the vault. Papal secrecy. Lucky for these guys that they are only sinners, not felons."

"Well, Martin, they are felons and the world is going to catch up with them and all the high and mighty bastards that protect them. Pardon if I am being disrespectful of your dear father, but these bishops are all in it together. I don't think the folks will take it much longer.

"And, have you ever thought of what has been going on in Ireland for years and years, and the poor young mothers with the old nuns in those God-forsaken laundries, giving up their babies for the American bishops to hand out. The Irish church has much to answer for, and as you know, the church runs the government."

Graham told me that he wanted to discuss something else that related to this issue, but he'd feel more comfortable back at his office. One thing that kept Graham from being boring was you just never knew what he had cooking in that magnificent mind of his. Or as they say, "A spur in the head is worth two in the heel".

We crossed back across the Tiber on the narrow *Ponte Cavour* and followed the *Via Crescenzio* right up to the walls of the Vatican.

307

His office had changed little with the stacks of papers, reports, magazines, and reprinted articles, tomes covering the shelves, tables and floors. He did have a new computer and couldn't hide the fact that he was rather proud of his agility with a 20th Century item.

He knocked some books off a chair and invited me to sit. He pulled his chair from behind his desk and we both put our feet up on his desk. The old pipe came out and I began to feel like I was a student again, sitting at the feet of a learned Jesuit, learning what I needed to know to be a priest.

Graham lit the pipe and again I smelled the turf fires from home. I knew he had something important to tell me, but didn't quite know how to begin. He showed me a picture of a woman, surrounded with black kids. "Here is my sister, Molly, the one that your Uncle Paul Sweeney delivered that old night back home. She is a doctor now, working in a village in Kenya with the Maryknoll sisters. A real trooper, she is!"

I took the picture in my hand and looked closely at Dr. Molly Byrne. My uncle had actually delivered her, with no training at all, and the order sending him to the tip of Donegal, punishing him for his drinking. God rest his magnificent Jesuit soul!

Graham then asked me what I understood about a Social Contract and had I studied it much. I told him that we covered it in Philosophy 101 when I was in Mundelein before I came to Rome. I understood it to be an implicit agreement between two parties, wherein the lesser obeys and the more powerful one protects. He smiled as he nodded assent with his grand silvery head of hair.

Graham then proceeded to remind me that the philosophers Plato, Aristotle and Socrates and the French Rousseau and English philosophers Locke and Hobbes, Rawls of recent years, had all struggled with that most fundamental aspect of our civilization. The Social Contract was the basis of all law. Thomas Aquinas, Dominican theologian and Doctor of the church, wrote that if a government becomes tyrannical, its authority may be revoked or limited by that community that has given its authority to them.

The heart of Social Contract theory is that those who are governed have an implicit agreement with those who govern: those who are governed will obey (by voting, paying taxes, following traffic signals) and he who governs will keep them safe. This holds true from the earliest times that man walked the earth right up to the present.

Graham relit his pipe and I excused myself and headed for the toilets. I needed a break from this heady stuff and I had a feeling I knew where he was going. I can't believe how young I was when I'd spend time in this very office with dear Graham. I was like a son to him.

"Now, Martin, you know where we are going with this, don't you?"

"Like I know the back of my hand, Graham, but do continue. I'm right with you, every step of the way."

Graham then began to draw a simple parallel with the church: We the people follow the rules, try to be good Catholics, and the agreement of the bishops is that they will keep us safe. The *Social Contract* of Political Theory becomes more of a *Sacred Covenant* when applied to the People of God, as the church was defined by Vatican II.

I interrupted Graham, "So if a bishop pays the people whom the church has damaged, kicks the priests out of the church, goes to confession and even resigns his position, he still has not fulfilled his part of the *Sacred Covenant*. Why, Graham?"

"You tell me. But we need not to forget that the church runs in a perfect hierarchical agreement, more like the *Divine Right of Kings*. I think this is the beginning of bringing the powerful aspects of a most *Sacred Covenant* up to the front. This has to be resolved, one way or another. You are much closer to that world than I am. I just read about it, hear about it, think and pray about it.

"I think the bishop in that situation would have done the right stuff, but in one way, it is all on the outside and does not really impact him as deeply as he allowed the people to be unsafe, harmed, damaged. He really owes more to his people, to God, to the Universe, more of the essence of himself, as befits the gravity of his neglect."

"You got it, Martin. Do you have any idea of what a bishop who perpetrates this damage on his people can do to truly, spiritually, soulfully, make restitution?"

"Kill himself?"

"You're getting closer. Think it through, Martin. Use your head."

"Prison?"

CHAPTER 47
To Your High Altar I Once Came

My father was still in his clerical suit and I was in my civvies. I hadn't asked him about what had happened with the Pope and he hadn't asked me about Graham. The stewardess had served us our tea and biscuits and we closed our eyes for our three-hour flight back to Shannon.

Jeremiah and I had so little real history together that I felt we were treading on strange, foreign soil. Now was the time to either put down roots for our relationship to grow deeply or it would prove to be quick-sand and that would be the end of everything. I didn't know what to do and all I could think of was "less said the better".

My father asked me to lower the shade a bit, as the sun was bouncing right off the snowy Alps and right into our eyes. He sipped his tea and ever so slightly nudged my arm. We had always been so careful not to touch each other, lest we convey a familiarity that was absent from our still somewhat stilted relationship. And of course, an Irishman could never touch another Irishman, unless it were a punch in the face or a slap on the back.

"So, Martin, how's your old Graham Byrne? Anything new in the Canon Law department?"

"He's the same, just a bit older. His office is piled high with stuff and he's still puffing on that old pipe."

"I was in many classes with Graham at the Gregorian. We never really took to each other, but we'd be sniffing around each other like two sheep dogs. Guess I was trying to see which of us had the most power and he was looking to see which of us were the brightest. We each went on the path that was the best for our talents and energy."

"As I was leaving, he told me a strange thing. He said that within the next 50 years that they would elect a Jesuit pope and the whole thing would be radically different. What do you think about that?"

"Well, as I've just told you, Graham and I have always been on different frequencies. There is no way in the world that the College of

Cardinals would pick a Jesuit to run the church. The Curia would chew him up and spit him out in less than a day."

"I don't know either, but I know him and I know you. I'm the link between the both of you. Graham, in a most bizarre way, has his finger on the pulse of the church. Like those Oriental doctors that can make a diagnosis for hidden diseases by just putting their finger on your pulse. Those doctors can feel three pulses at the same time. Graham Byrne feels what's coming in the wind."

My father got the attention of the stewardess and asked for some more tea and biscuits. He looked out the window and I saw him unobtrusively bless himself, as now we were probably over the Dauphine Alps and the Devitts snowy old bones.

"Bet you Five Quid, Da, that we get a Jesuit pope before 2020."

"Sure, I won't be around by then – Graham and I'd both be 104. If it happens before 2015, then you will win. I'd only be 99, and a young man by anyone's standard!"

That seemed to take the starch out of our spines and we began to relax. Graham Byrne had always been not exactly a 'bone of contention', but almost a repository for our hidden histories. Graham shared some of both of us and it was easier to speak of him than of ourselves. But perhaps that wasn't fair to Graham, nor to each other.

"So what did the Pope have to say on that bright day at the Vatican?"

"Now, don't get fresh. Don't get disrespectful to the Holy Father. Nor to me, Martin."

"I'm truly sorry, Da. I am. I want to know and I just don't know what to say."

"Well, that is a little more honest, Martin. The Holy Father sent his finest regards to the finest priest in all Chicagoland!"

"Did he really?"

"Do you think he even knows you exist?"

"Well, he ought to know. Why didn't you tell him?"

"That's none of your goddamn business and we're going to keep it that way."

Back home when I was a kid and Packy and I were rolling on the floor and Biddy was singing and Lizzie was snarling, Grannie would hum, over and over again, *"The stars make no noise...the stars make no noise."* and strange as it seems, it would quiet us all down, at least for a few minutes.

"I no longer have my ring." My father held out his hands and his fingers were bare. There was a slight tremor in his left hand. His right hand covered his left hand on his tray-table as he noticed me looking at them. "The Holy Father has it. He was shocked. Cardinals don't resign. They don't just quit."

I placed my right hand over my father's hands. I could feel his old hands moving, not on their own volition. He didn't shoo me away. I loved my dear old fool, more than he could ever love me, his young old fool. We both sat with tears running down our cheeks and the stewardess ran for more tea.

My father whispered to me, "I could get out of Chicago, out of the States, return to Ireland or England. He offered me the position of Archbishop of St. Mary Major, the largest basilica devoted to the Blessed Virgin in the city of Rome. I could sit on more Curial seats, have a big part in promoting cardinals and bishops in America."

I kept my hand over his. He was simply weaving for me a cloak of papal seduction that the Supreme Pontiff had held up for him to grab. Uncle Tom would have said, *"Hold on to the bone and the dog will follow you"*. My father was not a dog and he was not following the papal bone. "I'm proud of you, Da!" I whispered back.

Jeremiah continued, "I told him that I was thinking seriously of leaving the priesthood. He asked me not to. He felt there was more work for me to do and that I could do it only if I were still a priest. At that point he looked me right in the eye and I knew without a doubt that the decision was mine. I had led my life pleasing others. I know that the dear Lord Himself will guide me. Actually, I've already made my decision, as you know from my last Mass."

I held tight to this good man. He made it clear that he was not to be seduced by the most powerful man on the planet. I thought how the devil had tried to seduce Jesus after he was tired and hungry from fasting and praying for 40 days. 'Be gone, Satan!'

For all the years I had searched for my father and then for the many years I had hated and loved him, I never thought we would be

313

in a position for him to teach me anything, let alone lessons of the spirit. There was no price to be had on his soul, not even from the pope. There was no longer any space to hide behind *obedience;* his obedience was to God, not to any human stand-in.

We landed back at Shannon in the early evening. As all the summers in Ireland, the days take long to wind down. It was still bright as we pulled into Kitty Whelan's B&B down the road from Tom and Patch. We had stayed there since we had arrived, as there was no room for the both of us, and to be honest, the filth of the place made us sick.

Kitty had never seen Jeremiah in his clerical clothes. She knew who we were and our relationship with the Sweeneys, but to see him in full garb threw her off her game. Kitty was in charge of everybody and everything, but now the odds were off when it came to clergy vs. laity. She had called him "Jeremiah", but now it was "Fr. Devitt this and Fr. Devitt that…" She nodded to me – she'd get me in my right place and have us all sorted out by tea time.

We changed out of our travelling clothes and headed out to Lahinch for something to eat. Jeremiah and I were pleasantly tired and growing fond of each other's company. He reached over for my arm as the sun was slowly setting over Liscannor Bay. We were all talked out and this was his way of thanking me.

"So, right now, you're still a priest. We'll have to buy you another stole, Da, as you burned yours at your last Mass. What kind of a priest would you be without your stole?"

"And what kind of a priest would I be without my own flesh-and-blood son?"

We made our way to the comfortable dining room at the old hotel on the main street there in Lahinch. The sun had set and the narrow streets and alleys were suffused with the peachy-mauve of Grannie's big old roses back at home some 40 years ago.

****

I found myself feeling tender towards my father and he was becoming easier with me. I had always been aware of his power, but now he was becoming vulnerable, yet with a strength that arose from within himself, not from outside himself. He was intelligent and

314

worldly in a way that seemed to fit him. On me it would have been a farce.

I have spent many hours dwelling on the application of the concept of the Social Contract and *how* and *if* it applies to the church. Inherent in this agreement is the premise of *safety*, the basic need of every living thing. I like *Sacred Covenant* better, as those words seem to evoke the sacramental dimension and the more impenetrable mystery that is church.

I'm out here trying to refit the gray stones for our old Irish walls and thinking of the fact that there is something missing from my father's journey to innocence. He was up to his neck in all this child abuse by his priests, actually facilitating their access to kids, so just quitting the job doesn't quite retroactively make him innocent. There is something big missing from this picture.

For me there is something atavistic stacking up these old rocks, balancing the round with the sharp, the dark with the light, the smooth with the rough, just like old Martin Sweeney did long before the Famine of 150 years ago. Like trying to put the picture together whether this horrible issue could or would ever be healed.

The key right now in my thinking is in his failure to keep the implied promise of *safety*. Plainly, Jeremiah Devitt did not keep the children safe from the predators. He had put them in harm's way, again and again and again.

His failure will be felt in families for generations to come. Apologies and big checks don't really work. How does he atone for such sins? How does he fill the black, gaping void where love and light should dwell?

Regardless of what the doctors at the treatment centers said, it was clear that these priests would repeat and repeat. He threw them right back into other positions of access, filled with innocent kids and their trusting mothers. Like a guy goes into treatment for alcoholism and when he is finished, they make him take a job in a bar.

My father has now done the easy stuff, but he has not truly answered for his decisions to save the church and sacrifice the kids. This void cries out to be filled, or at least addressed. Like the Nazi criminals who had to answer at Nuremberg, but they were just doing what they were told to do. Like the My Lai Massacre with 500 innocent villagers killed, Lt. William Calley just doing what he was told to do. Like the Archdiocese of Chicago with hundreds of kids destroyed for life, and Cardinal Jeremiah Devitt just doing what he was told to do.

This may sound crazy, but I think these lumpy gray rocks trust that I'll know what to do with them and where they will go. Maybe not where they have been for hundreds of years, but in the right place now for the last part of the 20th century. They feel comfortable in my hands, even though my nails now are nothing but crumbs of keratin.

I'm feeling closer to my father and I don't think he is going to bolt on me. We are locked in this forever. I've got his back and he has mine, even though Kitty Whelan across the road is driving herself crazy trying to know who we really are. We're having fun keeping that all from her – a whisper in Kitty's ear is louder than a bellowing from a cow fallen into a well.

If she ever knew what's going on inside my head, it would give her enough ammunition for the rest of her days. So innocently fixing the wall, so shrewdly defining atonement for Cardinal sin.

I kept thinking that Jeremiah does not have to atone for all the dictates of *Crimen Sollicitationis* and the havoc it has wrought; he must simply atone for his own sins and pay back to society for his felonies.

As I slipped a nice, round speckled rock into a ready opening in my newly constructed old stone wall, I understood. His sins have been addressed; his felonies are unanswered. Not unanswerable, just not answered yet. Something has to change radically, or darkness will continue to cover the earth.

CHAPTER 48
The Pilgrim Soul in You

It was good to get back home. We were gone for only three days, but it felt like three weeks. Jeremiah was a new man, the burden of office off his shoulders. Kitty Whelan was like a hen on a hot griddle, wanting to know what was going on. Both Tom and Patch wanted to know, but they pretended that it was of no importance.

I needed to get back to my fields and fruit trees. My cows and goats. My stone walls and my sturdy plow. I've heard that every cell of our body remembers and as I'm out there doing an honest day's work, my cells are weeping within my sweat. I'm cleaning up my strange and twisted past, getting ready to return to my work as a priest, whatever that might be.

It is so good to finally have a flesh-and-blood father. My feet are now on the ground and as the muddy streams engulf my feet, I know I am a man in the world. I am no longer 'a man among boys; a boy among men'.

The church has taken a beating with all the secrecy and privacy and threats of excommunication. We are bleeding money, and that is only as it should be. We have a hell of a lot to answer for.

With my pale, white skin and flabby muscles and gross ignorance of how things work, I've turned our poor, ramshackle little house and farm into something we can be proud of. It was wrong of us to neglect it and let the house go to hell. Patch seems sober and is connected to the Program. Tom is on the mend with his depression and despondency.

Even though I've been back to Ireland for a short time, I've learned. The earth has taught me what it means to be a man – how to be strong and gentle and humble. I can't force animals or plants to grow, but I can ready the soil, pray for rain and hope the sun does her part. I'm ready to go back to Chicago and to do something to heal our poor, wounded church, our poor wounded children.

Jeremiah asked me to go back to Kilkee so we could plan what we were doing next. We settled ourselves on the porch at the Stella

317

Maris Hotel and were served a pot of tea and some fresh, brown bread. I had never felt my father so at ease.

"Martin, I have a lot to answer for. There's nothing I'd like better than to go to prison for 'endangering children', 'aiding and abetting', 'harboring fugitives'. I've spoken at length with Babe Nathanson, both before we left and just this morning."

I couldn't make eye-contact. Could he have been reading my mind? I looked far out to sea and the waves seemed sharp and reckless. "Go on, Da."

"Babe says that there is no Illinois statute that would cover my crimes. No attorney would take it (meaning herself), no prosecutor would agree to it, no judge would allow it in his courtroom. There is no room for a plea bargain if there is no prosecutable crime."

"While that is not how I feel, that is how it is. I have given a lot of thought and prayer as to what I need to do next. I need to get back to Chicago and clean everything up. All those boxes of evidence need to be carefully marked and stored, as I know they will be subpoenaed in the future."

I reminded him that a few of the priests had gone to law school, so they could take care of that. Jeremiah nodded with a smile. Of course, he had thought that all through. We were quiet now, with a comfort in each other's presence that we had never felt before.

"I've been thinking seriously of going up to the Cistercians in Tipperary. They run Mt. St. Joseph in Roscrea. They have taken an old Benedictine monastery and kept it up. A life of work, silence, solitude and prayer. I think I have secretly wanted that my whole life. If I can't go to prison in Illinois, then I'll be a monk in Tipperary."

"That's not good enough, Da. You'll be gone again and we'll end up being strangers to each other. If you have to go to a monastery, I'm sure there are some in Illinois or Wisconsin. Being locked away in Tipperary sounds like an easy way out. You don't belong there. I think I have a say in the matter! That's just not going to work!"

I closed my eyes. I felt the old lump in my throat. I'll be in Chicago and he'll be in Roscrea! He put his hand on top of mine. "I know, Martin, but I've spoken at length with the abbot and we will get together every six months for as long as we'd like. We'll have a special little Devitt fund for that."

"Absolutely not! This is chickening out. You have to go back and make your reparations with the all the people you caused trouble to! Absolutely not! No way in hell are you locking yourself away like that. I agree with the pope that you have more work to do. Doesn't faith come in here somewhere?"

After that out-burst, we were quiet again. People were coming in, heading to the bar in the back. I had never spoken to anyone like that. There was a subtle shift of power between us, as if I were now the parent and he were my son. I liked it this way.

"Now, about you, Martin. Do you see yourself getting back in parish work again?"

"Well, I don't suppose I've had all this information ...or commotion ...for nothing. I'd like to do something with all the Harry Hogans – to keep them safe and to keep the rest of us safe. I'm not sure what, but I do love the farm and the earth. I can't figure out how to put that together, but I'm not going to the Cistercians."

"No one asked you to."

"I know it, Da. Just being funny...'a nod is as good as a wink to a blind horse'.

"A thought came to me last night in prayer. There is no place for these guys to go who truly want to do penance for their sins and crimes. They've all been abused themselves, and while that is no excuse for what they did, they may begin to heal just the way you have healed, pushing that old plow, planting the seeds, taking care of your cows. Getting out of your head and into your body."

"What are you talking about, Da? You making this up?" I thought the man was getting a bit too monastic for me. "Where is this place?"

CHAPTER 49
You Will Go a Long Journey

I stayed in Quilty as the weeks turned into months. Finally, I had healed myself and the land and it was time to return to my life, my priesthood in Chicago.

The days and weeks that I had spent at home with Tom and Packy, honoring the land, honoring my own body and mind, growing in sobriety and simply growing up, had profoundly changed me. I had lost 20 pounds, my skin was darker and my hair was lighter. My body had definition and my eyes were clear - direct and confident, not beguiling, or even seductive.

When I walked through the gates at the International Terminal, Jeremiah was waiting for me. Unlike so many of the other Irish men who awkwardly shook hands with each other, we embraced and were not ashamed of our love for each other.

As we were headed back into the city, I shared with my father my dream of a holy place, a monastery, a place for reparations and atonement for the sins of the bishops and priests. None of this would have happened if the bishops had a care in their heart for kids and their families.

Jeremiah was silent as he negotiated his way down the Kennedy to Fullerton. I looked over and caught my father smiling and nodding.

"Is that what you've come home with now?" asked Jeremiah.

"I think the Good Lord has a different use for me now. I just can't see going back to a parish with all that's going on. But I still want to be a priest, that will never change," I chided my father, with a slight poke in the ribs.

"Let me think of this for a while, Son. You know, I still have all that old Devitt money that I've never really touched. I never had a reason. Let me think...you might be on to something, Martin. You still sober?"

"Sure, it's been a good eight years since my last drink. One day at a time, one day at a time. I love the AA meetings over there, but I'm anxious to get back to my home group. Up on Addison. They're all the same, but they're all different."

We exited the Kennedy for Fullerton. Everything looked the same, just somehow fresher. Perhaps it was me who was fresher. "How's Sheila?" I inquired off-handedly.

"I was waiting for you to ask me, Martin. Sheila is fine, her health, I mean, but she still misses Joel a lot. I've asked her to stop working so we can spend our time together…and when my papers come through, we're going to get married. She still lives in Skokie and I have an apartment in Evanston."

"Da? You sure? I thought this might happen. You sure?"

"Right as rain. I think now that the Pope wants to get rid of me fast, so Teddy Szymanski said that my papers would be here before Christmas. Some of those guys in the Vatican can tie me up forever, but I'll give them until the first of the year and then we'll get married, with or without my papers."

"Martin, I want to think more about your idea. I worked with a Benedictine Scripture scholar when I was in Rome. They're fine men. They have a place up in Wisconsin. Maybe we'll take a ride up there before the leaves turn."

****

Pulling their hoods up around their heads against the wind, the old monks walked the lush green hills like a herd of black Angus cattle. We stood on the Wisconsin bluff with the Abbot, Fr. O'Connor, an old man with thick, white eye-brows that sat defiantly above his rheumy black eyes. He'd wipe his veiny marble face with the worn sleeves of his stained black habit. In his prime, Father Abbot was well over six feet tall – now he was small and bent as an old beech tree against the wind.

As there had been no novices in over 30 years, the Benedictines were an aging community with no one under 70. The Abbot himself was nearing 80 and there was no one to take his place. The monastery had been built for over 100 monks; there were less than twelve.

As I worked the farm at home, I grew to respect the sheer simplicity and profound prayer of achy muscles and dirty hands and sweaty arms. How much closer to God could I be as I broke the hard earth beneath me and loved it into wheat and oats and flax?

I learned again to care for the weakest of the calves and to harness the strength of the horses. I became the man I had always wanted to be, fearless in the face of nature, humble in its majesty. Yet I was ignorant and fumbled as I learned the old ways. Tom Sweeney, knowing that I was struggling but would not ask for help, would say with a twinkle in his eye, "Now Martin, don't go mistakin' the beard of an old goat for the tail of a fine black stallion."

What if Harry Hogan had had the opportunity to breathe the wild wind as it tore across the earth and to cleanse himself in the searing rain and break his back with honest-to-God labor? What if Harry could have lost himself in community prayer, not in a pathological dissociation from the reality of life?

What if Harry could have entered into deep contemplative prayer and could have truly sought and received forgiveness? What if Harry could have become a monk, of sorts, to atone for his sins against children?

What if Harry could have forgiven himself? His brothers? His parents? His friends and superiors who did not stop him? The parents who slapped their son's face when he told them what Father Hogan had done to him?

As the Marshall Plan provided financial and physical resources to rebuilt Europe after World War II, why could not these priest-penitents rebuilt the community of Faith that they had so cleverly dismantled and destroyed? Did these old monks, faithful to their vowed life, deserve simply to atrophy and die?

What if Harry and the other priests-abusers could have stormed the heavens with grief and sorrow and repentance? What if these men had spent their days making reparations, spiritual reparations for their sins against children?

And these restitutions would be restitutions of prayer, not money. The reparations would be those of grace and healing, as the priest-abusers would enter daily into communal prayer and hard, physical work to restore the lands that the old monks were no longer able to care for and to nurture.

I shared this vision with the old Abbot who grew silent as he looked toward the over-grown fields, the empty barns, the decrepit sheds. He knew that the day was not far when there would be but the one monk left to blow out the last candle.

For well over 60 years, the Abbot's life had been governed by the Rule of St. Benedict, written in 528, the oldest rule for religious orders in the church. He had been elected Abbot for life when he was 55 and daily read from the Rule: *"An Abbot who is worthy to govern a monastery ought always to be mindful of the name he bears…for he is regarded as holding the place of Christ in the monastery."*

Had the Divine Design now deem that this already sacred space which was no longer needed for the daily life of the monks, now be used to renew the face of the earth and to heal its gaping wounds through the conversion and prayer of the abusers?

A Benedictine monastery was designed to be a haven for meditation. Who is there who could not be caught up in the very Presence of God as he worked the fields, prayed, chanted the Divine Office, meditated, obeyed the orders of his superior, supported his brothers?

Harry had made it clear to me that a child molester could never again be near a child, so this remote space, far apart from families and the young, would provide refuge for them, refuge from the onslaught of their addictions, their compulsions, their sins.

I knew well that those who abuse a child have been themselves abused, but that nearly all who themselves have been abused do not abuse other children.

So many days back in Ireland, I would wipe my brow and look inward from the sea to the many small farmlands distinguished from their neighbors by the old stone walls, rolling and folding with the contour of the land.

And when a willful sheep or blind donkey would bring down the wall, a farmer would quickly replace the fallen stones so as not to alarm a neighbor as to a slow take-over of his property. Generations of families had become and remained enemies over the stealing of land.

323

The great stone walls marked the boundaries where one farmland ended and another one began. When these boundaries were violated, hatred and violence broke out, neighbor upon neighbor. So much more precious than soil, the very boundaries of a child's body and mind and soul were disregarded, trampled by the compulsive needs of an addicted, sneaky pervert.

As I broke the soil and planted the seed potatoes, I wondered how many children were being abused by priests or ministers at that very minute and how many of those priests or ministers had been abused themselves. My very own father had been abused, Harry had been abused, three of the priests at Guest House admitted to having been abused by older priests.

There were lawyers who pursued jail sentences and financial settlements from priest-abusers and their dioceses. There were therapists who attempted to heal the broken hearts of young children and adult children and to restore a semblance of faith where all trust had been destroyed. There were social and political groups that spoke out to the media and marched to protest irresponsible Bishops and Cardinals.

There were treatment centers specializing in the treatment of pedophiliac priests. Too often the warnings of the staff were ignored and these men were returned to their dioceses only to strike again. Or to be sent to other unsuspecting or naïve Bishops to begin their "march to the sea" with a fresh crop of boys and girls.

In some of these places, the flawed, addictive nature of their minds and actions was seen in a moral context, and once a priest "repented", he was forgiven his sins and sent back to hurt more children. It was like sending an alcoholic to work in a bar, hoping he wouldn't drink.

There was nowhere that a Harry Hogan could spend his life, away from children, in hard work and deep prayer, healing the skin of the earth. Harry Hogan's death was in vain, as well as the deaths of all the other abusers. At the hands of others or by their own hands. Their sins were so great that they deserved not to live. Was the gracious Mercy of God not imaginative enough to save them?

****

324

The Abbot directed us into his office. He needed to discern if we were the Sundance Kids, there to wrestle control of the monastery from him, or were we an answer to the prayers that the monks sent up, "from their lips to God's ears," knowing that their days on earth were numbered.

Fr. O'Connor asked who we really were, what our relationship was, what did we see for the future of the monastery and would the old monks be cared for. Would the monastery still be Benedictine after all the monks were gone?

He closed his eyes and lowered his voice, "But the most important thing of all, it's all of us lying out there beyond that first hill, as the land slopes a bit to the east, that nothing ever disturb us lying peacefully under the sod with the old trees protecting us and Our Lady Herself waiting there to bring the rest of us home to her Beloved Son. I don't want a shopping mall or a cheap housing development to crush the old bones of our brothers, just for the sake of money and 'progress', you understand?"

Jeremiah began to speak, but I placed my hand on my father's knee. I was now in charge. I began to address the old monk's concerns of the present and his fears for the future of his entire community. I was clear in my vision of how the monks' needs would be met by an on-going community of priests, perhaps from all over the world, which would spend their lives in atonement for abusing children.

I continued, my voice clear and certain, "Secular priests, priests from religious orders, Bishops and Cardinals, and even the Pope if he feels so called. There is no place for these men to go and there is no work for them to do. They're all so sick with their addiction to kids and the only remedy for addictions is the 12 Step Program."

"You know, Fr. O'Connor, this is not going to be a dumping ground for any guy who just wants to avoid jail or for any bishop who just wants to get rid of a problem priest. They are going to have met the legal and prison sentences if any have been adjudicated. They will also have to meet our rigorous standards. It's going to be tough to be accepted, and after a trial period to see if they fit in, they won't want to leave."

I had never spoken with such forth-rightness and I was aware of my new leadership, as it sounded in the tone and depth of my voice.

The Abbot's eyes were closed and his old head was nodding. We didn't know if he were asleep or meditating. I stopped speaking. "Sure, now, Fr. Sweeney, go on, go on!" the Abbot chided.

As I spoke lovingly of how the land would be cared for, tears ran down the old Abbot's cheeks. "Ah, you know, Lad, the land is the Lord's good land and He'll see that it's always in good hands, but the old monks are my charge and we can never turn our backs on our good men who have spent their lives, the only lives they'll ever have, in the service of the Lord."

"Fr. O'Connor, we'll take good, good care of your men. They'll even have a new life as these holy grounds come alive with cows and pigs and ducks and horses and corn and wheat and the "sweat of their brows" as these penitents set things right with the Good Lord! The bees will be buzzing in our flowers, butterflies will cover the fields, the little birds will find their way back home to us."

The old Abbot opened his eyes, stood up and shook out his twisted black scapular, the long garment which was placed over his black habit, a tunic belted around the waist. The scapular was the width of his shoulders and went over his head and down to his feet in the front and back. Both his habit and scapular were frayed and stained, like an old man with no one to care for him.

He glanced at Jeremiah and extended his thin, gnarly hand to me. "Sure, now, doesn't the old pipe give the sweetest smoke? You might be an answer to our prayers, Fr. Sweeney!" I smiled down at the Abbot.

The Abbot squeezed my hand harder. "But on the other hand, you might not be, so don't go getting yourself all pumped up that you landed this nice, big fish! I'll tell the monks about you and what you want to do and we will all have to vote. Did you know that the Benedictines are the oldest democracy in the world?"

He ushered us to the door. "So now, this is the first step and there'll be many more before you become our 'guests'. You know, that's what you'll be called, unless any of you want to become Benedictines, but that's not necessary at all."

The Abbot walked us to our car. He pointed to an area beyond the large lake which was part of the monastery. "You see, over beyond there. There is another whole section. It's a large house that faces our lake…you can't see it from here, because of the trees."

"And an old dried up well, sunk deep into the ground. I think of her all the time and why she dried up on us. I think of her…maybe you'll know what she wants, I sure don't know. Be off with you now and we'll stay in touch, Fr. Sweeney." He nodded to Jeremiah.

As we circled around the drive and made their way down the road past the cemetery, the Abbot raised his hand in blessing and thought of the strange ways that the Good Lord answers all our prayers.

I had finally become a man. Jeremiah Murphy, sitting beside me, had at last come into my life to pull me out of my long dimension of boyhood, where I was vague, passive, afraid, and to pull me into the realm of manhood. It began on the porch of the *Stella Maris* in Kilkee when I told him he could not go to the monks in Tipperary. I was now, at nearly 50, beginning to be an authentic man.

CHAPTER 50
That Beautiful, Beautiful, Beautiful God
Was Breathing His Love in a Faraway Bog

1993. I turned from my desk and looked out my office window down to the lake. The lines from Gerard Manley Hopkins played again in my mind, *"What I do is me, for that I came."*

The Angelus bell was going to ring soon and the priest-penitents would be dropping their work to pray and then they would make their way, over the hills, from the fields and barns and kitchen and library and storage places to gather to chant in Latin the Divine Office – Prime, Tierce, Sext, None.

After that would be their main meal, grown mostly from our own green fields and rich, plentiful orchards. It was not an easy life they had chosen – one of hard work, silence, prayer, surrender, complete isolation from the outer world with no television, no computers, no newspapers and magazines.

No clocks except for the ringing of the monastic bells, summoning them to wake, to prayer, to work, to sleep. No mail. No visitors except family members twice a year who brought no gifts.

On my large dark walnut desk was a small framed picture of Harry Hogan on the day of his ordination. Harry never had a chance to atone, to make right the wrongs he had done to the children and their families, the wrongs that he had done to me personally. His death amounted to nothing - as much as an old withered stump of a tree that had to be extracted from the ground and burned.

*"What I do is for me, for that I came…*And Harry, old buddy, I'm doing this for you, too. You never had a chance to pay your debt; it was just death row for you. You never had a chance to make up for all the kids you hurt and the families you destroyed and the faith you crushed. You paid your debt with your blood, Harry. It was all wasted - Right down the drain."

"I was not wise, Harry, but at least I'm sober now and maybe a bit wiser. Then was not the time, for so many other things had to line up before we could begin to do the right thing for all of us. I'm sorry, Harry, it was just too early and I was not ready to take this on, to be able to listen to the voice of the Lord calling me to this ministry."

The Abbot came out of his office and walked with me down to the chapel. Neither of us spoke. I dipped my hand into the Holy Water and offered the Abbot some to bless himself. The Abbot shook his head and dipped his own hand in the font. He wasn't dead yet.

Fr. O'Connor, the Abbot. Jesus prayed to his Father, "*Abba, Father, all things are possible unto Thee.*" *Abba* in Aramaic means "Daddy" or "Papa." Fr. O'Connor was still the Big Daddy, despite his many years and frail body. I thought often that Fr. O'Connor would not die until he really trusted me to run the place properly and to take care of the old monks. It was four years already and I was still on probation in the old Abbot's eyes.

The new chapel slowly filled with the old monks in their black habits and the priest-penitents in their blue jeans, tee shirts and flannel shirts, black slippers as their dirty work boots were left at the door. The animal sweat of the younger men and the musty smell of the old monks mingled with the fragrance of old incense and pure wax candles. Sheila Levy called it our "Heavenly Bouquet".

Three men had sought admission to the monastery the first month it was opened. One was asked to leave after the first week. Soon there were six, then ten and soon the numbers were up to 93, with eight on the waiting list. Two were from Ireland and one from Australia and one from Kenya.

Word was getting around the country that there was a place for these priest-abusers who sincerely wanted to expiate their sins. They needed a place and way of life that would keep them away from children and direct them in a life of penance and sacrifice and atonement.

Many dioceses housed them together in places, frequently on the grounds of their seminaries, where their needs were well taken care, where they were not monitored and they could come and go at pleasure. What do you do with a pervert?

Was this a minimizing of the horrendous deeds they had done? Were their sins so great that even the bountiful Mercy of God could not touch them? Had we forgotten the ancient place held so dearly in the tradition of the church for penance and for restitution and reparation for harms done? Were we so detached, in such denial, that we could not enter into a creative redemption for these men?

The Benedictine Monastery of Atonement, as it was now called, was not a frivolous place and the sins of the priest-penitents were not frivolous acts against frivolous children. These sins were those that cried out to heaven for vengeance. These priests were truly pariahs, deserving of the hottest and deepest place in hell. I hope not forever.

As I grew in my wisdom and in my own sobriety, I could take one look at someone requesting admission to our monastery and I would be able to take his dimensions immediately. "It takes a con to know a con," as they say in AA.

But sometimes I got fooled. The younger guy with acne from Delaware, trying his charm on me got as far as my office door and was asked to leave. Another guy who thought he could escape the rigors of cleaning out the cow byre – he wanted to work in the library, the *scriptum scriptorum,* because he was a Canon Lawyer. The Bishop who wouldn't give up his cigars and brandy. They were out the door so fast that they didn't know what hit them.

I had long ago left my beguiling, charming, passive-aggressive way. Guest House and AA had knocked that out of me. And I was no longer vague, over-whelmed with self-pity and dissociated from the crunch of life. Working and sweating and plowing the hard earth at home knocked that out of me. I was now a man worthy to be entrusted with serious work. My protracted adolescence was over.

Being a Canon Lawyer, Jeremiah knew church law regarding monastic property and the legal intricacies of housing the priest-penitents. Brendan Sweeney and Tim Armstrong did the legal work needed to protect both the monks' interest and the newer mission of the church regarding the need for physical and spiritual atonement.

The Devitt fortune, long tied in trust for Jeremiah, was used to restock the farm and orchards and lake, as well as making repairs to the buildings and property. "Sure, there's another tide in the sea,"

Jeremiah would pray gratefully, as he wrote the checks to fund the mission. And there were yet plenty more tides, as the monies had been well invested over the years and it would well pay for the second life of that holy place. And for his second life.

My father waited for his papers from Rome releasing him from active duty in the priesthood. It was rare that a member of the hierarchy made such a request. Thank God for Bishop Teddie Szymanski who hurried them along. Teddie was soon to be made the first Polish Cardinal in Chicago. Jeremiah legally changed his name back to whom he really was - Jeremiah *Murphy*. No more *Devitt*.

The former Cardinal of Chicago, Jeremiah Murphy, married Sheila Levy in the chapel of the monastery with both myself and Rabbi Richard Fiebelman officiating. It was a quiet ceremony with only the monks and some of Sheila's family and friends. Babe and Lizzie, Brendan and Tim Armstrong. None of the priest-penitents were in attendance.

According to the ancient Jewish tradition, a *chuppah*, a canopy of cloth, had been set up at the foot of the altar, directly under the open sky-light that filtered light into the sanctuary. Before going under the *chuppah*, Jeremiah covered Sheila's face with a veil, as Rebecca covered her face when she first saw Isaac.

Under the *chuppah*, Sheila, accompanied by Babe and other cousins, circled Jeremiah seven times as a sign of protection for him. This is according to the myth of Lillith who was a gorgeous spiritual being who caused men to spill their seed in lust for her. By circling him seven times, the bride is symbolically herding back the groom's already spilled seed and claiming the groom and his seed as her own.

The old monks neither dozed nor dreamed, but sat upright with their eyes ablaze. They didn't know what was happening right in their own chapel, but, as always, they were their "guests" and no inhospitable thought would go their way. The Benedictines welcomed all.

Rabbi Fiebelman then blessed the wine and the marriage. Both Sheila and Jeremiah drank from the cup. Jeremiah then declared in fluent Hebrew, "With this ring you are consecrated to me as my wife in accordance with the law of Moses and the people of Israel."

He slipped on her finger the thin gold Claddagh ring that his mother had worn all her life. It was that same burnt ring that had appeared at his feet after his last Mass in the remnants of the old cabin by the sea in Quilty. He had it dipped to restore the original gold, to rid it of painful times.

Smiling down at my father and Sheila, I began the Catholic part of the ceremony. "Since it is your intention to enter into marriage, please join your right hands and declare your consent before God and his Church."

My father looked directly at Sheila, "I, Jeremiah, take you, Sheila, to be my wife. I promise to be true to you in good times and in bad, in sickness and in health. I will love you and honor you all the days of my life." Sheila returned the act of commitment, feeling his hand tremble and seeing tears in his eyes.

I cleared my throat, "You have declared your consent before the Church. May the Lord in his goodness strengthen this consent and fill you both with his blessings."

The second part of the Jewish ceremony, the *Ni' suin,* continued with the *Sheva Brachot,* the seven blessings recited for the bride and groom over a second cup of wine. As there were only three of Sheila's cousins present, seven of the old monks came out of their stalls, as a *minyan* of ten was required.

After the three cousins recited their blessings, Brother Thomas, in a husky, dusky voice read, "Blessed are you, Lord, our God, King of the universe, who created man." He handed the prayers to Brother Gabriel who read his blessing in a soft, effeminate voice and then Brother Justin concluded in a strong, clear voice, "Blessed are You, Lord, our God, King of the Universe, who created joy and gladness, love and harmony, peace and companionship."

As the monks stood looking for directions back to their stalls, Jeremiah raised his foot and crushed a clear, crystal goblet, a reminder of the broken fragments of Creation and the need to repair the world spiritually. This was the perfect place!

The sounds of the breaking glass reverberated throughout the chapel and Brother Gabriel held his ears. Enough was enough!

CHAPTER 51
The Grieving Madonna

I noticed my father kneeling in the chapel more and more often. Many of the older monks spent hours in quiet prayer and meditation, but they seemed to fade into the stained-glass windows, the Stations of the Cross, the long pews. What would a monastic chapel be without monks?

I set aside times for my own prayer, time apart from when the community gathered for the Divine Office. I genuflected and moved into a side pew. My father waited a respectful amount of time, then walked over to me and told me that he wanted to speak with me.

I concluded my prayer and headed back to my office, but Jeremiah guided me to the small conference-room off the chapel. We sat ourselves down at the round walnut table where no one was at the top and no one was at the bottom. I never knew what to expect from my father and he could come up with anything!

Jeremiah smiled at me and I smiled nervously back. Jeremiah shared with me that he had received the gift of prayer, so late in life, but "I've heard that the Good Lord is never late." I added, "And He's never early, either."

Prayer is elusive. How do we define a union between the Creator and His child? My father's admission to me was an act of total intimacy, of leaving himself vulnerable to my comments, judgments. I am sorry that I even commented on what he said.

Prayer to me is a total abandonment of our selfness to God – out of love, desperation, remorse, regret, grief, joy, happiness. God is as close as the air we breathe, or the blood that runs in our veins; He is as distant as Arctic ice, Hawaiian volcanoes, Kenyan tea groves. For most of us, it comes out of a desperation, or as the old nun once said, "When it's dark enough, we can see the stars".

Through the presence of the priest-penitents and the Wailing Well, Jeremiah had grown to understand that the Church had, indeed, been plunged into the throes of grief and that the Church's grief was different from the personal grief that anyone who had been abused experiences. It was a collective grief, one that hung on the shoulders of every member, active or absent, like a dripping pall, wet with tears. The church was no longer holy. The church was no longer sacred.

Primarily, there had been unbridled *Denial*, especially with the Cardinals and Bishops. "Martin, I was in total *Denial* of how rampant and how horrible the abuse was. All of us Bishops drove the 'get-away cars' for these guys, chauffeuring them from one parish to the next, from one diocese to the next. And reports and letters were coming out from all over and we ignored them all. Talk about Nixon 'stone-walling!'"

"But we are still *Bargaining*. If we give them enough money, it will all blow over. If we still act ignorant or focus on the rubrics for Confession or how deep to bow before we receive Communion, then we can divert attention from the real thing and it never really happened."

I didn't know where my father was going, but I listened intently, fearing I would miss something important. It wasn't often that my father spoke of the church at large and with such intensity.

Jeremiah gestured widely, "You know, Martin, these guys didn't operate alone. It took all of us, the 'Guilty Bystanders,' as Thomas Merton wrote. We had to keep our eyes closed and our ears blocked. Six million Jews were murdered and F.D.R., Churchill, and Pius XII were blind, deaf and dumb. These things don't happen in a vacuum, but in a protected space of looking the other way."

"What we are doing here is grieving and atoning and we must never, never forget that. I have been communicating with an old friend of mine, Luigi Nicolini in Florence. I want him to make us a sculpture of Mary weeping, grieving for all that has happened, for all that we allowed to happen. Not a Pieta with the body of Christ in her lap, but a Madonna with the broken bodies of all her abused children in her heart, in her hands. A Madonna for all of us, as we are all one and what happens to the least of us, happens to all of us. Right?"

Jeremiah showed me six sketches he had made for Luigi. A beautiful woman, bending with grief, her arms raised and fingers splayed about to cover her beautiful face contorted in agony, distraught at the violence done to her children. A grieving Madonna. No bargaining or denial. No pretending. No lies and half-truths.

I laid them out and carefully examined each face of the Madonna. They were all the same – a woman so beautiful it she took my breath away. I looked at my father. "Who is she, Da?"

Jeremiah closed his eyes. "My mother…your grandmother…your Grannie. Her name was Molly Murphy. I'm so sorry you never met her. My Mammie would have loved you to pieces, Martin."

I caught his breath. "I didn't know what she looked like. She is beautiful, Da."

"You never had a chance to meet her and she never had a chance to know you and watch you grow into the fine man you are today. Your Grannie would have loved you, Martin," Jeremiah smiled at me through his streaming tears.

"And if the truth be known, Lad, I was a bad son to my mother. She gave me nothing but love, and I turned my back on her. When I was small, she'd give me small pieces of tile and a marker for me to draw on and when I was finished, she would smile and kiss me, wipe it off and give me a clean tile to begin again. She knew I was an artist."

Jeremiah choked as he continued, "I was a bad son and she didn't deserve any of it. I could have talked to her and she would have welcomed me with open arms, but I shut her out. I thought I was better than she was. She went to her grave with a broken heart and I'm the one who broke it. I stomped on her feelings, on her motherhood, on her goodness to me all my life. If I could take back one moment with her, I'd give the rest of my life for it."

I closed my eyes to give my father privacy as the tears streamed down his old cheeks. I watched him blink slowly, praying that his old tears would cleanse him from that remorse and regret that plagued his every breath.

Part of the Devitt fortune was to be used for our Grieving Madonna.

****

335

It was in late winter when the Madonna finally arrived. Luigi Nicolini accompanied her to Wisconsin so he could direct the setting up of the statue, a polished bronze work that was six feet tall and five feet across. She was delicate to behold, yet massive in her dimensions, as befitting the sorrow she carried.

My father and I had driven to O'Hare to greet both Luigi and the Madonna. The statue had been carefully crated for her flight out of Florence, across the ocean and into the Midwest. Although Luigi was happy to see his old friend, Fr. Devitt, his main concern was for his bronze Lady and how she had survived the trip. He worried about the rumbling of the plane and the radical change in temperature which could damage the bronze he had chosen for her.

The huge statue was carefully fork-lifted onto a flat-bed truck and anchored down with ropes and chains. Two drivers were needed in case anything happened to their precious cargo. Another truck with a fork-lift and a crane would meet them the following day at our monastery.

The three men followed the truck out of Chicago and up into Wisconsin. It was getting dark and Luigi grew quiet, fearing the worse for her at the end of her long journey. I tried to make conversation, but Jeremiah nudged me to be quiet. The artist had his concerns and that was what they were paying him for. Nothing could happen to his Madonna at this stage.

The truck drivers and Luigi were shown to their rooms at the monastery. All were our guests in true Benedictine hospitality. Luigi couldn't sleep with the worry and asked for a bottle of wine. When I brought him the wine, I was tempted to tell Luigi that everything would be alright. But how would I know? That was the old, vapid me, assuming the powers of prophesy that I did not possess.

In the cold February morning, the Madonna was lifted off the flat-bed truck and ever so carefully, lowered at exactly the right angle to the waiting two-foot concrete rest in front of the arched portico at the entrance to the monastery. When Luigi was satisfied that she was correctly placed, the job of loosening the tight crating began.

When the Grieving Madonna was finally released from her wooden wrap, she was there for all the world to see her crushed in sorrow, mourning the death of her children from the hands of their priests and bishops. Make no mistake, the church was deeply grieving for her own sinfulness, for the loss of her holiness.

Slowly, l walked around the statue with my father. The snow was gently falling over the hard fields of the monastery, against its gracious gray-stone buildings, onto the jagged lake and The Welcome Home, on the laboring priest-penitents in their blue denim habits, onto the still loved and remembered monks who lay cold and still beneath the soil in their own graveyard.

Snow fell on the new Madonna as she slowly grew accustom to her new home far from the dank copper and tin mines of the Balkans, from the lusty sounds and smells of Florence, from the care and precision of Luigi Nicolini's fine, deliberate hands, and finally onto the receiving earth of the Benedictine Monastery on the frozen white breasts of Wisconsin.

CHAPTER 52
The Young Colors of Dawn

Jeremiah and Sheila lived in the long, ranch house across the lake from the monastery. This was a place for anyone who had been abused by a priest to come. In former days, it had been used by a community of Benedictine nuns, so there were many private bedrooms and baths.

In keeping with the Benedictine spirit of hospitality and sanctuary, The Welcome Home asked no questions of their guests, but both Sheila and Jeremiah were there for them to come and heal. Along the drive was a small sign: **Expect a Miracle!**

Word was slowly getting out through the various organizations that spoke out about abuse that there was a place of refuge for anyone who had been abused. No one from across the lake could come to The Welcome Home, so it was consciously protected from any of the old abusers, even though they were now priest-penitents. These guests had never known safety in a Catholic world.

When they wanted to go to the monastery, Jeremiah and Sheila would row their little red boat across the waters of the lake in good weather and drive their Jeep around the property when the lake was frozen and the wind howled. The priest-penitents were forbidden to cross the lake, much less to put a foot on The Welcome Home land.

Jeremiah never asked Sheila to become a Catholic. How could a tiger shed her stripes? As someone steeped in the Jewish tradition, Sheila understood sin and atonement probably better than Jeremiah himself. *Aveira* was the Hebrew word for sin. There were three types of sins: *Pesha* – a deliberate defiance of God; *Avon* – a sin of lust or uncontrollable emotion; *Cheit* – an unintentional sin.

While the priest abusers certainly defied God, the root of their sin was lust, *Avon,* an addictive obsession with sexual pleasure. Yet the horrendous harm each one did to a single child or many children still cried out to Heaven for vengeance. The sin of the Bishops was *Pesha,* for they deliberately, with fore-thought and total disregard for the lives of the children and their families, defied God and His Creation.

Sheila had been taught that God was merciful, even to those not deserving of His Mercy and that God is gracious, even to those not deserving of His grace. She understood well the penance that had accrued by the sins of the priest-abusers and the need they had for a perpetual *Yom Kipper*.

But Sheila had spent her life in restaurants, waiting, serving, cleaning up, schmoozing. Knowing when to schmooze and when not to schmooze. She had no fear of the pain of the priest-survivors, for hadn't her own mother and aunt survived Birkenau and lived to tell it?

She had always thought that there must be something more than just 'survival', for her mother's life had been hell, another Birkenau even after coming to Skokie, the northern suburb filled with Holocaust survivors. Was there no healing in the world to deliver these child sexual victims from their own private Holocaust?

The dried up old well stood beside their guest house. It went deep into the ground and had been covered with a round wooden top for safety. The Abbot mentioned this again and again to Sheila, as if she would somehow know what to do with it. She would push the cover slightly to the side, and with a shudder, peer into the blackness with her flashlight and see nothing. She would drop a stone into the well and listen for it to hit, but there was never a sound. The well had no bottom.

Sheila knew of the Wailing Wall in Jerusalem. It was all that survived of the Temple of Solomon. People wrote their prayers on small pieces of paper, folded them up and placed them in the small spaces between the holy stones, an act of Faith that God would hear their prayers. And they would leave their prayers there at the Holy Wall. But women were excluded.

Her old well would be called the Wailing Well and into it would be cast any remnant of a victim's abuse – a letter, shirt, gift, money, a stone. Once the object of abuse leaves the hand, it can no longer be retrieved. It is gone forever.

The abuse is over and it can stop and the memories can heal. Never to be forgotten, but healed. *Healing means that an injury can no longer cause pain.* And when the time would come, perhaps even to be forgiven. But recovery from sexual abuse was never hurried, never demanded, only when the stars were aligned perfectly.

People began to call it "Sheila's Well" and packages and letters would come from all over the country and beyond. On the outside would be scribbled, typed, printed, "For Sheila's Well." She would immediately run to her well, shove the wooden top to the side and toss the object into it. She never once heard it drop. She then went to the fresh-water spring that ran into the lake and washed her hands and knelt and prayed for whomever had sent it. No records were kept.

On some days, there would be 10 or 15 packages. Other days, only one or two. But there were always some, as if the wave of releasing trauma was hitting her door and it was her sacred responsibility to discard it forever. Sheila was the Mother Rabbi of Healing, who watched over the Wailing Well and remained faithful to that until the end of her days.

CHAPTER 53
Entertaining Angels Unawares

I knelt in prayer. My heart overflowed with gratitude that I had been called to do this work. *"What I do is me, for that I came."* The Benedictine openness and hospitality was just like in Ireland when there were no locked doors and everyone was welcome, for you never knew whom your guest might be, for it might be 'angels unawares'.

It was my 57th birthday, December 17, 1995. I smiled as I prayed, for I was much too young to be that old. My dear mother had not even seen her 40th birthday, and here I was, with many more days allotted than she ever had.

I felt peaceful. After all the years of mourning the absence of a father, my very own father lived right across the little lake and I saw him every day. It had gotten to be a habit, Jeremiah and Sheila and me. I reached in my pocket for my grandfather's old Rosary, broken and repaired so many times.

I blessed myself and began the five Glorious Mysteries. Fr. O'Connor shuffled into the chapel and motioned for me. He told me that there was an emergency on the phone from Sheila. I thanked him, genuflected and walked quickly to my office.

She spoke the word: TUSH! That meant, "Get your tush over here quickly! We need you! Drop whatever you are doing! Come quickly!"

I ran to my car, drove over the curb, up onto the lawn and back down with a shudder. The grieving Madonna held her breath. I righted myself and made my way around and up the long drive to The Welcome Home. The priest-penitents in the fields watched from far.

Parked in front of Welcome House was a new blue BMW. Illinois plates. I parked, knocked and opened the door. Sheila came out of the small, private room adjacent to the kitchen and brought me in to meet a man in his middle 40's. He was short and nearly bald. There was no fat on him, but neither did he look fit. He stood and Sheila introduced him to me.

His name was Harry Smith and he had heard of The Welcome Home. He had been abused"…300, 500 times by my uncle who was a fuckin' priest."

I asked Harry if he wanted Sheila to stay. Harry Smith asked me if I were a priest and when I said yes, he definitely wanted Sheila to stay. He could never be alone with a priest and he hated the church. He hated God for what He had put him through and how He had destroyed his life.

Harry Smith's life was a mess. He was a lawyer, "like everyone else in my family,: but he hated his job and had been fired three times. He drank, hated having sex with his wife. He loved his wife, but he was unfair to her. He thought he might be gay. They had three kids and he couldn't stand to be with them.

He had nightmares and couldn't stop thinking of what his uncle had done to him. Sometimes he'd actually feel his uncle's hands on him or up his ass. All he could think of was killing himself. He had tried it twice, but lost his nerve at the last minute. He was always sick with a bad back, the flu, sinus headaches. Today, his back 'was killin' him.

He knew about the Wailing Well and wanted to jump in and never come back. He had tried therapy and all he heard was that he had to forgive his uncle and then he'd get over it. He wanted to kill himself. No way in hell would he ever forgive his son-of-a-bitch uncle? His mother, Mary Kay, was his uncle's sister.

Sheila asked him if he had anything with him that reminded him of his uncle. Harry stared at Sheila. "Yeah, as a matter of fact, the golf clubs. Hush money, you know. He'd always call and say, 'How's about a round of golf?' and I knew that I had to go with him. I tried to tell my father, but he cracked me across the face and told me never to talk about my uncle or any priest like that."

Sheila told him that the Wailing Well was waiting for the clubs. "Ya know, Harry, they got bad juju all over them! Let's get rid of them right from the beginning!" Sheila and Harry walked to his car. As he opened the trunk, there was a dirty yellow shirt under an empty bottle of scotch.

Sheila placed her hand on his arm. "What's that? The bottle? The shirt? Whose shirt? What else is in this mess?"

"Uncle Harry always wore yellow shirts. I was afraid if I threw it away, something bad would happen to me. Family loyalty, or something like that."

Sheila looked him dead in the face, just like I imagine God will on the Day of Atonement: "Harry, I want it all! Unless you need to hold on to all this stuff, to all this pain. My mother could never erase her tattoo from Birkenau, but you can get rid of this crap and let the good earth just swallow it up. You uncle still has power over you as long as you keep it. Bad juju, right from the start!"

Harry and Sheila carried the clubs, the shirt, the bottle over to the Wailing Wall. She took off the cover and asked him if he wanted her or if he wanted to get rid of it himself. Harry didn't answer her, but dropped the golf bag and clubs, the shirt and the bottle down the well.

Sheila started to cover the well, but Harry ripped off his uncle's Rolex watch and threw it in. There was no sound, only a distant song from over the hills. She hears it every time she opened the well, but never told Jeremiah or me. Sheila carefully placed the cover back on the well

Arm in arm, they went up the small hill, back to The Welcome Home. Harry asked Sheila if he could take a shower and get "all the guck" off. She took him to a private room near the back, handed him a large, soft white towel and told him there was pure soap and clear shampoo from a farm up in *Door County.*

Harry Smith winced, remembering what had happened to him at the Hogans' compound up in *Door County.* Harry asked her to get him different soap and didn't explain. Sheila was adept at adding up the invisible numbers and told him it was no bother at all. She winced at all the triggers that get pulled unawares.

After he had showered, Harry returned to the small room. I was waiting for him. His face was flushed. He didn't know what he was going to say. Sheila asked Harry if it were alright with him if she went into the kitchen to make our lunch. She would be just in the next room and if he wanted her, she would be with him.   Harry said it was O.K., she could go.

I could not look Harry in the eye. "Harry, I knew your uncle. I knew him very well. We were at Quigley and Mundelein at the same time. I knew the Hogans. I knew your family."

I stopped talking. Harry Smith looked at me. We could hear the clock tick and Sheila stirring in the kitchen. I gasped, trying to hold down a tidal wave of grief that was about to strike me.

"I saw you when you were a little boy. At the Deer Path Inn. I wasn't a priest yet. I had too much to drink. Anyway, I saw you and talked to you. You were with your uncle."   Harry Smith began to cry and I began to cry.

"I'd see you up in Door County at your place up there. I had a funny feeling that something was going on, but I didn't know what. I didn't make it my business to find out what. I saw you up there, Harry!"

Harry was gasping for air and sobbing into his hands. "Go on, go on, Father. Tell me more! Tell me what happened, Father!"

"I was charged with what your uncle did to a little boy, but then it got cleared up and your uncle went to prison instead of me. You know that, don't you?"

Harry Smith nodded and added, "I didn't know it was you. I know the story and he got killed. He got what was comin' to him, I know that!"

I sat silently. Harry Smith needed to hear this part of the story or he would never be healed. I vowed to tell him the whole story and to keep nothing from him, even if I had to yank it out of myself with a pair of sharp, pointy pliers.

I told Harry of visiting his uncle in prison, down in Hillsboro, and that was the last time I saw him. He was murdered soon after I saw him. There was no place for him to go to atone. At that point, I think he was too sick to even think about atoning. That's why now there were priest-abusers doing their penance at this monastery.

I continued and Harry cried. His uncle Harry Hogan had been sexually abused by many of his brothers in their mansion down by the lake. It went on for years and years and no one stopped it. Then Fr. Harry Hogan began abusing other little boys, because that was all he had ever known. It didn't make it right, but that was the reason.

Suddenly, I rose and went over to Harry. I fell on my knees and held young Harry's head in my hands. I began slowly, but certain, knowing this must be done.

"Harry Smith, I am asking forgiveness from you in the name of the whole Catholic Church. In the name of your own uncle who was a priest and who hurt you and hurt you and hurt you.

"I ask you to forgive me for not protecting you and for not knowing what was going on. I ask your forgiveness, Harry Smith, for all the sins against you through the church. I only ask your forgiveness if you are ready and willing to forgive. I am a priest and I am asking your forgiveness."

Like a bishop, laying his hands on the head of a young man to ordain him a priest, Harry Smith placed his hands on the top of my head. He held them there firmly, waiting for any doubt or fear to clear before he spoke. I felt a wave of strength soar through his veins. He got very clear.

"I, Harry Smith, forgive you and I forgive my uncle and I forgive the whole church for the sins you have committed against me. When I was a child, when I was a little boy, when I was a big boy, when I was a very young man. I forgive you, not because I want to, but because you all need my forgiveness."

"And in the name of all us kids who got fucked by all you guys, I forgive all of you. You need our forgiveness more than you will ever know, more than you will ever know."

Harry took his hands off my head, stood, went into the kitchen, kissed Sheila on the cheek and walked out the door.

From over the far soft, green hills, Sheila heard the sweet, clear *Hymn of the Universe* as she had never before heard it. It mingled with the strong chanting of the priest-penitents and the Benedictines and it lifted far above and beyond to be heard deep in the souls of all the children who had ever been hurt by a priest.

And it went beyond the souls of those children into the souls of any child who had ever been abused, to any child who had learned not to trust, to keep dark and dirty secrets, to hurt themselves so they could feel alive, to learn to punish themselves for the sins of another, to split off so they didn't hurt feel the pain.

And the chanting of the priests and the Hymn of the Universe mingled with all the prayers of the mothers and fathers whose hearts had been broken because a child of theirs had been abused by someone they trusted.

And slowly, almost like the thin band of crimson that comes before the bright sun rises over the sea, the very waters of atonement stirred and brought forth the wondrous, lilting *Hymn of the Universe* to begin a healing for the whole world that could not be stopped, a wondrous breath of grace and love that emanated from the simple act of Harry Smith placing his hands on my head in forgiveness.

And God saw everything that He had made, and behold, it was very good.

To the Clergy, Religious and Faithful of the Archdiocese of Chicago

Dearly Beloved in Christ,

I have requested that this letter be read at all the Masses on Sunday, December 10, 1988. The Holy Father, Pope Thomas I, has reluctantly accepted my resignation as Cardinal-Archbishop of Chicago and from my position in the College of Cardinals.

My reason is that during my 25 years as head of the Archdiocese of Chicago, I have allowed our children and our families to be abused by our predator priests. I have sent these priests for treatment, only to have them return and I have then reassigned them to unsuspecting parishes. I have treated these priests as sinners, to be dealt with mercy; I have shielded them from the law, denying the fact they were criminals, felons.

I had a choice: I could defend the church and shuffle the priests; or I could protect our children from sexual abuse at their hands. I choose to protect the priests by sending them repeatedly for treatment and when they returned, I sent them to other unsuspecting parishes where they had a fresh cluster of children for their pleasure. Neither the pastors nor the people were warned about the presence in your midst of a predator.

These unholy and criminal actions are costing the Archdiocese millions of dollars. While other bishops may deny it, this money comes directly from the money you contribute weekly. Your money has purchased the insurance against such damages incurred by these predator-priests; your money has bought property that has increased in value that we were forced to sell; the hard-earned money from your grand-parents, immigrants from Italy, Poland, Ireland, and Germany, that built our beautiful inner city parishes and schools that we are now closing to pay litigation against us.

This cost is rising into the tens of millions and will only increase as victims find their voice and confront us through the legal system.

This is a time of horrendous sin committed by your priests and hierarchy. We have lied to you, ignored your legitimate complaints, interfered with police work, and stolen your innocence. We have shaken your faith in God and in the Roman Catholic Church.

We have been culpably ignorant of the profound and intractable illness of these abusive priests. Sexual addiction to the abuse of a child is a mental illness that cannot be successfully treated and put into remission. These men can only be educated as to the nature of their wrongs.

They are like recovering alcoholics who cannot take another drink. They cannot ever be alone in the proximity of children; a parish priest, by definition, is near children.

For this I am grievously sorry. I am not worthy to occupy this sacred office of Cardinal. I have been unfaithful to the promises I made to you at my installation 25 years ago. The predator priests have acted out of lust, addiction, insanity; we who have protected them have acted deliberately, rationally, and with a clear intent to protect the priesthood, upon which the Mass and sacraments of the church reside.

I have asked Fr. Martin Sweeney, a priest in the Archdiocese, to establish a residence for penitential priests and bishops at a Benedictine Monastery in Wisconsin. It will be opened not only to Chicago priests and bishops, but to any throughout the world who find themselves ready to make reparations for these priestly crimes against our own people.

A retreat center will be established for children (regardless of age) and families who have been abused by our priests and bishops.

This will be a center for spiritual and emotional healing. If anyone chooses to meet with his or her abuser, Fr. Sweeney will arrange such a meeting. These meetings will be conducted with the utmost privacy.

For as many days as I have left, I will ask God's forgiveness for the great harm I have caused, for the misuse of my sacred office, for the broken promise I made to you to care for the most vulnerable of my flock.

If you have it in your hearts, please forgive me. I truly repent of all the harm I have caused and for my infidelity to my vows. I will do penance every day of my life for these sins.

Jeremiah Cardinal Devit

Made in the USA
Lexington, KY
06 October 2018